Sa... gaspi... shrin... coughed ..., ... the spasm. One of the black knobs on the old goblin's neck had ruptured and was oozing an ugly, green pus.

Direfang held his breath and looked at the once-proud clan leader. The coughing subsided and Saro-Saro tried to speak again. His voice cracked, and the words sounded like leaves blowing across a dry riverbed.

Saro-Saro managed to rally and struggled to sit up. The old goblin had dug his claws into Direfang's legs, poking through the thin material of his leggings and finding flesh beneath. Saro-Saro pulled himself close the hobgoblin even as Direfang tried to shove away. Saro-Saro scratched Direfang's chest and spit in his face.

"Die too, Direfang," Saro-Saro rasped. "Join me in death." A thick line of blood dripped over his lip. "Should have died on the mountain, you. Were supposed to die there."

"Should have died, Direfang, so Saro-Saro could lead this army," Uren hissed. "If Saro-Saro cannot lead, Direfang will not either!"

THE STONETELLERS

The Rebellion

Death March

Goblin Nation
(August 2009)

DEATH MARCH

THE STONETELLERS
VOLUME TWO

JEAN RABE

The Stonetellers, Volume Two

DEATH MARCH

©2008 Wizards of the Coast, Inc.

Published by Wizards of the Coast, Inc. DRAGONLANCE, WIZARDS OF THE COAST, and their respective logos are trademarks of Wizards of the Coast, Inc., in the U.S.A. and other countries.

Printed in the U.S.A.

Cover art by Matt Stawicki
First Printing: August 2008

9 8 7 6 5 4 3 2 1

ISBN: 978-0-7869-4917-5
620-21820740-001-EN

U.S., CANADA,
ASIA, PACIFIC, & LATIN AMERICA
Wizards of the Coast, Inc.
P.O. Box 707
Renton, WA 98057-0707
+1-800-324-6496

EUROPEAN HEADQUARTERS
Hasbro UK Ltd
Caswell Way
Newport, Gwent NP9 0YH
GREAT BRITAIN
Save this address for your records.

Visit our web site at www.wizards.com

ACKNOWLEDGMENTS

Many thanks to Cam Banks and Jamie Chambers for providing background on the New Sea and for keeping my Dark Knights in line.

To Trampas Whiteman for passing along his sage wisdom about Schallsea Island and the Citadel.

To Doc for once again feeding my wizard.

And to Chris Pierson, who can read maps far, far better than I. Without the help of Chris, my goblins might still be stranded in the mountains.

DEDICATION

For Pat and Margaret,
who invited me to dance with
Krynn's goblins

1

HONOR

The sword cleaved into the goblin's side with enough force to sever its spine.

"To the deepest corner of the Abyss with these things!" cried Bera Kata. The Dark Knight commander thrust her heel against the dead goblin's hip and yanked hard to pull her blade free.

She was covered in blood, none of it her own. She pulled up the hem of her tabard, using the underside to wipe off her face. After a deep breath, she plunged forward into the mass of goblins again.

Bera thought she heard one of the goblins cry, "Stop!" in the Common tongue. She knew them capable of language and recognized the clacking, snarling gibberish so many of them used. But as far as speaking her language? She considered them parrots repeating words taught to them by owners; they were not able to understand.

Goblins were stupid, pathetic creatures, lower than common animals, Bera knew. Filthy and annoying; the only good goblin was a dead one . . . or a slave.

She snarled when a pot-bellied goblin darted forward, a dagger thrust out as if the puny weapon were a spear. She let the creature in close as she raised her sword high above her right shoulder and brought it down in an executioner's swing, slicing through the goblin's neck and lopping off its ugly head.

1

Around her the battle raged.

She felt her heart thrumming and the surge of blood to her face, her chest tightening and breath coming faster—all sensations she relished. Her arms grew warm, and she clenched the leather-wrapped pommel of her sword with both hands to put more power behind her swings.

"Dance with me," she cooed.

Bera was never more truly alive than when she fought—real battles, not the mock combats she staged to keep her men fit and their skills reasonably honed. Fighting kept her mind away from all of her other concerns. She enjoyed the emotional and physical rush it provided. It was the danger she savored, the real danger, the chance that with each step forward she put her otherwise-staid life at risk. It was why she let two of the goblins come at her, raising her sword so they could dart in beneath the sweep of it.

Bera spun, presenting her back to them for just a heartbeat. But when she completed the pivot, her sword low and whistling, her blade sheered into the thigh of one of the goblins, maiming it.

"Sing!" she taunted. "Sing and dance!"

The injured goblin howled and grabbed at its leg as if by pressing its bony hands against the gushing wound it could keep the blood inside. "Mercy," she thought she heard the goblin say. "Please."

"Sing louder! Wail for all you're worth! The gods won't listen to you." She left the crippled goblin on the ground, considering it no threat and sparring with the other one. It backed up, the dagger held in front of its scrawny body mimicking a defensive stance.

"Rats, no better than vermin you are!" Bera couldn't have said where her hatred of goblinkind came from. She'd never associated with them on any level other than what she was doing—fighting and killing them. She'd never been posted to the Nerakan mines or to other compounds where they were used for slave labor. Thank the gods for that, she thought, as it would have been difficult to live close to them. They were so far beneath humankind.

DEATH MARCH

Their appearance alone was enough to justify slaughtering them. They smelled horrible and were hideous, and they chattered in a vile-sounding language that reminded her of wild dogs yapping. What clothes they wore hung on them in tatters, their eyes were yellowed as though they were deathly sick, and their skin was bumpy and scabrous, as if they carried some foul wasting disease.

She spit as she advanced on the goblin, tasting her own sweat in her mouth and trying to rid herself of it. She knew that she needed to finish it quickly and move on. There were so many other goblins to deal with that prolonging any one segment of the battle, no matter how much she enjoyed the contest, put her—and, more important, her men—at risk.

The thing continued to chatter, lips curled up and eyes narrowed, making it a grotesque sight that sent a disgusted shiver down her back. She couldn't understand it and could barely hear it; everything else was so loud in comparison—the shushing sound swords made against goblin ribs, the screams of the dying goblins all around, the whoops of the youngest knights, the victory shouts of the older ones. Too, there was the thunder of feet stomping against the ground and the occasional clang when a goblin weapon was raised in successful parry.

Her own foe managed that just then, somehow barely deflecting her blow with its dagger. Luck, she thought; goblins could be lucky, but they were not so skilled.

"Not again, you. No more will you block my blade and no more will you suck in my air." She crouched when she swung the next time, her blade biting deep into the goblin's arm and causing it to fumble its dagger. It grabbed futilely at the gaping slice with its good hand, the wounded arm useless and hanging gruesomely by a bit of muscle. She swung again, slaying the foul creature, and she raised her gaze to survey the scene.

Despite the growing shadows from the mountains ringing the valley, it was easy to pick out her men; even the shortest among them towered above the puny goblins. Her Dark Knights were dressed in fine plate armor with black tabards and cloaks spotted with dirt and blood. Some of the goblins possessed armor, pieces of this and that they'd cobbled together into breastplates and greaves to comical effect. Many of them wielded weapons that had been taken from a Dark Knight mining camp; Bera saw the rose and lily etchings on some blades and the black-leather-wrapped pommels. Also, she spotted Dark Knight tabards on a few of the hobgoblins in the mix, confirming her belief that she'd been successful in locating the escaped slaves.

"Kill them all," she breathed. "All but one or two. Monsters to parade before Lord Baltasar Rennold!" That last she shouted. "Save one of the hobs!" She recalled someone telling her that hobgoblins were slightly smarter than their small cousins, and she knew a handful of them had been used as foremen in the mines.

She inhaled deeply, pulling the battle scents into her lungs, tasting the blood and mud and the stink of the goblins. She held the breath briefly, struggling to take all the excitement in.

Her eyes gleamed as she glanced over her shoulder. One of her men joined her, Eloy. He put his back to hers and without a word met the rush of a broad-shouldered hobgoblin with a sunken chest. At six feet, she matched Eloy in height. She turned back to face her own assailant, a yellow-skinned goblin wearing a chain mail shirt that dangled above his knobby ankles and weighed him down. He wielded a short sword, the first goblin she'd seen toting something other than a mere dagger or the sticks they tried to use as clubs.

The colors of the creatures had always perplexed her. Some were yellow, but most were various shades of mud-brown, a few of them red, with one or two in the mix gray. All of them were the shades of molds that grew in the woods, she mused as she drove her blade forward with enough strength to part the links of her opponent's mail and pierce his heart. Their color was always the same on the inside: blood red.

Out of the corner of her eye she saw one of her men fall, four goblins swarming on top of him.

"To Gare!" she shouted.

"Aye, Commander! Together, then."

Fighting back-to-back, she and Eloy worked their way toward the downed knight.

Bera hadn't joined the fight until it was well under way. She'd watched at a distance for several minutes, wanting to appraise the skills of her newest knights. She commanded a force of sixty-two, nearly a third of them freshly assigned to her just twelve days past in the capital of Neraka. Though not the first battle for them—according to the records she'd reviewed—it was the first time they'd fought against something other than humans and the first time they'd worked as a blended unit with her previous charges. Her new knights had earlier been stationed south of Jelek, at an outpost that had fallen into a rent in the earth when the first of the earthquakes struck; they were the only survivors.

One of those men had caught her eye from the beginning. She studied him as he entered the fray, wielding a double-edged battle-axe that swept with the regularity and appearance of a pendulum. He was the largest in her unit, easily seven feet tall and heavily muscled, looking formidable in his suit of plate mail, with his chest evidencing some bluing—atypical for his low rank. She speculated that he had some ogre blood in his veins, but he'd not specified it in his records. He'd told her that he was twenty-six, but she put him at least five years younger; his face was boyish, unlined. In any event, she knew he came from a reasonably wealthy family; his bearing told her that, as did the battle-axe she'd allowed him to retain—a keepsake from his grandfather, he'd claimed. The Dark Knight wizard in her company whispered that it was enchanted.

That he hadn't risen up through the stations was due to several documented incidents of insubordination. Lesser men would have been drummed out for half the number of offenses she'd found in his records before leaving on the march. No doubt his fighting skills, coupled with the losses the Order suffered from the recent earthquakes and volcanic eruptions, preserved his job. He'd not shown her disrespect or balked at any of her commands . . . yet. And his courage and apparent bloodlust impressed her.

Zocci was the name he went by among the knights, though his full name was much longer—Zoccinder Angeda Redstone of . . . —a long name, so she would settle for Zoccinder. She'd left all the papers about Zoccinder in Neraka, along with her husband and nearly-grown daughter. Bera had seen less and less of her family in the past few years. The Dark Knights were more of a family to her; she'd been raised in the Order and would die with it.

"But not die this day," she'd murmured to herself, watching the battle unfold at the outset. "Not to these grimy rats."

She'd taken a position on the rise and ordered her men to fan out through the mountains. Her scout had discovered the goblins resting in that narrow valley, settling in as the sun was setting. Bera directed her most experienced knights to sweep around and come at the goblins from both ends of the valley, where a narrow pass cut through the hills, effectively trapping the enemy while the bulk of her force descended. Despite their heavy armor and weapons, the knights had moved at a stealthy pace, alerting the goblins only after the pass through the valley had been sealed.

Zoccinder had been among the first to rush into battle, and even from her lofty post, she'd heard his feet pounding across the earth, or perhaps she'd only imagined it. But she'd enjoyed hearing the first scream as his axe cut through a skinny hobgoblin.

She was pleased by the spectacle below. A grim tableau, some would describe it, but to her it was a glorious sight. There were six or seven times the number of goblins and hobgoblins compared to her knights, she guessed; it was impossible to count them. But her force didn't need to outnumber them. The goblins were unskilled, most of them unarmored and without weapons; they were disorganized. Their screams of pain and disbelief roiled up the side of the mountain and tugged her down to join the lopsided battle.

DEATH MARCH

"If Gare's finished, Commander, those monsters—"

"Will pay with their lives, Eloy," Bera finished.

They raced toward the fallen knight. Bera couldn't see Gare's chest rising and falling, but that didn't mean he was dead; the plate mail could conceal his breathing. Gare was facedown, with two goblins standing on his back, one yanking aside his tabard. Two others were on the far side of him, grabbing at his weapons.

She snarled and swept wide with all of her strength, slicing through the waist of the first goblin, cutting him in two. The blade continued on its path, lodging in the chest of the other.

One of the other goblins had managed to free Gare's sword. The goblin tried to wield it like a lance, clearly struggling with the unfamiliar weapon.

"Take care!" Bera warned Eloy.

He leaped over Gare and the two she'd slain.

The goblin drove the sword forward, but the weight of the blade caused him to lose his balance; the blade dipped down and speared the earth. Eloy cleaved the goblin's shoulder, drew back, and ran it through just as Bera joined him and slew the other one.

"There's traitors with them, somewhere," Bera said. "Keep an eye out for the traitors."

"I remember, from your briefing," Eloy returned. "This is a mission of honor."

Honor on many levels, she mouthed. Bera put her back to her comrade again and caught her breath. "Dark Knights, one of them an officer—and a wizard too, remember? Face scarred, I was told. An Ergothian priest, too, big as a barrel. Did I mention the priest was an Ergothian? A man of the water in a desert-dry mining camp?"

Eloy nodded. "Haven't spotted them," he said. "I can't see any humans beyond us among this mob." The knight was winded from the exertion. "Hiding somewhere in the rocks, maybe, they are."

Eloy was young, half Bera's age, and she was disappointed to note his weakness. She would force him and a handful of others to double their drills and exercise later.

She left him behind as she rushed toward a trio of goblins harrying another of her knights.

"Where are those damnable traitors?" she said to herself. "I see only dying goblins. Too bad they don't have better weapons. This is really too easy." She drew a deep breath and thrust her blade through a small one's chest. "Leave one hob!" she shouted to her troops, reminding them in a shrill voice.

In the end, they managed to leave alive three goblins, the hobgoblins having all fought to the end, refusing to surrender.

2

Eyes on a Fallen Knight

Zoccinder guarded the three captured goblins, though his presence was not really needed. The trio was bound with heavy twine, lashed with their backs together and stripped of the semblance of clothes they'd worn; Bera could not stomach the creatures wearing what had obviously once belonged to humans.

The goblins hadn't the strength even to snap the twine. One of them had a broken leg; the bone protruded from its thigh, and the blood congealing on it drew flies.

She paced in a circle around the three, occasionally pausing to grind the ball of her foot against the hard-packed ground. That the vile creatures vaguely had the forms of men grated on her. Legs, arms, toes, fingers, all in roughly the same proportions—though certainly not the same size—as a human's. Their heads were rounder, the face of the female in the trio was heart shaped, and their wrists and elbows stuck out as if the skin had been stretched over their bones. Their eyes were small and dark, sinister, with bony ridges that shadowed them like a hood, and their teeth were pointed like a rat's. She'd touched a goblin only once before, years past, one time, purely out of curiosity. She'd found its hide like leather, scaly in places and with little clumps of hair sprouting here and there that felt bristly like a stiff brush.

9

"These smell no better alive than dead," she muttered.

"Stink to be certain," Zoccinder answered. He settled himself on the ground opposite the biggest goblin and took off his helmet; a thick mane of red hair spilled out on his shoulders, strands sticking together with sweat. He tugged off his gloves, shook them out, and folded them, tucking them beneath his belt. Then he ran the backs of his hands across his face. "Stink more in this heat, the rats do. Shouldn't be quite so hot this time of year."

Bera stopped her pacing and met his gaze. He had large blue eyes that possessed an unusual hardness. "Yes, we need to find water when we're done here," she said.

"Larol and a scout are already looking," he replied.

Another few circles around the goblins, and Bera squatted in front of the female. The goblin tried to avert its gaze.

"Do you understand the Common tongue?" Bera removed one of her gloves and struck the goblin with it, quick and hard. "Do you understand?"

The goblin cast its gaze down but nodded pitifully.

"And can you speak it?"

A shake of its head.

"What about you others?"

The goblin with the broken leg whimpered and shivered. Bera couldn't tell if it was frightened or had lost too much blood and was in shock. She shifted so she was directly in front of the wounded one.

"I can get you healing help. I've a battlefield medic in the ranks, and I can order her to mend your leg." She wondered if the wounded goblin could detect the falseness in her voice. When it didn't respond, she continued, "I asked, do you understand the Common tongue?"

It looked at her with a glazed expression on its ugly, pinched face.

"May I try, Commander?" Zoccinder asked. Then, without waiting for a reply, he rattled off words in a tongue she couldn't identify. Bera knew it wasn't goblin; she'd heard enough of that guttural variation before.

One of the goblins understood and haltingly replied.

"This one speaks Ogrish," Zoccinder explained after a moment.

Bera raised an eyebrow. Perhaps there was indeed some ogre blood in Zoccinder.

"What do you want to know, Commander?" he continued. Again without waiting for an answer, he began conversing with the goblin.

Bera drew her lips into a fine line and stood. The wounded goblin in front of her watched her, trembling more noticeably.

"Where is the Dark Knight—former Dark Knight— Guardian Grallik N'sera?" Bera demanded, interrupting Zoccinder. "Ask that. Say he is a wizard, heavily scarred."

Zoccinder cocked his head, asked, and waited. No answer came from the trembling goblin.

"We have a witness who says the wizard fled the mining camp and joined with the goblins," Bera continued, waiting for Zoccinder to translate for the goblin. "He left his post and chose to live with the slaves instead of the Order." The words hissed out. "He left my father and the other knights to die. Where is the traitor Grallik N'sera?"

Zoccinder spoke once more in the odd, deep-throated tongue. The exchange went on for several minutes, and midway through it the Dark Knight, losing patience, stretched his arm forward and dug his fingers deep into the goblin's thigh. The goblin stiffened and spasmed, hissing a stream of words.

Finally Zoccinder released the goblin and leaned back, tipping his face up to catch the slight breeze that found its way down the mountainside. There was little natural light left in the day. Well away from Zoccinder and Bera, knights were building a large fire using the scrub they'd been gathering along the eastern edge of the valley.

"The goblin's name is—"

"I don't care what its name is."

"He's of some tribe—clan he calls it, Hurbear's—this clan split from the main group. But all of these were from Iverton."

"Steel Town," she said, supplying the nickname the Dark

Knights had called the place. Her father, Marshal Montrill, had been in command of Steel Town before the earthquakes erupted and destroyed the mines and camp. He died of injuries he suffered while trying to save his men, so she'd been told.

"What about the traitor Dark Knights? Zoccinder, the creature is not telling us all it knows."

Zoccinder spoke in the ogre language again, and Bera found herself concentrating, trying to pick out familiar words in the strange tongue. The conversation went on too long. Her legs started to cramp, and she shifted back and forth on her heels, her thumb worrying over the pommel of her sword.

Eventually Zoccinder stopped and stood and worked a kink out of his neck. He fixed her with his blue eyes, which looked black in the lantern light. "This fellow doesn't remember any Dark Knights joining with them, though he says he remembers that a group of goblins came back after the first earthquakes and killed plenty of Dark Knights in a surprise raid on Steel Town."

Bera curled her lip. "Ask it about the rest of the goblins that escaped. Which way did they go? The traitor knights must be with them."

"I did ask that. Says he doesn't know where the larger group went, just that his clan, and some other clans, came this way instead. Says his leader"—Zoccinder gestured to a mound of dead goblins. More were being heaped on the pile as he watched.—"his clan did not want to go wherever the large group was headed. He says if there are more Dark Knights, like us, hunting for goblins in the mountains, then they will probably be found."

"Yes, that will be their fate," Bera said. In truth there was only one other unit, not quite as strong in numbers as hers. "Tell it that all of the escaped slaves will be hunted down and killed. Escaping is an affront that will be punished, making an example for the rest of the Order's slaves. Tell it death is the penalty for running. Tell it . . ." She paused and ran her hands through her short brown hair, feeling it stiff with blood spatter. "Forget it. Tell it nothing else. Kill the one with the broken leg, Zoccinder. The other two will be marched back to Jelek in the morning. Lord Adjudicator Galen Nemedi asked we spare only a few for questioning and to be made examples of at another labor camp. More than that will burden our travel. And we have more work to do." She took a dozen steps and looked over her shoulder. "And leave the dead one tied up with the two living ones."

Bera sat apart from the men, her back against a spike of rock on the western side of the valley. She listened to the steady buzz of conversation, the occasional outburst of laughter from those around the fire, and above it all the deep voice of Zoccinder, who was singing. He sang on almost every night that she didn't order a quiet camp, usually offering hymns to the gods, but his choice that night was a battle song about the blue dragons and their riders who had died in the Chaos War. She could see his huge silhouette against the fire. She watched him and the specks of red that popped off the burning wood and floated away like fireflies.

Zoccinder was starting in on the second chorus when a figure approached her, blocking Bera's view.

"Commander?"

"Isaam." Bera nodded a greeting and gestured for the wizard to sit next to her.

"I was listening to Zoccinder," Bera murmured. She kept her eyes on him, even when the wizard sat so close that their shoulders touched. The wizard was a slight man, only five and a half feet tall, with an oddly pudgy face that reminded Bera of a bulldog's.

"Yes, a remarkable voice Zocci has," the wizard admitted. "Quite the repertoire too." Together they listened until the song finished, to the mild applause of the other Dark Knights who'd been lulled into paying attention. "I understand you do not want me to burn the dead goblins, Commander."

Bera shook her head. "No."

"They draw bugs. Have you been over to the mound of dead? The gnats are thick as river fog. And there are beetles."

13

"Insects don't bother me, Isaam."

"It is customary to burn the bodies. We always burn goblins." The wizard had been under Bera's command for nearly a decade. He was her second, and so she allowed him to argue with her from time to time. "We should accord them the honor of burial . . ."

Bera chuckled softly. "You don't know all that much about goblins, do you, Isaam?"

"No. Do you?"

"I know enough."

"To hate them. I know you hate them, Commander."

Bera smiled. "Aye, they are rats to me."

"So far from humankind, you've said. I agree. Repulsive little things."

"And their practices are barbaric." Bera held her hand up, briefly halting the discussion as Zoccinder launched into another song. She'd heard that one a few times before, and when he reached the chorus, she continued. "I've had you burn goblins before; I well know that. But this time is different. This time we leave two survivors to tell the tale of this night. Don't you understand, old friend? They prefer us to burn the bodies of their dead. It is not enough that bodies are dismembered, shredded, the bones broken. They must be burned. Otherwise, they believe, goblin souls will come back, returning to broken, rotting bodies."

Isaam's eyes grew wide. "In all my years with you, I've not heard you speak of this."

"I've had no reason to, old friend. We're not slavers to capture goblins, and so we've not left any survivors before. As you say, we've burned them before."

"But we've never before camped in such close proximity to the dead either. By all the gods, the stench and bugs—"

"We'll move on at first light, Isaam."

The wizard gestured toward the pile. "And so if their bodies are burned, the souls are freed, eh?"

"That is what they believe. Otherwise the souls will return and be trapped in rotting corpses. But when the bodies are burned, the souls are free to move elsewhere and start a new life in a goblin baby being born," Bera finished.

"What an insipid belief," the wizard pronounced.

"They are insipid creatures." Bera wriggled her nose in disgust. "And so the dead ones can draw bugs, and so the two we've left alive stare at the mound of corpses in terror, thinking the souls are seeping back and reinhabiting the bodies, becoming trapped."

The wizard nodded. "A horror story you've birthed."

"The two survivors will be taken to a slave encampment when the Lord Adjudicator is done with them. They'll be quick to tell the slaves there about the massacre of their fellow escapees. And they'll tell them that the dead were left intact so the souls would come back to be ensnared forever."

Isaam shuddered. "I understand the policy now."

"Use their own beliefs against them."

"The Order needs hundreds more slaves to rebuild Iverton." Isaam rubbed at the stubble on his chin. "Perhaps we should not kill so many; we could bring back many more for labor."

Bera made a growling sound in her throat. "My orders were to spare only a few, so the tale of the mass killing could be spread, so slaves elsewhere will know that escape only leads to death and damnation." She gestured to the northeast. "Already ogres and minotaurs work to gather more slaves for the Order. They look to the north, where your magic says the escaped slaves did not go."

"Yes. That is correct."

"Good."

Isaam studied Bera for several moments. "I think you are enjoying this assignment."

"Yes, old friend." Revenge, Bera thought, vengeance for my father. Vengeance for the Order. "On many levels. Slaves dishonor the Order by escaping." Bera clenched her hands so tightly that they ached. "It cannot be tolerated."

"And renegade Dark Knights . . ."

"They are even worse," Bera corrected. "No traitors to the Order should escape punishment. They must be hunted down too."

Isaam pointed toward the fire. Zoccinder stood with

his back to it, staring at them. After a moment, he started walking their way. Isaam got to his feet.

"The wizard too," Isaam said.

"Grallik N'sera," Bera said.

Isaam pulled an empty bottle from a pocket of his robe. "This is all I have to follow him with, all that was salvaged from where he lived in Iverton. The ink in it has dried, and the top is melted. But Grallik N'sera used it, and so I am using it too." He replaced the bottle. "It is enough of a link that I can scry upon him. It and my spells tell me he is still with the goblins. In these mountains, somewhere, Commander. These vast, vast mountains."

Bera stood too, eyes on Zoccinder, who had come up close to them, ignoring Isaam even as she spoke to him. "But not with this group of goblins."

Isaam shrugged. "Unfortunately, no."

"Then we resume our search at first light," Bera commanded. "Would that your magic were more precise, old friend. Would that it could lead us directly to him."

Isaam took that as a dismissal and headed toward the fire, giving Zoccinder a wide berth. The big knight turned to watch the wizard, then turned back to face Bera.

"Commander?"

"What do you want, Zoccinder? It is late, and the men are settling down for—"

He bent and his warm breath tickled her forehead.

For a moment, Bera considered berating him for his insolence.

3

GRALLIK'S AIM

Grallik N'sera sat cross-legged on an uneven patch of dirt, staring straight up and trying to ignore the pebbles that bit into the backs of his legs.

The sky looked as flat and gray as the iron he used to leech from the rocks in Steel Town, the same shade as the fine robe that once served as a badge of office, the one he'd given to the goblins as an act of surrender.

There were no clouds or birds to catch his attention, no breeze to tease his filthy, matted hair—just an unending emptiness that cast a gloomy pallor and masked the time of day. It could have been morning or early evening for all he knew; he'd lost track of how long he'd walked before being allowed a respite.

"Was this a mistake?" he whispered.

He was on a mountain trail in the company of hundreds of goblins, most of them milling behind him, resting their ugly little feet. He wished they would rest their tongues instead. Grallik could not shut out their galling chatter, which sounded like locusts swarming. He couldn't fathom their crude language and had no desire to learn it.

His head pounded horribly from the annoying din and competed with the burning ache that suffused every inch of his body.

"Was this a mistake?" he repeated.

17

Throwing in his lot with the once-slaves? Leaving the Dark Knights? Abandoning decades of work for an Order he'd been unswervingly loyal to?

The goblins could kill him at any time; his magic could not best their numbers, and he knew they all hated him. Had he brought about his own demise by practically groveling to join them?

He dropped his right hand onto his knee and rubbed at the thin material of his undertunic, finding a hole and absently worrying at the frayed threads. The goblins had let him keep the utterly dirty and snagged garment, along with his boots, which he'd taken off the corpse of another Dark Knight. One heel was cracked down the middle and would break soon, and the sole of the other had worn through in places and birthed painful blisters. It hurt to wear them, but he knew it would hurt far worse to go barefoot over the rocky ground.

It hadn't been a mistake to leave Steel Town, he told himself.

There couldn't be much left of the Dark Knight mining camp. What the earthquakes hadn't ruined and what the escaping slaves hadn't destroyed, the erupting volcanoes had no doubt finished.

Shattered, melted, buried . . . all of it.

He'd barely escaped the lava himself, following the slaves south into the mountains before magma covered everything that had been important to him. Sulfur still hung heavy in the air, and that, coupled with the stink that rose from the goblins like an omnipresent specter, threatened to send him into another fit of retching.

Grallik worked up some saliva, swallowing hard and frowning when he was unable to dispel the taste of the sulfur and dust and his own reeking sweat. He felt his skin pulling here and there from thick scabs forming, on his left arm in particular, where yesterday he squeezed against a jagged outcropping on a narrow part of the trail. He'd cut himself rather deeply.

Horace, a Dark Knight priest he'd lured along on his mad venture, had tended him, but Grallik had opened the cut again that morning. Grallik focused on his wound, hoping that its sting would take his mind off the rest of his miseries and swearing when the attempt was unsuccessful. He let out a hissing breath and lowered his gaze to the sleeping form of Horace an arm's length away.

The priest was dressed only in leather breeches, which had been stripped from the corpse of a young ogre and given to him by the goblins before they'd started their march. Like Grallik, the priest had surrendered his Dark Knight tabard, along with his chain mail, which a stout hobgoblin had claimed.

Had it been a mistake to bring the Ergothian priest with him? Grallik wondered. And for that matter, should he have invited the only remaining member of his talon?

Should he have headed north or east and found a Dark Knight outpost, accepted another posting?

No, he told himself not for the first or last time, eyes focused on the regular rising and falling of Horace's ample stomach. "None of it was a mistake."

Grallik had followed the once-slaves for purely selfish reasons. It wasn't to save himself when the world shook and the volcanoes erupted, but to better himself. And he hadn't so much as followed the slaves as he'd followed one slave—her.

He could see her when he leaned forward and looked around—a gaunt goblin wearing a Dark Knight tabard.

She was a diminutive, red-skinned thing with a flat face and wide eyes threaded with tiny veins. Her small mouth was drawn forward in a pensive expression. She commanded a discipline of magic that Grallik didn't understand but desperately wanted to learn and control. When he'd watched her in the slave pens back in Steel Town, he'd seen her combine her magic with that of another goblin. She was doing that at that moment, kneeling across from a mud-brown creature a head taller than she was, a goblin with a mottled, bumpy hide that looked like a piece of the trail come to life. Together they rocked back and forth, slowly, fingertips brushing the ground.

Back in the mining camp, their magic had created a

hole beneath the slave pen that their fellows could escape through. He wondered what magic she and her mud-brown companion were casting.

More, he wondered when he would get an opportunity to speak with her. The thought of a lowly goblin teaching him anything was at the same time appealing and demeaning. The wizards he'd studied under in his youth would consider his notion blasphemous.

Goblins were so far beneath men!

But that one goblin . . . she was special. She was why he had risked everything. No human or elf wizard Grallik had studied under had been able to join magic with another, with the earth, in the same way.

Grallik needed to get her alone—or as alone as possible amid that malodorous mass. She knew a smattering of the human tongue, so he felt certain he could make her understand what he wanted.

Would she consent to teach him?

By the dark gods, she had to; otherwise all of his humiliation and agony would be for nothing.

But it might be days before he could find the right opportunity. The crowded mountain trail certainly wasn't the place. So meanwhile, he would continue to watch her and wait until they left the trail and returned to flat ground, where the goblins and hobgoblins would spread out and he might find her alone.

"Patience," he whispered to himself. "It will happen." He stifled a yawn and glanced back at Horace, the priest's stomach still rising and falling in sound sleep.

Grallik envied the Ergothian, who seemed to have no trouble dropping off peacefully any time the goblin horde stopped their march. The priest had told Grallik it was Zeboim's will that he slept deeply, so that he could better face the rigors of each day.

But no god seemed to will that Grallik should sleep—at least, not long enough to do him any good.

Despite his exhaustion, Grallik couldn't bring himself to close his eyes; he didn't trust the goblins not to slit his throat as he dozed. His wounds ached. His feet hadn't stopped throbbing since he joined with the goblins. His head constantly pounded as loudly and rhythmically as a blacksmith's hammer. His legs were beyond sore; sometimes he couldn't feel them.

Grallik's magic was powerful, but he didn't know a single spell that could ease his wracked condition. In Steel Town Grallik's spells enabled the work of the great smelters, and he fashioned glyphs and wards that shot columns of flame into the sky and kept the slaves in check. Fire spells came almost effortlessly.

Horace *slept* effortlessly.

Grallik tapped the fingers of his left hand against his temple and studied the priest's face. Horace's expression was serene. But in the passing of a few heartbeats, beads of sweat dotted his smooth forehead, and his eyelids twitched as if he were lost in a troubling dream. Moments more passed, and the sweat became a fine sheen that covered all of his face and traveled down his neck to settle on his bare stomach. The priest's breathing became ragged. The goblin wearing the Dark Knight tabard turned to stare. She grunted something Grallik couldn't understand, wiped her nose on her arm, and closed her eyes.

A smile tugged at the corner of Grallik's lips as Horace's discomfort increased. His sleep was no longer so peaceful. The wizard had no intention of harming the priest, just making him a little uneasy. It wasn't fair that Grallik should suffer without company.

Grallik stopped worrying at the thread on his undertunic just as Horace bolted upright, gasping. The priest placed the back of his hand against his cheek, as if to check for a fever, then slowly turned and glared at Grallik.

But the wizard did not meet the priest's gaze. He had returned his attention to the red-skinned goblin. Her arms were thrust into the hard-packed earth nearly up to her elbows. It was as if the ground had turned to liquid around her.

"No, this was not a mistake," Grallik said to himself.

4

MUDWORT'S REACH

Mudwort let out a ragged sigh, wrinkling her nose at the pungent scent of her own breath. She watched Boliver leave, wending his way past a lean hobgoblin and disappearing in the mass of bodies milling on the mountain trail. Mingling their magic had not yielded what Direfang wanted. In fact, it had not worked at all.

Her fault, she knew. She was too unfocused and listless, her mind wandering freely into the earth and thinking only about the earth itself. Boliver had been right to give up on her.

The earth had shaken so fiercely in days past that it had caused the mine to collapse and the volcanoes to erupt. She had predicted the disasters, sensing the nervousness in the rocks. She had marveled at the earth's power, pleased that its violence had led to their freedom, worried that it had forevermore become a wobbly, uncertain, distrustful thing. Above all, she remained curious.

How soon would the earth tremble again? Would great rents appear soon and suck down more goblins and hobgoblins and the three Dark Knights who were their prisoners? Would bulges in the land arise without warning to block their path or push them off the mountain? Would the volcanoes breathe their hellish fire once more?

Her fingers teased the rocks that did not feel nervous.

They were smooth and sleeping, and the longer she touched them, the more relaxed she became.

"Perhaps the ground is tired and done," Mudwort said to herself. "Perhaps it will not bounce again." She, too, was tired, and the soothing pebbles lulled her toward sleep.

A muffled wail startled her. Glancing up the trail, she spotted Direfang cradling Graytoes. The once-delicate features of the young goblin with skin the color of sunflower petals were twisted in pain as Direfang held her, and she sobbed over the loss of her mate, Moon-eye. She had been sobbing practically every minute she was awake. Moon-eye had tarried behind the column, and a scout searching for him the previous day reported seeing a big cat feasting on his corpse.

Graytoes was as worthless as her dead mate, Mudwort decided—worse than worthless, as she was commanding Direfang's attention and pointlessly caterwauling all the time. It might not be such a bad thing if the earth opened up and swallowed Graytoes.

Mudwort missed Moon-eye too, or rather, she missed his abilities. His senses had been keen, and he had tracked better than anyone she knew. If he were alive, Moon-eye would have been tasked with her present assignment.

Graytoes wailed louder.

"A bag of flesh with a sad, sour mind, Graytoes is," Mudwort muttered. She cocked her head and heard Direfang talking to Graytoes, no doubt trying to calm her. She also heard the Dark Knight priest blathering to the Dark Knight wizard in their horrid-sounding tongue, and she picked out pieces of other conversations between goblins and hobgoblins—all of whom should be resting rather than bothering her by crowding the air with their unimportant prattle. She dismissed the jumble of words and returned her attention to the earth.

Direfang had given her a task. It was past time she tended to it.

She pushed her arms even farther into the earth, which her mind had willed to be as soft as clay. She stopped just short of her shoulders, her face pressing close. Breathing deep, she welcomed the smell of the dirt, far preferable to her own odor and the stench of sulfur that still filled the air. She held the dirt-scent deep in her lungs and relished it, again becoming distracted.

The task! Mudwort cursed herself for being so easily sidetracked. Do what Direfang asks!

She closed her eyes and imagined she was an ant scurrying down her arm and into the ground, leaving the noisy mass of her kinsmen behind and following a maze of thin cracks plunging down, down. In the back of her mind she saw rock shards and the husks of dead insects, all pleasantly cocooned by the dirt.

Deeper and farther south she traveled, in the direction Direfang was leading them. She detected tiny bones, likely those of a bird, and the desiccated dung of some creature. There were cracks everywhere her ant-mind wandered, some reaching up to the surface, others leading to mysteries she craved to explore. She felt hooves atop the trail and up a rise, and was curious as to their source.

She felt heat, residue from the volcanoes—their touch noticed even there, though the lava was many miles behind them. Small nests of grubs and pockets of beetles caught her attention; those she lingered on. Her stomach rumbled with hunger. She was thirsty too, and the thick, juicy insects would help to sate her. But there were only handfuls of squirming things here and there—not enough to be of much use. Certainly not what Direfang had tasked her to find. She should look closer at the hoofed things up above, she thought again.

Was Direfang watching her as she worked? Was he upset that she'd not come up with anything yet? Or was empty-Graytoes still bothering him? For an instant the buzz of conversations from the hobgoblins and goblins intruded on her consciousness. Someone complained of aching legs. Another speculated the Dark Knights might be tasty.

The task!

Once more she forced the chatter away and continued her earth-journey. She let the dirt press down on her, embracing the smothering sensation and the darkness. A calm settled in her core, and all the goblin sounds melted to nothingness. Mudwort held her breath.

Calm.

She exhaled slowly, the scent of the blessed dirt nearly overwhelming her. She continued to slip to the south, leaving her body and the hundreds of other goblins far behind and taking her senses on an amazing journey.

So perfect things were down in the earth, she thought. The world around her had thoroughly receded, and there were only granules of rich dirt, smooth pebbles, small roots of long-dead plants, a colorful egg-shaped insect, and much, much more. Everything was so interesting and perfect. Even the cracks her senses crawled through intrigued and pleased her.

She brushed against something cool and hard, and she peered closer. It was a crystal embedded in a chunk of ugly grayness. Pretty, it was a transparent blue-green with six sides and thin grooves that would do well as a decoration. A few such similar pieces had been found in the Dark Knight mines and been fashioned into jewelry. Beryl, she remembered the crystals being called. It was odd that humans had names for rocks. But then, they seemed to have words for everything.

Perhaps the crystal was not terribly deeply buried and she could dig it out. Just where was it? She willed her ant-mind to spiral outward and up, so she might learn precisely where the pretty stone was buried, ahead on the trail.

Suddenly a crack widened below, and her mind slid away from the crystal and felt the tug of something secret.

What is this?

What Direfang wanted would not lie so deep, she knew, and so she should not pursue that secret. Instead, she looked for the hoofed creatures she sensed farther down the mountain trail, but she hoped not too far. If Moon-eye were alive, he would be helping her see all of that, she reflected, and she would be free to roam and unravel the beckoning secrets in the belly of the world.

"Should not do this," she told herself. "No time for this." But she allowed herself to be tugged away from her task regardless. "Just for a little moment. Direfang will not know."

What would be the harm?

She could take just a quick look at the mystery. Then she would help Direfang, herself, and all of the goblins and hobgoblins stuck on the mountain trail, help them find something to eat. One quick look. No one need know.

Besides, Direfang had empty-Graytoes to occupy him.

The crack widened the farther down it she went.

"Share the secret," she murmured, unaware that she had spoken the words aloud above the earth, drawing the attention of Grallik and the Dark Knight priest. "What is the mystery?"

She spied a cavern in the distance, and though so far underground it should have been blackest-black, she could make out myriad details. The walls were granite in places, a common enough stone. But sections were cut through with beautiful dark red crystals, some filled with spiderweb-fine cracks.

"Fragile rocks," Mudwort guessed. "Fire-colored and pretty as beryl."

The floor was likewise granite, but there was an oval patch that was smooth and deliberately polished, reflecting light that spilled out of a tunnel she hadn't immediately noticed. A cluster of short, prismatic crystals, dark green and gleaming, sat in a copper bowl in the center of the smooth patch.

A smile threatened to break out on Mudwort's face. That was far more interesting than what Direfang had asked her to look for. What wonderful secrets the earth hid!

Just where was that cave? Was there a way down from the mountain trail? Could Mudwort physically reach that secret place?

The cave floor felt cold to her senses, and air stirred, coming from the tunnel. The air on the mountain trail was dead and gray and reeking of sulfur. Below, it carried the scents of the rocks, of water that trickled somewhere out of sight, and of something that seemed familiar but was not quite familiar.

A part of her wished that Boliver had not given up on her so soon and that he could see that amazing place. But a greater part was glad that she was alone, so she could keep the precious secret to herself. Her secret!

"Where is this place?"

She started toward the tunnel, slowly so she could take in everything. There were carvings around the polished oval on the floor, odd symbols that might have been a language or were simply pictures. Stick drawings of animals, perhaps. She studied them a moment and picked out what might be representations of bears and bats. But she could make no sense of most of the drawings. There were more such markings on one wall of the tunnel, and the flickering light made the crude carvings appear to move.

The tunnel floor was smooth, though not polished like the oval, worn perhaps from feet—just like places in the Dark Knights' mines that were worn from the feet of goblins who had labored there for so many years.

The light grew brighter as she continued down the tunnel, the scents intensifying. The odors of the familiar-but-not-quite-familiar thing, and water—definitely water— filled her nostrils. Direfang would be interested in the latter discovery, Mudwort thought. All of them were so thirsty. And so he would not be upset that she'd let the earth distract her, tug her. She heard the splash of something. A moment more, and she heard voices.

It was a language she could understand!

"Mudwort!" Direfang was growling her name, drowning out the conversation she heard below ground. "Mudwort find anything?"

She fought to keep her mind in the tunnel, but the hob-goblin tapped her shoulder then jostled her, threatening the spell.

"Mudwort find something?"

"No," she said as she tried desperately to concentrate on the cavern. "Find nothing."

He nudged her once more, and all traces of the cool air that had stirred around her senses vanished. It was replaced by still air filled with the stench of sulfur and the tang of sweaty goblins and hobgoblins. She felt the clay her arms were thrust into hardening.

"No!" she shouted. "Found nothing!" The cavern below disappeared from her mind, the spell completely broken. Damn Direfang! She'd wanted at the least to find out where the mysterious cavern was.

She heard the Dark Knight priest talking behind her, his ugly-sounding words coming so fast, she couldn't understand what he was saying. Direfang continued to question her. Graytoes still sobbed, though not as loudly as before. There were other conversations and other sounds, the whisper-soft bleat of something . . . of several somethings—the hoofed creatures.

"Mudwort find anything?"

She tugged her arms out of the earth, the clay thoroughly hard and as dusty-dry as it had been before she used her magic.

"Something?" she snarled angrily. "Yes, found something, Direfang." The hobgoblin had ripped her mind away from the marvelous secret.

"Find what?" Direfang asked, looming over her.

The hobgoblin was nearly seven feet tall, easily twice Mudwort's height. His hide was dark gray and hairy, but there were spots on his chest and upper arms that were heavily scarred and where no hair grew. "Mudwort find what?"

"Sheep, goats," she returned, trying to keep the anger out of her voice. "Feel the hooves against the ground. Find food. Found just what Direfang wanted." Mudwort futilely tried to brush the dirt off her arms then scratched at her chin and pointed down the trail. "Farther south, but not too far. And there are not many."

"Food," Direfang repeated, sounding pleased. He motioned for the goblins and hobgoblins to stand and pointed south. "Good Mudwort found some food."

5

THYA'S CLAN

The mountainside was high and steep, but the rocks were jagged and provided plenty of tiny hand- and footholds for the goblins climbing it. Thya chose that section because it was so sheer; the ogres that had been pursuing the clan could not fit their large, thick fingers into the crevices the goblins used and were, therefore, stuck at the bottom. However, before the ogres had given up, they had managed to catch a dozen of the goblins who hadn't scaled the rocks fast enough.

"A smart one, Thya is," a pale gray goblin pronounced when the clan finally reached the top. "Smart to find a path the ogres could not take. Not many clansmen lost."

It was midmorning, and the sun struggled to chase away the chill that wrapped around the peaks. There were no clouds, and the bright, blue sky was almost hurtful to the goblins, who had spent their lives in the caves to the north, emerging in only the evenings to hunt.

There were nearly two hundred clansmen, all of them panting and out of breath, some of them fearful of the height, most of them shielding their eyes from the brightness.

"Never climbed like this before," one of the young ones said. Her arms were wrapped around a spire, her eyes closed. "Like the low places much, much better. Like the dark better too."

29

"Arms so sore," Rockhide complained. He was the oldest goblin, the one who had insisted the clan leave their home. The earth inside their main cave had told him the ogres were coming. "Need to rest here," he continued. "This clan needs to sleep and—"

"Sleep later, Rockhide. Sleep now and this clan might never leave this peak." Thya had threaded her way through the crowd. Perched as they were on a narrow part of the mountain, there was little room to maneuver, so she used great care.

"Understand? This clan must move now. Sleep later when it is safe, Rockhide." Thya was overly tall for a goblin, nearly four feet, and her skin was the color of pine bark. Her face was long and narrow, her nose wide, the center of it pierced with a silver ring she'd taken from the corpse of a merchant a few years back. She wore his shirt too, gathered at the waist and tied with a leather cord that had been around the merchant's neck. A charm dangled from the cord, a jade dragon's claw that she rubbed each morning as a luck ritual.

"Move now!" she shouted, raising her right fist, small finger crooked outward. The finger had been broken—along with other bones—when she'd fought for leadership of the clan eight months past. The finger was the one thing that hadn't properly mended. "Move now, or stay here and die."

"Safe here," Rockhide argued. "Safe so high where the ogres cannot come."

She bent until her face was inches from his. "Do the stones say it is safe?" She hadn't meant it as an honest question, more as a taunt, but the old one looked dazed and worried.

"So tired," he answered. "Thya, just rest a little—"

"The ogres are not tired," she returned, raising her voice so plenty of other clansmen could hear. "The ogres did not climb the mountain, and so are not tired at all. The ogres will look for an easier way up here and could well find a path. The ogres will not give up. A smart goblin does not need to talk to the ground to know that." She stood and squared her shoulders, tipped her chin up, and shook her fist. "South now, or wait for the ogres. Wait to be taken and sold as slaves."

She picked her way back through the throng, nodding to each one as she went and telling them to be careful treading on the rocks. The goblins had as many of their worldly possessions with them as they could carry; most were items looted from trappers and goatherds who had ventured too close to the clan caves. A few goblins, such as Thya, had more valuable treasures from raiding the merchants who came through a pass to the north.

She was pleased there was no real challenge to her command to keep moving. Even Rockhide was edging his way along the summit, though he still grumbled about it and rubbed at his arms. Her arms hurt too; her legs and feet ached. But Thya could not show any weakness.

"South," she said. "The mountain goes south, and so does this clan."

"Why south?" That came from a youngling standing directly behind her. The small goblin had little trouble with the terrain, but he blinked furiously because of the harsh sunlight. "What is south, Thya? Are there more ogres to the south?"

Thya shrugged. She was not one to lie to her clansmen. Her father had taught her from an early age that the truth was easier and could always be remembered. Lies were easy to get tangled in.

"Maybe more ogres, maybe minotaurs, maybe worse," Thya said. "But maybe peace too. That is what the stones say, that peace lies to the south. That many goblins are massing to the south, and that clans are banding together for safety."

The youngling tugged on Thya's shirt as she continued on her way, following the spine of the mountain.

"Cannot hear the stones, Thya. Cannot listen—"

"Then listen to Thya, little Rawdon." A stoop-shouldered goblin nudged the youngling along. "Thya can hear the stones, and that is enough."

Thya listened to the stones as she led her clan south, heard the voice of the earth coming up through the soles of her aching feet. She was not as proficient with earth-magic as her mentor, Rockhide, and she had not heard the warning about the ogres coming. But she had, days past, heard the summons and been touched by the mind of a goblin called Mudwort. She'd thought little of the call then, having no desire to leave her comfortable cave. But the ogres changed that, and she listened more intently to the earth as they traveled. It told her the northern lands were not safe, and that ogres and minotaurs hunted her kind. They were to be sold as slaves, she knew. Though Thya had always lived free, she'd lost many friends and kinsmen to slavery.

What the Dark Knights did not want to do for themselves, the goblins were forced to do. And stories said the Dark Knights paid the ogres well for strong, young goblins.

"South," she said. "There is safety to the south." It wasn't a lie she spoke; Thya firmly believed they were going to a better place.

6

THE TYLOR

Dragon! Dragondragondragon!" called the goblin named Knobnose, a potbellied youngster whose yellow skin marked him as one of Saro-Saro's clan. He stood on the ridge, pointed down to the huge beast at the base of the foothills, jumped, and waggled his fingers. "Dragondragondragon!" he repeated, spittle flying from his quivering lips.

"That's not a dragon," Spikehollow said. He shoved Knobnose back so the youngster wouldn't tumble down the ridge; then he motioned the first wave of goblins forward. "But it might as well be a dragon for its size," he added to himself. He drew a deep breath, swallowed hard, and brandished a long knife he'd taken days past from a dying Dark Knight. "Be fast! Be deadly!"

Spikehollow's feet slapped against the stone as he whooped and urged more than one hundred of his fellows to follow. Their cries of "Be fast! Be deadly!" rose to a deafening din, and the gravel crunched under their heels as they barreled down the ridge toward the beast.

It made no move to flee.

The sky was copper from the late-afternoon sun, and it painted the goblins and the ground with broad, shimmering strokes, blending everything into earthen hues, including the creature they swarmed toward.

33

It stretched more than sixty feet from snout to stubby tail tip, with a mottled brown hide that made it look like a huge living hill. Its toes were as big around as tree trunks. And it had thick, blunt talons the color of eggshells that were split along the edges from digging in the hard ground. Its curved horns gleamed white like a bull's, and its head looked vaguely like a dragon's but was too wide and short. Its saucer-shaped eyes were set in the front of its skull, rather than perched toward the sides where a real dragon's would be. When it moved, there was a flash of green along its flanks and at the base of its tail.

"A green dragon," Grallik observed from the top of the ridge. A second wave of goblins descended, at least two hundred. The wizard leaped back to keep from getting swept up in the rush.

"That is not a green dragon," Horace said after another group went hollering down the rise. The priest stood farther back from the edge, a safer perch. He shook his head and pulled his lower lip into his mouth. "It is a tylor, Grallik. Not a dragon."

The wizard made a growling sound. "I know that, Horace. It is a spawn of a dragon and a hatori. Aye, a tylor. The Dark Knights had one hatori in Steel Town, which they forced to dig tunnels. The hatori escaped during the quake, slaying knights and goblins in its wake. In fact, Horace, I suspect . . ." The rest of the wizard's words were drowned out by the thunder of more goblin and hobgoblin feet pounding against the trail and over the side, the whooping and yelling growing to a painful cacophony.

The beast watched the oncoming waves with mild interest. More than half of Direfang's force was streaming toward it.

It laid its ears back and opened its maw, revealing a long black tongue and jagged teeth that looked like broken chunks of charred wood. It bellowed, the sound cutting through the chorus of goblin shouts, and it lumbered back from the base of the hill, allowing the horde more room to swarm around it.

DEATH MARCH

Away from the shadow of the hill, more green scales showed. Interspersed with the brown patches, it made the creature look like a massive piece of rotting meat. It had that sort of foul stench, which wafted up the ridge to Grallik and Horace and made them gag.

"An abomination!" Grallik shouted, his voice sounding like a croaking whisper. He coughed, his shoulders bouncing from the strength of the spasm. He'd developed the cough in Steel Town, and it lingered even though they were miles from the place. "That's what it is, priest, an utter abomination, a monster that should not exist!"

The priest shook his head again and mouthed something the wizard could not hear.

Below, the tylor's neck stretched, and its jaws opened and snapped shut with a speed that startled the horde. Its teeth pierced one goblin, then another, and it threw its head back greedily as it swallowed them.

Suddenly dozens of goblins and hobgoblins shrieked in terror and fled from it, letting their knives and swords slip from their sweat-slick fingers.

"Feyrh!" they shouted. Flee!

On the rise, Direfang stared in disbelief.

"It is a rare creature of magic, Foreman. The tylor's second skin is fear," Horace said.

Direfang had to strain to hear the priest's words. The hobgoblin leader had moved up between the two Dark Knights. He still held Graytoes, who continued to whimper. Anxious goblins crowded around him and the Dark Knights. Direfang had held many of the goblins back from the fight; they were too young or too old or weaponless. The hobgoblin leader had remained behind only because of Graytoes.

"Explain, skull man," Direfang shouted. He scowled at the goblins continuing to flee and gestured futilely at those scrambling back up the ridge. They ignored him, continuing to climb.

Horace screamed to be heard above the din, the panic, and the thunderous growl of the tylor. "It is part dragon, and so it exudes magic! Fear! It terrifies your army with a thought. You were a fool to order it attacked, your rumbling bellies be damned! It will kill them all!"

"Then help, skull man," Direfang shot back. He held Graytoes with one arm, his free hand shooting out to clamp itself around Horace's neck. "Help now!"

Horace tried to wriggle free of the hobgoblin's grip, but Direfang only squeezed tighter.

"Wizard, help too!" Direfang bellowed. "Burn that thing or die to it!" He made a gesture as though threatening to push the wizard off the ridge. "Use the fire magic."

"Can't breathe," Horace managed to gasp. "Can't . . ."

Direfang relaxed his grip on the priest only slightly. Horace gulped in as much air as he could, like a drowning man rising to the surface, and began gesturing with his fingers, pointing down the rise toward the goblins fleeing from the tylor. He tried to explain what he was doing, but only a croaking sound came out.

"He's stopping them from running, the goblins," Grallik supplied. "He's giving them courage."

"Fire, wizard. Now! Use the fire magic!"

Grallik brushed his hair out of his eyes and stared at the great beast below. Goblins lay dead around its front claws; three more were dying in its jaws. It tossed its head back and forth as it chewed, and even from that distance, Grallik could see the pleased gleam in its eyes.

"Not for much longer will you feast, abomination," Grallik hissed. He thrust his hands forward, angled down, thumbs touching. His left hand looked wet, the scars thick on it and glistening from his sweat. A moment more and his pale skin glowed yellow, then white. Fire crackled along his fingers and arced down like lightning to strike the tylor's head.

Flame danced around the beast's jaws and settled on its tongue. It howled and reared back on stunted legs, its front legs flailing and its stubby tail twitching.

Grallik repeated the spell, striking the armored plates of its stomach, turning the fire white-hot and causing the beast's natural armor to sizzle and pop.

The goblins who had not yet fled in fear redoubled their

efforts, massing close to the creature and stabbing viciously with the knives and swords they'd taken from Steel Town, jumping back to avoid the fire and the claws and darting in again.

The goblins and hobgoblins who had scattered in flight stopped running and turned to stare, bolstered by the priest's magic. Some shook their heads as if they'd been awakened from a bad dream. Spikehollow was among that group, and he blinked furiously and vomited from the stench of the burning tylor.

Above, the priest mouthed a prayer to Zeboim and tried once more to pull himself out of Direfang's grip, that time successfully.

"Sea Mother," Horace blurted, "give them strength and courage." There were other words he might utter, but they were much softer and not meant for the hobgoblin's ears. Then his voice rose again. "Fill their hearts with courage, their blood with ire. Help them . . . by the goddess!"

Below, the beast shimmered; then suddenly it vanished. A heartbeat later it reappeared a hundred or so feet to the west. It whirled to face the goblins that immediately charged toward it again. Then it raised its head and locked eyes with the priest on the ridge.

Horace trembled. "I told you, Foreman, it is a creature of magic, that tylor. Smart, too, and far more than your little friends can deal with. It could—"

The tylor roared and iridescent waves rolled out of its maw, striking the ridge and shattering it where Direfang, Graytoes, and the Dark Knights stood. Horace and Grallik dropped with the collapsing rise. Direfang, Graytoes, and the rest of the goblins fell at the same time, choking dust billowing everywhere.

Fist-sized rocks pounded the wizard and the priest as they tried to scramble to their feet. Grallik could find no purchase and clumsily somersaulted down to the bottom, cutting himself on jagged shards and opening the gash on his arm even wider. A coughing fit struck him as his shoulders slammed against the ground, and he sucked in a mouthful of dirt and stone dust.

Suddenly hands pulled him up, and more slapped at his back. Direfang and another hobgoblin had come to his aid, the latter chattering at him in the ugly, clacking language of goblinkind.

"Breathe, wizard," Direfang growled.

When Grallik was able to do just that, Direfang grabbed his shoulders and whirled him around to face the tylor, which, down below, was busy ripping through one goblin after the next.

"Fire magic, wizard. Use it now!"

Something raspy and unintelligible came out of Grallik's mouth. He spat, tasting only dirt and blood, his tongue flailing around amid broken teeth. The wizard's head pounded, and the right side of his face felt warm and wet; his blond hair was matted with blood and sweat on his forehead, hanging down in his eyes. He tried to look around to see what had happened to Horace, but Direfang forced him to return his gaze to the tylor.

"Now!" Direfang growled louder. "Now or die!"

It wasn't that the hobgoblin would kill him, Grallik realized, as he called up one of his more familiar fire spells. It was that if he didn't act, the tylor would kill them all.

Concentrating, he sent a thin column of flame lashing down on the beast's back. Not enough to penetrate its scaly hide and hurt it very much, but enough to distract it from its goblin feast. Direfang's army took advantage of Grallik's spell and swarmed in tighter, stabbing fast and furious, desperately.

A dozen feet behind the wizard, Horace was struggling to pick himself up. The priest's bare chest and arms were covered with welts and cuts from his plunge down the shattered ridge. One eye was swelling shut, and a few ribs were broken, making it painful to breathe.

"Zeboim, mother goddess, save us," he whispered. He held his right arm in close, clutching his broken ribs, while he gingerly sucked the dust-choked air into his lungs and began a spell.

Around the priest young goblins were picking themselves up, some crying, the rest too frightened to make a sound. One who looked barely old enough to walk hung tightly to Horace's leg. A few could not raise themselves up because they were dead or dying, and their fellows stared around sadly at them.

"Tottle is not moving," one goblin said.

"Tottle will never move again," another said sadly.

"Three-toes is dying, and Drak and Bosky too," a slight female wailed.

"Mother goddess," Horace croaked, trying futilely to speak louder than the goblins milling around him. "She who is called the Darkling Sea, the Maelstrom, Rann . . . turn the ground beneath the tylor's feet to blessed, thick mud."

Sweat beaded thick on the priest's face as he forced all of his energy into the enchantment. A moment later the glow ran from him like melting butter, settling in a spreading pool around his feet.

At the same time, the earth softened beneath the massive claws of the tylor, and slowly the creature began to sink.

"Zeboim, mother goddess, she who is called Zebir Jotun, Zura the Maelstrom, and Zyr, now turn the ground beneath its feet to stone." The glow around Horace's feet brightened, scattering the young goblins who were able to move. "Mother goddess, stone, I pray!" He sank to his knees, spent, and pitched forward, his face buried in the dirt and scree. The glow faded, and the young goblins carefully returned, poking and prodding the priest, one beckoning an elder goblin to come close.

At the same time, the hobgoblin took a step toward the tylor. "The skull man's magic!" Direfang yelled. "Take advantage! Slay the monster while it cannot move!"

Behind Direfang, Grallik struggled to his feet. "I've nothing left," he said to himself. Despite that, he started gesturing feebly at the beast, desperately trying to summon more magic.

The tylor had dropped into the soft earth, covering up the first joints on its legs. Several goblins were caught in its sinking, and their shrill screams sliced through the air, suddenly, as the ground turned as hard as granite and trapped them as surely as the tylor. The beast screamed its rage, and tried to shimmer as it had before, when it moved itself magically.

But the huge beast went nowhere; it was trapped by the priest's spell. It struggled to pull itself free of the stone. Its thrashing head bludgeoned those goblins closest to it, snapping backs and necks. Then cracks appeared in the stone at its front feet, and a great ball of flame engulfed it, the whooshing noise drowning out the tylor's bellows and the surrounding goblins' screams.

The stench of burning flesh became unbearable as the fire died out almost as quickly as it had materialized. The goblins trapped in stone around the tylor had been incinerated, their smoldering corpses competing with the reek from the tylor's singed hide.

Still, the beast was not dead.

"More fire, wizard!" Direfang barked.

Another hobgoblin slapped Grallik on the back for emphasis. "Do what Direfang says."

"More fire now!" Direfang looked to the ground at his feet, where Graytoes lay whimpering. Abruptly he vaulted over her and drew his sword, one he'd taken from a Dark Knight he'd slain in the mining camp. He raced forward, roaring a battle cry, leaping over rubble and broken and dead goblins, hollering for his surviving kinsmen to join him.

"I've no fire left to give," Grallik muttered. But somehow the wizard was able to stand erect, focus his energy, and hurl another fiery lance, aimed straight at the tylor's open mouth. He had strength left for one more lance, which missed the mark and instead struck the beast's jaw. Then Grallik sagged back against a lean hobgoblin.

Grallik coughed deeper, the hacking spasm painful, and he looked around, again searching for the priest. Grallik wanted Horace to tend to him, but he saw the priest was lying on his stomach, young goblins hovering nearby and jabbing at him. "Dead?"

The wizard glanced up to what was left of the ridge, seeing more goblins streaming down, including Mudwort and the one he thought was named Boliver. The two had been watching from a high perch, out of reach of the tylor's rock-shattering breath.

A sharp intake of air drew Grallik's attention back to the tylor. It was ready to loose another one of those earth-rending breaths, and the wizard flattened himself against the ground in preparation for the blast. But the tylor angled its head down, sending the shimmering waves to break apart the stone that gripped it.

"Be fast! Be deadly!" Direfang shouted as he closed. The cry was repeated by hundreds of goblins in the swarm until the words swelled to a roar that echoed off the mountains and added to the hellish din.

The hobgoblin leader raced straight toward the tylor's snapping mouth, his sword pointed like a lance and his free hand waving the goblins in front of him out of his path. Direfang threw back his head and howled something in the goblin tongue. An instant later he drove the sword into the beast's tongue, the blade sinking through to its bottom jaw and lodging there. Unable to pull the sword free, Direfang snatched up a knife lying by a goblin corpse and darted to the beast's side, barely missing a blow from its wildly swinging head.

Direfang scrambled over stone that was breaking apart at the tylor's feet, jumped in to strike powerfully with his knife, and leaped back.

"It is free!" That came from Spikehollow, who was wielding two long knives dripping red with the tylor's blood. "Be fast! Be deadly, Direfang! The monster is loose!"

The tylor shimmered brightly, and Direfang and Spikehollow charged in unison, stabbing repeatedly at its side and finding that the mottled green-brown patches were softer. They worked at a frenzied pace, urging their fellows to do the same, all caught up in the bloodlust.

The beast started to fade, and for a moment it seemed that it would disappear and shift away to safety, but Direfang continued his relentless assault, as did Spikehollow and the others.

Then the tylor stopped shimmering and opened its

maw and released an ear-splitting howl so loud and painful that it dropped the nearest goblins to their knees. Direfang momentarily lost his grip on the knife, pressed his palms against his ears, squeezed his eyes shut, and stumbled back.

Another lance of fire shot down, and the tylor crumpled.

"It is dead!" Saro-Saro cried. "The dragon is dead!" The cagey old goblin had remained at the edge of the throng, standing on a mound of rubble from the collapsed ridge. He continued to shout, but the cheering of hundreds of his kinsmen blotted out all other sounds.

Saro-Saro climbed down from the rubble and pushed his way through the press of goblins. Age granted him respect, and his kinsmen moved aside. Spikehollow helped him to climb up on the tylor's side. The old, yellow-skinned goblin balanced on the beast's shoulder, raised his arms, and waited for the clamor to subside. It took several moments.

"A feast this night," Saro-Saro began, waiting again until the cheers dwindled. "A feast in the memory of fallen friends." He pointed to the bodies scattered around the tylor. He patted his stomach and lowered his head as if in reverence.

"A feast!" Spikehollow echoed. "Saro-Saro calls for a feast!"

Direfang watched the old goblin pontificate atop the dead beast. Direfang's head pounded from all the noise, and he ached all over, though he knew his injuries were not so bad as many of his fellows'.

He spotted a young goblin named Chima cradling a broken arm, her dark orange skin marking her as a member of the Flamegrass clan.

Another goblin of the same clan, Olabode, rocked back and forth on his hips, bottom lip held between his teeth to prevent him from crying out. A piece of bone jutted up through his thigh.

All around, others were nursing similar and worse wounds.

Death March

"Priest!" Direfang called, craning his neck this way and that. "Skull man! It is time to render aid!"

But Horace did not answer and was nowhere to be seen.

7

SECRETS

Mudwort found Horace beneath a mound of goblin children. She thought the priest was dead and tried to roll him over so she could get at the jug of water that hung from his belt. But he was heavy, and after a few attempts, he groaned and startled her.

."Should be dead," she muttered. "Too bad the skull man's not dead." Louder, she said, "Direfang!" Mudwort gestured to the hovering children. "Get Direfang, now!" Mudwort poked her finger at the tallest to get them moving. "Be fast!"

They scurried off, only two of them heading Direfang's way, the rest scattering. She glanced once more at the priest, who was making a snuffling sound against the dirt, and wrinkled her nose. He smelled of sweat and blood. Though he wasn't much more stinky than her kinsmen, he carried the aroma of a Dark Knight. The smell reminded her of the mine where she'd slaved for too many years.

"Hate the skull men," she hissed. She spit at the priest, kicked his leg, and turned to survey the bloody scene. Saro-Saro had put his clan in charge of butchering the tylor, and the yellow-skinned goblins were busy scrabbling over the carcass that was silhouetted by the setting sun.

Mudwort had watched the battle against the beast from high on the ridge and managed to avoid any injury when part of it collapsed. She'd thought the tylor a hideous monster then, but it looked worse in death, glistening from the hundreds of wounds the goblins and hobgoblins had inflicted on it. Pieces of hide hung loose, the edges fluttering in the breeze. A rib showed at its middle where a hole had been hacked so the goblins could get at its insides. Insects swarmed around it, thick like a haze, and she would swear she could hear the incessant buzzing even at that distance.

There'd been insects in the mine too, tasty beetles mostly. There had been more insects around the slave pens too, at times thick as ooze, biting and getting in the goblins' eyes and mouths. Perhaps there would not be so many flying insects in the Qualinesti Forest, she mused. And perhaps she would ask Direfang or one of the young goblins to bring her a nice tasty piece of tylor meat so she would not have to stand in the bug-cloud and wait for her turn.

Direfang intended to lead all of them to the Qualinesti Forest, a place she had discovered in one of her earth-visions. The Dark Knights said the place was distant, far across a sea. Perhaps the bugs stopped at the sea.

She watched members of the Flamegrass clan drag the dead goblins into a pile quite a ways from the carcass. Insects were swarming there too.

Less than one hundred goblins were dead, she guessed, maybe sixty or seventy—a hefty loss but not terrible. It was bearable. She knew someone in the Flamegrass clan would count the bodies, and someone else would try to collect names for the remembering ceremony. Certainly she'd known some of the goblins who had been killed by the beast, though perhaps she had not known them by name.

Mudwort had not been close to any of them.

A loner, she counted only Direfang as a friend, and that was because he had forced his friendship upon her. When he was a foreman in the mines he had taken it upon himself to make sure she ate and stayed strong. He had recognized her magic and respected her ability, believing in her earth-visions.

In Steel Town she had claimed a corner of one of the slave pens, and though she was never afforded much space, the other goblins and slaves for the most part left her alone. She knew that many of them considered her mad, though she also knew that she'd gained in their esteem since she predicted the earthquakes.

Only a handful of them claimed to understand her magic, and they were goblins with a similar talent. Moon-eye had special magic in him too; she wished he had not lagged behind and died. She would miss mingling spells with him, and she would miss his bad singing.

Boliver could easily mingle his magic with hers. She drew her face into a scrunch as she peered at the food lines and searched for him. She didn't spot him in the milling mass, and for a moment she feared that perhaps he was among the pile of bodies. But a few seconds later she spotted him, nearing his turn at the carcass. She thought it possible Boliver had more talent than she did. Was he keeping the true extent of his power a secret from her?

Mudwort heard murmured conversations from the goblins standing in line and from small groups moving away from the carcass, sated for the moment. She saw one of the younger goblins, Knobnose, point to her and heard a one-armed goblin claim that she was to blame for all of their troubles, all the many deaths, that it was she who had found the tylor, after all.

But she hadn't killed anyone, she told herself with a frown. She had only directed the goblins there, hadn't forced any of them to swarm the beast. They'd all been looking for something big to kill and eat, and all she did was discover the tylor with her earth-magic. They should be praising her rather than blaming her. The half dozen goats she'd found yesterday had satisfied only the older goblins and the children. Direfang had allowed only the weak and vulnerable to eat the goats. The others had watched jealously. She'd found water after that, with the help of Boliver.

It was their own grumbling bellies that had killed them, she decided. Their hunger clouded their minds like the insects clouded the dead tylor. And it caused them to attack a creature that should have been left alone. So their empty bellies and the creature were to blame, not her.

"Dards," she whispered to herself. "Fools, the lot. Dead to hunger and stupidity."

Besides, it was only sixty or seventy that had died, she guessed. The earthquakes and the volcanoes had killed many, many more.

The tylor had not killed her friend Direfang, thankfully, and it had not killed the principal clan leader, Saro-Saro, and so no real harm was done. She smiled. The great carcass would feed the eight hundred goblins left alive. Her own stomach rumbled, and she patted it.

"Later," she told herself. "Eat later." Mudwort had no intention of standing in line and being jostled by her hostile kinsmen and swarmed by the bugs. "There will still be plenty left later. So much left that—" She looked up to see Direfang looming over her.

"The priest?"

"Found him, Direfang, see? Not dead, the skull man," she gestured. "But dying, maybe. Dying, hopefully."

Direfang slid past her, knelt, and carefully rolled Horace over so that he was facing the sky. The water jug the priest had tied to his belt had shattered. Pieces of it had sliced through the leather leggings and were lodged in his hip and leg.

"Dying, definitely, Direfang. One less Dark Knight to watch and worry over," Mudwort declared flatly. "Only two left soon, the wizard and the other one." She pointed to the base of the ridge where the human named Kenosh was helping the wizard to his feet. Kenosh was the last surviving member of the wizard's talon. She wrinkled her nose. "Hate Dark Knights. Hate them more than anything."

"It is a good hate," Direfang admitted. The hobgoblin carefully pried the jug shards out of the priest's leg and scowled when one of the wounds started to bleed freely. Direfang looked to one of the goblin children who had returned to hover. "Chima and Olabode have water. Spikehollow has water, Leftear too. Go get water." The largest child hesitated only a moment then dashed away.

"Direfang, why help a Dark Knight?" Mudwort turned her back to the priest and sat against him.

"Because this Dark Knight is a skull man." Direfang carefully prodded the priest's side, cocking his head when Horace twitched. "Saving the skull man saves goblins. This skull man is a very good healer."

"What is good is that Direfang leads this army," Mudwort said. She closed her eyes and tipped her head back, letting the last rays of the sun warm her face. Her fingers drifted down to bury themselves in a small patch of ground she had willed to soften like clay. "Unfortunately, Direfang also heals the hated Dark Knight."

Direfang's reply was muffled by the earth she'd let her senses slip into.

Leftear followed the goblin children to Direfang. One long-fingered hand was wrapped around the neck of a water-skin, the other around a stringy piece of tylor flesh he'd grabbed. He shoved the bloody chunk into his mouth and thrust the waterskin at the hobgoblin. Direfang took it, and Leftear hurried off to get another piece of meat.

There wasn't much water in the skin, so the hobgoblin poured only a little into his cupped hand and dribbled it on the priest's face. He spread the water around with his fingertips, an oddly gentle gesture, and he opened the priest's mouth and poured a little water down his throat.

Direfang heard the crunch of boots and, out of the corner of his eye, saw the wizard approaching, leaning on Kenosh for support. Spikehollow followed them, warily watching the pair, knife held ready.

Direfang returned his attention to the priest, giving him more water, then leaned back and waited.

Noise swelled around Direfang—goblins still whooping in victory, a few arguing over chunks of meat, Saro-Saro barking orders, and finally the priest coughing loudly. There was a great sighing sound, and for an instant Direfang feared the beast had come back to life. But when he heard it again, he realized it was just a gust of wind coming down what was left of the ridge and stirring the dust at the bottom.

DEATH MARCH

Direfang helped the priest sit up as the wizard shuffled closer. The hobgoblin got Grallik's attention and pointed to the pile of bodies. "Wizard, use the fire magic on the dead ones."

Grallik shook his head. "I can't. Not now. There's nothing in me, Foreman. Later, though. I'll burn all of them for you later. I promise."

Direfang growled at the title of foreman. He had been a foreman in the Dark Knight mines for several years. The title afforded him a few favors, though he was treated little better than the rest of the slaves. The position had also forced him to push his kinsmen to their limit, garnering him some permanent enemies. "Then help the skull man, wizard. Find the strength to manage that, at least."

"I'll help him." That came from Kenosh, who had eased Grallik down next to the priest and slid into Direfang's place. The middle-aged knight had a careworn face, and the wrinkles across his forehead were deep with concern.

"Be fast about it, then." Direfang handed the waterskin to Kenosh. "Spikehollow has more water." He trundled toward the tylor carcass, intending to eat his fill before all the choice parts were gone.

Mudwort was distracted by all the talk. She pulled her fingers out of the dirt and shuffled away. Finding another patch of ground and sitting on it, her fingers boring in again.

————— S —————

The priest watched Direfang leave before he gestured for more water. When he'd drained the skin he rocked upward and struggled to his knees. He placed his hands on his knees and started praying. Spikehollow stepped back, suspicious.

"Zeboim, called Rann in my homeland, give me strength and health." His fingers glowed orange, the color quickly spreading to his leggings and rolling up to his bare chest. Expending the magic made Horace sweat, and Kenosh used the hem of his tabard to wipe the priest's face.

"Zeboim, Sea Mother, heal my battered body." The glow brightened and crept up his neck, then disappeared.

49

He moved his right hand to his thigh, where the blood still pulsed. He pushed against the worst cut, the blood welling up through his fingers. Again his hand glowed orange.

Spikehollow dropped his waterskin, snarled with disgust, and headed back to the carcass for more tylor meat.

"Zeboim, if I have not angered you by throwing in my lot with these creatures, aid me. Mend my wounds." After a few moments, he moved his hand over his chest, where he suspected his ribs were broken. The glow darkened over the worst injuries, and he pulled his hand away. The blood had crusted and the cuts had sealed. "Help me up, would you, Kenosh? Zeboim has blessed me, and now I must tend to the others."

Grallik had been watching the priest intently. "Horace? So you are well?"

"Aye, reasonably so. I'll mend you first, Grallik, before the hobgoblin comes back. Else he'll insist I heal the goblins first." The priest edged toward the wizard, his hand starting to glow again. "Fools they were to attack a tylor, you know that."

"You should have let it kill them," Kenosh said angrily. He was staring at the goblins still slicing chunks of meat off the carcass. "Guardian Grallik, I think this all a . . ."

"A . . . foolish thing we've done by being here? No, we're better off with the goblins," Grallik said. He kept his voice low as there were goblin children within earshot. He doubted the young ones knew any of the human tongue, but he should be careful regardless. "When the earthquakes ripped Steel Town apart, and the lava buried what was left, there was nothing to be done but leave."

Grallik paused and hung his head. He sucked in a sharp breath when Horace prodded his ribs and arms. "I faced a demotion because Steel Town was lost under my watch and because my wards failed and the goblins escaped. Kenosh, you would have been demoted as well. You call me Guardian, but that title was buried with Steel Town."

Kenosh nodded, his eyes still fixed on the feasting goblins.

"And Horace's loyalties were not with the Dark Knights," Grallik continued. "You know that as well as I. Clearly they were not." He saw the priest frown at his comment, though he said nothing. "Horace, you wanted to return to Ergoth. You told me such."

Horace was sweating again, as he worked the healing magic on Grallik. The orange glow that had spread from his hands covered practically every inch of the wizard. Grallik's undertunic was ripped in several places from his tumble down the ridge, and much of his pale, scarred flesh showed through. The priest could do nothing about the long-existing scars, but his spell closed the most recent wounds. Grallik began to breathe easier.

"Aye, I intend to return to Ergoth," Horace stated. His hands moved to Grallik's arm. "This is broken, but it is a simple break." He worked to set the bone, just as Grallik worked not to cry out in pain. "And I intend to return when the first opportunity presents itself. I know, Gray Robe, that you've got some secret reason for joining with these escaped slaves. You can tell Kenosh and I that it's for our good, all for the best, that we're safer in their company. And safer we are. But you've got your own reasons for all of this. And I cannot ken those reasons."

Grallik did not reply. A wave of dizziness was washing through him as the priest finished adjusting the broken pieces of bone. The priest's hands were overly warm against his arm.

"Your bone will mend, Grallik. Do not move, else it will not heal straight." Horace had shifted so that his back was to the throng of feasting goblins and the picked-over carcass.

Grallik gritted his teeth. The healing was an uncomfortable process. When the warmth receded and the priest started to release his grip, the wizard said, "My feet, Horace. Can you do something to ease—?"

"Skull man!" The bellow came from behind the knights. Between bites of tylor flesh, Direfang had noticed what they were doing. He shouted at the priest. "Healing work to do! Be fast!"

"You can tend to me later," Grallik said in a low voice.

Kenosh stepped away. "I am not hurt so terribly bad."

Horace let out a ragged sigh and clenched and unclenched his fists. "Zeboim tests me, Gray Robe. Perhaps it was she who set me on this course with the goblins, not you. And perhaps she will reveal her secret before you reveal yours." He brushed his hands on his tattered leggings and adopted a slight smile. He turned to face the hobgoblin and raised his voice to answer Direfang. "Until I cannot stand, Foreman, I will aid your people."

Direfang grunted and pointed to a slight female from the Flamegrass clan.

"Merely a broken leg," Horace muttered as he headed in her direction. Over his shoulder, he called, "Kenosh, if you would aid me please."

The knight hesitated only a moment and, avoiding Grallik's glare, followed the priest.

Horace spent the next few hours mending bones and closing deep cuts. There were some goblins he could not save, and those were added to the pile of bodies. When the priest was spent, the hobgoblin ordered remnants of tylor flesh brought to the Dark Knights.

The three knights ate alone, though Spikehollow watched them from his post on a flat rock. Horace and Kenosh were quick to consume their meager portions, but Grallik only nibbled at the raw flesh, wrinkling his nose and breathing shallowly.

"You need to stay strong," Horace scolded him. The priest wiped at his mouth with the back of his hand. "It doesn't matter that it tastes like leather."

"Raw leather," Grallik spat. "I've not eaten uncooked meat before."

"And none of us have been subservient to goblins before," Horace said. "Eat, Grallik. I've no healing left to give you, and that damn foreman—"

"Direfang," said Kenosh vehemently. "His name is Direfang."

Grallik took a nibble. "Using his name gives him a measure of respect, Kenosh. Makes him more of an equal. And a hobgoblin certainly is no equal to a man."

Kenosh shrugged and brushed his hands on his tabard.

Spikehollow climbed off his rock and headed their way. The sun had set, and in the growing darkness, his gray-brown skin looked almost black.

"Hard to tell one goblin from the other," Horace said. He looked to Grallik. "That one there. Do you know that fellow's name?"

"Spikehollow," the wizard whispered. "One of the few names I do know. It's odd, like the name of an ugly weed."

Spikehollow stopped a few feet short and pointed his knife at Grallik. "Time for the ceremony," he said. "Time to burn the bodies."

The wizard dropped the piece of tylor flesh and looked to the mound. His hands grew warm with the beginning of a spell. He shuffled toward the corpses, favoring his foot where the boot had worn through, and he pointed a slender finger at a little broken goblin at the edge of the pile. Flame arced from his index finger and touched the goblin's blood-soaked shirt. It smoldered for a moment before the fire took hold.

Spikehollow watched the flame spread and the goblins gather around the mound to remember their fallen kinsmen. The stink was strong from the burning bodies and all the blood, not to mention the tylor carcass.

The caws of crows mixed with the crackling of rising fire and the whispered conversations of goblins and hob-goblins. Insects still swarmed everywhere and created an annoying thrum.

Spikehollow bent and picked up the piece of tylor meat that Grallik had dropped. Not bothering to brush off the dirt, he stuck it in his mouth and then joined Saro-Saro for the ceremony.

8

RUFFEM'S FLIGHT

The hobgoblin's hide was crusted with blood, and flies swarmed him. He didn't bother batting them away anymore; he was too tired, and what little strength he still had, he needed for running.

Two other hobgoblins trailed him. He didn't know their names; he was a loner and knew the names of only a handful or so of his kinsmen.

"Slow, Ruffem," one called. "Slow, please."

Ruffem slowed several minutes later but only because the muscles in his legs refused to take him farther. They clenched and he dropped to his knees; a moment more and he fell forward, turning his head just in time so his face would not slam into the earth.

He registered the sound of his heart pounding, nearly in time with the slapping of the other hobgoblins' feet as they finally closed the distance and dropped down beside him.

"Free, Ruffem," one of them wheezed.

Ruffem couldn't tell which one was talking as he'd closed his eyes and tried to shut out the sound of his pounding heart and everything else. He'd never run so fast in all his young life, and he feared if his heart did not slow down, it would burst out of his chest.

He felt a hand on his back, jostling him gently. "Ruffem?"

Ruffem growled softly, a warning to be left alone.

54

But the jostling continued.

"Free, Ruffem," the one continued.

"But maybe not for long," the other hissed.

That got Ruffem's attention. He sucked in a breath, inhaling dirt too, which stuck to his teeth. He coughed and pushed himself up.

The other two hobgoblins were indeed from his clan; Ruffem recognized them once he looked at them, though he still couldn't put names to them. One had pockmarks on his face and neck from some malady of youth; the other had a head that seemed too large for its body. Both had mud-brown hides and wore boiled leather breastplates, marking them as clan warriors. It was the one with the pockmarks who had said they might not be free for long. Pockmark helped Ruffem to his feet.

"Too many minotaurs," Pockmark said. "Wise to run, Ruffem. Would that everyone had run."

"Others ran," Ruffem managed to gasp. Some part of him thought his cowardice was justified because he'd spotted some of his kinsmen fleeing. "Others ran first."

The hobgoblin with the overlarge head snarled. "Foul creatures from the pits, minotaurs. Man-bulls that should burn in the abyss."

Ruffem nodded in agreement.

The pockmarked hobgoblin brushed at Ruffem's chest to get the dirt and sticks off. "Hagam warned the clan about the minotaurs. Hagam days past said slavers were coming and that a shaman promised freedom to the south. Should have listened to Hagam."

"Hagam ran days past," Ruffem said.

The pockmarked hobgoblin prodded Ruffem's chest and stomach and picked at the blood. "This blood . . ."

"Belongs to a minotaur," Ruffem finished.

They got on either side of him and propped him up as they continued south, trying for a steady pace.

"A dead minotaur," Ruffem added as he shook them off and regained his footing. He grinned widely so they could see the blood on his teeth and gums. He made a snapping gesture, indicating he'd bitten the minotaur. The minotaur had held Ruffem in a bear hug, waiting for another minotaur to bring a rope to tie him. Ruffem had stretched up and clamped his teeth on the minotaur's neck, releasing a rush of blood. "A very dead minotaur."

"Should have listened to Hagam, though," Pockmark repeated. "None would be caught to be sold as slaves. All would be free."

"South," Ruffem said, pointing. His legs burned, but his muscles still worked, good and strong. "Run now."

Ruffem took off at an easy lope, the others following.

9

THE OTHER RED-SKINNED SHAMAN

Mudwort smelled the goblin bodies burning; the stench was so thick in the air and heavy in her lungs that she took only the shallowest of breaths. Although she'd smelled death often, it was an odor she'd never allow herself to get used to. Other goblins cast the smell off as commonplace; even Direfang seemed inured to it. But Mudwort thought it should always bother her, even if she had no special attachment to the ones who'd died.

The world was harsh and everything eventually died. But did goblins have to stink so badly when they stopped breathing?

She'd smelled nothing truly pleasant in a long, long while.

When she concentrated on the rocks and dirt beneath her fingertips, the odors from inside the earth grew stronger and helped mask the death scents, but it did not get rid of them entirely. The Dark Knights and goblins had moved away from her, and Direfang was busy helping the injured. So she relished the relative peace and silence that had settled around her.

When she was alone, it was easier to listen to the stone.

Exploring, she discerned traces of copper far below, and when she stretched her mind to the south, she found glistening fibrous blue crystals melded in bumpy, gray rocks.

57

They were mixed with dark green hairlike threads in places, and there was a taste to them that reminded her of early summer mornings from before she was a slave. She lingered over the bumpy rocks, which she'd not encountered before, and her mind teased the hairlike threads.

"What do the rocks say? What say?" She cocked her head. "Saying something, but talking too soft. Stop the whispering. Say something louder."

Mudwort heard crows cawing and angrily gnashed her teeth together. They'd inadvertently drawn her senses back to the surface. Many crows were circling, she knew, waiting for the goblins to leave the tylor carcass, waiting to feast on whatever was left . . . and on any flesh remaining on the goblins and hobgoblins that were still burning in the death pile.

"Stone saying something," she scolded the crows. "Saying something more interesting than crows and bugs and Dark Knights and goblins." She leaned forward and pressed her ear to the ground and twirled her fingers deeper into the dirt. She squeezed her features together, and her head started pounding.

"What say?" She jammed her knee hard against the ground in consternation. "What?"

It was a soft sound at first, for the most part words that were too indistinct for her to comprehend. But she picked out a few phrases in goblinspeak.

"Huh. Stones not speaking at all. Goblins are."

She strained to hear clearly, finally managing to block out the crows and concentrate on the distant whispers that had become insistent and were pulling at her.

"Goblins are talking of magic!" She let her mind flow like water through cracks and over slices of shale and around the gray chunks filled with the hairlike green crystals. Then she detected the cavern below and raced toward it, finding the familiar oval with the symbols around it that she'd spotted a few days past.

It was near! That cavern had to be close to where she sat in the mountains! It felt close, but Mudwort couldn't determine precisely where.

Her heart raced as she hurried down a corridor, spying a light ahead and focusing on it. She pressed her senses against the wall and instantly faulted herself for trying to hide. Whoever—whatever—was down there could not see her. She wasn't really in that place. She was still above the ground, too close to the Dark Knights and the rotting tylor and all the burning bodies. Too close to the ceremony for the dead that she knew was happening and that she had no interest in.

Only her mind was below the earth.

"Hurry," she urged herself. "Find the goblins."

She wound her way through one tunnel and the next, sometimes dipping down, other times rising toward the surface, occasionally doubling back. The maze reminded her of the tunnels in the Dark Knight mines in Steel Town, where she'd toiled for too many years. But the stone in the earth tunnels was different than that in the mines. There were more of the gray, bumpy rocks shot through with blue and green crystals, and sections of granite along the floor had been worn smooth and shiny by many passing feet. Yet there were none of the rocks the Dark Knights had coveted to turn into their steel swords and knives. And there were no slaves.

But there were goblins. She continued to hear them.

Mudwort better understood the words; they were coming louder. *Krood, dallock, slarn.* Hunger, dance, sleep. Hunger was repeated the most often. *Krood, krood, krood,* she heard. Goblins were always hungry.

The tunnel she glided down widened ahead, opening into a chamber filled with goblins and lit by guttering, fat-soaked torches that had been rammed into crevices. The air was not pleasant; it was filled with smoke from the torches and the sweaty odor of goblins. But it was better than the air around the tylor, so Mudwort pretended that she was breathing the underground air.

The goblins down there were all of the same clan, likely, as their skin was the same color. It was red but much darker than hers, the shade of dried blood, almost black in places. One goblin had a gray patch on her back that Mudwort found curious. A mark from birth, perhaps?

The goblins milled anxiously as Mudwort observed them, and she grew anxious too. Thirty, she counted, or close to that number; they constantly moved, so it was difficult to know just how many there were for certain. They walked with shoulders back, proud like the Dark Knights who once paraded around Steel Town. Their chins were tipped up, faces set in grins, nostrils quivering. And their hides were relatively smooth; Mudwort could not spot many scars or a single sign of injury. Not one walked with a limp. Clearly, from their tall, full frames, they were not oppressed slaves. Not one of them was skinny. And not one of them wore a scrap of clothing or carried a weapon.

She saw the one with the gray patch look straight up, and Mudwort followed her gaze.

"Amazing," Mudwort whispered to herself. The chamber they were in had a natural domed ceiling that she guessed was more than a dozen goblins high. It was covered with crude drawings and symbols, or perhaps they were words in some sort of language, the etchings darkened here and there from the smoke the torches gave off. Had the goblins made the drawings? she wondered. And if so, how could they have climbed the walls to make them? The chamber looked at the same time primitive and elaborate. The flickering torches placed at their odd intervals chased shadows around the dome and made the drawings move, which made her dizzy.

She wished she could be there in body, not just in mind, to join with the fat, happy goblins and feel the smooth granite beneath her feet. It would be so much more pleasant than walking on the hurtful trail where she led Direfang's army from one meal to the next and where the air was so foul. She wanted to talk to the goblins, mingle with them, learn more about them.

What did they eat, those fat goblins? And where did they live? Certainly not in that chamber; it was too clean, and there wasn't a single animal skin for them to sleep on. Two more tunnels led away from there, and maybe the answers were down one of those tunnels. She would explore the tunnels later, she decided. All of her attention was directed to watching the red-skinned goblins, clearly larger than any in Direfang's army.

Her belly rumbled, and she cursed. Thinking about what the goblins ate made her remember that she was very hungry. She smelled something strong and pleasant in that instant—nothing from aboveground, where she still sat, but from the chamber below. The smell wasn't instantly recognizable, it was something . . .

"Delicious," she said. "What smells so wonderful?"

A loud *bong* suddenly sounded, and four goblins brought in a large wooden platter with the cooked carcass of a boar. They placed it in the center of the chamber, and Mudwort watched as the goblins crowded around it and fell upon the meat.

Despite their full frames, they acted as ravenous as her starving kinsmen, pulling loose the flesh and skin and stuffing it down their throats. Their manner was wild and frightening as they pried hunks off and barely chewed the flesh before swallowing it, some of them pushing their fellows out of the way and arguing over the largest pieces.

Mudwort could hardly believe the scene. She'd seen her kinsmen argue over the meager rations doled out in Steel Town before but never in such a barbarous fashion. There was a ferocity about the red-skinned goblins that excited and disturbed her. Their behavior seemed extreme, exaggerated, and she thought perhaps she was sleeping and that it was a dream. But when she concentrated, she could feel the dirt she'd burrowed her fingers into and could hear the crows cawing overhead. So she realized that what she watched in her magical vision was in some fashion real.

One of the four goblins who had brought in the tray—a tray she realized was a shield—wore a necklace of teeth and tiny bones. He thoughtfully chewed on one of the boar's ears and distanced himself from the others, leaning against the wall between two torches. He tilted his head to one side, as if listening for something. Mudwort listened closer too, hearing an annoying pounding in her head and, under the pounding, singing. It was good singing, in a female goblin voice, enjoyable and not at all like the discordant tune Moon-eye used to wail.

It was a song about the earth and magic and old, powerful things. And it grew louder as another goblin came into the chamber, a female. She was the singer.

The female was young, and she stopped singing when the feasters turned their attention toward her. Like them, she wore no clothes, but she had several necklaces of carved wooden beads and bats' feet that draped to her waist. She also had a wooden bracelet on her right wrist, cut with marks that resembled those Mudwort had seen carved into the dome.

"Little more than a youngling," Mudwort pronounced. "But one honored, it seems."

Indeed, the other goblins backed away from the boar, save four who removed it after making sure no scraps remained on the chamber floor.

The young female stood next to the male with the bone-and-tooth necklace.

"Those two with the necklaces wait for something," Mudwort guessed. "But wait for what?" A part of her wondered where they had taken the delicious-smelling boar. There was still a little bit of meat left on its ribs, and she suspected it would taste much better than the raw tylor meat. It had been many years since Mudwort had feasted on something that was cooked in such a style. Again her stomach growled, and again she cursed.

"Waiting for what?" Mudwort repeated to herself. Her curiosity nearly overwhelmed her, and she held her breath in anticipation. "Waiting for something important," she said when she finally released her breath and sucked in another gulp of air. "Something . . ."

Four goblins returned with the shield-tray, the boar carcass gone, and a skull-sized mass of crystals on the middle of it. Mudwort had seen crystals numerous times on her magical, mental forays into the earth, and she'd seen crystalline jewelry adorning some of the women in Steel Town. But it was the most amazing crystal she'd ever seen. Its base was a bowl-shaped chunk of the bumpy, gray rock, which had the green threads running through it. Dozens of finger-sized crystals sprouted from the rock in all directions.

The crystals were iridescent like quartz, but not so common as quartz. Clear at the tips of each protrusion, like water struck by the sun, they were milky at the base.

All of it was gleaming angles and planes. All of it caught the torchlight and birthed a rainbow of colors that flitted around the walls like maddened fireflies.

Mudwort barely noticed that all the goblins in the chamber were as captivated as she. Some turned this way and that, their eyes trying to follow the lights. Others simply stared, entranced, at the entire mass. That's what Mudwort did, stare, forgetting to breathe, and finally shaking her head and gasping to jolt herself back to consciousness.

She wished Direfang could see this amazing, beautiful thing—the most beautiful thing she'd ever seen in her entire life. She wished Boliver was with her, dipping his senses down along with hers and catching sight of this cavern and this crystal. But a part of her was glad she was alone and did not have to share this experience. She could show Boliver later. For the moment, she would keep this remarkable scene all to herself.

Mudwort drifted closer until the crystal cluster filled her vision. She saw the reflections of several goblins in the facets, their grinning visages looking broken in all the angles and planes. There was a wildness in their expressions, they looked primal. She hadn't paid attention to their faces before. Now she studied them. They were goblin faces, clearly, but they looked different than her kinsmen. More frightening somehow. More savage. More willful and powerful. They had thick ridges above their eyes and wide noses with snuffling nostrils. Perhaps they were not so quick or bright, but perhaps they were better in other ways.

This tribe was to be envied, she thought . . . because of their more powerful faces and stances and seeming fearlessness; because they were beneath the earth where the air was better. Because they were staring at this mass of beautiful crystals, some of them tentatively reaching out to touch it, when all she could do was look at it wistfully, seeing it and them magically from a distance.

She imagined feeling the coolness of the crystal shards

and suspected they would be smooth against her fingers, like polished granite. She tried staring inside the cluster and was practically blinded by the vortex of rainbow colors. Mudwort blinked furiously and willed herself to float back and up until she looked down on the goblin tableau from the top of the domed ceiling.

The cluster of clear and milky crystals was not magical, she recognized; she was certain she would have sensed any magic about it if that were so. Still, the cluster was breathtaking.

But there was magic somewhere in the chamber; she could feel the unusual magic. And after a few moments of searching, she realized it was in the young female goblin who wore all the necklaces.

Mudwort watched her approach the crystal and saw the goblins grudgingly part to allow her passage. The young goblin's fingers played over the segments of one of her necklaces then stretched out and touched one facet after another on the crystal.

"A shaman," Mudwort realized. "Like Boliver." And like herself, she added almost as an afterthought.

But the young goblin was not as sure of herself as Mudwort and Boliver. Her movements were timid, skittish like a squirrel.

"Learning magic, maybe," Mudwort guessed. "Using the beautiful rocks to help. The rocks are a focus."

Mudwort knew that her own senses moved more easily through certain types of stones and not at all through others. So the young goblin was not yet proficient in magic and was using the crystal cluster to augment whatever skills she had. Mudwort wondered what powers resided in the crystal and how the beautiful rock might help her.

"But where exactly is this cave with the wild-looking goblins? And the dome? And the young shaman?" Mudwort's brow knitted, her lips forming a needle-thin line. "Where, where, where?"

Mudwort watched the shaman for quite some time, not fathoming what she was attempting with the crystal, and finally deciding to leave the chamber. It was time to find out more, time to learn just where that cavern sat so she could physically go there. She willed herself to drift up through the dome then through one sheet of rock after another. She felt herself splinter when she passed through a thick layer of sandstone, just as the images of the goblin faces had broken apart in the facets.

Pieces of her consciousness skittered all over like bugs running from a disturbed nest. The sensation was unnerving, and as it lengthened, she briefly became terrified and could not tell where she was or where she was going. Her mind spun while she continued to splinter and splinter again. She felt like she was spiraling down, down, not rising to the surface.

Drowning in the stone.

"Mind going sour," Mudwort said. She only faintly heard her own words, as if they were spoken by someone else a long distance away. "Mind running away. Mind is shattered and broken and—"

She gasped, her head jerking back from the shock of someone roughly grabbing her shoulders. The slight shift she wore—a shirt that had once belonged to a human child in Steel Town—was thoroughly soaked and plastered to her slight frame.

"Fever," pronounced a voice, breaking into her thoughts. It was Horace. The priest and Direfang hovered over her. "She has a fever, Foreman, but no physical injury that I can see."

Mudwort crawled away from the pair. "Am fine," she told them, thumping her thumb against her chest and waggling her fingers.

Direfang looked concerned. "The skull man will—"

"Do nothing," Mudwort finished for the hobgoblin. "Fever will leave soon. Am fine."

The hobgoblin knelt, his eyes locked on hers. "Did Mudwort find something in the ground?" Direfang asked.

"Nothing," she replied. "Found nothing at all."

10

DIREFANG'S DISTRACTIONS

Grallik had told Direfang that the trees in the Qualinesti Forest were so thick in some places that their leaves blocked the sunlight. The hobgoblin had a difficult time imagining such a place, but he tried. Although he wasn't born a slave, he'd never lived far from the aridness of Neraka. All he'd known was scarred, scabrous land and a hard life. There'd been a few trees, but not a single one in Steel Town proper. He was looking forward to seeing so many trees that he would not be able to count them all.

Many days past, Mudwort's magic had told her that the Qualinesti Forest would be a good homeland for the goblins and hobgoblins who had escaped from Steel Town and followed Direfang through the mountains. He'd earlier believed that the Plains of Dust would be best. When he was a slave, he'd caught glimpses of the Dark Knights' maps, and the Plains of Dust to the south had always intrigued him. From listening to the knights, he knew the Plains were not as arid as their name implied, and he envisioned plenty of land for the goblins to spread out on. He heard more than one knight say there were few ogres in the Plains.

But he trusted Mudwort and had grown fascinated with the notion of the huge, thick trees of the former homeland of the elves. As he walked at the head of the long goblin column, he tried to picture such trees. The daydream

66

occupied him and kept his mind off the events that had killed so many of his kinsmen—the earthquakes, volcanoes, ogres, and most recently, the tylor. And it kept him from worrying about Graytoes, whom he carried.

His legs ached from traveling so many days with little respite. The soles of his feet were like leather from working in the mines for so many years. Still, they gave him much pain. The mountain trail had so many sharp shards that they cut through his thick pads and made him dread each step.

Many of the goblins and hobgoblins had boots that they'd taken from the Dark Knights during the escape from Steel Town. Others had taken sandals and shoes from the ogres in a town they'd sacked high in the mountains. They'd obtained their clothing from both of those places, though Direfang thought shoes were the most important acquisitions. He had not taken any for himself, though he had been quick to take a tunic off a dead ogre. He'd left the shoes for the other, weaker ones, but he regretted not grabbing a pair for himself. His weary feet hurt.

He vowed to grab the next pair of shoes for himself if they came across another ogre village or patrol.

In the wonderful elf forest, perhaps none of them would need shoes. Perhaps the ground would be soft and comfortable to walk on, like a green carpet. And he hoped there would be plenty to eat. He would have to approach Mudwort soon about using her earth magic to find more beasts, a large herd of goats or sheep—something that would not be so difficult as the tylor to kill, something that would feed all the hungry goblins following him.

He stopped on a narrow promontory, staring down and ahead at what passed for a trail. Weeds grew in small pockets of dirt that had been caught in shallow depressions, but for the most part everything looked brown and dead. Some goats did come that way; he spotted their spoor, and if goats managed to negotiate that trail, goblins could too. But it would not be an easy path.

Direfang scratched his chin and glanced over his shoulder, seeing the three Dark Knights a dozen yards behind him and towering over the goblins. Even though the knights had been beaten down by the trek and were treated as slaves, they held their proud posture.

Direfang squared his shoulders and affected a similar mien. He looked as if he had been chiseled from a block of granite, compared to the humans. His features were rough and thickly scarred, his build was lean but muscular. The humans had smooth skin and features that seemed small and foolish. He didn't like knights, and he hated what they and their kind had inflicted on the goblins at the mine. Direfang's throat grew dry at the memories of watching goblins being whipped for not mining fast enough or not carrying enough rocks in their sacks.

He couldn't get some of the horrifying images out of his head, and tears threatened his eyes.

"At least free now," he muttered to himself. He'd tried to escape once before, many years earlier. And when the knights had caught him, they beat him until he couldn't stand and poured salt in his wounds. They'd cut off his left ear and hung it on a thong around his neck, and they'd forced him to return to the mines immediately. Those who had tried to escape with him were killed, and Direfang was certain he'd been spared because of his strength and size; he was too valuable a laborer to slaughter. Too, he was certain he'd been promoted to foreman a few years after that failed escape because the knights had forgotten who he was and what he had done. Hobgoblins and goblins looked the same to men.

Sadness and anger rushed through him in waves, and the images from the mining camp became more vivid in his mind. All of the past several years—the beatings, the torturous hours of toiling in the belly of the Dark Knight mountain, the scant meals, the stink of the slave pens—all of it overwhelmed him and he sobbed.

"Think about the trees," he told himself.

He brushed at the tears with his forearm and kept his back turned to the others so no one could see his weakness. It was a terrible thing for a leader to cry, he knew. It was bad enough that Graytoes continued to whimper over the loss of her mate.

DEATH MARCH

Direfang tried nurturing his rage over the Dark Knights' treatment of him and the others, over the number of goblins lost to the earthquakes and volcanoes, over the muddled attack on the tylor, and all the violent deaths at the hands of that foul creature. The rage inside him burned like a column of the wizard's fire and finally chased away his tears.

"Should kill the three Dark Knights maybe," he whispered to himself. It might get rid of some of the stench that hung in the air; the humans had a distinct, unpleasant odor, worse than goblins, Direfang thought. Direfang wondered if it was the scent of evil, as he knew of no more evil creatures than the Dark Knights who worked the slaves.

"Might feel better with the Dark Knights dead." But the knights might still come in handy. The skull man was necessary as none of the goblins possessed his ability to heal wounds. And the wizard's fire magic had proved useful. The one called Kenosh had not been particularly helpful, but he'd not yet given Direfang an excuse to kill him either. "Maybe kill some Dark Knights later," he said. "The wizard and the other one." That might help erase some of the terrible memories of being their slave at the mines. "But maybe keep the skull man for healing when we need it."

He shifted Graytoes to nestle in his other arm. She could walk, but when she did she shuffled along mindlessly, and Direfang worried that she'd get trampled by her kinsmen or might fall off the edge of the trail. He felt responsible for her, for all of them; they'd designated him their leader.

"Didn't want to be a leader," he said. Graytoes looked up at him quizzically. He spoke in the Common tongue of man—both for practice and because most of his kinsmen didn't understand the language. "Still don't want to be a leader."

Maybe the others followed him because they were used to him ordering them around in the mines. Or perhaps it was because of his size. At nearly seven feet tall, Direfang was an imposing figure, and the scars that riddled his body made him look even more intimidating.

"Moon-eye," Graytoes murmured. Her shoulders shook as she broke into another wail. "Moon-eye . . ."

"Is dead," Direfang finished for her, switching to the goblin tongue. "Moon-eye is dead and best left forgotten. Better to think about lots and lots of trees. There will be too many trees to count, Graytoes. And the shade will feel very good. We are going to a wonderful place, Mudwort says. Qualinesti."

At last, the image of the trees took precedence in his mind, Graytoes quieted, and he marched along with a measure of ease.

The trail was riddled with knifelike shards of shale and limestone, however. Direfang himself couldn't avoid all the troublesome spots, and behind him he heard goblins complain and cry out in pain; the wizard gasped and stumbled, the priest catching him. Good that the knights looked after each other, Direfang thought. Goblins might do well to look after one another.

"How much longer to the trees, Direfang?" It was the first time Graytoes had mentioned something other than her lost mate.

The hobgoblin shrugged. "Miles, Graytoes. Many, many miles."

He knew how to measure miles but had no idea how many miles they'd actually traveled or how many miles they had yet to go. The mountains began far to the north of Steel Town and cut south into ogre territory, running well more than one hundred and fifty miles, if his memory of the Dark Knight maps he'd studied was true. Flat on the map, nothing more than brown paint that looked like earthworms, there'd been no hint how imposing and difficult to cross the mountains truly were. He'd lived in the foothills before Steel Town; it was where a hunting party of ogres had caught him. Scattered villages of ogres supplied the Dark Knights with slaves.

But those foothills were not so difficult to traverse as the mountains, and the goblins in the line behind him constantly complained about the arduousness of the journey. A part of him wished they would all go their own ways and leave him alone.

He paused and closed his eyes and tried to picture one of

the Dark Knight maps. The Khalkist Mountains stretched into Khur, where ogres were the dominant population. Not even the large number of goblins and hobgoblins following Direfang would stand a chance against them. If he recalled one of the large maps correctly, the mountains curved like a fishhook around the eastern edge of the New Sea. He intended to lead the goblins around that edge and strike out west, avoiding the ogre country and cutting through the swamp.

"Wish I had a map," he muttered.

"Map?" Graytoes tugged on his arm. "What's a map? Direfang has talked about a map before. Is it a pretty thing?"

"A map . . ." He shook his head, eyes squeezing shut tighter, trying to figure out how to explain it to her. Graytoes wasn't stupid, but she had never seen a map. "Yes," he thought, ignoring her question, "a map would be very useful. It would show these mountains, and the Qualinesti Forest. And it would show how many more miles all the goblins must walk."

He opened his eyes again just as he took a misstep and slipped down the side of the mountain. The world spun one way, then another, as he fell. Holding Graytoes close and trying to shield her with his body, he briefly regained his footing but stumbled again. Clumps of dirt and scrub grass flew, and tiny stones bit him all over.

The wind was knocked out of him, and white pinpoints of light flashed in his head as it struck a rock, the sensation as hard as a hammer blow. He momentarily blacked out. When he came to, he was still rolling down the side of the mountain, but he no longer cradled Graytoes. Direfang bounced off a bush that had managed to grow in a patch of earth in a bowl-shaped depression. He flailed about with his arms, trying to grab onto something. The bush slipped past, but his fingers caught on a shale outcropping.

Direfang held on tight and regained his footing, scrambling to his feet and taking a few steps before the rock he held on to snapped off and he went tumbling again. He felt a few ribs break, and he tasted blood in his mouth. He spat as he continued to fall, sucking in dirt and gravel with a mouth already full of blood.

He thought he heard Mudwort calling for him and someone else shouting for Graytoes as he continued to bounce against rocks; Direfang's tumble to the bottom felt as if it were taking forever; he hadn't thought the mountainside that high, that precipitous.

Where was the bottom?

Something jabbed at his leg, and he briefly felt a sharp pain. But then the pain was gone and he felt and saw nothing.

"Direfang is gone," pronounced Saro-Saro. The old goblin carefully leaned over the side and looked down. "Cannot see Direfang. It is a long way down. Too far to see. So Direfang is gone and lost."

One of Saro-Saro's youngest clansmen, Pippa, leaned with him. Pippa was a human name that meant "one who adores horses." Pippa was named after a woman in Steel Town, the wife of a blacksmith who had died in the first earthquake. Pippa's mother hadn't known what the name meant when she chose it, only that she liked the sound of it. Pippa had recently learned the meaning and did not hide her disdain for it; Pippa hated horses only a little less than she hated Dark Knights.

"Cannot see Direfang either," Pippa said. "Direfang is dead, then. Graytoes is dead too," She crossed her thin arms and stepped back. "Careful, Saro-Saro. This mountain might be hungry still."

The goblins around Saro-Saro moved anxiously, some shifting back and forth on the balls of their feet, others wringing their hands, a few tittering nervously.

"If Direfang is dead." That came from Chima, a young goblin who still favored her ribs and her arm from her encounter with the tylor. "If Direfang is dead . . ." She looked nervously to Saro-Saro.

The old goblin puffed out his chest, making sure he had a safe perch. "If Direfang is dead—"

"Direfang is not dead." Mudwort cut Saro-Saro off. "The earth says so." She squatted and ran her fingers along the rocks at her feet. "The earth says that Direfang is not dead." She wrinkled her nose ruefully. "Graytoes is alive too. Empty, empty Graytoes."

Mudwort stood and peered over the side, seeing a navigable way down. "We should be done with this horrid, hurtful mountain," she said. "Tired of walking on all these mean rocks. We should join Direfang at the bottom where the ground is flat and not so hurtful."

Saro-Saro shook his head in protest. Pippa copied the gesture and stuck out her lower lip.

"Direfang is the leader," Mudwort insisted. She looked around the old goblin and his clustered clan members, seeing the three Dark Knights. She spat and growled. "Skull man, Direfang and Graytoes need help." She gestured for him to follow her.

Horace's face registered his skepticism at the notion of climbing down so steep a slope. "No," he said softly. "I do not think I can handle that. It is too sheer." But he carefully moved through Saro-Saro's clan, Grallik and Kenosh following. What passed for a trail was so narrow and precarious that Horace nearly pushed a goblin off as he went.

"Follow now, skull man," Mudwort scolded. She lowered herself over the side, finding handholds and footholds and skittering down like a spider. Chima was next, moving slower because of her still-sore side; Olabode, who still nursed his once-broken leg, came after. "Follow, skull man!" Mudwort hollered. "Be fast, skull man!"

"Maybe there will be time to rest at the bottom," Pippa said hopefully. She turned to Saro-Saro. "Need some help climbing?"

The old goblin stared at the Dark Knights who were slowly making their way over the edge. "It would be easy to push the knights off," he heard one of his clansmen whisper. That brought a rare smile to his wrinkled visage.

"Don't need help, Pippa," he said as he carefully lowered himself over the side and struggled to find his first foothold. "But thank you, young one."

Pippa hurried over to help him anyway, staying even with Saro-Saro as he climbed down slowly, and pointing out places that looked easy to grab. "Rest at the bottom," she repeated. "So tired of all the sharp rocks. Take care!"

Saro-Saro gave her a nod. "Rest at the bottom, loyal Pippa."

The climb down took several hours. One hobgoblin and two goblins fell trying to make the descent, the hobgoblin bashing his head open on a protrusion of granite and dropping like a rag doll. One of the two goblins disappeared screaming down a crevice, the other broke his legs and arms and was promised tending by the priest.

They spread out in the valley at the base of the eastern mountain range, looking up the western side at similarly imposing peaks. Grass grew in patches as far as they could see to the north and south, and the dirt was thick and cushioned their steps. Far to the south, black birds picked at something in the grass, seemingly oblivious to the goblins' presence. The air was still because the mountains on either side shielded the valley, and the heat of the afternoon sun was cut by the shadows from the western range.

"Should have come down the mountain yesterday," Saro-Saro said as he reached bottom. He dug the ball of his sandaled foot into the ground. "This feels much better. Not going back up into the mountains ever again."

While the Skull Knight saw to Direfang, the goblins searched in the dirt for grubs and sucked on roots they dug up. Chima stretched out on her back and rubbed her shoulders against the ground. Olabode lay nearby, snoring soundly despite the chattering of his fellows.

Saro-Saro scratched his rump and looked around for a good place to sit. The yellow-skinned clan leader was possibly the oldest goblin in the horde, and his age and position gave him a measure of respect; he would claim the best place to rest.

Pippa followed Saro-Saro and scanned the ground for a suitable spot for the old one. "Hungry, Saro-Saro?" He didn't answer her, but she continued. "Me terribly hungry. Mudwort needs to find more food. But never dangerous food again."

It had been two days since the tylor was slain, and finding no other great beast since then, they'd been eating the occasional few goats they'd caught and digging in the dirt for insects. Their course had followed a high mountain stream, so water had been plentiful, as had nightcrawlers buried in the mud along the banks. Spikehollow had caught a fish early that morning and had shared it with Saro-Saro. But the mountain stream was gone, and some of the goblins chatted nervously about their hunger and thirst.

The old goblin settled on a slab of limestone just as a hobgoblin was about to sit on it. He shooed the hobgoblin away and rolled his shoulders, tossing his head first one way then another, trying to work the kinks out of his old body. Many in his clan gathered around him. Not all the yellow-skinned goblins in the horde were of Saro-Saro's clan, but most were, roughly two hundred of them. Most of the time, they clung together.

Goblin skin tones ranged from yellow to dull orange to red to shades of brown. Most goblins in any given clan were of similar color, which also tended to mark them as from a specific part of the country. Hobgoblins were not so colorful; their hides were primarily gray or brown, and no features associated them with one clan or another.

Saro-Saro slowly regarded the goblins who sat around him, all of them giving him the respectful distance of an arm's length or more.

"Good to rest," Spikehollow said. He was always in the front rank, and stood at that moment shoulder-to-shoulder with Pippa before dropping to the ground. He wiggled his toes and cringed when the skin cracked and oozed. "This would be a good place to sleep."

Pippa nodded. "No more walking today. The skull man said Direfang needs to rest."

Their gazes shifted over to where Direfang was being worked on by the priest and wizard, Mudwort standing behind them, harshly exhorting them to hurry up and heal the hobgoblin leader. A whimpering Graytoes had been carried down the mountain and stood behind Mudwort, being shushed by her repeatedly.

"Spikehollow needs rest too," Spikehollow added with a sigh.

"And Two-chins," another goblin added. He referred to one of the goblins who had fallen off the mountain. "Two-chins is badly broken. Two-chins is hurt worse than Direfang."

Saro-Saro rested back on his arms and raised his head so he could look at the western peaks. "Resting is good," he admitted. He yawned wide. "Sleeping here will be good."

"Good that Direfang will be well," one goblin said.

Spikehollow softly growled, sharply glancing at the speaker. "It will be better when Direfang is dead and Saro-Saro leads us."

The old goblin kept his eyes on the peaks and smiled.

11

AN EMPTY BOTTLE

Isaam folded and refolded his blanket until it was thick enough to serve as a cushion. Then he sat on it and tucked his legs to the side. Around him the camp buzzed with activity. Larol had led a hunting party into a small gorge, and they'd returned with four large wild pigs, more than enough to feed everyone.

Isaam heard Zoccinder grumble that he would have preferred the pigs spitted and slowly roasted, the juice conserved and used to flavor the roots that also had been collected. But there wasn't time for that.

The wizard watched a half dozen men slice thin slabs of meat off the carcasses; they would cook quickly. Isaam did not like to eat animal flesh, convinced that, while it was tasty, it also dulled his mind. Still, on the march he had no other option; keeping his strength up was more important that sticking to a meager and not always reliable diet of vegetables and fruits.

He fumbled in his pocket for the empty ink bottle and brought it out, noticing that all the dirt and smoke smudge had been rubbed away against the fabric in his pocket. The early-morning sun made the clean bottle shimmer.

"Crystal," Isaam pronounced. "Not common glass." He'd not used it for scrying before when the light was bright enough to show its true nature. "Expensive, from the looks

77

of you." He wetted the tip of his index finger and ran it along the half-melted lip of the bottle until the motion produced a faint hum.

"Anything?"

The word was loud and startled Isaam. He'd been so intent on the bottle and on the scent of the roasting pork that he'd not noticed Bera's approach.

"Nothing yet, Commander." Isaam noted that Zoccinder, though hovering around the fire, was keeping a watchful eye on Bera. "Give me a few moments, please."

Bera plopped down opposite him, unmindful of the dirt and pebbles. She fixed her gaze on the bottle and sucked in a deep breath. "All right. Well?"

Isaam cupped his hands and brought them together so the bottle nested in them. He lowered his gaze until all he saw was the bottle. He didn't like others watching, particularly Bera, when he cast such spells. The enchantments were not always successful, and he did not want to appear a failure.

He pressed his thumbs against the sides of the bottle and focused on the little piece of his reflection he could see—one eye and the left side of his face. Isaam didn't need books and scrolls to cast his spells; they were ingrained in his memory. He needed only to summon up the enchantment in his mind.

Words tumbled from his lips, also not necessary to the spell, but something he did from habit, a ritual he'd acquired from an old mentor. The words were Elvish; Isaam's mentor had been an elf. And though Isaam was human, he enjoyed the melodic sound of the Elvish language.

As the final phrase faded, the crystal shimmered and Isaam's reflection winked out, to be replaced with the scarred face of Grallik N'sera. Isaam shuddered at the image, as he had each time he'd looked in on the wizard. The fire that had disfigured Grallik's face and the left side of his body must have been terrible.

"I . . . I think I see him," Bera whispered.

Isaam concentrated on the image until it expanded and hovered like a floating pool between himself and Bera. Then he willed the figure of Grallik N'sera to be smaller so that the wizard's surroundings could also come into focus. A rocky spire shadowed Grallik, but the magical vision had limits, and so Isaam could not see to the top of the spire or mark any formation that might give them a better view of the wizard's location.

Bera wanted to know precisely where the goblins and Grallik were, and so far Isaam's magic had been unable to provide that information.

"He would be handsome," Bera said, "were it not for the scars. They look painful besides ugly." She paused, and added, "I pray they are painful still. The traitor deserves to suffer."

The vision revealed nothing else but goblins, their numbers stretching away into the distance as far as the bottle permitted.

"Hundreds of them," Isaam said. "Hundreds and hundreds . . . and far too many for this force to take on." He did not see Bera shake her head in disagreement.

A cheer went up behind them, and Isaam realized the first of the pork was being served. It did not take long to cook meat cut so thin. The wizard was hungry and found his mouth watering at the smells wafting toward him. But the vision—and Bera's presence—held him.

He tried to shift the scrying scene by turning the bottle in his hands ever so slightly. Only more goblins were revealed, nothing of the land around them to help pinpoint the location. Some of the goblins wore Dark Knight tabards and bits of armor, and several had Dark Knight knives and swords strapped to their waists. He couldn't pick out any leader, unless Grallik N'sera was the leader, nor could Isaam see the Ergothian priest or any of the other Dark Knights reputed to be missing and probably in the goblins' company.

"Your magic is . . ."

"Worthless, Commander?"

Bera let out a deep breath that sent a ripple across the vision. "No. No." She rested her elbows on her knees and cupped her chin with her hands. "I appreciate what you can do, old friend. Magic is so far beyond me; I've truly no understanding of it. Pardon my frustration. I just want to find the traitorous Dark Knights and slay the goblins they escaped with. My orders—"

"Commander!" Zoccinder jogged toward her, wiping his mouth then his fingers against his tabard. "Our scout has spied goblins in a vale to the south, and they're getting ready to move."

Isaam stared at the image. The goblins there looked settled in and sluggish, not ready to move anywhere. He opened his mouth to say something, but Bera was on her feet and rushing away.

"Break camp," she called. "We move south now!"

The image of Grallik and the goblins folded in on itself, and all Isaam saw was an empty ink bottle in his hands.

12

REORX'S CRADLE

The dwarf screamed and the goblins charged, whooping and drawing their knives, their feet pounding loudly against the ground. The dwarf had surprised them, standing up on the far side of a stream she'd been kneeling at to wash clothes.

A copse of trees rose beyond her and the stream; willowy pin oaks and silver maples glittered pale green with dew in the early-morning sun. The goblins had been fixated on the trees, so they hadn't noticed the female dwarf at first.

They were thirsty, and the stream had been their destination; Mudwort had found it in a vision with her earth magic. But Mudwort had said nothing of the short, stocky dwarf woman.

If the dwarf hadn't screamed and startled them, they might not have killed her. They might have simply let her run away, or they might have tried to talk to her and asked where they were in the Khalkists; Direfang wanted to know how many miles they'd traveled since leaving Steel Town and how many more they had left to go.

But the scream rattled them and sealed her fate. And she wouldn't stop screaming, her cries getting louder and more hysterical as she waved her arms like an ungainly bird trying to take flight.

"Quiet!" Spikehollow had shouted at her in the goblin tongue. "Quiet now, short woman!"

But she didn't understand goblinspeak, so she screamed some more, eyes wide and staring at the hundreds of goblins who were marching through the valley straight toward her. Fear rooted her to the bank.

Spikehollow was the first to reach her, splashing across and driving his long knife into her stomach and killing her with a single blow. Pippa and Leftear were close behind and slashed at her too, not realizing she was already dead. The next few goblins were caught by the frenzy and turned her into a pulpy mass.

"Should have shut up," Spikehollow said ruefully, as he stepped away from the body and washed the blood off his hide in the stream. "That short, fat, ugly woman should have listened and shut up."

"The woman's clothes are ruined," Pippa said, frowning and pointing to the bloody rag that used to be the dwarf's shift. "Shoes all right, though. Short, wide shoes." She shouldered her way up to the body, crawling between the legs of a hobgoblin and tugging the leather slippers off. She sloshed them around in the water to rinse off the blood and pranced away with her prize.

Chima draped herself over a small basket near the body and clawed angrily at her kinsmen who were trying to see what was inside. Leftear growled at her and waved his knife, but she wouldn't budge from the basket.

"Enough!" Direfang had not been at the front of the column, and he'd been late to catch up with the dwarf killing at the stream. Since his tumble down the mountainside, he'd been forced to move slower because of a twisted leg and blurry vision. He'd nearly died back there, and the Dark Knight priest had saved him—just as the priest had also saved Graytoes and Two-chins. But the priest told Direfang some of the mending would have to come on its own, and that could take days.

"Leave Chima alone!" Direfang barked. He had directed Spikehollow to lead while he'd drifted back into the heart of his army, walking at a slower pace. Rustymane, another hobgoblin, had been charged with carrying the still-whining Graytoes.

Direfang plodded forward as fast as his sore leg would allow, stopping when his feet sank into the cool mud of the stream bank. He stared across to the opposite bank and at the woman's body, barely recognizable as a dwarf's. Then he glanced at Chima, who still protected the basket filled with clothes.

"Take one thing from the basket," he ordered Chima. "Only one."

She raised her lip in a protesting snarl but bit off any reply. Then she dipped her head in the basket and poked through it until she came up with what she guessed was a child's dress the color of wet saw grass. She pulled it on and stepped back.

"Saro-Saro's clan should have the basket now," someone behind Direfang said. "Saro-Saro—"

"Enough!" Direfang repeated. He whirled to face the goblins behind him, anger etched deep in his scarred face. "Savages," he said, waving an arm to indicate the dwarf. "There was no threat here. No weapon. One woman washing clothes! No reason for this bloodletting!"

"But the fat woman screamed," Spikehollow protested at Direfang's side, still wet from the stream. He cleaned his knife on the grass and sheathed it. "Screamed and screamed. And that scream could have brought men with weapons."

"Probably her screams will bring men." Chima smoothed at her dress and adjusted it around her hips until it lay properly, though it was too big and hung to her ankles. "The woman screamed a lot. That short, fat woman—"

"Dwarf," Direfang said with a sigh. He knew some of the goblins had never seen a dwarf. "That was a dwarf."

"Just one dwarf," Spikehollow added. He'd dropped his voice so only the closest goblins could hear. "One that will never scream again."

"One that might have been worth talking to." Direfang wiped a line of spittle from his lip.

More goblins splashed across the stream, some lingering

in the water to drink. The Dark Knights drank too, and washed their hands and faces.

"Talking to one dwarf would not have been much help."

"Need a map, Spikehollow. Need to know how much farther to the fishhook of mountains that goes around the sea. Need to know how many more days—"

"That dwarf did not have a map," Spikehollow said sulkily. He cocked his head and opened his mouth to say something else, but Direfang waved him silent.

The sound of goblins splashing in the stream grew louder, and many were pushed up on the opposite bank to make room for their fellows. Direfang moved farther away to avoid being jostled.

"Rustymane and Graytoes will pass out the rest of those clothes." Direfang gestured at the basket and snarled when some of the yellow-skinned goblins growled their objections.

Chima twirled to show off her dress. "There will be more clothes from other dwarf women. There will be more dwarves nearby. Dwarves are like birds, nesting together. Many dwarves, maybe."

"But not too many," Leftear said. "Don't want there to be too many."

"Look! Fat little men!" Rustymane shouted. "They're here now!"

Gravel-voiced shouts and the sound of branches breaking came from the south. Dwarves appeared, weaving around the trees and charging toward the goblins, their stubby legs churning up the loam.

"See? That short, fat woman should not have screamed," Spikehollow said triumphantly. "Look what comes now!"

A cheer went up from the goblins as they rushed to meet the dwarves' charge, while a shiver raced down Direfang's spine.

"More killing!" Chima exclaimed, her eyes sparkling as she raced to join the fray.

"Tired of all the blood," Direfang said. But he stood and watched and made no move to call a halt to it.

"Do not hurt the trees!" Pippa cried. She was sitting on

the muddy bank and trying to put on her new shoes, but they kept slipping off because they were too wide. Goblins swarmed past her, rudely bumping her aside on their way to grappling with the dwarves.

There were only fourteen dwarves, wielding hoes, rakes, and shovels, their beards swishing around their waists as they dashed toward the goblins. The dwarves' clothes were not so fine as what the men had worn in Steel Town, Direfang couldn't help but notice, and not one of them wore a piece of armor.

Direfang moved forward as his kinsmen started the killing.

The first dwarf fell before Direfang cleared the far bank.

The dwarves' battle cries were brief. Only one remained standing by the time Direfang lumbered to the edge of the copse. He was a young, stout dwarf, the hobgoblin saw, and the muscles of his arms bunched as he swung his hoe around like a scythe. The dwarf's wide arc caught Chima in the stomach, ripping through the green dress she'd coveted. He picked her up on the blade and effortlessly heaved her over his shoulder. She landed in the low branches of a pin oak, her arms twitching and rattling twigs as she died. Leftear howled his anger at his friend's death as the young dwarf ripped open the belly of another goblin, then one more.

To Direfang's eyes the dwarf was obviously more than the simple farmer he'd initially appeared and far more skilled than his dead kinsmen. The dwarf flipped the hoe around and struck a female goblin in the forehead with the handle, cracking her skull, then rapped her in the temple so hard that blood ran down her face and she crumpled. The dwarf spun the hoe again, once more using it as a scythe and slaying one of Saro-Saro's clansmen. Then he advanced on a hobgoblin, using the handle end of the hoe as a spear.

Goblins flowed around the last dwarf, trying to avoid the deadly hoe and awkwardly navigating through the trees, some of them stopping to stare up at the leaves and to feel the bark. Many of the goblins had been born in Steel Town and had never seen trees, save the pines to the far north of the camp, and they could not hide their amazement. Other goblins continued past their wide-eyed fellows, breaking through the copse and seeing a village shaded by the eastern slope of a jagged peak.

They whooped loudly at their discovery, and Direfang hurried to catch up to them. He glanced once over his shoulder, seeing that the defiant dwarf was finally being brought down by the odds, the hoe yanked from him as he was brutally torn apart.

Direfang lengthened his stride, ignoring the ache in his twisted leg and blinking furiously in a failed effort to clear his vision.

"Stop! No more killing!" he shouted as loudly as he could. "No more blood! Listen! Stop!" He wanted someone in the village left alive to talk to, to ask about the mountains and the land beyond them.

He shouted "Stop!" until he was hoarse. And eventually the goblins did stop—just short of the village. Anxious, the goblins raised and lowered their knives, shifted from one foot to the other, or craned their necks this way and that to get a better look at the dwarf homes. They whispered among themselves, the noise like a swarm of locusts. And though it was difficult to make much sense of what the goblins said, Direfang knew they were excited at the prospect of what might be gained and what they might kill.

Behind him, Direfang heard the whoops of the goblins still beating on the corpse of the last defiant dwarf and his dead fellows. He glanced over his shoulder and saw goblins stripping clothes and boots off the corpses and snatching the farm implements the dwarves had used as weapons. Farther back, other goblins were still splashing in the stream and drinking their fill.

They were more of a mob than an army, the eight hundred or so goblins and hobgoblins who followed him. They were difficult but not impossible to control. They had held together up till then, as he'd demanded. But they likely would not hold for long.

DEATH MARCH

Again, Direfang wished leading them were not his burden.

"Why stop?" Spikehollow had come up next to him, where Direfang had paused to look over the dwarf settlement. Spikehollow looked eager to charge into the village. "Why stop here, Direfang?"

Direfang didn't reply, but he limped forward, gesturing as he went that the goblins and hobgoblins should stay put. He reached the front of the mob and started counting the buildings.

There were fifty small homes, sturdily built from blocks that had been chiseled out of the mountains and mortared together with a white paste. The roofs were for the most part thatch, more tightly woven than any of the roofs in Steel Town had been. A few were made of slices of shale, also mortared together and looking like fish scales.

"Skull man!" Direfang bellowed.

None of the homes had wood doors, as the Dark Knights had used. But they all had goat or sheep hides covering the openings and more hides hanging across the narrow windows. Several of the hides had symbols painted on them—anvils and hammers and other things Direfang could not recognize. One house had a riot of purple and yellow flowers growing around it. Another had a large pot outside of its door that contained a bush covered with red berries. Smoke rose from the chimney of only one home, and the hobgoblin sniffed to tell if something were cooking over a fire, but the scent of his wet kinsmen overpowered all other smells.

A large garden filled the center of the village and wrapped around most of the homes, with paths cutting through it leading to doorways and toward the trees and the stream. The crops were thriving. Cornstalks in a section to the west stood taller than Direfang; bushbeans to the east were fully leafed, and each plant appeared as big around as a barrel. There were vegetables Direfang had never seen before: bright red and yellow pear-shaped bulbs, and bumpy, purple bulbs as big as his fist. One section was filled with dark red berries growing on slender, thorny vines.

"Why wait?" Spikehollow had edged up close behind Direfang. "Raid the village. Take the food. Take everything."

"Everything, everything, everything," Leftear growled, not far behind Spikehollow. "For Chima and Grok and Durth and Bignose," he said, naming the goblins the young dwarf had killed. "Everything."

"Skull man!" Direfang repeated. "Come here now!" He heard goblins grudgingly move out of the way for the priest, some of them cursing the Dark Knight and spitting, and others talking excitedly about the imminent raid on the pretty village. "Skull man!"

"I'm here, Foreman," Horace said, hurrying up, his dark skin gleaming. He'd cleaned himself in the stream, and water dripped from his shoulders.

Direfang pointed to the far eastern edge of the village, to what held most of the goblins' attention. Past the massive garden, a boulder had been carved into the shape of an anvil. It was roughly eight feet tall and a little more than that in width. Its sides were polished and shone darkly, and they were etched with symbols that Direfang suspected were words, but he was too far away to read them. Circling the anvil were a few dozen dwarf women and children, kneeling, eyes closed, and obviously praying.

"Easy to kill, those short, fat people," Pippa said gleefully. "Saro-Saro says that—"

"There will be no more killing," Direfang growled. "Skull man?"

"They are worshipers of Reorx," said Horace, staring at the huge boulder and the dwarves praying. "What else do you want to know, Foreman Direfang?"

Direfang raised an eyebrow. He knew about some of Krynn's gods, primarily Zeboim, from the priest; and Takhisis and Chislev, from some of the Dark Knights in the mining camp. But he'd not heard of that one, the god of the dwarves, Reorx.

"Is Reorx a god only for dwarves?" the hobgoblin asked. "Does Reorx demand the dwarves pray at that rock?"

"The gods are worthless," Spikehollow spat. All of the goblins and hobgoblins who followed Direfang considered themselves godless. The gods had done nothing for goblin-kind, had allowed them to be enslaved and to be bullied by practically every race on Krynn. "No god will save those dwarves. Attack now, Direfang?"

The hobgoblin shook his head irritably.

The goblins had spread out behind Direfang, stretching as far across as the village and standing several ranks deep, yet none of them dared to step past the hobgoblin. They continued to whisper, though, a shushing that was similar to the sound of the breeze rustling through the trees.

"Do the dwarves pray for Reorx to come down and smite this army?" Boliver had moved up next to the priest and was speaking now, with Mudwort close behind him. Boliver was addressing the priest; he was one of the few goblins to fluently speak the human tongue. "Or do the dwarves pray to have all hobgoblins and goblins spirited away? What can this god do, skull man? This Re-or-ax?"

"Nothing," Spikehollow softly muttered. "Gods do nothing."

"Gods . . ." Horace took a deep breath and tilted his head back, wondering where to begin. "Reorx is called Elian, the Anvil, the Forge, and the Weaponmaster. The patron of smiths and craftsmen across Ansalon, he is said to toil with Shinare to improve the lives of dwarves. The World Smith, with his hammer and under the direction of the High God of Krynn, he forged the stars and the world and shaped the souls of mortals from the breath of Chaos. Reorx is the supreme god of the dwarves, and gnomes and kender revere him as well. Reorx—"

"But goblins revere no gods," Direfang said tersely.

A young goblin jabbed Direfang in the back of his sore leg. "Do not understand," she hissed. "All this babble. Do not understand!"

Boliver tried to translate some of the discussion, which was relayed down the ranks. The goblins began chattering about what little they knew, all the talk about the strange dwarf creatures and their supposed god.

"What do the dwarves say, priest?" asked Direfang.

Horace wiped his face with his big hands, and brushed

at his leather leggings, which were still filthy despite his stop in the stream. He cocked his head, trying to make out the words.

"Never seen dwarves," Leftear whispered. "Are short, fat humans also dwarves?"

Horace listened. "I can't make out all the words."

"Bah! The words make no sense to me," said Direfang.

The wizard had come up behind the priest and the hobgoblin; his gaze flitted between the dwarves and Direfang. "I can't understand them either, Horace. I had no call to learn their language. But I'll wager they're praying for their souls. They know they're going to die. These goblins will—"

"No more blood," Direfang repeated. "Not this day, wizard. There's been enough blood today." He motioned again for his fellows to stay back then plucked at the priest's arm. "Come now, skull man. Talk to the dwarves." The hobgoblin shuffled down one of the garden paths toward the assembled dwarves and the stone anvil.

"Gray Robe, watch the homes," Horace cautioned over his shoulder.

"Just in case," Grallik added. "Just in case there are warriors waiting to spring a trap."

The dwarves continued to pray, some of the women's voices rising louder and the words coming quicker as the hobgoblin and the priest neared. When the pair came to within a few feet of them, an ancient dwarf with thin, gray hair tied loosely behind her head got to her feet with effort. She nervously looked between the priest and Direfang, and she kept mouthing her prayer.

"Woman," Direfang began. "Quiet, woman!" His words sounded like a fierce growl, and the hobgoblin half expected the dwarf to start at the sound.

But she didn't even meet his gaze, staring at his stomach while her lips kept moving in the prayer.

"Woman," Direfang began again. The hobgoblin looked back to the eager mass of goblins. "Dwarf . . ." He knew he needed to find a way to communicate with the dwarves soon, or his army would descend on that place and kill anything that moved. He'd need to prove the dwarves useful and worth allowing to live. He stretched an arm out and poked the shoulder of the frantically praying old female dwarf.

"Listen, woman!"

She looked up, her eyes meeting his and showing her anger. She stopped praying and spoke, but the words were still all foreign, except for Reorx, which she repeated several times.

Direfang let out an exasperated sigh. "Skull man!"

"Let me try something." Horace glanced uneasily at the goblin army. "You don't need to butcher these people, Foreman Direfang. They've no weapons. They all look to be simple farmers and—"

"Talk to the farmers, then, priest. Talk fast and tell me how simple they really are." But the priest might be right, Direfang thought; not even the sturdiest among the women had a knife or cudgel.

"We come to your village . . ." Horace tried speaking in the tongue of gnomes, a language with which he was more familiar; his words were halting, however. "We mean you no harm, and . . ."

Most of the dwarves had stopped praying. They still knelt around the stone anvil, but they were paying attention, staring at the priest. The expression on their faces revealed that they understood his words. The ancient dwarf shuffled closer and looked up into Horace's wide eyes.

"Harm? Mean us no harm?" Tears glistened in her eyes as she answered in the gnome tongue. "Your monsters butchered our men and our priest. Killed a divine man of Reorx! Your monsters will butcher us next. Reorx save our souls. And Reorx damn yours!"

Direfang found the language thick and fuzzy-sounding. It reminded him of the noise rocks made when they tumbled down the mountainside. Still, he listened closely, hoping to pick up anything he could understand.

"They are not my monsters," Horace told the ancient female dwarf. "At the moment, I am their slave. They've done me no real harm, though, and if you are careful, you will stay safe too. But you have to be careful. And you have to listen to me."

She narrowed her eyes and thrust out her chin, looking to Direfang and making a gesture with her fist. "Murdering monsters, they are. Reorx save us. Monsters come to Reorx's Cradle."

"That is the name of this . . ." Horace searched for the word. "Town?" he said finally.

"Reorx's Cradle."

"I'd have thought to find dwarves inside the mountain. You'd have been better off there. These goblins would not have found you." Horace closed his eyes and mouthed a quick prayer to Zeboim. "And my goddess and your god willing, perhaps what's left of your town can remain unhurt. The . . . foreman . . . is not as bloodthirsty as the rest of them."

She returned her gaze to the priest, balled her fists and set them against her hips. "I ask only that the young be spared, and one of the mothers be spared to lead them from this place."

Direfang, listening in frustration, catching only a few words at intervals, snarled and jabbed at the priest. "What does the dwarf say, skull man? Secret words are a dangerous thing."

The goblins had pressed closer, some edging into the garden to the west, eyeing the vegetables and the caterpillars that crawled on them, then eyeing the dwarves. Their chatter grew louder.

The priest quickly translated what he and the old dwarf had said. "There are no more men in this village. You killed all of them."

"But the homes?"

"Aye, they would suggest that more dwarves live here than we have been told, Foreman. You are smart to see that. This is not so small a village. Still, I can't explain why, but I think she is telling the truth."

Pippa and Leftear had made it to the garden and were plucking beans off a bush and stuffing them into their mouths. Saro-Saro was near them, on one of the paths, and he pointed to the nearest home and turned to his clan.

"The strange talking, it is done," Saro-Saro proclaimed. "It is time to take. To take everything."

A cheer went up.

13

LOOTING THE CRADLE

Direfang shot past the priest, grimacing with each step, his twisted leg still agonizing. He should have ordered the goblins back when he spotted the first one slipping into the garden.

In a heartbeat he reached Pippa, furiously plucking her up and hurling her over his shoulder back into the crowd of goblins who were moving into the garden. Olabode went next, landing at Leftear's feet, and Direfang threw a potbellied goblin hard into Saro-Saro, knocking the old clan leader down.

"Enough!" Direfang raged at the mob, spittle flying from his lips. A handful edged forward, knives out and ready to challenge him. A goblin called Knobnose looked defiant. But the hobgoblin did not back down. He slammed his fist into Knobnose's throat and grabbed a small goblin who had rushed in, picking her up and tossing her over the heads of the front line. "I said no killing! No more! Fighting these dwarves—women and babies—is tainted blood. Only weak and stupid goblins draw tainted blood."

He picked up another goblin, threatening to throw him too, and the crowd stopped moving. Some stared in disbelief that Direfang would threaten his kinsmen; some mumbled that his words made sense. Finally he released the goblin and shoved him away, keeping one eye on the crowd as he turned back to the priest and the old dwarf.

"Skull man, are these all the dwarves left in the village?"

The priest had a quick exchange with the woman. "No. She says there are a few in the homes, babies and a sick old man. She's worried that—"

"Other dwarf lied! No more men in the village, that dwarf claimed." Direfang beckoned to Boliver.

"No more men that could stand up to you, she says," Horace continued. "Only one very sick man, and old, and she cautions you that—"

Direfang said to Boliver, "Gather some clansmen and search the homes." Then he pointed to the hobgoblin Rustymane, who still carried Graytoes. "You. Search the homes, and take food, weapons, anything useful. Leave the women no weapons. Gather sacks for carrying." He paused and stared at the dwarves still circling the stone anvil. "Take everything. Everything! But no killing. No more blood. Swear it!"

"No blood," Rustymane agreed. The hobgoblin nodded to the goblins surrounding him, most of them light brown members of the Fishgatherer clan. They followed him as he headed toward the nearest home, chattering excitedly.

"No blood, Direfang," Boliver repeated. "No more killing. Only taking." He repeated the command in the human tongue for the benefit of the Dark Knights, and he selected several of his clansmen and scurried off. "Take everything!"

"Everything!" they echoed.

The dwarves had started praying again, their voices shaky with fear. Direfang heard Horace talking in the unknown tongue again. From his expression, the priest was trying to reassure the ancient female dwarf who appeared to be the leader of the small band of survivors.

Saro-Saro had picked himself up and was scowling at Direfang. A line of drool spilled over the cagey old goblin's lip, and he glared menacingly at the hobgoblin. Then his expression softened, and he awkwardly bowed, acknowledging Direfang's leadership. But when Saro-Saro turned and went back to his clan, the harshness returned to his eyes.

"Flamegrass!" Direfang shouted, instantly capturing the attention of the orange-skinned goblins belonging to that clan. "The gardens are yours. Find sacks and blankets, anything to put the harvest in." He glanced at the priest. "Are there animals? There must be. Skull man, ask the dwarves where the animals are."

There was another quick exchange between the priest and the old woman.

"Foreman," answered Horace, "she says there are pens south of the homes. They keep quite a few goats and—"

"Goats!" blurted Truak, a hobgoblin nearly as tall as Direfang. He knew only a few human words, but *goats* was one of his favorites. "Goats taste good! Big, bloody goats!"

"Slay half of the goats," Direfang ordered Truak, clapping him on the shoulder. "Spikehollow, make sure only half the goats are killed. The old goblins will eat, then the others."

"Only half the goats?" Truak sounded disappointed. "Can't slay all?"

"Half," Spikehollow said firmly. "Direfang will save the other half for later."

Truak grinned and thumped his fist against his chest. "Yes. It will be good to have goats now and goats later. Direfang is wise."

Direfang wasn't done delegating the many tasks that were necessary. He eyed the mass of goblins, registering the ones with hostile expressions; those he would remember and dress down later. He picked three young goblins and pointed to the trees.

"See to the dead," he told the three. "Take the wizard and make sure only the goblins burn. The dwarves can bury their men later or do whatever it is dwarves do with the dead." Direfang repeated his instructions in the human tongue, so Grallik would understand.

The wizard started after the goblin funeral detail, Kenosh following his fellow former Dark Knight.

"Only the wizard," Direfang said.

An unsmiling Kenosh returned to Horace's side as the priest continued to converse with the old dwarf, calming her.

DEATH MARCH

Saro-Saro fumed silently as he watched all the activity, narrowing his eyes on Direfang as the hobgoblin limped toward the stone anvil. That his clansmen, save for Spikehollow, were given no important duties in the village was a serious insult to him. It was as if Direfang had physically struck Saro-Saro. The old clan leader growled from deep in his belly as Direfang stepped between a pair of goblin children and approached the big stone.

"What do?" one of Saro-Saro's clansmen asked him, sidling up to him. "What do here?"

Saro-Saro wiped at the drool that clung to his lips. "Nothing do here now. Do nothing but wait."

"Wait?"

Saro-Saro nodded. Wait and plan, he mouthed. "Wait and watch Direfang," he whispered.

Even close to the stone, Direfang could not read the writing carved on it. "Priest?"

"I cannot read it either, Foreman. It is Dwarvish and from the looks of it quite old."

"Make the woman read it, then. I want to know what it says."

The priest shrugged, touching the old dwarf's shoulder and turning her so she could face the anvil. She glared defiantly at the hobgoblin. But Horace implored her to do what Direfang wanted, and breathed a sigh of relief when she whispered the words she read. Horace translated.

"The anvil is an altar, Foreman, carved by her ancestors when this village was founded. The original settlers were miners, for gems, I understand. When a quake rocked this part of the mountain range a few hundred years ago, and subsequently brought down the caverns they lived in, they took it as a sign from Reorx. They moved aboveground and for the most part became farmers or herders."

Direfang snorted. "In a few hundred years, one would think there would be more dwarves than this in this place. Dwarves must breed slowly."

"Some moved away, obviously," Horace said dryly.

"Because Reorx said to?" Direfang scoffed. He raised his

hand to touch the top of the altar, his gesture drawing gasps from the female dwarves.

"Ask where this 'Cradle' sits in the mountains. How far from Steel Town is it, does she know? How far is it to the sea where the range wraps around the shore like a fishhook? Ask the woman those things, skull man."

Direfang was not pleased with the terse answers of the wary dwarf woman. His army had perhaps weeks of travel ahead of them to reach the border of ogre lands, she said, and even longer to reach the swamp.

"A year?" he wondered aloud. It sounded as though it would take longer even than a year to reach the Qualinesti Forest—two, maybe. He tried to picture the mountains and the swamp and the Plains of Dust. His army did not dare to follow any major roads for fear of alerting cities of enemies who could outnumber and outfight them, and the knights who were bound to be tracking them.

"A fool to take on this foolish quest," he muttered to himself. The horde of goblins would be noticed—somewhere along the trail—and men would come after them.

"A map, priest. Is there one in this Cradle?"

"No, Foreman," Horace replied after talking to the dwarf elder. "But she says her sister can draw you one. If the goblins agree to leave quickly, her sister will cooperate. Her worries are genuine and I share them, Foreman. The longer we stay here, the greater chance these women and children will be—"

Direfang waved away the rest of his words and traced the etchings on the anvil with his fingers. "Reorx had done little to help these dwarves," he mused to himself. He turned and set his back against the stone, relishing the cool smoothness that seemed to draw some of the pain out of his body.

"Priest, tell the woman . . ." Direfang folded his arms across his chest and carefully detailed his instructions.

The priest knelt in front of the old dwarf, so she would no longer have to look up to meet his eyes. He spoke slowly, as he did not know all the intricacies of the gnome language.

"Your village will be thoroughly looted. The goblins will take every scrap of food, every piece of clothing, all of your shoes and anything they consider valuable. Do you understand?"

The glaring old dwarf woman nodded.

"They will take anything that might be used as a weapon because they need more weapons and because they do not want to leave you with anything that you might come after them and attack them with. Though you are few in number compared to this army, they do not want you following them and posing any threat."

She nodded again. The light had gone out of her eyes, and the wrinkles in her face had become more pronounced. Tears streamed down her cheeks.

"They will kill half of your animals now, and they will feast and celebrate before they move on. The rest of the animals they will take with them, so they can feast later." Horace's voice quavered as he delivered the last of the harsh news. "They will strip your garden, trampling every last plant in the process. They will carry it all away and leave you nothing to eat, but at least they will leave you your lives. I know that they will leave you that much . . . Foreman Direfang has promised."

She shuddered and hugged herself as if a freezing wind were whipping around her.

"Do you understand?" Horace repeated.

"May Reorx send your souls to the deepest part of the Abyss," she answered flatly. "May his Cradle be your demise."

Irritably Horace turned away from her, addressing Direfang. "There must be some parchment in one of those homes . . . for your map."

The hobgoblin was watching the hundreds of goblins milling at the edge of the garden. Some were sitting, a few sleeping, but most were agitated and felt constrained by his orders to stay put. Their eyes were begging, questioning, accusing. Well past them, a wisp of smoke curled up through the trees, signaling that the wizard had begun burning the dead goblins. After the goblins feasted, Direfang would hold a brief ceremony for the few who had died.

"Chima," he mused, remembering. She'd been rash, and she had chattered often when he preferred quiet. But she had been a hard worker in the mines, never complaining to his face, never accepting her lot. He would miss her. "Too much blood." He sighed.

Direfang's face turned dark and hard. He needed to feed his army, and to clothe them—as goblins coveted garments of any kind, which accorded them marks of respect. And so it was good they'd come upon that village, which had been unable to defend itself. At the same time, the hobgoblin leader felt sad for the few surviving dwarves. Their homes would soon be empty.

"Priest, yes, find this parchment," he answered Horace finally, "and find something to write with. A map is important." He paused. "And make sure the map drawn is true. No deception from Reorx's children." Direfang saw the old female dwarf had heard his words and bristled at his mention of their god.

Horace lumbered to his feet and looked at the houses, unsure of where to start. Goblins streamed in and out of them, the latter with canvas sacks over their shoulders or baskets in their arms. Some dragged blankets bundled up and stuffed with junk.

"Mudwort, go with the skull man." Direfang wanted to make sure none of the looting goblins hurt the priest—and also, the hobgoblin leader wanted the priest watched. "Mudwort! Be fast!"

The red-skinned goblin had plopped herself down in front of the crowd, watching the priest talk to the ancient dwarf woman and observing Direfang as he dealt with all of the preparations.

She jumped up, her face an unreadable mask. Mudwort made her way up one of the paths that cut through the garden, plucking a tomato as she went. She studied it for a moment, then tossed it to the priest, following her, who did not hesitate to eat it.

Direfang watched the pair walk off. He wanted to search the homes too, thinking there might be something tasty or useful inside them, some little treasure he could claim . . . perhaps some leather he could fashion into shoes. He'd been curious about what the Dark Knights had kept in their homes, and he wondered the same about the dwarves.

But he couldn't leave the dwarves unguarded at the anvil; the goblins surely would descend on them. Only his presence would keep the mob in check. So later he would ask Mudwort and Spikehollow to describe what they saw and smelled, and later he would look through the spoils and perhaps find something left over.

The dwarves around him were praying again, whispering in their gravelly voices, a few rocking back and forth and closing their eyes so tightly they looked as if they were in pain.

The goblins were chattering, their prattle mingling with the dwarves' praying and making Direfang's head hurt. The bleats of terrified goats and sheep and the squeals of pigs cut through all the noise. The goblin voices rose in excitement.

"Food soon," he said, too softly for anyone to hear.

Direfang did not see Saro-Saro slip deep into the goblin crowd and gather his most trusted clansmen close.

14

TREASURE

Mudwort brushed by Spikehollow and Leftear and selected one of the more promising homes that didn't appear to have been ransacked yet. The priest followed her without a word.

The home was tilted to one side, as if the dirt on one end had gotten tired of holding the stones up. It was a ponderous and ugly building, she thought, carved bricks as dark as an overcast sky, all squat-looking like the people who lived there. The only spot of color was a painted symbol on the hide door, and that was cracked and weathered. She stopped in front of the hide door and smoothed out the folds. The painting was an outline of a stern man's face. Like the dwarf men who'd been killed outside the village, he had a long beard. She put her nose against it and made out tiny drawings of hammers and anvils entwined in the beard.

"Silly," she pronounced it as she moved the hide aside and went inside. After a moment, Horace followed her. The home consisted of one room, a low table in the center separating the kitchen from the sleeping area.

"Reorx," the priest explained. "On the hide, that is a drawing of their supreme god. It is said he dared to refer to Chaos as the Father of All and of Nothing." After a heartbeat, he added, "But I understand that the gods mean nothing to you."

She gave no indication that she'd heard or understood him and moved past the table and straight to a chest at the end of a short four-poster bed. If the priest had not come inside, Mudwort would have tested the bed, having had nothing comfortable to sleep upon for years and years; she wondered how soft it and the pillow were. She ran her fingers over the edge of the chest, eyes on the quilted coverlet that draped over the bed and fell to the floor.

She sniffed the air. It was musty and dead-smelling in that place, and Mudwort instinctively knew it hadn't been lived in for a while. Yet there were possessions everywhere—ceramic dishes on a counter, a tall mug banded with copper, a small cask that might have held ale. The table had what she guessed was a shrine in its center: a totem of the same dwarf depicted on the hide, Reorx, circled by smooth stones she guessed came from the stream.

Whoever had moved on had left more than a few possessions behind. Maybe there was something interesting in the chest. She opened it, and out of the corner of her eye watched Horace step to the kitchen counter. The priest walked stooped over as the ceiling was low. He reached for a towel and wiped the juice from the tomato he had just eaten off his hands and face.

Just then two goblins rushed in, chattering and looking around for things to take.

"Out!" Mudwort spat.

They swung about and went elsewhere.

"The foreman is in a hurry for some parchment," Horace said. He opened a cabinet door, bent over, and peered inside. His voice came muffled. "One of those women is going to draw him a map. He wants us to be quick."

Still, Mudwort did not let on if she understood him.

Horace repeated the gist in her tongue, and she nearly dropped the lid on her fingers in surprise. So that much was clear; she had not known that he understood goblinspeak.

Quickly she turned away, sorry she had let him know that she understood him at all, in any tongue.

He shrugged, continuing to search. She heard him moving things around in the cabinet. Over her shoulder she stole glances at him, finding him more interesting—at the moment—than what might be in the chest.

"Why come here?" she asked finally in goblinspeak.

"In here? With you?" he replied, not understanding.

"No."

"With you and the rest of the goblins? When Steel Town was destroyed?" He stopped poking around for a moment. "I'm not sure . . . Mudwort. Perhaps because the Gray Robe asked me to. Perhaps because Zeboim gave me the nudge. Or perhaps because following all of you goblins seemed like the most attractive option at the time." He returned to searching through the cabinet. "Ah, books!"

He retrieved three small volumes, bound in the dyed hide of some animal. Two were red, like Mudwort's skin, the other was faded blue. Horace set them on the counter and leafed through the first.

"I don't read Dwarvish," he said, half to himself. The next seemed equally perplexing to him, and so he set it aside. But the faded blue one was blank. "This will work." He squatted and searched through the cabinet, a moment later finding sticks of charcoal tied together with a strip of cloth. "The foreman is in a hurry," he repeated. "I should take these to him now."

"Yes, go. Take those things to Direfang. Be fast." She peered inside the chest. "Leave me alone."

Horace left the home without another word, and Mudwort breathed a sigh of relief to be rid of the foul human. She could give her full attention to the chest's contents. A thin summer blanket was folded on top, and that she took out carefully, thinking it a prize. Underneath the blanket rested a jumble of things that brought a pleased gasp. She reached for the things, eager like a child receiving birthday gifts. Her fingers danced over carved wooden dwarves, depicted standing straight like soldiers—one with a crown, another in robes, one a woman. She thought they might be toys or playing pieces for some game. She scooped them out but wrapped her fingers around the woman-piece.

The descriptive detail was incredible, and Mudwort brought the woman-piece close. Even the eyes were carved finely, wide and open, the carved expression looking wise and kind. Mudwort sniffed it, barely detecting any scent, and placed it carefully on the blanket.

Whoever lived there either died or left in a terrible hurry to leave behind such precious belongings. She decided the set of carved dwarves must have some value. Two sets! Below the first were more figures, carved from a darker wood and shining with some sort of lacquer. There was a woman-piece among that set too, and as before she inspected that one and set it aside. There was also a pipe and a small pouch of tobacco that smelled sweet. Maybe the skull man would like those items; he was plump and so given to fleshly excesses.

There were several small, empty pouches made of soft leather. She put the pipe and tobacco in one, the two women-pieces in another. She found a belt, woven of strips of leather and decorated with green and red wooden beads. It was more colorful than any worn by the dwarves she'd observed outside, and so it must be clothing for special occasions. She tried to put it on, but found it much too big. But when she wrapped it twice, it worked, and she tied the leather bag containing the woman-pieces to it.

There were no clothes, else Mudwort would have replaced the dirt-stained tunic she wore. But there were other interesting objects at the bottom of the chest—beads. Her fingers flew to them, and she brought up string after string. One was a necklace of simple beads, polished and roughly round, carved from some tree with wood so dark it looked almost black. She draped it around her neck and looped it twice because it was so long. Another string was much shorter and made of beads carved into the shapes of animal heads: boar, bear, wolf, ram, and a vicious-looking cat. The eyes were tiny stones that glinted dark blue. The string went quickly around her neck too. Some of the neck-laces at the bottom were made of clay beads that were old and chipped. One string was broken, and the beads bounced across the floor before she could catch them.

"Beautiful." The rare word came out as a croak. The last strand she brought up from the bottom of the chest was made of tiny golden links festooned with small blue stones that caught and held the light that came through the high, narrow window. That strand she held against her bosom for a long moment before putting it in the pouch on her belt. She knew better than to wear something like that and draw too much attention to herself.

The chest stood empty, but she continued to study it; something about it didn't seem right. She leaned into it and thumped its bottom; the chest did not look as big on the inside as it did on the outside. She was rewarded with a hollow sound, and she tore at the bottom until a piece of wood came loose. Under it were seven leather pouches, so old they were cracked like a parched riverbed.

At that moment Leftear came into the home, grunting and shuffling. "Direfang says take everything that seems valuable," he said, barely sparing her a glance. He didn't see her treasure, nor her scowl at him or her waving him away. Instead he went over to the cabinets, roughly breaking a door when he carelessly pulled it open. Then he began grabbing mugs to dump into a canvas sack, along with other things he didn't bother to take the time to identify.

Mudwort opened the pouches and looked inside.

"Lots of valuable stuff here," she whispered to herself. She spilled the contents of three of the pouches onto the floor, and it was that noise that caught Leftear's attention.

"Rocks," he said, looking at her dismissively. "Just lots and lots of rocks." He went to the table and plucked the carved wooden Reorx off it and dropped it in his sack. "These rocks are bigger, prettier." He scooped up some of the polished stones that had ringed the idol and dropped them into the sack. "Might be worth something."

"Precious rocks, mine are," Mudwort said with a tinge of awe, looking away from the hobgoblin and stirring the stones. They were not faceted, like ones in a fine lady's gemstones would be. But they glimmered nonetheless, blue like the surface of a lake when the noon sun hits it. "Humans would have a name for these rocks," she mused. "Humans have names for all sorts of rocks."

She managed to fit the rocks into one of the pouches, hooking it to her belt. Then she spilled out the contents of the other four. One contained more of the uncut stones, but the other three contained cut gems, the facets catching the light and drawing a gasp from Mudwort. There were, perhaps, two hundred or more of the cut stones.

"No food in here." Leftear knocked over a shelf in his search for something to eat. "Going back to the garden," he told her grumpily. "Going to fill up the rest of this bag with onions."

She was quick to scoop up the remaining stones, redistributing them so they fit in two more bags, and those she also fitted to her belt. Then she climbed onto the bed and stretched out momentarily. It would be so easy to sleep here, she thought. Even though so many sounds from outside were drifting in—goblins gathering things, more goblins rooting through the garden, all of the noises running together. She thought she could sleep deeply regardless. The pillow was soft, and she thought she might take it with her but then thought better of it—one more thing to carry.

She pushed herself up, deciding she'd better leave or she would get left behind. She slipped off the bed and hesitated, then grabbed the pillow, shaking it out of its case. She took one more look around, and, seeing nothing else of interest, tucked the case under her arm and stepped outside.

Spikehollow poked his head into a home, one near the section of the garden filled with potatoes. He had made sure the goblins he supervised were working hard in the garden, and he saw his chance. He'd seen a few Flamegrass clansmen go into that home and quickly rush out again earlier. Nothing interesting to be found, they thought, as they'd only taken one sack from the place. Or perhaps the Flamegrass goblins were not observant and had missed something tasty.

"A quick look," Spikehollow told himself. "Then back to the garden."

He pushed the hide aside and darted inside but stopped as if he'd struck a wall. "Stinks bad," he muttered. He made a choking sound and turned to leave, then changed his mind.

"Stink kept the others away. The stink protects good things, maybe."

He held his breath and picked through the shadows. It was dark in there, though it was bright outside. A tattered hide covered the lone window, and little light slipped in around its edges. Spikehollow made out a low table and two stools, a fireplace with a big pot hanging in it. A few logs were under it, slightly charred, but looking as though a fire hadn't burned in it that day. He sniffed the air and recoiled; whatever was in the pot smelled bad, but it wasn't the only thing contributing to the stink.

Three small beds were against the far wall, only one occupied; the other two had been stripped bare to the wood slats. Spikehollow sniffed again. "Stinky dwarf smell. Stinks worse than . . . than anything. Should leave and breathe the better air outside. Leave like the Flamegrass clansmen left—quick."

But he was still curious and so inched closer. The dwarf on the bed looked old, his wispy white hair and beard resembling a mass of cobwebs. A colorful quilt was pulled up to his waist, and his chest was bare and ruddy in places. The quilt was made of yellow, red, and green squares, some with stitching on them. Even with the goblin's superb vision, there wasn't enough light to distinguish the intricacies of the stitches, but his fingers traced the outline of a flower in a vase, a bird, and a butterfly.

"Lots of wrinkles, an old, old man," Spikehollow said. "A stinking one. A sleeping one. Sweating too. Sweating too much for a quilt." The goblin pulled it off him. "Too stinky and sweaty a dwarf to waste a very nice quilt like this."

Spikehollow wished for a treasure to take away from the village, not just something to eat. He wanted something to keep for himself, or perhaps he would give it to Saro-Saro. The old goblin might enjoy a quilt as fine as that. As he carried the quilt to the door, he spotted two more blankets on a shelf, one loosely woven and dyed green, the other gray and frayed. He carefully folded the quilt and set it down and pulled the gray blanket off the shelf.

Then he returned to the old dwarf and covered him with

the frayed blanket. Even though Spikehollow meant well, he felt bile rising in his throat and he gagged.

"Worst stink ever."

Holding his breath, he stared at the dwarf. The dwarf's eyes never opened, and the goblin had to look closely to make sure the dwarf was indeed alive.

"Not breathing much," Spikehollow decided. The dwarf's chest rose and fell only slightly. "Dying, maybe. Old things die. And dying old things don't need any lovely blankets." The goblin cocked his head, noticing a swollen black spot on the dwarf's neck, like a knob on a tree trunk. Spikehollow scowled. "Ugly, stinking, dying old thing."

The stinking old dwarf with the black spot on his neck didn't need the gray blanket, Spikehollow decided, and so he removed it, with the dwarf still sleeping. Spikehollow folded it and set it atop the fine, colorful quilt. Then he pulled the green blanket down too, deciding that was the one he would give to Saro-Saro. He would keep the butterflies and birds and flowers in vases quilt for himself. Satisfied, he took all three out into the sunlight.

Rustymane and Graytoes were heading toward the longest and narrowest home. It was their third stop on their explorations, and they had bulging pillow cases and satchels that they set outside the door. The work had kept Graytoes occupied, and she'd not whimpered or mentioned Moon-eye since they'd started foraging.

"Could live here, in this village," Rustymane was saying. "This place tall enough. This one house anyway." The other two homes the pair had looted had low ceilings, and the hobgoblin had had to stoop.

"Could live in the Qualinesti Forest, like Mudwort says," Graytoes said, more cheerfully than she felt. Then Graytoes slipped inside, her eyes adjusting to the shadows and spotting movement. "Another dwarf." She pointed, adding, "No more killing, Direfang says."

Rustymane pushed past her, growling when the young female dwarf started shouting. She was the height of a goblin, though stockier and smooth all over, marking her as a child. The hobgoblin couldn't understand her angry words, and so he shoved her against a wall.

"Quiet! Quiet, quiet!" He pinched his lips and bent until he was face-to-face with the short female dwarf.

The dwarf stopped yelling and started shaking, beads of sweat sprouting on her wide forehead.

"Stay!" he ordered, pressing his hand against her shoulder. He pushed, and she sat.

"Stay, dwarf!" Graytoes parroted. "Stay quiet!"

"There's food in here," Rustymane announced, looking around. "Lots of it, Graytoes. All of it mushy and sweet." The hobgoblin leaned over a table, where several large bowls were filled with a pulpy mixture. He thrust two fingers in a bowl, and using them like a spoon, shoveled the pulp into his mouth. "Can't put this in a bag, Graytoes. Might as well eat it." He continued to feast, using both hands. "Want some?"

He didn't see her shake her head or squeeze past him. Neither did he see what filled the rest of the one-room building. Small beds and cradles. Rustymane slurped the porridge so noisily that he didn't hear the wave of soft gurgles and sighs or hear Graytoes coo back at the eight dwarf infants inside the place.

The goblin went from child to child, looking each one over and tentatively touching their chins and noses. She giggled when they smiled, and she tucked the blankets up around the ones who'd kicked theirs loose. She couldn't tell precisely how old the younglings were; she'd never seen a dwarf before coming to that village. But she knew they were young; it didn't look as if any of them could walk yet.

"Which one?" she asked Rustymane, though he wasn't paying any attention to her. He was busily slurping up the mixture that Graytoes realized was food for the babies. Frowning, she looked around the table and spotted a jar and spoons. She left the babies and gathered up a jar and the prettiest silver spoon.

Moving to a bowl that Rustymane hadn't yet delved into, she spooned the porridge into the jar and tightly stoppered it and carried it outside and squeezed the jar into a satchel. Then she went back inside happily.

"Which one?" she mused, that time to herself.

Rustymane didn't hear her anyway. The hobgoblin's slurping was louder than all the little sounds the infants made.

The young female dwarf still sat against the wall, quivering and looking timidly between Graytoes and the hobgoblin. The female dwarf wailed when Graytoes started lifting up blankets and counting the infants' toes and looking to determine their sex.

"Boy," Graytoes said. "Boy. Boy. Girl." She halted at the cradle of the baby girl dwarf. "A girl, and the smallest one here." She reached inside and picked up the baby. It gurgled pleasantly. She made sure the blanket was wrapped tightly around it, and she held it close. "Moon-eye always wanted a girl."

Larger than a goblin baby, the dwarf infant was cumbersome, but Graytoes managed to cradle it lovingly. "The best treasure," she said. "This is the best treasure ever."

She left the building, ignoring the frightened young female dwarf who wailed her protest. Rustymane's feasting sounds diminished behind her as, with some difficulty, she shouldered the satchel she'd nestled the porridge in while still carrying the child.

Graytoes struggled only a little with her burdens. The acquisition of a baby had given her strength and purpose.

15

DIREFANG'S MAPS

The moon was full, and its light was bright enough that Direfang could study the series of maps one of the dwarves had drawn. Rendered in charcoal and spread out over the small pages of the book, the maps were not near as detailed as the Dark Knight maps he'd admired in Steel Town. But then, he'd never been allowed to get too close to those precious maps. He had to be careful with the charcoal drawings too because the pages of the book were thin and the lines smeared easily.

He desperately needed a real map, one large and sturdy and drawn by men who'd been over the terrain. But he did not know where to get one.

The hobgoblin sat in the center of a wide trail that ran south of Reorx's Cradle. He'd intended to peruse the crude maps while he was in the village, perhaps pass a few nights there and give the goblins more time to dig through the garden and truly relax. He certainly could have used the time to rest his leg and his foggy eyes, and to ask the old female dwarf more about the mountains. But he worried too much that the dwarves would provoke his charges into killing the women and children. It was bad enough when one of the dwarves saw Graytoes carry away a baby; the dwarf became hysterical, and her fellows had had to restrain her.

The priest had pleaded with Direfang to leave the baby in the village. "She belongs with her own kind," the priest had argued.

But Graytoes wanted the child badly, and the mewling thing seemed to make her happy. So Direfang let Graytoes keep it, and he ordered the goblins out of the village to keep the surviving dwarves safe.

Why did he care about the dwarves to begin with? he wondered. What kind of spark of weakness, deep inside him, stopped him from letting the goblins slay every last dwarf in Reorx's Cradle? Was it the same spark that had kept him from sending the goblins after the Dark Knights in the infirmary in Steel Town? Was his heart too soft?

"Weakness," he grumbled. "Helpless and empty of fire." He returned his attention to the maps.

He'd demanded the mapmaker put a scale to her drawings or something to roughly indicate the passing of miles or days' travel between one place and the next. But she added only landmarks that he might notice on his journey south, not seeming to understand precisely what he wanted. So Direfang still had no clue where exactly they were in the mountain chain and how much farther it was to the sea.

"Maybe two years' travel," he mused. "Could it really take that long, two years? Or could it take more? The world is so big."

"Two years for what?" Boliver asked. The earth-colored goblin scratched his head, listening to Direfang. Then he scowled as he understood. "Two years to reach Mudwort's forest? Two years?"

"To the Qualinesti Forest," Direfang said. "Maybe. Hard to tell. More than a year, probably. Maybe two. A long time in any event. It is on the other side of the world from Steel Town. There's a mountain range and a swamp, and then more mountains. The world is very, very big, Boliver."

Boliver shook his head in disbelief. "Don't think all the clans will walk for that long. Saro-Saro is old and might not live that long anyway. Besides, the clans are tired of walking in these mountains. The forest would be good, though, at least the forest I saw in the vision Mudwort conjured. Lots and lots of trees there. But the clans may give up before the forest. Before two years, surely, Direfang. The clans will give up long before one year."

"Yes," Direfang replied. And that wouldn't be such a bad thing, would it? he mused to himself. He imagined how good it would feel to be left alone . . . or to be traveling with just a handful of goblins he truly liked. But there was no safety in small numbers. The ogres and minotaurs would capture the goblins and hobgoblins and resell them as slaves to the Dark Knights. Their only hope was to cling together in that massive force.

Not even the tylor had defeated them.

Direfang's finger hovered above the spot where the map-making dwarf had drawn an X to represent Reorx's Cradle. But she hadn't known where Steel Town was—the Dark Knights had kept the place as secret as possible—and so he still had no way of knowing how far they'd come from the ruined mining camp.

How many days had they traveled? At first Direfang had tried to keep count, but the numbers were lost. Since his tumble down the mountainside, some things were difficult to recall.

He looked toward the bottom edge of the page, where the dwarf had drawn the peaks more tightly packed. The priest had translated that those represented the Southern Khalkists, which consisted of the Onyx Teeth, on the border of the swamp, and the Ogre Peaks, which Direfang desperately wanted to avoid. Nearby stretched what she'd called the Reorxcrown Mountains, which essentially formed the border between Khur and Blöde. She'd claimed that her village was in the central Khalkists, near a group of mountains called the Suncradles, from which came the name of their village, Reorx's Cradle. The dwarf had said she'd never traveled beyond those ranges, and so could not draw a map of anything else.

"One thing sure. A long way to go to the Qualinesti Forest," Direfang repeated. "Too long."

Boliver, looking over his shoulder, tried to make his own sense of the maps but finally gave up. "Maybe Mudwort can find a better way," he proposed, "one that would not take two years. Maybe one that would not involve walking over more mountains."

Direfang raised his head. "Yes. Maybe Mudwort can."

"I've been watching you," Grallik said, "for some time now." He sat opposite Mudwort, though not so close that he might spook her into fleeing. "Can you understand me? Understand anything I'm saying to you?" He sat with his back straight and his shoulders square, traditional military posture. He tried to show some pride, even though he wore filthy rags and his hair was a tangled, matted mess.

The red-skinned goblin regarded the wizard slowly. Her nostrils swelled, taking in his fetid scent, and she drew her lips into a line, her brow furrowing and her veins tightening along the sides of her head. Her eyes were tiny, dark points as they fixed on Grallik, but the wizard was uncertain if she was really looking at him or through him. She seemed to disappear inside herself, breathing shallowly and not even acknowledging his presence.

"Mudwort," he tried again.

Not even a blink did he get.

The air was cool and had a dampness to it, and the faint breeze brought the scent of wildflowers that grew in patches of dirt on the eastern slope. But the breeze also bore the redolent stink of hobgoblins and goblins. There was a distinct odor to the mountains themselves too, the peaks rising to the east and west and stretching as far south as they could see.

Grallik let out a deep breath and placed his hands on his knees, the fingers of his right hand finding one of the many holes in his undertunic and worrying at the threads. He kept his eyes on the goblin shaman, resolving to engage her, communicate with her. It was the first real chance he'd had to talk to her.

"I know you can speak a little of the human tongue. I heard you warn a guard back in Steel Town about the coming earthquakes."

She scowled. "Warned the guards about something." The human words sounded raspy and foreign coming from her, and he had to concentrate to understand her. "Did not know about what you call . . . earthquakes. Just knew the stones in the mine were anxious. Felt something bad was going to happen, but the Dark Knights would not listen to me. Now those Dark Knights are dead."

"You knew the volcanoes would erupt too, didn't you?"

She scooted farther away from him and looked around, seeing groups of goblins nearby; there were so many in Direfang's army that true solitude was impossible. She watched Pippa smoothing at a shirt she'd fashioned into a dress and trying to brush the dirt out of it.

Grallik craned his neck to see what she was looking at. Pippa was also wearing the slippers she'd taken off a dead dwarf; she'd tied them around her feet with cord she'd found somewhere. They made slapping sounds as she moved. The young goblin had also tied a cord around her waist to hold her shirt up so she wouldn't trip over its hem. Grallik thought the goblin looked absurd, comical, and he returned his attention to Mudwort.

"Your magic . . . ?" Grallik had rehearsed several speeches he'd planned to deliver to Mudwort, but the right words eluded him at the moment.

She turned to look at him, again her small eyes staring, her expression heavy with distaste. She folded her spindly arms in front of her, relaxed them and interlaced her fingers. After a moment, she rubbed her thumbs together, a gesture that might have seemed nervous but that Grallik took for boredom. He feared she might get up and leave him at any moment.

"Mudwort . . . I want to—"

She wrinkled her nose and spat. "Hate Dark Knights." Those words were clear; he had no trouble understanding. "Mean men, hateful men." Still, she made no move to rise, though she glanced up for a moment.

The moon was directly overhead, silvery and hazy with a rain ring.

"The Dark Knight tongue is ugly sounding," she added

matter-of-factly. "Don't know much of it. Don't want to. The words are as ugly as the men."

"But some of it, the language, you know. That is good." He paused. "Listen, please. I'm not a Dark Knight anymore, Mudwort." Grallik spoke slowly, hoping that it might help her understand his words, trying to emphasize his sincerity. "I left the Order when I left Steel Town. I'm just a man now and—"

"A hated man." She spat again. "A slave now."

"Mudwort, teach me your magic." He ground his teeth together, angry at himself for rushing into his plea. He'd not intended to bring up the subject until after he'd established some sort of rapport with her—days or, at the outside, weeks from then. He'd planned to compliment her on her skills, try to get her to warm to him. But he'd clearly ruined any chances he might have had. His skin suddenly felt as dry and brittle as old parchment; the damp air seemed to pull all the life from him. His face and hands felt chafed, and his fingers ached so badly that he stopped worrying at the thread.

All around them goblins chattered, but he could understand none of their guttural exchanges. For all he knew, they could be nattering on about the baby the little yellow-skinned goblin had stolen, arguing over the spoils, or simply discussing the weather.

Grallik couldn't see Kenosh or Horace, but he suspected they were nearby, watching him warily. Kenosh was loyal and never strayed too far. Grallik had put all three of their lives in such disarray that there might never be a future for them beyond slaving to that tribe of little monsters. The wizard silently raged against the world and himself for his stupidity.

What have I done? he mouthed.

He raised a hand and pressed it against his forehead, let his fingers trail down over his face. He didn't need a mirror to register his appearance. His cheeks were sunken and his chin pronounced, the scraggly beard not enough to cover it. He'd practically been starving himself since leaving Steel Town. Grallik had always been thin, in part due to his half-elf heritage. But he'd never been gaunt before. The goblins had not been giving him more than meager handfuls of nourishment, and he hadn't been able to eat some of it—raw meat, insects and grubs. The one tomato Horace gave him from the dwarves' garden had exploded inside his stomach and made him feel sick, he was so unused to food.

He was weak from hunger, and he blamed his weakness, his hunger, for his fumbling mistakes, asking Mudwort so bluntly about her magic. He should have scavenged in the village, as everyone else had.

"I'm sorry. I . . ." He shook his head in resignation. "So hungry. So hungry, I'm not thinking right."

"Then eat, wizard," Mudwort said brusquely. "Ask Direfang for food to fill that ugly little belly. Beg. Beg to be given something."

"Beg?"

"Like the slaves in Steel Town begged," she answered. "Like the skull man begs."

Grallik looked around, finding Horace easily then, standing amid a group of goblins, staring at him and Mudwort as though he were listening to every pathetic word. Had the priest begged for food?

"Go beg," she said. "Like a slave. Then come back and talk about magic."

---&---

Thoroughly broken, Grallik begged and Direfang took pity on him.

The goblins chittered happily as the wizard groveled before Direfang. The begging, though embarrassing, netted the wizard a basket heavy with tomatoes and potatoes, a handful of berries that set his mouth to watering, and a jug of what might have been dwarven ale.

Grallik took his prizes to a side of the trail where there were only a few goblins, who watched, pointed, and whispered about him. He was careful not to eat too much too quickly. He intended to ration the contents of the basket; it could last several days. There were many white crackers dotted with fennel seeds that were stuffed in the side of the basket and felt as firm as bricks—dwarven hardtack, he suspected. It was fundamentally tasteless but useful and nourishing. He bit into one and chewed it gratefully.

When he returned to Mudwort, carrying the basket protectively close, he saw that the other earth-skinned goblin was sitting across from her, their fingers sunk into the dirt and their eyes closed. They were casting magic together, he was excited to see.

Direfang loomed over Mudwort, however, and several other goblins hovered nearby, all of them clearly curious. With a scowl, Direfang waved the wizard away.

Grallik sighed with disappointment, knowing he'd missed an opportunity to talk to Mudwort and an even greater opportunity to observe her working her strange magic. He turned to seek Horace's and Kenosh's company.

"Sit," Mudwort said, surprising him and the others.

Grallik wasn't aware she'd seen him and wasn't sure she was even talking to him. But then she repeated her command, her head turned ever-so-slightly toward him. Perhaps her eyes were not completely closed after all. Or perhaps she had heard him return. He drew his eyebrows together thoughtfully.

Or perhaps she'd sensed him walking on the path as her fingers were buried in it.

His hesitation was brief. He sat cross-legged next to her and the brown-skinned goblin. He sat closer to her than before; he could reach over and touch her if he tried. Direfang and the others stepped back, giving them space.

"Boliver," Mudwort said, introducing her companion goblin to Grallik. "A clan shaman in the Before Time. Boliver is a stoneteller."

Grallik didn't know what the Before Time was, nor a stoneteller, and neither goblin explained further.

Boliver nodded without opening his eyes. His lips were working, like a babe suckling, and the muscles in his arms jumping.

"Boliver, this is the hated Dark Knight that watches," Mudwort continued. "The one who wielded the hated fire magic in Steel Town. The one that burns the bodies. The one that wants to mingle magic." She spat at the ground near Grallik's knee. "The dirty, smelly Dark Knight with all the fire-scars."

Grallik felt unnerved by Mudwort's description of him.

She cocked her head toward the wizard, as if she were waiting for something. Grallik didn't know what to do or what she expected.

Was he allowed to speak?

He set his basket in his lap and put his hands on his knees, finding a hole in his clothing and once more worrying at the threads. He coughed once and a deeper, brief hacking followed. He'd not been able to entirely shake the cough he'd developed in Steel Town, but he noticed it had been getting better the farther away from the mine they traveled.

"The hated Dark Knight hesitates. Frightened maybe?" That was Boliver's statement. The goblin chuckled mirthlessly.

"I . . . I don't understand," Grallik said. "What should I do?"

Neither goblin responded, their fingers sinking deeper into the hard-packed ground. A moment more, and their hands disappeared below the surface. Mudwort leaned forward until her head touched Boliver's.

Gravel crunched and Grallik looked up to see Direfang edging closer again. The hobgoblin's gaze was fixed on Mudwort.

"Mudwort," Direfang began. "As I said, the maps the dwarf drew are not enough to go on, and the mountains stretch too far. This army stops in the Plains of Dust—"

"Unless there is a shorter way," she finished. "Yes, I know. You seek a better way to the forest."

"Mudwort's forest," Boliver said.

Grallik glanced at Direfang, then returned his attention to the two goblins. He stretched a hand forward, tentatively, and touched the ground in front of him. It felt as hard as stone.

"What magic do you possess?" he whispered, half to himself, half to Mudwort. "How can you possibly—" He gasped as his fingers suddenly slipped down into the earth, the ground becoming soft and malleable as wet clay. It was nothing he did himself, he knew, as he'd cast no spell, nor even searched his memory for one.

It was all her doing, he decided, gasping again when her fingers grabbed his beneath the surface and tugged his arms deeper still. Grallik set his other hand upon the ground, feeling it solid at first, then yielding. More fingers grabbed that hand, and he couldn't tell if those belonged to Mudwort or Boliver.

Grallik struggled for air, feeling a painful tightness in his chest, as if the goblins meant to suffocate him in the dirt. He felt dizzy as his mind spiraled down into the ground. A heartbeat later, and he felt as if he were rising. Though his eyes were wide open and staring at Mudwort, an image superimposed itself on his vision; he realized he was staring down at the two goblins and himself from a point high above them on the trail.

He opened his mouth to ask "How?" but he couldn't speak. It was their spell, he realized, Mudwort and Boliver's; and they'd pulled him into it somehow, maybe using his arcane energies to help power it. That would explain the dizziness, the feeling of being siphoned. He closed his eyes as the view became clearer. As if he were a bird soaring on some thermal updraft, looking down on the world. He rose, and the image of himself and the two goblins, of Direfang hovering and goblins upon goblins stretched out along the trail, became smaller and smaller until all were specks.

In his precious spell tomes in Steel Town, there was an incantation like the spell he was experiencing. It was not joined magic, of course; before watching the goblins, he'd not thought it possible to join magic. But the "distant view," a spell like that stirred a memory. Arcane eye, arcane vision, magic sight . . . something like that was the name of the enchantment. He'd cast it once or twice, a long time past. He'd collected the necessary words for it during his study with the black-robed wizards before the Chaos War. He had written them down in a precious spell tome, lost when the earthquakes hit.

He'd never had a reason to use such a spell since his early

years, so preoccupied had he become with his destructive fire enchantments. Amazing spellcraft! he thought as his mind floated higher, and vaguely he registered that he was growing weaker still. Mudwort is definitely feeding off me. The spell was parasitic, evidently. But Grallik didn't care. She and Boliver were tugging him along, and he savored the experience.

He spied a river running parallel to the mountains, on the other side of the western ridge. Grallik knew Mudwort would tell Direfang about the water and that they would look for a shortcut to reach it. They were all so thirsty, despite drinking out of the stream near Reorx's Cradle. The river he saw was wide and dark with night, with the moon reflected in it, the shimmering ripples stark against the black water, adding to the wizard's dizziness.

There seemed no more mountains west of the river. Grallik released a sigh of relief. He was so tired of all the damnable rocks that rose all around him and the sharp little ones along the trail that bit into his painfully-aching feet. There were low hills farther west, but they evinced gentle slopes. The land beyond them smoothed to a plain divided by a winding road.

He wanted to linger over the inviting countryside, but Mudwort didn't seem too interested in the area.

The image of the river returned, and the goblins' magic followed it south. The river narrowed, with pines growing along its banks. The roots of the pines looked like black snakes slithering into the equally black river, the tall trees cutting some of the moonlight and making the scene look eerie.

Startled, Grallik heard the splash of some fish and the rustling of branches as a great horned owl took flight. There was a smattering of the sound of smaller wings—blackbirds that had been disturbed by something. He could smell the river; then the goblins' magic took him low across the clear water. Grallik tried to hold the refreshing scent in deep and memorize it. That helped to banish the vestiges of char that had clung to his nostrils since he had burned the last batch of goblin bodies.

DEATH MARCH

Before he could make out all the details of the scene, they were climbing again, and the scent of the pines mingled with the night air. Another wave of dizziness crashed against him, and his physical form fought for balance. The pines gave way to oaks, some of them ancient things with gnarled trunks as twisted as bent old men. Their branches overhung the river, creating a canopy, and the goblins passed through it, dragging Grallik's senses with them.

He swore he could feel the leaves tickling his skin and the wind cooling his face. He delighted in the soft sounds.

Farther, and the river widened once more, meandering through a stretch of rocky land dotted by smaller trees. Finally the river straightened, miles and miles from where they'd started their journey. And judging by the whorls and ripples on its surface, Grallik could tell the river's current had picked up speed.

Ahead was a sheet of blackness, speckled here and there by moonlight. The New Sea, he realized. There were a few deepwater docks at a port town to the west, a few lanterns glowing in windows . . . so tiny, the dots looked like fireflies.

"Not all that far to get to the sea," Grallik heard Boliver say. "A few weeks to the water. No longer than that. Maybe less. Maybe only days. Hard to tell how long it will take to walk there. But not all that far."

"But it is the journey after the end of the river that Direfang will worry over," Mudwort said. "Isn't that right, Direfang?"

The hobgoblin didn't answer.

Grallik felt exhausted by their magic spell, the ordeal. He struggled to stay awake and to protect the basket of precious food he held in his lap; he could not afford to have some goblin steal his food while his mind continued the journey with Mudwort and Boliver. And yet he couldn't afford to break away from the spell either.

They floated over the sea for some time. The wizard could not tell how long the enchantment was taking—minutes or hours. It didn't matter; he was still caught up in the thrill of it. They followed the eastern shoreline of the New Sea, where the mountains rose high again in a formation like a crooked finger that beckoned them toward the heart of ogre territory. In the distance to the west, great shaggy trees, shadows upon shadows, loomed. The swamp. Grallik shuddered at the thought of braving the harsh, wet land.

Direfang had said he intended to take them that way, through that wet hell so different from the arid desolation of Steel Town. Cypress trees dominated, giants that stretched well more than a dozen men tall. There were maples and oaks too, but mostly cypress and willows. Old black willows and willow birches stood tall, their lofty trunks surrounded by dark water that smelled stagnant.

Grallik thought the place should smell worse, all the standing water and rotting wood. Instead, the odors were heady and not terribly unpleasant. He smelled flowers everywhere; the flooded forest teemed with them. The odors from the largest—where the goblins hovered near—made him feel drunk. The wizard decided he wouldn't mind journeying through that place on foot if it meant keeping company with Mudwort. He just wished he could do it magically rather than slogging through the difficult place. He was not looking forward to the physical journey.

He heard Boliver say something in the goblin tongue then repeat it. "Very, very far, this place is. Two years, Direfang thinks. Too far indeed. The clans will not walk so far."

Grallik agreed. His feet—his desperately aching feet and desperately tired legs—could not carry him there.

"So tired," Grallik whispered. The words twisted around his ears as if the wind had blown them.

Then the goblins drew the last of Grallik's strength to continue powering their spell, and the wizard pitched forward, falling heavily to the ground. Grallik was sound asleep well before Pippa stole his vegetable basket and pranced away.

16

DISSENSION

Saro-Saro wore the green blanket around his shoulders like a cloak, fastened with a silver pin in the shape of an anvil that he'd polished with a little spit. Pippa had taken the pin off one of the dead dwarves and given it to Saro-Saro as a gift. "For the greatest clan leader of all." The old goblin also had replaced the tunic he'd stolen many days earlier from an ogre village with a better and cleaner one that had been taken from the dwarves.

Dyed a rich brown, the tunic was made of a heavy, coarse material. He liked the way it felt against his chest, and it was one of the finer garments brought away from Reorx's Cradle; it was only right that Saro-Saro should have the best. It fit much better than his old garment, which was infested with fleas. It was slightly big around the waist, but he tied it with a thin cord to keep his legs from getting tangled. The small bumps in the fabric formed patterns of swirling lines that he thought might be drawings of vines. He'd also been given a pair of nice dwarven sandals, the straps tightened enough so they would not fall off.

While Direfang remained engrossed with some spell Mudwort and Boliver were casting, Saro-Saro met with Spikehollow and other goblins who were angry the big hobgoblin had not let them kill the females and children in the village. They'd wanted to kill everything.

125

"Should have killed everything," Spikehollow complained.

Saro-Saro quietly sowed his dissension. He was wily, and knew that many, many goblins were loyal to Direfang because he'd fomented the rebellion in Steel Town. If Saro-Saro spoke to the wrong goblins about his plans and word drifted back to Direfang, there would be trouble.

Saro-Saro had secretly made an alliance with the leader of the Flamegrass clan, an aging female who did not like the prospect of walking "more than a year," the phrase that had been whispered down from Boliver. She'd told Saro-Saro she didn't want to walk more than another day.

"Patience," he told her and Spikehollow. "When Direfang takes this army away from the mountains, the time will be right."

"To leave?" she asked. Her name was Cattail, and she wore no clothes, disdaining them and calling them "Dark Knight trappings." She had shoes, however, small ones that had been taken from a child's corpse in Steel Town. Cattail made it clear she hated shoes too, but there was the matter of the rocky trail they'd been following. "The Flamegrass clan will leave after the mountains. Go its way or go with Saro-Saro."

Saro-Saro shook his head. "Leave, yes. Together, yes. But after Direfang dies—regardless of where in the mountains that is."

Her face was darker than the rest of her, and it had a shine to it, like mist on a rock. She moved with a grace Saro-Saro found incongruous considering her years, and she had not so many wrinkles as himself. Were he not so venerable and preoccupied with plans for the army, he might woo her for a mate. It could be an advantageous pairing, melding her clan with his. He tugged at a wiry hair that protruded from a mole on his face. Perhaps he would pursue her anyway after Direfang was dead and they broke away and headed for the Plains of Dust. Pursue her or Pippa, who was considerably younger, a mere child. Pippa adored him, and Cattail more or less considered herself Saro-Saro's equal.

He would need a queen eventually, he mused.

"Kill Direfang?" Cattail had drawn closer, the musky

smell of her becoming distracting. "Why not just leave? Hurbear's clan left this army long days ago. Why not leave like Hurbear's clan did?"

Saro-Saro tugged harder on the stubborn hair protruding from the mole on his face until it came out. "Killing Direfang is necessary."

"That would make Saro-Saro the king." That came from Spikehollow. "With Direfang gone, all the clans would follow Saro-Saro."

Cattail's eyes narrowed as she considered that possibility. "Maybe," she said after a few moments. "Maybe Direfang's death makes Saro-Saro the king. Maybe it makes Saro-Saro hated." She paced in a small circle, her musky scent growing stronger. "Maybe killing Direfang is a smart thing to do. But maybe it is stupid. Many goblins like Direfang. But Direfang—"

"Prevented all of those dwarves from dying," Spikehollow said angrily, sitting next to Saro-Saro. "It was bad to let some of the dwarves live. Direfang let Dark Knights live in Steel Town's infirmary. Direfang is weak and has a soft heart. This army should back down from nothing."

"Should kill everything in its path," another clansman softly added.

Spikehollow wrapped his colorful quilt tightly around him. "Mudwort and Boliver are searching for a shorter way to the Qualinesti Forest. But it looks like there is only a long, long walk through more mountains and then through a swamp."

"A death march Direfang demands," Saro-Saro said.

"A foolish thing," Spikehollow whispered. He was careful to keep his voice down as on the surface he'd championed Direfang's decisions. "So many clansmen already dead. The living ones tired of this walk. Direfang should instead march on more villages. Killing everything. Taking everything. Taking a village to live in." Even though it was warm and the air dry, Spikehollow shivered.

Pippa bent over Spikehollow, running her fingers along his forehead. She did not see Saro-Saro raise a jealous eyebrow over her ministrations.

"Hot," she pronounced. "Spikehollow is hot."

"Sick?" Saro-Saro adopted a concerned expression. "Spikehollow is sick?"

Spikehollow wrapped the colorful quilt even tighter around himself and shook his head, beads of sweat flying off his brow. He coughed once. "No, just tired, worn out like a pair of boots full of holes." He laughed at the image and coughed harder, until his shoulders jumped and he gasped for air.

Saro-Saro grew truly concerned. The young goblin was loyal and a good spy. The cagey old goblin needed him to be healthy. "Spikehollow is sick. That is a bad thing."

"A little sick maybe," Spikehollow admitted when he stopped coughing.

Pippa felt his forehead again. "The skull man will help. Direfang will make the skull man tend Spikehollow. Direfang will make—"

Spikehollow and Saro-Saro shook their heads in unison. Both goblins did not want to ask anything of the hobgoblin right then as they intended to betray him as soon as possible.

"Then Spikehollow should rest," Pippa scolded. "Sleep long while this clan—and the Flamegrass clan—talks about what to do. Yes, Spikehollow should stop being part of the talk and start sleeping. Then the sick will go away."

Spikehollow agreed, stretching out on the trail a few yards from Saro-Saro, cocooning himself in the quilt, the wings of the embroidered butterflies moving in time with his rising and falling chest.

"So Direfang must die," Cattail finally agreed. "Spikehollow will do it." She had no trouble volunteering someone outside of her clan. "Spikehollow is strong and crafty. It can't look like Saro-Saro did it. Nor can it look like any goblin in the Flamegrass clan is responsible. It should look like an accident."

"Yes, Spikehollow will do it. Spikehollow will think of something. Maybe push Direfang off a mountain."

"And this time," Pippa cut in. "This time Direfang will not be so lucky. This time Direfang will die on the way down." She smoothed her shirt, trying to work out a wrinkle, and she flapped around in her too-big dwarven shoes. "Saro-Saro will be king, and Cattail queen. And Saro-Saro will take us . . . where?"

The old goblin did not have an immediate answer to that question, though he tried to display a wise expression.

Mudwort had to hurry. She knew Direfang would leave early in the morning and that he intended to head toward the Plains of Dust. She and Boliver had not found a shorter way to the Qualinesti Forest through the seeing spell, even though they had tried very hard by pulling energy from the Dark Knight wizard. There were mountains and swamps and more mountains in the way of her forest, she knew that. Direfang was right; it could take more than a year to reach Qualinesti—the world looked very big. So maybe the forest wasn't such a good idea after all, but she still wanted to go there. For some reason it was important.

She needed some rest. She needed to think.

First she wanted to scry on the cave with the young female shaman, so she'd best do it. There was little privacy in the pass Direfang's goblins sprawled in, so she climbed up to a ridge. There was a recess in the stone, and Mudwort settled herself inside the recess so she couldn't easily be seen from below. Her back felt good against the granite as she rubbed gently against it. She felt the energy of the mountains radiating through her. There was no more pain and nervousness to the stone, as she'd felt before the earthquakes struck and the volcanoes erupted.

"Finally at peace, the earth, maybe," she mused. A small part of her was disappointed. Though the earthquakes had been terrifying, they'd also been interesting, and she was glad to have witnessed the destruction and happier to have lived through it.

She reached into the smallest pouch at her waist and pulled out the dainty gold necklace dotted with the cut blue stones. Mudwort put on the necklace, her fingers squeezing some of the dainty stones. They grew warm to her touch, something all true stones did, and she searched to find the pulse in them. It was there, so faint she might have imagined it. She wished the young shaman from her vision could see the necklace and that Direfang and Boliver could see it too, not to mention the collection of cut and uncut stones in her pouches that she took out to admire when she hoped no one was watching. But if she showed Boliver the necklace and stones, that might mean that other goblins would hear of her treasures. Those stones, the necklace in particular, were things of greed, and so someone might steal them from her. She took the necklace off and replaced it in the pouch, and she stretched her hands to the rock she sat upon and magically began searching for the young shaman and her cave.

"Should have done this earlier," Mudwort said to herself. "Might be sleeping, that shaman. Might not have anything interesting to watch."

Below in the pass, most of the goblins slept. It appeared that even Direfang was resting. The Dark Knight priest and the wizard slept too, the latter because she'd robbed him of all his energy. The one called Kenosh looked over the other two knights.

"Loyal," she pronounced the knight.

If the wizard wanted to learn her magic, he would first have to share his knowledge and craft. "The fire spells I want . . . before the wizard gets more from me. The fire spells before anything."

There was no patch of dirt there for her to dig her fingers into, but she didn't need dirt. She only burrowed her fingers into the ground because she liked the feel of it. So instead she drummed her nails against the stone she leaned against.

The young shaman . . . Mudwort concentrated. The one with red skin, but a different red than her own, the one who wore necklaces and nothing else and who might be sleeping, as late as it was.

"Probably sleeping, but hope not." Mudwort closed her eyes, and the cavern appeared, the one with the domed ceiling and all the symbols carved in it. The place looked . . . different, and she studied it closely until she figured out what had changed. There were not as many torches as before, so it was a little darker. But her eyes were keen, and aided by her magic, she could pick out details. The carved symbols—there were more of them! They were not just on the dome, but high on the walls and stretching into the shadows.

It hadn't been that long since she'd last looked in on those goblins. How had they been able to carve so much since then? Some of the newer symbols were darker, cut deeper into the stone. It wasn't writing, not like the language of men or the language the dwarves had carved into their anvil-altar. Not that Mudwort could read any language. Goblins did not have a written language. But the newest symbols showed stick figures of hills and goblins, and there might have been marks that represented the passing of time and seasons, such as the images of the sun that were depicted in various sizes.

She gave up on deciphering the carved symbols and turned her attention to the cavern's occupants, most of whom were indeed sleeping. Mudwort didn't notice the young shaman at first glance, but there were plenty of goblins stretched out on the stone floor—more than had been when she looked before.

"Where is the shaman?" Mudwort rubbed her back against the stone a little harder, focusing, and the mountain's pulse radiated a little stronger.

There were no familiar faces that she immediately recognized, but then, Mudwort remembered only paying close attention to the shaman and the large crystal that had been carried in on the shield. The goblins all looked so . . . primitive, she thought again; no clothes or shoes, crude spears at their sides, none of them with a metal blade of any sort. Likely they'd never raided a human camp for forged weapons.

Mudwort had not carried a weapon before their journey, but she wore a small knife in a sheath as they walked the trail. It was hooked on her belt between two of her pouches. Boliver had given it to her earlier that day, said he'd found it in one of the dwarf homes, found several of the knives and that she should have one. He took a slightly larger knife for himself, and he did not tell her what he'd done with the others.

She continued to scan the goblins, all of them seemingly well fed, many of them plump, a few even proportionately as thickset as the Ergothian priest. To never want for food—like those cave goblins—would be a good thing.

Ah, there she was! Mudwort recognized the necklaces that hung from the young shaman's neck. She was sitting against the cavern wall, just like Mudwort, who continued to sit with her back against the mountain. The young shaman's head was down, chin touching her chest, so Mudwort knew she was sleeping.

There was nothing interesting in watching her counterpart sleep. Mudwort thought about ending her spell and getting some sleep herself.

"A few moments more," she decided. "Then sleep." She concentrated, hearing the snores of many of the goblins in the cave. They sounded so much like her kinsmen sleeping along the trail below. But they did not repulse her as much as her kinsmen did; they did not carry the stink of sweat and dwarf and tylor blood. They did not—

The shaman stirred, picking up her head and yawning. Mudwort's attention flew back to the shaman, eyes widening when she saw that it wasn't the same shaman after all. She had wrinkles at the edges of her eyes, and her face was not so smooth. Her nose carried a thin scar, and another scar ran from her ear to her jaw. There was a bone hoop in her right ear, recently stuck there as it was crusted with blood from the piercing, and there was a feather and a bead on a string hanging from the left.

"Not the same shaman." Though the necklaces were the same. The disappointment was thick in Mudwort's voice. "No, not the same—"

Or was it?

The eyes were similar. So was the face, though it was older. The shaman's mother perhaps?

"Years and years and years older. But how can that be?"

Mudwort tried to get more comfortable, pressing herself

farther into the niche, and settling in to watch and puzzle out the age problem.

"A curse? A disease that withers?"

The goblins below called the shaman Saarh, Mudwort had understood on her previous magical visit. The name meant "prized one" or "treasure" or "princess." Saarh rose and stretched, clenching and unclenching her fists, and picking her way through the sleeping goblins to stand in the center of the cavern under the dome. She twirled slowly, the beads around her neck clacking and the feather and bone hoop that hung from her ears fluttering. She was graceful, the most graceful goblin Mudwort had ever seen, and she moved so quietly that only the beads made any noise.

Saarh moved her fingers in a pattern as if they were spider legs and she were weaving a web. In response, some of the symbols in the dome glowed, winking on and off and throwing an odd, ghostly light over the goblins sleeping below.

How had Saarh aged so many years in such a short time? The question gnawed at Mudwort. Very, very curious, Mudwort thought. She still couldn't say where in the world the cave was.

"Or when in the world," she said, sudden realization dawning.

Mudwort shivered with the thought.

"When, when, when."

Well more than a few days had passed in that cavern, that was for sure. It had been more like twenty years, judging from Saarh's wrinkles. The shaman was middle aged. Mudwort couldn't tell how she knew, but she realized that she wasn't looking at the present. No curse or disease was responsible for Saarh's aging. It was simply time.

Somehow, it must be that Mudwort had glimpsed the past when she first touched the cavern with her mind, and she was looking at the past still. The cavern and Saarh and all the goblins with their crude spears were not a part of Mudwort's world.

Her mind had journeyed through the stone and into the past.

The stone of the earth was ancient, and its memory long. Mudwort guessed she was borrowing those memories by looking in on the cavern.

Another shiver passed through her. It amazed even her. So she could use her magic to look not only across distances, but across ages. She could peer through time.

Just what else was she capable of?

She'd become distracted by her realization, and the image of the shaman and the cavern started to fade. Mudwort fought to retain the images, feeling the pulse of the mountain quicken against her back. She focused on the shaman, on those dark, magical, and mysterious eyes. What had they witnessed through the years? What did Saarh know? How long ago had she lived?

What did the cavern look like in the present? Not ten years earlier, or twenty, or whenever Saarh breathed. But at that very minute.

Seizing on that impulse, Mudwort turned her attention to the cavern itself, the decorated walls and the dome. She put all of her energy and efforts into bolstering her seeing spell and was promptly rewarded with blackness.

Mudwort raged and raged. She thrust her head back, striking the rock and hurting herself. There was nothing there at all. Nothing . . . she concentrated harder. Her mind was still in the cavern, she could tell that, but she was staring at darkness. Then shadows began to separate as her keen eyes probed. At the same time, she listened, hearing nothing, no snoring goblins. She heard only her own breath and, after a few minutes, the flutter of bat wings.

The cavern was empty of goblins.

The markings were still on the walls, more numerous than when she saw them before; they stretched nearly to the floor in places. It wasn't so much that she could see them as that she could feel them, her mental fingertips tracing the various cuts and curves made in the stone. She let her senses drift to the granite floor.

It was smooth and polished but more so than before. The feet of decades had made the floor cool and pleasant to the touch.

Mudwort searched and searched, finding only the small crevices where the torches had been, no traces of the wood that once burned. Guano was thick directly under the highest point in the dome; bats had lived there for quite some time.

"Where is the shaman? Dead?" Mudwort wondered. Dead and burned a long while ago?

"When was the shaman?"

Mudwort finally ended her spell.

She was exhausted, as if she'd walked miles and miles and miles over the ugly terrain of that ugly land.

She opened her eyes and looked up, expecting to see the moon with its rain ring.

Instead she saw the lightening sky.

Mudwort had passed hours inside her seeing spell.

17

SARO-SARO'S SCHEME

Direfang awoke shortly before dawn, carefully picking his way through the sleeping goblins to the head of the column. Mudwort had said the pass would end soon, but she'd found a trail of sorts that wound up the western ridge that they could follow to the other side to reach the river. Direfang decided to take his charges along that trail and follow the river to the New Sea.

He walked south alone for a short while, seeking rare solitude. He was far enough ahead that he could no longer hear the snores of those still sleeping or the chatter of the ones just waking up. All he could hear was the whisper of the wind edging over the ridge and stirring the dust at the bottom.

How many days had he walked? How far had he come from Steel Town?

Hell Town—he'd heard the wizard call it that once.

Indeed, the Abyss could have been no worse than the Dark Knight mining camp. Direfang wore the years he'd spent there in scars. They were so thick in places on his chest, arms, and back that no hair grew there, making him ugly, a grotesquerie as far as humans and hobgoblins alike were concerned. He scratched at the left side of his head, where his ear had been; a small, jagged piece of flesh remained. His appearance and size had helped make him

136

a formidable foreman in the mine. His arms and legs were thick with muscles from the hard labor in the camp, his hands and feet callused. He'd hoped to find shoes in Reorx's Cradle, but he'd not had the opportunity to look through the homes. His first responsibility had been to keep an eye on all the goblins, keep them from rampaging or squabbling.

Besides, his feet were not hurting as badly as they had been earlier. Either the calluses were growing thicker or he was becoming used to the constant dull pain.

A large bird flew overhead, banking slowly and circling. It was a hawk of some kind, dark brown and with white tail feathers. There were other birds higher up, black specks seen against a pale gray sky. Direfang watched them for a few moments and savored the sweet air. There'd been birds around Steel Town, mostly scavengers. The large one that still circled was a predator.

Direfang dropped his gaze and opened the book filled with the dwarf's charcoal maps. He guessed at where he was in the range, not far out of Reorx's Cradle. He saw where the pass ended, probably a few hours of walking ahead, and there was a thin line indicating the trail that would take them over the western range. Mudwort had confirmed the authenticity of the map with her spell the previous night.

The Plains of Dust? He'd been thinking about that place lately, wondering if they should go there.

Mudwort had tried to convince him the Qualinesti Forest was a better destination. She and Moon-eye and Boliver had delved into the earth and searched for a good goblin home for the long-term future. They'd agreed on the Qualinesti Forest. Mudwort was undoubtedly right about the forest, Direfang mused. The forest would be the goblins' best opportunity to build their nation.

But it was so far away. He tried to picture it on the maps the Dark Knights had stretched out across their long table. The forest was a world away.

Direfang had slept little the previous night, thinking about the long, hard journey ahead. He'd come to a difficult decision just a little while earlier—not one that would sit well with Mudwort. They would travel around the fishhook of mountains to the swamp, spend some time there hunting and resting to recover from the arduousness of their trek thus far, then they would head to the Plains. It would take them weeks and weeks to get to the Plains, maybe a few months. But the Plains were not so far from the forest . . . if he recalled the Dark Knights' maps correctly.

That way, he could investigate the Plains, and Mudwort could have her way too.

Direfang closed the book and gave a last look up at the hawk, which still circled, but farther west and higher. He headed back to his charges, his twisted leg not bothering him as much anymore and his vision much improved over the previous day.

As he drew closer, he stared at the rag-tag army, all of them waking up—more than eight hundred, less than one thousand. There had been more before Hurbear's clan broke away many miles earlier. About half of his charges wore clothes and scraps of armor taken from Dark Knights, ogres, and, just yesterday, the dwarves.

Few of them had been afforded the luxury of clothes in Steel Town. Neither had any of the goblins there had possessions. Since then, many wore clothing and all coveted various things they'd hauled away from Reorx's Cradle and the other places they'd looted. The possessions had given them pride.

It was almost funny, Direfang mused. One goblin had claimed a stool half as tall as he was. It was awkward to carry, but he'd stubbornly refused to part with it or to trade it for smaller and perhaps more valuable things. Other goblins bore empty flowerpots, pans, ceramic mugs too big around to comfortably hold in their hands, books they could not read, vases, gardening tools, sacks of seeds and bulbs they probably would never plant, toys they'd snatched from dwarf children's beds, sacks of flour, and many other things that Direfang had no names for. One old goblin led a pig on a leather leash; some held chickens and geese they'd stolen from the dwarves, and others tugged stubborn goats. A few of the bigger, plumper goats were protected from slaughter, and they were in the Dark Knight Kenosh's care.

Death March

The Dark Knight priest said Graytoes' stolen baby required milk, which the goats could provide. Direfang suggested the goblin younglings in the throng could also benefit from the milk. Hence a few goats were saved.

The entire army looked like refugees streaming from some village with everything they owned on their backs.

Indeed, they were refugees, and Direfang intended to find them a home.

Saro-Saro and his most prominent clansmen had claimed a wide spot in the trail, one where a rocky overhang sheltered them. Direfang stepped around members of the Woodcutter clan and beyond Graytoes, who belonged to no clan. She held the baby close, rocking it and singing an old song to the youngling that Moon-eye used to sing to her. She smiled at Direfang and immediately returned her attention to the baby.

Several Flamegrass clansmen were mingling with Saro-Saro's clan. Direfang thought it good to see the two groups getting along.

"Saro-Saro."

The old goblin snorted and got to his feet. He adjusted a green cape he wore over his shoulders, his fingers wiping off a silver pin that held it on. He nodded to Direfang and suppressed a yawn. Around him, members of his clan stood and stretched, some of them beginning to eat vegetables they'd harvested from Reorx's Cradle.

"It is time to go over the mountains. The pass will end ahead where a trail leads up and to the west. It will be a few hours of walking to that trail." Direfang pointed to the western range. "A narrow trail and probably difficult to climb. But there is a river on the other side."

"Thirsty," Pippa said. She sniffed at herself. "And dirty. Cleaning in the river would be good."

Saro-Saro looked thoughtful. "A mountain trail. Steep?"

"Looks to be steep."

"Dangerous?" Pippa asked.

Direfang shook his head. "Dangerous only to those who are not careful."

The hobgoblin did not notice the glimmer in Saro-Saro's eyes.

"This river," Saro-Saro said. "The one on the other side. It leads to the New Sea Mudwort talked about?"

Direfang nodded. "Spikehollow?" Direfang looked around. He expected the goblin to be somewhere near Saro-Saro, as he usually was. "Where is Spikehollow?"

Pippa scowled and tugged on Direfang's arm. "Spikehollow is a little sick," she explained. "Maybe more than just a little sick. Maybe Spikehollow should have talked to the skull man last night. But Spikehollow—"

"Is fine," Spikehollow finished, emerging from between two burly, yellow-skinned goblins. He still wore his quilt, but he'd tied it around his neck, wearing it like a cape. It looked garish, the colorful thing fluttering around his shoulders. "The sleep helped a lot, Pippa."

Direfang turned and walked toward the front of the column. "Spikehollow will lead this army," he said over his shoulder. "For a while. At least until the pass ends and the trail up the mountain begins."

"The very steep trail," Pippa whispered. She rubbed her hands together gleefully. "And when Direfang reaches the top . . ."

Saro-Saro's voice became barely audible. "Spikehollow will push the big, ugly hobgoblin down the mountain." He paused. "And this time Direfang will not survive."

Spikehollow, nodding to them over his shoulder, followed Direfang. But the young goblin did not walk as fast as usual, and he was shivering despite the warmth of the early morning. He breathed shallowly to keep from coughing.

"Feel better," Spikehollow said to himself, "but not much." He tugged the quilt tightly around him and tried to pick up his pace, stumbling when he bumped into a goat tethered to the Dark Knight named Kenosh. He hurried around the three Dark Knights and avoided Graytoes. Spikehollow didn't want the others to see him sick.

"Saro-Saro is old," Spikehollow mused, knowing he stood a very good chance to inherit the clan at Saro-Saro's passing. "Saro-Saro might not live to reach the New Sea. Spikehollow lead now, but soon it might be Spikehollow's army truly."

He passed a brown-skinned goblin he'd befriended in Steel Town, one who often worked the same shift as he in the mine. He'd given the goblin, Bugteeth he was called, the gray blanket he'd plucked from the home in Reorx's Cradle. He stood tall as he passed him, not wanting to appear as sick as he felt. He smiled and gestured.

Bugteeth smiled a greeting, then turned and coughed and wiped a speck of blood off his lips.

18

HOPE

Graytoes ran her finger along the baby's bottom lip. It was soft, softer than anything she'd touched before. The goblins who walked at her side said the baby was an ugly thing. Its skin was too light and uninteresting; it was all smooth with no bumps or growths. And it cried for seemingly no reason.

At least its nose was wide, one goblin told her, and its eyes were reasonably large.

It didn't have much hair on its head, another pointed out. So while it was a dwarf baby, it didn't look like any of the dwarves in Reorx's Cradle; they were all hairy creatures.

Graytoes knew the speakers hadn't seen the other babies in the house. None of those babies had much hair, and admittedly the one she had taken had the least. She hadn't picked that baby because of that fact; she'd picked it because it was the smallest and would be the easiest to carry. And she picked that one because she liked the cooing and gurgling sounds it made when it seemed to be happy. She told herself that the baby would be far happier with her and the rest of the goblins than stuck in a village that had been plundered to the point where nothing of any value remained.

She looked forward to naming the child. But what should its name be? A dwarf name might be appropriate,

142

but Graytoes had never seen a dwarf before Reorx's Cradle, and she did not know any of their type of names. Goblins and hobgoblins were often named after their physical traits or acquired habits or sometimes for the area in which a clan lived. Her dead mate, Moon-eye, had been given his name because one of his eyes was a solid white, overlarge orb that looked like a full moon. Bugteeth ate bugs, probably from a very early age, and often legs and wings got stuck to the front of his teeth. She had no idea how Mudwort got her name, as she was red skinned and did not at all look like any patch of mud.

Then there were goblins named after ancestors, such as Saro-Saro. She'd heard him say that his grandfather Saro was a clan leader, and because he was the second Saro in the family, they doubled the name. Spikehollow said he thought he was named for the tall, scratchy reeds that grew around his home. Some goblin names made no sense to her, seeming to be sounds more than anything else. Other names likely had a significance known only to the parents or the clan.

If Graytoes had a name when she was a youngling, she couldn't recall what it was. She'd acquired Graytoes in Steel Town, working in the mines. Her feet were often gray with stone dust, in stark contrast to her yellow skin. Graytoes didn't want her baby to be named for her slave work or her bug-eating or Baby Graytoes. She needed something special to call the child.

Wide-nose, she could call her baby that.

Or Large-eyes . . . no, that would always remind her of Moon-eye, and that would make her sad.

Smooth-skin. That would be a good choice, except as the baby got older, its skin might not stay so smooth.

Sabak, that was the interesting name of an old goblin hero she'd heard a story about in Steel Town. Maybe Sabak.

Direfang-Direfang would honor the hobgoblin who led the escape from that hated mining camp. But that was too long a name, she decided after running it around on her tongue a few times.

Hmm . . . Paxtan, that was a goblin word for traveler, and

the baby would be traveling a lot before settling down in the forest Mudwort had told her about.

"Lek," she finally murmured aloud.

A goblin at her shoulder cocked his head. "Small one?" That was what lek meant.

"This baby needs a name," Graytoes explained. "A very good one."

"Lek," the goblin repeated. "It is small, that baby. But it will get bigger. It might get bigger than Graytoes."

"If it lives," said Pippa, who had drifted close out of curiosity.

The goblins had reached the end of the pass, and Graytoes looked up to see Spikehollow start to climb the trail. Her eyes narrowed as she saw the challenge ahead, and she shook her head. It would not be an easy climb, especially with the baby and the satchel on her back, but she would manage. It would be more difficult for Direfang with his twisted leg and for Saro-Saro because he was old. At least the goats would be fine, which concerned Graytoes because she wanted plenty of milk for the baby.

"Sugi?" Graytoes said, trying out another name.

"Big tree?" Pippa scratched her head. "That's not a good name for a baby, even for a dwarf one."

"Sugi also means blessed." Graytoes had learned that from Hurbear. It was a word that had not been uttered very often in Steel Town as there had been no blessings there.

Pippa shrugged. "It also means a big tree. But there will be plenty of big trees in the elves' old forest. So Sugi would work."

Graytoes wrinkled her nose, thinking. "This baby needed an important name."

Deva meant . . . special. The baby was that.

Or Sheel . . . meaning quiet . . . the baby was indeed quiet.

"Pippa-Pippa," Pippa suggested helpfully.

Graytoes scowled as she started her climb. It narrowed to the point they had to go single file, which suited her fine. Pippa stayed behind her. Good. Graytoes didn't need help naming her baby.

Her baby.

A Dark Knight priest had magically ripped one from her belly after the first quake in Steel Town. The priest had been tending the wounded, and Graytoes had indeed been injured in the mines when a support beam had fallen across her legs. The priest deemed that her real trouble was the child inside her; it was turned incorrectly, he'd said. He had solved the problem by killing it. Then she'd lost Moon-eye, her mate, too.

"Umay," she decided when she reached the halfway point in the climb. Graytoes held the child close, both arms wrapped around the young one. If she stumbled, her arms might protect Umay. She couldn't bear to lose anything else in her short life.

"Umay?" Pippa had caught up to her, close. "Hope? You would name the baby that?"

Graytoes nodded. Umay indeed meant hope in goblin-speak. It was another one of those words that hadn't been used very often in the slave pens. But that's what the baby had given her: hope.

"Umay," Graytoes repeated. "It is a very good name."

Pippa muttered something Graytoes could not hear then added, louder, "Pippa-Pippa would have been better."

———— S ————

Spikehollow wondered when he would find an opportunity to push Direfang off the mountain. He felt a little conflicted about Saro-Saro's plan, as Direfang was not a bad hobgoblin and had never done anything so very wrong in his eyes. Direfang had helped the goblins all escape from Steel Town, led a rebellion against the Dark Knights . . . yes, but he also had brought them to that hellish stretch of steep mountains that seemed to go on forever.

The goblin couldn't hold the quilt around him as he climbed. He needed at least one hand free to grasp rocks for support. The fingers of his other hand were wrapped around the cord of a canvas sack he'd taken from one of the younger clansmen. Inside were a few potatoes, some shiny, colorful vegetables that were bulbous and hot-tasting, squares that he'd heard the wizard call dwarven hardtack, and a fist-sized rock carved in the shape of an anvil—a miniature to the one that stood east of the expansive garden in Reorx's Cradle. Spikehollow didn't intend to worship Reorx with the thing; he thought it might make a good tool for pounding.

Right then, however, it was his head that was pounding. Spikehollow admitted to himself that he was still feeling sick. He realized he should have sought out the help of the Dark Knight priest, who seemed able to work healing wonders. But he didn't want to look weak in front of the other clansmen, and looking for help from a hated human could indeed be construed as weakness. He had to look strong and act decisively, especially if he intended to take over Saro-Saro's clan when that old goblin died. Saro-Saro would surely die soon. Spikehollow was the obvious leader for the clan then, which he intended to rename the Hollow clan.

The trail disappeared two-thirds of the way up, and the goblin had to wedge his fingers into small crevices and use his hands and feet to pull himself up a sheer rock wall. He nearly dropped his bag of treasures. Maybe he wouldn't have to wait long for Saro-Saro's demise. The old goblin might not have the strength to follow the arduous climb. Spikehollow's muscles bunched as he levered himself up onto a ledge. His arms and legs ached more than ever, and again he barely managed to hang on to his canvas bag. He sucked in a couple of deep breaths and coughed. Then he looked over the side and motioned the goblins to follow.

He spotted Direfang, quite a ways behind, down the trail. The hobgoblin was still favoring his leg. Spikehollow would have to wait for Direfang at the top, find a way to engage him in some conversation, perhaps waylay him when he was still recovering from the climb. Spikehollow couldn't risk the wrong goblins seeing him push Direfang, so he would have to be very careful. But the high ridge might provide the right opportunity; there might be no better one.

The goblin continued his ascent, pausing to pick up the hem of his quilt and wipe off his face. Though he felt chilled on the mountain—no doubt because the air was colder high up—he was also sweating unaccountably. It was because of the exertion, he told himself. That was why. But a shiver passed through him, and he had another coughing spasm. He would have to rest after killing Direfang. But everyone would want to rest. He knew everyone would stop to grieve, and so he could sleep a little and get better.

He slowed down, though the trail was a little easier to navigate toward the top. He had started to ache all over—not just his head or his legs, but his stomach and sides too. Had he eaten something from the dwarf village that had made him so sick? That had happened once before in Steel Town, when the Dark Knights had given some of the hardest-working slaves scraps of meat. Tasty scraps, but they hadn't sat well in their stomachs, and the slaves had vomited and curled up into feverish balls and were unable to work the following day. Spikehollow hoped there was nothing wrong with the food in his treasure bag. He would be hungry later. He wasn't hungry at that moment. Odd, but he hadn't wanted anything to eat since shortly after leaving Reorx's Cradle.

He'd earlier heard a hobgoblin say that the women dwarves had cursed them for the destruction, wailed for the goblins to go to the Abyss. But Spikehollow didn't believe in curses or the Abyss.

It was probably some bad bit of food he had eaten.

When Spikehollow reached the top, he steadied himself. He was at a place where there was nothing to grab on to, and he felt a little dizzy, so high up, so weary, and so sick-feeling. He redoubled his grip on his treasure bag and stared down at the pines far below. He couldn't see the river; it probably ran too close to the base of the mountain and was hidden from his view. But he knew the water was there. Boliver and Mudwort talked about seeing it, and he swore he could hear it rushing along. The colors were intense up there so high, such a change from the drab browns and grays of the mountain. The pines were a vibrant green, the color of the blanket he'd given Saro-Saro, the sky bright blue against thin, wispy clouds. The air was blissfully free of the smell of goblins, though that would change soon, as hundreds were climbing behind him.

Spikehollow would have liked to savor the scenery. But he was feeling worse and worse, and the matter of Direfang weighed heavily on him as well. He heard a clatter behind him and whirled in time to see a stool bouncing down the side of the mountain; the goblin carrying it had lost his grip. Other things were dropping too, sacks and chickens, and a small table—some deliberately, some accidentally. A few minutes later, a piglet squealed shrilly.

"Direfang chose bad, this route," said the first goblin who crested the top and started down the other side. He struggled with a big flowerpot filled with potatoes and radishes. "Direfang should have picked an easier way, Spikehollow. Bad way, this."

The goblins might not miss Direfang so much after all, Spikehollow mused, hearing the flowerpot-carrying one's complaint. He pointed down the opposite trail toward the forest and Leftear appeared at the top, not far behind the flower-pot goblin. Leftear paused and looked curiously at Spikehollow, still pointing.

"Not coming, Spikehollow?" Leftear asked. "Not leading the way down?"

Spikehollow shook his head and explained he was staying on the top so he could help all of the goblins up to the top and steer them in the right direction. His words came out jumbled and quick, so he repeated them.

"Spikehollow is smart and kind," Leftear said as he started down the other side.

Goblin after goblin passed Spikehollow, some of them chatting as they went by, some cursing at the loss of possessions they'd abandoned. Graytoes struggled up the trail, holding her baby, which had started to cry, and panting under the weight of the dwarf child, added to the satchel on her back. "Umay," was all she said to Spikehollow as she passed. She sang softly to Umay, and that seemed to ease her own burden. She kept going, not even stopping briefly to admire the view.

Pippa followed Graytoes, but she paused at the top, stared at Spikehollow, and felt his forehead. She was careful not to pronounce him "sick" with so many other goblins around, but the concern in her eyes was not lost on him.

Bugteeth had to be pulled up the final few feet to the top. Like Spikehollow, he was shivering, but he seemed even sicker. When he coughed, pink frothy bubbles formed at the sides of his mouth. Raised ugly patches had appeared on his arms, and the goblins supporting him avoided touching the ugly pieces of skin. Spikehollow noticed that a few other goblins were coughing too. If the Dark Knight priest tended to Bugteeth and the other sick goblins, Spikehollow would ask for help from the priest too—secretly if he could. He remained resolute in not wanting to appear weak, but more than anything he wanted to feel better.

As more and more goblins came up one side and started down the other, Spikehollow grew sicker and dizzier. The goblins became a blur of colors, with their red, yellow, orange, and brown skins, the drab to garish clothes they'd pilfered, and their odd assortments of belongings and animals. He managed to find a place to the side of the trail where he could sit, where no one would bump into him and possibly knock him down the mountain. He felt better sitting; the world wasn't spinning so much, and he didn't cough so frequently. He closed his eyes for a few moments then opened them when he heard the frightened bleat of a goat.

The Dark Knights were passing by him, the one called Kenosh leading three goats. The pudgy priest was in the front of the trio. He didn't look as winded as Spikehollow had expected; all the walking and climbing had built up the human's stamina. Close behind the three came several members of the Flamegrass clan.

Direfang had obviously lingered somewhere on the trail, probably helping goblins and hobgoblins up in difficult spots. He didn't reach the top until well more than half the goblins had topped the rise and started the climb down. Spikehollow thought the hobgoblin looked drained; he was clearly favoring his leg.

It will not be so hard to do this thing, Spikehollow thought. One good shove and Direfang would have a long fall.

"Should wait up here," he told Direfang. "Until all the goblins are over. Wait and make sure that none are left behind."

The hobgoblin frowned but nodded, saying nothing. Spikehollow could tell Direfang was tired and distracted by the view; his quivering nostrils were taking in the scents of the forest.

Beyond the small pine forest, the land leveled out and was covered with tall grass and summer wildflowers. A small herd of deer grazed, and a white-tailed hawk circled above them. Spikehollow could hear birds singing, but he couldn't see any other than the lone hawk. The lead goblins descending were swallowed up by the trees and the land and could barely be glimpsed.

"Probably nested in the pines, the singing birds," Spikehollow said. His voice cracked and he used the quilt to wipe his face again then his arms. The tunic he'd acquired many long days before from an ogre village they'd raided was thoroughly soaked with his perspiration. He plucked it away from his skin and tried to shake it a little to dry it.

"Spikehollow is sick." Direfang did not phrase the statement as a question.

"Yes." He did not see a problem confiding his weakness in someone who would soon be dead. Spikehollow was looking over the top of the crag, pretending to enjoy the scenery, and he thought he had found just the spot where Direfang should stand. Now to lure him over here, he thought. "Bugteeth is sick too, and a few others."

"Spikehollow should see the skull man." Direfang crossed his arms as if making a grand pronouncement.

Many other goblins had passed and finally the last of them were making their way over the top, several of them wheezing and grumbling, only a few of them stopping to glance at the magnificent view.

DEATH MARCH

"At the bottom, I will." Spikehollow closed his eyes again. "After the skull man sees to Bugteeth and others. At the bottom of this mountain. I am still strong. Can wait." He didn't see Direfang nod with approval.

"A malady swept through the slave pens some years ago," Direfang said. "Many goblins died to a strange sickness."

Spikehollow did not appreciate that dismal reminder of a bad episode he had blocked out of his memory. He let out a sigh and rubbed at his eyes with his free hand. They were matted, the lashes stuck together. He brushed at the sweat on his face again. "Just a little sick, Direfang," he said as he stood. He took a step toward the promontory and bent his knees to keep from falling. The rock was just the right size for Direfang to stand on.

"Beautiful place here," he said, gesturing.

"The skull man will deal with this malady," Direfang said, again sounding as though he were making a grand pronouncement. Spikehollow winced at the self-important hobgoblin, the loudness of his words. "The skull man will help Spikehollow and Bugteeth."

"Look at this," said a pleased-sounding Spikehollow, pointing down at nothing in particular. Indeed, he was pleased. Things were working out well. He and Direfang had lingered long enough. All the goblins were gone. There would be no witnesses. And no one would doubt his story. "Direfang, come look at this."

He heard the crunch of rocks as the hobgoblin approached. Direfang was ever a curious sort.

"See something interesting, Spikehollow?"

Spikehollow nodded and gestured more firmly. "Yes, Direfang, very interesting. There is a—" The rest of his words were lost as suddenly the sickness came at him from all sides—his leg, his stomach, his head—a rush of pain and dizziness. Spikehollow dropped to his knees then pitched forward, his treasure bag falling over the side of the mountain. With dull eyes, he watched it bounce down the rocks out of sight. He felt himself slipping, slipping, and felt strong fingers circle his wrist and, miraculously, pull him up and off his feet.

"Spikehollow is not just a little sick," Direfang corrected. He lifted the goblin, cradling him close to his chest, wrapping the quilt around him. Spikehollow had the image of Graytoes and the dwarf baby in his mind; for the moment he was as helpless as that child.

Grunting with his new burden, Direfang carefully picked his way down the trail.

19

THE SONG WITHOUT WORDS

Spikehollow, waking in the shade of pine trees, heard a constant whoosh in his ears. The river flowed nearby, whooshing incessantly.

Conversations filled the air, competing with the squawk of blue jays objecting to the goblins' presence. The crunch of twigs added to the hubbub, someone violently stomping on a dead branch to split it. There was also music nearby, a tinkling sound that was not rhythmic but was engaging. He wished the latter noise were louder to drown out the birds and the talking. Then he heard another whoosh, but it was different, signaling the start of a fire.

Were goblin bodies being burned?

Spikehollow bolted to his feet then tottered and nearly fell.

Pippa, hovering over him, tugged him down so he plopped on the ground in a sitting position. Saro-Saro was nearby, the old goblin holding court with members of his clan, who were responsible for the loudest chatter. Saro-Saro glanced at Spikehollow and sucked in his lips in a disapproving expression. He shook his head for good measure then looked up at the mountain.

It was clear to Spikehollow that Saro-Saro was angry with him for not killing Direfang when he had a good chance. It was also clear to Spikehollow that Direfang had

153

saved his life and had carried him down the mountain. Squinting as the late afternoon sun hit the side of the mountain and made the granite in it sparkle, Spikehollow looked up the hard trail they'd just come down; it was just as steep as the one on the other side.

He blinked furiously when he realized there were dozens of goblins nearby who he did not recognize from the march. Where had all the new ones come from? Was he imagining them in his fever?

"Hunter's Ridge clan," Pippa explained, patting him on the shoulder. "More than two hundred, Direfang said. Came from these trees, said the clan answered Mudwort's call. Said more are coming."

Spikehollow groaned. His legs ached even more than before. He was still cool from his damp clothes, though the bad chill had left him and his head had stopped pounding. Other than his aching legs, he felt a little better.

He heard the crackle of a fire starting to take a good hold and turned, craning his stiff neck over his shoulder. Leftear had spitted a pig and was roasting it. Spikehollow anticipated a fight as the pig was not big enough to feed even the smallest clan.

"The skull man did some tending," Pippa said. She edged closer and felt his cheek. "Not burning so much now. The skull man helped Spikehollow some. Feeling better?"

Her face loomed large, her eyes shiny and wet, as if she'd been crying over something. Spikehollow thought about asking her what was bothering her, but he knew Pippa. She was talkative and would tell him soon enough.

"Bugteeth is dead," she said finally.

So that was her unfortunate news.

"Bugteeth didn't fall," she added. "Bugteeth got sick like Spikehollow, and the skull man couldn't help. The skull man didn't tend Bugteeth soon enough. Direfang had the skull man tend Spikehollow first. Bugteeth couldn't wait for healing."

Spikehollow glanced around Pippa and saw Saro-Saro still scowling. Bugteeth had been the most loyal to the old clan leader.

DEATH MARCH

"Where is Direfang, Pippa?"

"Still alive. Talking with the Hunter's Ridge clan leader." Pippa helped Spikehollow up when it was clear he was refusing to stay put. "Should wash those clothes, Spikehollow. Stinky stinky." She held her nose for effect and pointed to the river.

Spikehollow ignored her for the moment, wanting to find Direfang and the source of the odd music. He stepped away and looked to the river. Goblins were lined up along the bank—some resting, some of them bathing, many of them drinking their fill, most all talking. It was like a carpet of bodies stretching to the north and south, some of them grouped into clans. They spread back into the trees too, and the music was coming from there. He didn't see Direfang, so he decided to pursue the music first.

He tried to follow the odd notes, Pippa shuffling behind him.

"Spikehollow should wash those clothes," she insisted.

He waggled his fingers behind him, hoping to silence her. Both hands free, he remembered he'd lost his treasure bag. A small price to pay, he decided, for breathing the air of life. He would not be able to kill Direfang. Spikehollow had a sense of honor, after all. Saro-Saro would have to find someone else in the clan to tend to the matter . . . or handle it himself.

Spikehollow still intended to see to Saro-Saro's demise, but he didn't need to worry about that just then. He was grateful he was no longer dizzy and the priest's ministrations had helped. He still felt a little tired, and there were the aches that plagued him. But he was recovering, it was certain. And he'd not really showed signs of weakness to any of the others; he hadn't been the one to ask the skull man for help; Direfang had done that for him.

The pines smelled heady. Even with hundreds of goblins around, the trees had a strong, sweet smell that was like nothing else Spikehollow had experienced in his life. The young goblin had not been born a slave and, in fact, had spent only a relatively short time in the mines of Steel Town. But his native land was filled with rolling hills and saw grass, and the trees had broad leaves and thick trunks. There were pines north of Steel Town, but he'd never got a close look at them or smelled them before. In the mining camp, all he smelled was sweat and dirt, the harsh scent of iron being drawn from the rocks, and sulfur when the volcanoes smoked.

"It smells wonderful," he said, walking deeper into the forest.

"Yes," Pippa agreed. She came up to his side and touched his arm. Was she trying to claim him? "Is this the forest Direfang was leading us to? Saro-Saro said it was much farther away."

"Not this forest," Spikehollow said. The trees were tall and grew close together, but from his view on top of the mountain, he knew it wasn't a very large forest, just a strip of pine trees that paralleled the river. "But this is a good forest."

"Why not stay here, then? Saro-Saro's clan could stay here; the Flamegrass clan too. Might not have to kill Direfang then. Direfang can go on to that other forest. Why not stay here?"

Spikehollow thought it a reasonable question. But there were too many goblins for the small forest; it was too close to Neraka and the Dark Knights, and also too close to ogre territory.

He shook his head. "There is a better place for goblins, a safer one. Maybe Mudwort knows best."

She pursed her lips, considering that, and her fingers trailed up and down his arm. "Good that Spikehollow is not sick anymore."

"Yes, it is very good." He stopped when the odd music grew louder, and he looked up, seeing bottles hanging from a tall pine. Its lowest branches were at least six feet off the ground, and as the breeze rustled the branches, the music came from the bottles.

"Why would anyone hang bottles from a tree?" said Pippa, releasing Spikehollow's arm and coming to stand directly under a dark blue bottle with a long, fluted neck. It was tied to the tree with a piece of leather. "What a silly thing to do."

DEATH MARCH

Nothing else hung from the tree save pine cones, though farther up were several birds' nests, old ones that had not been used in years. Spikehollow looked from one bottle to the next. Some were tiny, no bigger than his thumb, others were as big around and as long as his forearm; the bigger ones were tied on with multiple leather strands.

Some of the bottles clacked dryly against branches; others made rustling sounds against the needles. But the ones close to other bottles clinked merrily against each other in the breeze and made whistling noises from the wind sweeping across their open tops. There were more bottles than Spikehollow could count.

"A good, not silly, thing to do, hanging all of these," Spikehollow corrected her. "It sounds good, all these bottles."

"But why do it?" Pippa was more interested in why someone would hang them from the tree than in the bottles themselves or the silly sounds they made.

The sun cut through the branches, making some of the bottles look golden. Most were clear, but there were a few of the dark blue ones, and some were so close a shade of green to the needles that it was difficult to separate them from the foliage. There was a yellow one that was in the shape of a bird with its wings folded close to its side. The leather thong that held it to the tree was wrapped around an open beak that Spikehollow guessed someone once drank out of. Two were the color of milk and were as big around as they were tall, looking more like fat globes than ordinary bottles. The corks that used to stopper all of them were strung on threads on branches. Their movement added to the music.

"Go get Direfang," Spikehollow told her. "Find Direfang somewhere near the river." He moved closer to the trunk and stared up. "Direfang should see this."

"What about Saro-Saro?" Pippa tapped her foot against the ground, making a crunching sound against the many dropped pine cones. "Saro-Saro should see this first."

"Then go get Saro-Saro and Direfang." Spikehollow unfastened the quilt from his neck and laid it on the ground.

Then he sat on the forest floor, still gazing up at the unusual sight.

He spotted a dark red bottle, the only one of its color. It had a knob at the bottom and top, and was thinner in the middle, almost shaped like an hourglass. He thought that the prettiest one, the sun making it look wet and inviting like a sweet apple.

Several minutes later, a crowd of goblins had gathered around the tree along with three hobgoblins Spikehollow had never seen before. He heard one with a pockmarked face call the young one Ruffem. Saro-Saro arrived, muscling his way to the front and snorting scornfully.

"Stopped eating for this?" he asked, glaring at Spikehollow. "Stupid to stop eating for this. Lots of empty bottles. So what?" The old goblin spat and ground the ball of his foot against a pine cone. "Stupid Spikehollow." He turned and retreated a few yards, pushing his way through the crowd. But he didn't go far.

Direfang had arrived, and everyone awaited his reaction, which was different. The hobgoblin stared thoughtfully before he stretched up and grabbed a bottle, a long-necked clear one. He tugged, which set the bottles on the same branch to clinking and whistling in the breeze. The sounds were melodious; he tugged again and again to the oohs and ahs of the young goblins around him. Finally the bottle came loose, and he inspected it in his hand. Fashioned of heavy glass, it had a maker's mark on the bottom and some sort of raised lettering that had been rendered when the bottle was formed. He hefted it in one palm, showing it to everyone around him who gawked at the pretty musical bottle.

"Wizard!" Direfang shouted several times before Grallik materialized. He tossed the bottle to Grallik, who in his surprise caught it awkwardly, just barely keeping from being struck by the flying object. "Huh. What is the meaning of this bottle tree?"

"A waste!" That opinion came from Saro-Saro, who had turned around and was standing, glaring at Direfang. "A waste of time is the meaning of it. This tree has nothing to do with goblins." The old goblin spit again and turned, ambling slowly toward the river.

Grallik looked at the bottle in his hands, his fingers tracing the raised words. "It's a glass tree," he said finally, handing off the bottle to a tall goblin. "I'd wager it was started quite some while ago, judging by how rotted some of those leather strips look." He pointed to a green bottle hanging from a cracked leather cord.

"A glass tree," Spikehollow whispered to Pippa, translating the wizard's tongue.

"What's a glass tree?" Pippa wondered aloud.

Direfang translated her question, which was also the very next thing he intended to ask.

The wizard brushed his hands against his threadbare undertunic. "Elves probably were responsible for this one, given the fact that it's in a forest. A glass tree was a tradition started by some Nerakan merchants many, many years ago. They'd hang bottles and pieces of glass from the few trees they passed on their trade routes. The wind blowing across the tops of the bottles was said to ward off evil influences, such as bandits. Some elves adopted the practice to ward away foul forest spirits and the like."

Spikehollow said, "The sounds are nice, like a song without words." He repeated the wizard's explanation in goblinspeak to the many others collected around him.

The wizard had wound his way through the goblins and come up to the trunk, careful not to step on Spikehollow's quilt. He pointed to a symbol carved at his eye level. "Elven for certain. Some of the homes . . ." He paused, caught up in a memory of his young years. "The homes where I grew up. They had these symbols carved on door frames or somewhere in their shops. It essentially is a wish for good luck and boon times."

Direfang joined him. "Can hardly see it, that faint symbol."

"The bark's growing over it. I don't believe there have been any elves around here for years. There are more carvings higher, but they are even harder to recognize. Some are names, some of them symbols."

"So the bottles belong to no one. Not any longer." The hobgoblin scratched his head and reached up, and standing on his toes was able to grab one of the darker blue bottles. He yanked it hard, and the cord snapped, the motion again setting many bottles to clinking and whistling. "Wouldn't matter if the bottles did belong to elves." He turned to face the crowd. "Take everything. The bottles will be good to hold river water when there is no more river to drink from."

Direfang pulled down a few more then returned to the river, passing by a group of Hunter's Ridge clan members who called out to him about how pleased they were to join the hobgoblin's army.

Pippa came back to Spikehollow. She touched his arm gently and nodded to the tree. "Which bottle for me, you?"

"The red one," Spikehollow said. "The only red one on the tree."

She brushed her hand against his cheek, scampered to the trunk, and tied her shirt around her waist so it would not tangle in her legs. Then she started to climb.

Some goblins stood on their taller kinsmen's shoulders so they could reach the lowest-hanging bottles. Others followed Pippa's example and climbed. Grallik watched them for a moment then reached toward the tall goblin he'd given the first bottle to. He plucked it from the goblin's hands.

"This one is mine," the wizard said flatly, looking around fiercely. "Foreman Direfang gave it to me." Not waiting for an argument, he left. "And someone best tell Horace and Kenosh they should come here—soon—if they want their own bottles."

20

MUDWORT'S PRICE

The sky was as red as Spikehollow's bottle. The setting sun had colored the low-hanging clouds crimson, and the goblins stared at it, oddly quiet. They'd left the shade of the pine trees days before and were at a point where Mudwort said the river would soon widen and head straight to the sea. More goblins and hobgoblins had joined them, the army's numbers swelling to close to two thousand.

Where had they all come from? Direfang asked Mudwort days past.

Mudwort shrugged and found something to busy herself with. She did not want to tell Direfang that she'd been calling through the stone to their kinsmen, summoning them to join the horde.

She sat apart from the rest of the goblins, her thoughts churning. Direfang had confessed to her that he'd changed his mind about the Qualinesti Forest. It was too far away; the clans would drift apart long before they reached the place. And she hadn't been able to find a faster route to travel to the forest.

"There are too many of us now," he told her. "We will attract attention if we march directly to the Qualinesti Forest. So we will go first to the Plains of Dust . . . if this army will walk that far."

Mudwort wanted—needed—to reach the forest. She

161

couldn't tell Direfang why because she couldn't provide a solid reason to herself. But her mind had touched something there when she'd been looking for a home for the army, when she'd mingled her magic with Moon-eye's and Boliver's. And that something lured her; she couldn't say why, but she couldn't resist.

Her fingers drummed across the ground, twirling in the grass as she softly hummed. She'd heard some of the newcomers speculate that something bad was coming because the sky had turned the shade of blood.

They were silly to be superstitious.

There was no nervousness in the ground, so Mudwort was not worried about any "bad somethings." She was instead worried about Direfang turning his army of goblins away from her goal.

It had become so easy to let her mind drift through the earth and flow like water in any direction she wanted. It was easier still when she held one of the uncut blue stones from her pouch. There was an uneven fracture to that particular stone. It was the color of one of the blue bottles that had been plucked from the glass tree, but it was clear on one end and darker at the bottom. There were others in the pouch that were prettier, but that one had already warmed to her touch; she held the blue stone pressed against her palm.

She thought she might look in on the shaman Saarh, journey through the stone and years and find the cave again. But since she had established that the cave and the shaman were lodged in the past, that wasn't an immediate concern. There would be time for such matters later. She had a much more important mission at the moment.

Her mind traveled southwest, flowing through the sea when she came to it and hurrying along—she didn't like the sensation of being surrounded by water. She touched the shore of the swamp and continued due west. Faster and faster she traveled through the earth, ignoring all the interesting things she came across that had been buried in the ground by men or by time.

She came upon another range of mountains, and her

senses rose as she touched them, feeling limestone that had been veined and pocked on the surface by heavy rains and deeper by underground streams. There were sections of sandstone too, and graywacke, basalt, and obsidian, the last of which was cool and smooth and almost tempted her to stop her travels so she could enjoy the sensation.

Abruptly she reached the forest, which began on the other side of the range. Her mind skimmed the surface of the ground, weaving around the trunks and slowing to feel the pulse of the land.

"Where is it?" she whispered to herself. "The very special something is here. Somewhere here."

Mudwort was so engrossed in her search she didn't hear the wizard and Kenosh approaching her. Both had been sitting nearby, watching her. Grallik cautioned Kenosh to keep quiet as they crept closer.

She'd only journeyed there once before, that time when she and Moon-eye and Boliver had looked for a land for all the goblins to live in. They were inside the top of a mountain when they cast that seeing spell; she couldn't recall the name of the place in the mountain, but the skull man had told it to her—a place of religious or arcane significance for humans. She couldn't remember why it was so important. But she remembered the priest said it was a repository of power, and the magic had come easily to her there.

"Where is it? What is it?"

Refusing to give up, she sent her mind deeper into the ground, teasing the very ends of the roots of the great trees. She felt water rushing over her, the earth damp and rich there, and she passed through ground that was so hard packed it could pass for stone. Mudwort was growing tired; she had put so much energy into her spell. Her palm ached from pressing the blue stone so hard against it.

"Where?"

At last she found it, the place where the pulse grew so strong that it sounded hard and harsh in her head. She stopped humming and sucked in a breath.

"What is it?"

Her mind wrapped around the power. Yes, it was magic,

terribly unusual and potent magic. Like a bug attracted to lantern light, she slipped toward the magic. She would ascertain how deep the magic was hidden later on, as well as where precisely the magic was in the forest. She would make a second trip, perhaps, for that information.

Something was wrapped around the magical thing, a rotting cloth that at one time must have been fine and elaborate. There were thin, metallic threads running through the cloth—silver and gold and platinum. Tiny pearls had been sewn into a pattern, the details of which she couldn't make out. Someone had treasured the powerful artifact, burying it so no one else could find it and wrapping it in such a fine, fine piece of fancy cloth. A dark thought flitted through her mind: was the something so powerful that someone feared it and buried it to keep it out of the wrong hands?

"Doesn't matter," she muttered. "These are the right hands." She happily twirled her fingers in the dirt and basked in the eldritch aura of the wrapped object. She tried to peer past the cloth but could see very little beyond the wrapping. The something was wood, but it had metal bits in it, and gems.

When exhaustion claimed her and she finally released the spell and opened her eyes, she spotted the wizard nearby. He was talking to the Dark Knight Kenosh, asking him how he felt.

Kenosh didn't look so good, Mudwort thought. His face was flushed, beyond the sunburn he'd developed, and he was sweating even though it was not overly warm. He was coughing, and his nose was bleeding.

Mudwort got up and put more distance between herself and the sick knight. She had no intention of catching whatever malady was going around. Until she'd seen Kenosh, she thought the bug was limited to goblins and hobgoblins. Spikehollow had been one of those sick in days past, but the skull man had cured him.

However, in the past day or so, more goblins had come down with the strange illness, all of them sweating, coughing and shivering. Their suffering made Mudwort nervous. Too bad there were not a dozen skull men to tend to the sick.

The wizard followed her. She crossed her arms and tapped her foot, all the while still holding the blue gem against her palm.

"Mudwort . . ."

She glared at him.

"Your magic . . ." The wizard swallowed, looking her up and down. "I . . . You've tempted me, Mudwort." He looked her in the eyes, the first time he'd done so without glancing away. "You took me along on your spell the other night and I am grateful. You have tempted me sorely with your magic. I want you to teach me, Mudwort, teach me how to combine spells with another, how to work the earth magic with another . . . wizard."

"Shaman," she corrected him. She liked the sound of that word better.

"Yes, well, shaman, then. I want—I need to know how to wield this magic." He swallowed hard again and coughed—not the same type of coughing sound the sick ones made, more like a nervous cough, Mudwort thought. "I followed you, all of you, from Steel Town just to learn this magic. I've risked everything, Mudwort, to learn this amazing magic." He knelt down so he was eye level with her. "Teach me. Please."

She let a silence settle between them. In the silence she heard the chatter of goblins watching the sunset. The sky was full of birds, and she heard their faint, melodic cries. She heard Kenosh coughing and others making sick sounds, and there was Direfang calling for the skull man. Saro-Saro called for the skull man too.

"There is a price, wizard, for this magic."

"Grallik. My name is Grallik."

"A price." She didn't care about his name.

He nodded. "Any price. Anything . . . anything within my power." The wizard was begging her as he'd begged Direfang for food.

"Direfang does not want to go to the forest . . . Grallik."

"The Qualinesti Forest. He has changed his mind?"

"Yes. Direfang says it is too far, that the clans will

splinter before that. Says the Plains of Dust is better for now. But Direfang might stop the march even before the Plains of Dust. Might stop soon because of the sick ones. Might stop because feet are sore and goblins are tired." She hunched forward.

"And you prefer to go to the forest."

"It would be a good place for goblins," she answered almost too quickly.

"So this price . . ." Grallik did not take his eyes from hers. "This price for learning your magic . . . ?"

"Is to make Direfang go to the forest," Mudwort finished, huffing for emphasis.

Grallik laughed. "I am a slave here, Mudwort. I've no power over Foreman Direfang. He'll not listen to me, and getting Horace to charm him with a spell—if that's what you are thinking—wouldn't last very long. I've watched Direfang. He listens to you all the time. You're the only one who could convince him."

"Not this time," she shot back.

Kenosh coughed louder and longer, a wracking spasm that caused Mudwort and Grallik to turn and look at him. Kenosh was doubled over, a bloody line of drool trickling from his mouth.

"Kenosh," Grallik said in a hushed voice. "The last one of my talon."

"He is sick like goblins are sick. The skull man will mend the Dark Knight after mending goblins. If there is any mending left."

"I will talk to Foreman Direfang," Grallik whispered.

"Talk well," Mudwort said. "Be convincing. That is the price."

When Grallik turned back to look at the red-skinned goblin, she was gone.

———— s ————

Horace worked late into the night, moving from one goblin to the next, shaking his head ruefully when inspecting each patient but offering sympathetic words in the goblin tongue.

"The skull man learned goblinspeak fast," Direfang observed, hovering close behind the priest.

"I have a talent for languages," Horace replied. He was kneeling next to Spikehollow, who was wrapped in the colorful quilt. "I tended you before. I'd thought the sick chased away from you."

Spikehollow opened his mouth to reply, but nothing came out. His lips quivered in his chill, and pink bubbles formed at the corners of his mouth. His teeth clacked together as he shivered all over.

Pippa stood nearby, darting in concernedly to touch his forehead. "Spikehollow burns," she said to the priest. "Sweats and shivers. They have come back. It is a bad sick, isn't it?"

Horace nodded. "Bad. Yes, very." He pulled back the quilt and lifted up Spikehollow's tunic, the words to a healing enchantment tumbling out as he worked. His hand glowed orange. "Oh, my."

He stared at Spikehollow's waist, and his eyes traveled up and locked onto the young goblin's neck. Horace could see well that evening. There was a riot of stars overhead, and along the riverbank there was nothing to block the light from twinkling down.

There was a swollen black knob on Spikehollow's neck, another in the pit of the goblin's arm, and one protruding from his side.

"This is a very bad sick," Horace echoed.

21

THE BLACK SPOTS

Horace's dark skin gleamed with sweat. It wasn't from the sickness, but from exertion. He'd been tending ailing goblins for so many hours that he was nearly at the point of collapse. He was numb all over, and his legs felt like lead weights.

At least the Hunter's Ridge clan had not come down with the illness, nor any goblins from the other two clans that had joined them that morning. That was curious, the priest reflected, and might be important. He was too tired to think about it, though.

He stood propped against an old maple, Direfang in front of him, scowling and muttering in the goblin tongue. After a few moments, he spoke slowly so Horace could more easily understand him.

"Not done yet today, skull man," the hobgoblin leader grumbled. "Not close to done. There are many more—"

"No, Foreman, I'm not done. I'll well admit that. But I do need a break, a brief rest. And I need to see to myself or there'll be no helping any of you. If I catch this malady, there'll be no more healing to give."

Despite Direfang's snarl, the priest raised a glowing hand to his own chest and mumbled a prayer to Zeboim. "Goddess, grant me strength," he breathed. "Keep me well so that I can serve these creatures' health." He placed his

168

fingers over his heart, and the glow melted into his skin, radiating up his neck and down his arms and traveling to the waistband of his tattered leggings.

His chest rose and fell more rapidly as the glow brightened, and he gasped for breath. The hobgoblin stepped forward, ready to catch him. But Horace waved him away. His breathing slowed after a few moments, and he tilted his head up, finding something in the branches to stare at.

"Sea Mother, I am your humble servant and . . ." Horace continued his prayer, his voice rising and falling as his fingers danced over his skin.

Direfang stepped back and shook his head.

"You disapprove of Horace tending to himself?" That came from Grallik. The wizard had come up behind him, leading the three goats that used to be in Kenosh's care. He looked with distaste at the animals tethered to his wrist and let out a sigh when they dropped their heads to munch on the grass at his feet.

"This Mother Goddess—"

"Ah, that's what you disapprove of, Foreman Direfang. You don't believe in the gods. None of your kind do, it seems."

Direfang shrugged.

"What matters is that the skull man is mending the goblins for you. And what he's doing now, Foreman, is bolstering his body against whatever disease ravages them."

The light was thin, filtering through the maples and oaks, and it made the leaves and branches look brittle. The forest had narrowed and changed considerably along that section of the river; the pines had all but disappeared. There was more space between the trunks, and trillium and ferns covered most of the floor. Along a branch of the river that split and pointed to the west, beavers had built a dam. But the little creatures were long gone, and the mound of twigs and mud was falling apart. The hobgoblin took a deep breath, smelling the moldiness of the rotting dam and finding it far preferable to rotting goblin flesh and the smell of the Dark Knights.

Direfang looked away from the priest and stared at a

dying black willow, its bare branches dangling over the river and over the many goblins lying beneath it. Thirty-seven, he counted, all of them in various stages of the bad sickness. Spikehollow was one of the worst of the victims. Direfang watched as the young goblin coughed fiercely and tried to retreat deeper into the once-colorful quilt that had become stained with blood and mud. Swollen black spots were clearly evident on his neck. The hobgoblin could see more black spots on those who did not have the benefit of blankets to cover them. There were spots on legs and under armpits, along their waists—everywhere on their bodies, it seemed.

The hobgoblin shuddered and looked back to the priest. He breathed deep again, but he couldn't catch the moldy scent of the dam anymore. He could only smell his rotting charges.

"The sick need more help," Direfang said, interrupting Horace's prayer. "Need more help right now. Pray to your goddess, tend to yourself, but be fast." The priest had finished with his own ministrations; the glow was gone and his hands had relaxed at his sides. "Some are dying, skull man. Be fast and be good."

Horace met Direfang's gaze. The priest's red-rimmed eyes looked small on his fleshy face, but there was something hopeless in them that sent a shiver down the hobgoblin's spine.

"I know some are dying, Foreman. I'm not blind." Horace crossed his arms in front of his chest. "And you must know I have done—and will continue to do—my very best not because you demand it, but because Zeboim does."

Direfang opened his mouth to say something, but Horace cut him off.

"This is a profound sickness, Foreman. And not even the healing that comes from the Sea Mother may be enough. Divine magic cannot cure everything." He paused and looked over toward the black willow. "Do you understand that? Do you?" He didn't wait for a reply. "There are some illnesses that magic simply cannot defeat. It is as if the gods have decreed that—"

"Goblins do not believe in the gods."

"Aye, Foreman," Horace said. "You've mentioned that to me on more than one occasion."

"That dwarf . . ."

"In Reorx's Cradle?" Horace still watched the sick goblins under the tree. He had thought about the dwarf too. "The old one, you mean, who cursed us all and begged her god to send us to the deepest pit in the Abyss? The one who rendered your maps?"

"Yes, that one."

"I believe in the gods, Foreman Direfang. But I do not believe any mortal can call down such a malady. That dwarf, she is not responsible for this sickness, and neither is her god, Reorx." He wrung out his big hands and pushed away from the trunk. "I will be famished when I am done for the day."

"Pippa will bring you some food," Direfang said. "And skull man?"

Horace paused.

"Be fast with the magic. Make the goblins well."

The priest shuffled over to the black willow and knelt next to Spikehollow. "Sea Mother," he began.

"Best to keep your distance from the sick, Foreman Direfang," Grallik advised the hobgoblin leader, putting an arm out to stop him from following Horace. "Wouldn't do for you to succumb to the black spots."

Direfang raised an eyebrow, as much as asking "Why would you care?"

"I'd not fancy being led around by that old yellow goblin," said Grallik, meeting his eyes.

"Saro-Saro," Direfang supplied.

"He seems an ill-tempered soul."

"With no tolerance for Dark Knights," Direfang added.

Grallik dug the ball of his foot into the ground and grimaced. Both of his boots were falling apart. "Yes, Foreman. I feel I would be safer with you. I fear that old yellow goblin will not realize how useful I can be. His indifference worries me. And his ambition."

Direfang cocked his head.

"And his contempt for magic, save for what Horace offers," Grallik further explained.

"Goblins hate Dark Knights for good reason," Direfang said. "Saro-Saro has good reasons too." He waved a hand to indicate he was finished talking to the wizard and headed toward the river, pulling his tunic up as he went.

"Wait, Foreman."

Direfang slowed but did not stop.

"I know of a much shorter way to the Qualinesti Forest," said Grallik, hurrying to follow the hobgoblin leader. "Shorter, safer. Certainly a shorter journey than even to the Plains of Dust."

Direfang turned. He held his tunic loosely in one hand, shaking the dirt from it.

"Mudwort found the way, actually, though she didn't realize it at first. She and that bumpy, brown-skinned—"

"Boliver."

"Yes, the other night in fact. They found a much shorter way with that spell they cast. I was part of that spell, remember."

Direfang snarled. "This faster way, wizard," he said skeptically. "What is it?"

Grallik tugged the goats to follow him as he walked along with the hobgoblin. "It will take a little explaining."

Horace's face was a stoical mask. He'd learned long ago not to let patients see his concern; it only added to their worries and worsened their chances of recovery. But he almost couldn't help himself after easing himself down next to Spikehollow and touching the back of his hand to the goblin's forehead.

He almost yanked his hand away. "So hot, you are."

Spikehollow's eyes fluttered, and his head turned slowly as though he were trapped in a bad dream. His fingers wrapped around the top of the quilt, clenching and unclenching.

Horace tucked his chin close to his chest and prayed in Ergothian, wanting no one else to hear his desperate words.

"Sea Mother, such a sickness I have never tended. This could well be beyond me. Sea Mother, hear my—"

Nearby, a brown-skinned goblin coughed so hard that his body shook against the ground. He turned onto his back and vomited a spray of blood that spattered against Spikehollow and the priest. Tremors wracked the goblin's thin body, and Horace briefly stopped his work on Spikehollow and turned to aid the brown goblin. He moaned in pain and retched again, and Horace grabbed his shoulders and turned him onto his side so he would not choke on his own vomit. Then Horace tilted his head so he could breathe easier. The priest's hands glowed orange, and he rattled off the words to a healing spell he'd been casting frequently—with diminishing results.

Blood seeped from the goblin's mouth, though he stopped shaking as Horace's spell progressed.

"Shad bleeds inside." That was spoken by a yellow-skinned goblin propped against the trunk of the black willow. She had black spots on her neck, but they had not yet abscessed. An old, gray blanket was draped over her legs. She'd taken it from Bugteeth after he had died. "The sick is deep with Shad, isn't it?"

She spoke in the goblin tongue, her voice so soft and raspy that Horace had to listen hard to pick out the meaning.

"A deep, deep sick, isn't it, skull man?"

Horace nodded but kept his face a mask and slowly answered in her language. "Yes, this one is bleeding inside—his lungs. But my healing spell—"

"Shad will die, eh?"

The priest shook his head. "Not if I can help it." His hands glowed bright, but the glow didn't spread far across the brown-skinned goblin, as though the illness fought back against the priest. Horace redoubled his effort and was rewarded with a shower of blood when the goblin vomited again. The thin body shook once more, then stopped moving. Horace bowed his head and closed the goblin's eyes.

"Shad is dead?"

Horace didn't answer. He futilely tried to wipe the blood off his robe and hands and returned to Spikehollow. Horace was particularly concerned about that goblin, whose name he couldn't remember, despite Direfang telling it to him more than once.

"The sunlight is too bright," Spikehollow croaked. He raised an arm to shield his eyes. "Skull man, it is too, too bright. Painful."

Horace looked up through the branches. The light was still thin and should not have bothered Spikehollow. But the disease seemed to make the goblins acutely sensitive to light and noise and temperatures, Horace reflected.

You were among the first to get sick. Why? Horace hadn't spoken aloud; the question was in his thoughts. He didn't think the goblin knew the answer any more than he did. What, the priest mused, do you have in common with the others? The answer might go a way toward healing you and stopping this from spreading further.

Horace stared at the goblin, then more closely at the quilt.

The others who were among the first sick also wore blankets and quilts taken from the Reorx's Cradle, Horace realized. He recalled the ancient dwarf who had cursed him and all of the goblins for descending on their village; he couldn't get those frightening words out of his head. Yet the priest could not believe that the sickness was Reorx's doing. A god wouldn't meddle in something as petty as goblins raiding such a small—

"Small village." Horace's eyes grew wide. Even Foreman Direfang had noted that there were far more homes than necessary for the number of dwarves living there. And the garden was much larger than was needed to support the population. The village had certainly been larger at one time, but it hadn't shrunk because of dwarves moving away, as the priest had heard the goblins speculate.

The population had dwindled because of the sickness.

The ancient dwarf had tried to warn him at one point, when he was translating Direfang's demands. But she stopped short, no doubt hoping all the goblins would catch the malady and die.

As some of them already had.

He stared at the patterns in Spikehollow's quilt, not really seeing them, seeing instead the village with its too-many homes.

"Goblin, tell me what you're feeling." Horace spoke those words aloud, in the human tongue, having heard that goblin speak in the language of humans before. He didn't want all the goblins under the tree to listen and understand their conversation.

"Head hurts," Spikehollow began in Common. "Hurt for a few days now." He coughed and a line of blood thickened over his lips. "Back hurts, arms and legs hurt . . . ache so bad. The light, it is much too bright. Hot, feel hot too. Very, very hot."

Swallowing his fear and disgust, Horace examined the lumps on Spikehollow's neck. They were hard, same as the ones under his arms. Black as coal, one had split open and was oozing blood and a greenish pus. He pulled back the quilt and saw that one lump on the goblin's leg had grown to the size of an orange.

"By the Sea Mother," he whispered. The mask of stoicism melted into a look of horror. In all his years working with the Dark Knights, and before that with the sailors on the coast of Southern Ergoth, Horace had seen nothing as terrifying as what lay before him. He fought to keep from retching, so horrid was Spikehollow's appearance.

There was blood in the goblin's urine and feces, blood pooling under his skin; black spots and painful-looking boils dotted his chest and upper arms. That close his stench was unbearable, and Horace finally lost his battle to ignore the stench, turning and emptying the contents of his stomach on the ground. Then he pulled the quilt back up so he would no longer have to look at the worst of Spikehollow's lesions.

The priest wiped at his own lips. The goblin was feebly reaching under the quilt for something at his side and, after a moment's work, pulled out a knife. Horace leaned back, thinking the goblin meant to kill him, angry that the curing spell had not worked. Instead, the goblin pressed the knife to his own chest.

"Don't . . ." Horace began. The priest didn't have to finish the warning. Spikehollow didn't have the strength to end his own life.

"Hurts too bad," Spikehollow gasped. Then the goblin's fingers slipped from the pommel, and the knife fell aside. The goblin gave a great rasping breath, clutched at his throat, and died.

The priest stared glumly. Then he noticed the knife, snatched it up, found a scabbard under the quilt, and sheathed the small blade, putting it in the pocket of his leggings. The handle stuck out, but he hoped no one would notice that he'd acquired a weapon.

Horace worked well into the evening, spending his spells on those who were not yet so badly afflicted; they seemed to respond best to his divine magic. There had been nearly forty when he'd started that afternoon; he looked around and saw there were at least double that number of goblins who were hobbled by the sickness. By nightfall he'd given so much of himself that he could barely raise a hand, and he could no longer coax a healing glow. He stumbled away from the black willow and dropped to his knees on the riverbank.

The moon was high and bright and set the water to sparkling, but the priest couldn't appreciate the beauty of the scene. Fire crackled behind him; the bodies of the dead were being burned in a clearing. He'd insisted that they be burned immediately—their clothes, their possessions, everything should join them in the fire. What couldn't be burned had to be buried beneath the earth. He considered all the goblins scavengers, and he prayed to Zeboim that they had enough sense not to loot the diseased corpses for clothes and blankets.

Remembering, he reached in his pocket and pulled out the knife; the scabbard and the leather-wrapped pommel would also be thick with disease. He nearly tossed it into the river. Horace would be taking a chance if he kept something like Spikehollow's knife, probably as disease-ridden as the dead goblin. He should throw it away, he knew.

Instead, he replaced it in his pocket; it was too precious a thing to give up. One knife would do nothing against that many goblins. But he wanted the knife so he could end his own life if the first symptoms of the disease appeared. Horace would not allow himself to suffer the way the sick goblins were suffering.

Horace listened to the river shush by as he slipped his hands into the cool waters to wash them off. A chorus of whistles and what sounded like birdsong rose. Frogs or toads or both, the happy noise was a relief compared to the moans of the sick and the wails of the mourners. He splashed water on his face and edged out into the shallows, nearly slipping on an algae-covered stretch of slate. He scrubbed his arms and chest and waded out until the river reached his waist. He felt the insistent tug of its current, and for a moment he considered wading out farther still until the current pulled him under and ended his despair.

He was a devoted man and believed that Zeboim would send his soul to the place where spirits drift for a pleasant eternity. Death could well be preferable to his existence. Damn Grallik for talking him into their escapade! Better that the earthquakes had sucked him down or the volcanoes had buried him in ash. Better such a fate than watching the goblins suffer so and finding his divine magic impotent.

Yet the soothing waters revived him a little.

He stood in the shallow part of the river for quite some time, his back to the goblins and eyes cast down at the moon's reflection. After a while his head bobbed forward, and he felt impossibly weary. He could fall asleep right there and drift away down the river. Again, he thought, drowning might not be so bad.

But for some reason Zeboim had tasked him with his terrible situation, had indeed nudged him to follow Grallik in his mad plan to join the goblins. If the Sea Mother had put him on his course, he had little choice but to see things through.

He returned to the bank. His wet leather leggings clung like a second skin and made his legs feel heavier still. Even in the moonlight, he could tell the river had not washed all the blood out of the leather. He should burn the leggings; they were no doubt thick with the disease. But he had nothing else to wear. As tattered and germ ridden as they were, they were all he had. And his pride would not allow him to go naked among the savages, those goblins.

Horace let the water run off him and focused once more on the trills and melodic croaks of the frogs. The breeze cooled and energized him.

"Zebir Jotun, Zura the Maelstrom," he began. His fingers glowed orange as he returned to the black willow and the goblins beneath it. He eyed the closest ones, evaluating which to try to work on next. "By the silvery hair of the precious Sea Mother . . . no!"

Horace had healed him just the day before, thought for certain he'd erased the last vestige of disease. Yet there he was again; it was Kenosh, stretched out between a goblin and a hobgoblin.

The Dark Knight coughed deeply and shivered. And even in the shadows of the dead tree, the priest saw the black spots on the man's face.

22

SAARH

She wore eight necklaces that morning, all that she owned, along with her earrings and an armband that had been a recent gift from a consort. Around her waist was the skin of a cave snake that she'd caught and gutted in a ceremony some time ago. It was a special day, so it was important to look her best and wear everything she owned.

The longest necklace hung just below her waist. It consisted of carved wooden beads, most of them round, but a few were cut and shaped to look like bats. The beads of another necklace had been painted with dyes made from lichen; Saarh seemed to favor that one, and she worried at the beads with her slender fingers.

The most beautiful necklace was the shortest one, barely fitting around her head. Irregular-shaped beads the color of a full moon shimmered in the torchlight. The beads were smooth, and along their surfaces streaks of blue, pink, and green glistened. That necklace, and the others, marked her prestige in the clan.

Saarh was the clan leader. It had taken her well into middle age to earn the position, but her kinsmen followed her without question. She stood in front of them—several hundred goblins squeezed into the domed cavern and spread into the tunnels that led away from it. Most of them

179

were red-skinned, like herself, but there were some brown-skinned goblins too, and a few tinged orange.

Several wore necklaces made of wood and stone and the teeth of small animals that lived underground. Some boasted feathers and bits of bone on leather cords, and other goblins displayed pieces of bone pierced through their ears and nostrils.

They whispered among themselves, their voices sounding like the wind that sometimes found its way through the upper tunnels and whistled sonorously. But they stopped their quiet chatter when Saarh raised her arms and demanded their attention.

"These caves are too small," she began. "For some time the clan has known this. The food is too sparse. Hunger begins to rumble in the younglings' bellies." Saarh had a rough voice that often cracked and made it sound as though speaking were painful. "This day the clan leaves the underground so it can grow larger and thrive."

"Saarh, Saarh, Saarh!" The chant swelled and reverberated off the dome, and the torches flickered as all the goblins joined in. The light played across the carvings and made everything seem to shift and waver.

When she again had their attention, she said, "This clan is large, safe in its size, fearless."

"Saarh, Saarh, Saarh!"

"Strong and terrible this clan is." Saarh's eyes gleamed darkly, and some of the symbols on the wall behind her glowed. "This day, the clan claims the surface."

"Saarh!"

She slipped between the tightly packed goblins, each one bowing as she passed. Taking a last look at the great dome, she glided down a wide tunnel, the goblins falling in behind her and continuing to echo her name.

Saarh ran her fingers along the wall as she went, picking up the pulse of the stone and coaxing its ancient energies to trickle into her mind. Behind her, goblins copied her gesture, though they could not understand nor use the power held in the earth.

The torchlight from the cavern didn't reach there, so

DEATH MARCH

Saarh relied on her keen senses to guide her through the darkness. She found something comforting in the shadows and the dampness of the cave; she would miss both of those things. She knew she could retreat there if necessary, but she also knew she never would choose to do so. The challenges of the surface world would not be so great that she and her clan could not endure them.

Her journey lasted hours, so deep in the earth were the goblin caverns nestled and so winding were the tunnels. Her legs were tired by the time she reached a narrow slot that was little more than a crawlway. The goblins moved in single file there, scraping their shoulders on the stone, none complaining. Some of them had been that way before with her, when food had become so scarce they had to hunt above. But most had never seen the sky.

Finally she stepped out of the darkness, the air wrapping around her and making her shiver in its chill freshness. She stood on a high ledge atop one of the range's tallest peaks, taking in the scenery below. The land was green and lush, almost hurtfully bright in the midday sun. Tall grass and small trees stretched as far to the west as she could see. The scents of the foliage drifted up and mingled with the more subtle odor of the stone.

The chatter behind her grew louder, and she climbed down so her kinsmen could emerge behind her. Saarh glanced up to make sure they were following close. The brown cliff that stretched above her was streaked with sunlight, the hollows in the rock gray with shadows and looking like pockmarks on an old goblin's face. High and to the south was a formation that looked like a rearing cave bear, the top of it crimson and the center sparkling with some sort of crystal. She hoped to climb there later and investigate that place.

First she had her people to worry about. She continued to descend, the green of the young forest seeming to reach up and tug her down.

So many goblins, it took them a long while to filter out from the narrow tunnel. Most of them dallied on the ledges, both frightened and amazed by their new surroundings, all of them blinking furiously, their eyes were not used to so much glare. They would get accustomed to the light of the sun, Saarh knew. They would get accustomed to the forest too.

She picked up a hint of rain when she reached the bottom. Saarh had been outside in a storm before and so recognized the first delicate traces of water in the air. Far to the west, she spotted high, misty white clouds, and beneath them floated larger ones with swollen gray bellies. She hoped to push her clan deep into the young forest before the rains came, else they might flee back into the caves out of fear and a desire for safety.

From her new vantage point at the base of the mountain, Saarh could look up and take in much more of the heights. The range looked like the spine of some great beast, and it stretched north and south, rising up high in the middle section, where it was shot through with bands of almost-white stone set against red and brown strips and a line of rock that looked almost black.

Hematite, Mudwort knew. That's what the brown and black layers were. She'd seen enough of the stone in the Dark Knight mines to recognize it. The mountain Saarh gazed upon was heavy in the center with the iron ore that stained the rock around it. Above it were bands of sandstone and limestone, and time and heavy rains would eventually winnow those away. But the hematite would stay until the Dark Knights or some other group of men found it and dug down and broke it out to make their swords and shields.

Mudwort watched Saarh and her goblin horde with fascination. The shaman was not leading quite as many goblins as Direfang, but Saarh's force was nonetheless impressive . . . formidable.

Mudwort had been looking in on Saarh and her clan for what she guessed were several hours. The spell was taking its toll on her, but the goblins' activities were far too interesting for her to break away. Mudwort had been trying to puzzle out just how long ago Saarh had lived. One clue was in the forest and the mountains.

In an earlier seeing spell, Mudwort's senses had passed through that range before she'd come upon the Qualinesti Forest.

Saarh was in that very Qualinesti Forest, but the trees were very small, and there was so much grass and space between the trunks.

The forest was in its youth.

"Centuries ago," Mudwort decided. That was when Saarh had lived and when she brought her clan to the woods. Mudwort was awestruck by her magical ability to visit the past, awed that she could draw from the earth-memory so easily. "And the goblin caves and the dome, they are in that big range of mountains, deep in the heart of the earth. A long, long time past."

She smiled, pleased that she'd finally learned something vital about Saarh and her clan . . . about where the caves were and when those goblins had been alive. Her smile broadened. Just as Saarh had brought her clan to the woods, Mudwort would lead Direfang's army there. She peered closer through her vision.

———S———

Saarh's goblins spread out, investigating their new surroundings but keeping their natural curiosity under control, careful not to venture too far from their shaman.

Saarh stood shoulder to shoulder with an aging goblin with a crooked face. One of his cheeks was higher than the other, and his lower lip drooped as if the muscles in his jaw didn't work properly. While his appearance might have suggested he was stupid, his eyes were filled with rare intelligence, and the four necklaces he wore suggested he was important to the clan.

He stared at the mountains then slowly shook his head. "Is this the right thing? For certain, Saarh?"

She nodded.

"Too long this clan has lived in the earth. Fathers and grandfathers and farther back than that."

"Food is short now in the earth," she added. Saarh's voice still cracked, the words running coarsely together. "The clan is larger, and many females have swollen stomachs. They will deliver younglings soon. The need for food and space weighs heavy on me, on them. That is why the clan had to move."

"But the clan must return someday, Saarh. Goblins belong to the earth."

"Yes," she agreed. "That is also certain, a return."

"Goblins were meant to live under the press of the dirt and stone."

The sky darkened suddenly and lightning began to flash. Many of the goblins had never witnessed such a display and stood transfixed. Some were terrified and ran for reassurance to Saarh and the goblin with the crooked face.

The air was electrically charged and the wind gusted, setting Saarh's beads to clacking and the young trees to bending. Thunder boomed, and a few goblins screamed in response. When the lightning came again and again, forking brilliantly and followed by more thunder, some of the goblins streamed toward the mountain.

"Stop!" Saarh cried. But her pained voice was too soft.

The crooked-faced goblin added his voice to hers, telling the clan to stop, and the goblins nervously returned.

"This is a storm," she explained. "Chislev's touch. Nothing more."

———— S ————

"Chislev." Mudwort spat. The goblins long ago revered some gods, that clan recognizing Chislev apparently. She spat again.

"S'dards! Fools, the lot." But she scratched her chin thoughtfully. Perhaps the goblins of long ago were unaware that the gods had no regard for their fate. Perhaps in that faraway time they'd not experienced slavery yet, had not been hunted and maligned by Krynn's more powerful races.

But they will learn the falseness of the gods, Mudwort mused. "A bad, sad, painful lesson." She looked up, still keeping her senses locked into the seeing spell and focusing

on the shaman. At the same time, a part of her registered
Direfang approaching, a stern expression on his craggy face.
She dropped her gaze and held tight to the scene from the
past, angry with herself that she had not done her "seeing"
farther down river where the hobgoblin wouldn't have
spotted her.

Saarh raised a fist the next time there was a crack of
lightning. The lightning illuminated her proud, determined
face, her wide, wild eyes glistening with excitement. "It
is Chislev calling this clan to this place. The lightning is
Chislev's touch."

"Chislev, Chislev, Chislev!"

"Saarh is Chislev's claw!" That was intoned by the
crooked-faced goblin. "Saarh rules here! Rules for Chislev."

"Saarh, Saarh, Saarh!"

The sky opened up at that very moment, the rain pattering against the ground and the goblins, loud and insistent;
many who had never seen a storm were startled.

"No fear!" Saarh tipped her face up and opened her
mouth, drinking in the fresh water and knowing that many
of her people would do the same to imitate her.

"Saarh says 'no fear!' " The crooked-faced goblin moved
behind the shaman and rested his hands on her shoulders.

"There is more here, in this little forest, than food and
space to grow," Crooked-face whispered softly into her ear.
"There is more, isn't there?"

"Yes," she hissed. "There is much more."

"And that something more is . . ."

"Is Chislev's gift to goblinkind. There is power here. The
pulse is too strong to be denied."

The lightning flashed, a wide, bright stroke, and the
thunder boomed even louder.

Direfang nudged Mudwort with his foot.

She cursed as the spell slipped away and the image in her
mind of the infant forest and the shaman melted away.

"Mudwort, the wizard says there is a faster way to the Qualinesti Forest." Despite the news he brought, Direfang looked positively glum, thought Mudwort.

She got to her feet, excitement on her face. "Yes, the forest that the elves used to call home. That would be the best home for Direfang's army. The forest . . . the one I saw in the vision . . . the forest . . ."

"But the skull man does not want to leave this place," Direfang interrupted, his face growing even more solemn. "The skull man says this sickness is a plague, and that the plague must not travel elsewhere. Says it must end here with the goblins."

Mudwort cursed again. "The skull man does not lead the goblin army; Direfang does. It is what Direfang says that matters, not what a hated Dark Knight says."

Direfang looked north to the dead black willow tree. "Mudwort, soon there may be no one left to lead. Even though more and more goblins arrive, everyone is getting sick. Everyone might die."

23

THE PLAGUE TREE

Rain clouds scudded across the moon, hiding the river and thickening the darkness beneath the black willow. Lightning flickered high overhead, but it was brief and did nothing to cut the shadows, and the thunder that followed was little more than a whisper.

Leftear didn't need the moon to see by. He found Horace tending a retching goblin, waited until the priest was done with that patient, then stepped in and picked the priest up by the throat and pressed him against the willow trunk. He cursed at him in the goblin tongue and shook him.

Horace was so spent, he couldn't defend himself. He feebly kicked out at Leftear, but his feet didn't reach the goblin, who squeezed harder and drew blood.

Still holding the priest, the goblin balled his free hand and rammed it into Horace's stomach, grunting happily at the dull thud.

"Again," Pippa urged him. "Hit the skull man again, harder! Break the skull man! Make the man bleed."

"Kill the skull man," that from a one-armed goblin called Upana. "Be fast!"

Leftear grinned widely and hammered his fist into the priest's stomach again and again, careful as he did so not to step on his sick kinsmen sprawled under the tree.

187

Pippa was a few yards behind him, dancing between two ill goblins, deftly avoiding pools of vomit and blood while watching Leftear maul the priest. She'd briefly mourned Spikehollow's passing on that very spot a scant few hours earlier and had instigated the attack to avenge his death.

"The skull man did not save Spikehollow!" she hollered. "Kill the skull man! Get revenge for Spikehollow in blood!"

"Stop! Leave him alone, you monsters!" Those words were spoken in the human tongue, coming from the wizard rushing up to them. Though the offending goblins didn't comprehend the language of the man, they well understood that Grallik was also their enemy and, without releasing Horace, Leftear turned to threaten the newcomer, snarling in defiance.

"Stop this now!" Grallik pulled his three goats as close as he dared, staying well short of the first rows of the sick. He strained to see through the darkness, but saw only black shapes shifting and groaning. "You're fools, the sorry lot of you! Horace is your only chance to survive this plague!" When it was clear they didn't fathom his words, he realized none of them spoke the human language; desperately, Grallik searched his memory for a spell.

"What say?" Pippa called to Leftear. "What does the foul wizard say?"

Leftear grunted happily and turned and punched the priest again.

"The wizard wants Leftear to stop hitting the skull man," Upana, who had caught the gist of the human words, explained. "The wizard is stupid. And the wizard cannot see in the dark." The one-armed goblin laughed loudly and made a punching motion to imitate Leftear.

More words tumbled from Grallik's lips, those uttered in an arcane language that none but he could decipher. "I begged you," the wizard said. "I warned you, you vile little things."

Grallik waited for the lightning to flash again, and when it did and he could see his target, he pointed his free hand at Leftear. Fire shot out, striking the hobgoblin squarely in the back and pitching him forward into Horace. The two fell in a heap at the base of the tree, while Pippa howled in rage. The goats tried to bolt, nearly pulling Grallik down, but he spread his feet and kept his balance, searching his memory for another spell and praying for another fork of lightning so his tired eyes could better spot his next target.

"This will damn me," Grallik muttered. "Kill me. Those flea-ridden monsters will—"

"The wizard killed Leftear," one of the hobgoblin's friends cried. "Kill the wizard! Revenge in blood!"

"Yes, Leftear is dead. Stinky dead." Upana grabbed at Leftear's waist, gagging on the scent of burned flesh that mingled with the stench of the sick. He pulled free a long knife and rushed at the wizard. Keen as the goblin's eyes were, he didn't see a pool of blood near a coughing hobgoblin. Upana slipped in the ooze and fell down but was quick to struggle to his feet.

"Stay away from me!" Grallik shouted. "I'll not touch that blood! Keep your damnable sickness to yourselves!"

Upana continued his charge, just as lightning flickered again, and the wizard blasted him with a ribbon of flame. The impact propelled the goblin back into a sick kinsman who was trying to rise.

The fire and commotion caught Direfang's attention. He and Mudwort had been too far away to see Leftear attack the priest, but he could tell there was trouble brewing beneath the tree.

Another column of flame lit up the night. The flash almost blinded the hobgoblin, but it also served to reveal a group of goblins swarming at Grallik and toward the black willow.

"Stay put," he ordered Mudwort. "Stay away from the plague tree!"

He lumbered forward toward the column of flame. Fingers of lightning again illuminated the wizard, who was being pulled down and pummeled. Another flash showed the glint of several blades.

Direfang ran as fast as he could, not to save the Dark Knight, but to stop a brawl in which who knew how many goblins might be hurt. He was at the scene in a few heartbeats, and started pulling knives out of goblins' grasps and hurling them into the river. Then he tugged the goblins off the wizard, who in such a short time was already badly beaten and cut.

"What is the meaning behind this?" Direfang bellowed. Staggering, the wizard put his back to the hobgoblin's. "Speak fast!" Direfang demanded.

More goblins were rushing toward the black willow, all of them anxious to be a part of whatever excitement was happening.

"Speak now!" Direfang screamed so hard his voice broke.

He was answered by dozens of explanations that ran together and made no sense. The sound of the brawl at the tree, the goblins' chattering, the river rushing by, and the thunder coming louder rose to a painful cacophony. The wizard was also trying to explain, and Direfang could pick out only a few of Grallik's words.

"Horace . . . attacked . . . monsters."

Direfang howled again, and the growing number of goblins around him hesitated and backed away. One risked darting in to slash at the wizard, but Direfang was faster. The hobgoblin spun, his big hand reaching out and closing around the goblin's wrist. He picked the offender up and hurled him into the river.

"This . . . ends . . . now!" Direfang snarled. He pushed his way through the mass of goblins and headed toward the base of the tree. "This ends now!" he howled again and again.

The goblins edged back, cowed by his fury. Direfang carefully stepped between the ill and neared the trunk, pulling curious goblins aside until he reached Pippa. Her dress was covered in blood; her companions were just as blood soaked.

Direfang threw a hand over his nose and mouth, but that couldn't keep out the foul odors.

"Leftear," Pippa pointed. "The wizard killed Leftear."

"Burned Leftear and Upana," another goblin interjected. He muscled his way past Direfang and took a stance on top of the unconscious priest. "All to protect this useless skull man. Goblins died to the wizard's fire for no reason!"

Direfang knocked the goblin off Horace's stomach and kicked Leftear's body away. He saw that the priest was still breathing. He bent and carefully picked him up, placed him over a shoulder, and struggling under the priest's weight, carried him down to the riverbank. The hobgoblin laid him down at the water's edge and put his own face inches above the water.

He breathed deep, trying to clear his lungs of the terrible stench of burned flesh and rotting goblins. "All of this ends now," he said when he finally stood up and faced the many who had followed him. "No more fighting. This isn't worth it, none of it. No more bleeding."

"Direfang leaving?" one of the older goblins murmured. "Direfang angry and leaving?"

He listened to a wave of similar questions before finally shaking his head. "No one should leave until the sickness runs its course. It must not spread beyond this place."

"Direfang not leaving!" a relieved goblin shouted to the crowd.

"But the skull man must pay for not stopping the sickness!" Pippa had threaded her way to the riverbank and prodded Direfang with her finger. "The skull man—"

The thunder boomed loudly, and Pippa stopped talking. Rain began falling, gently, and the goblins looked up and closed their eyes, letting the water sluice over their faces. It was quiet for several minutes, save for the pattering sound the rain made against the goblins and the river.

"Leave the skull man alone," Direfang said. There was little power behind his words, however. *And leave me alone,* his dour expression seemed to add.

The rain came down harder, swelling the river and soaking Direfang and all the goblins gathered. Within the passing of a few moments, the sound of the rain grew until it seemed hurtful in its intensity. The ground began to rock, and the river shuddered when the thunder grew louder still. Direfang arched his back and let the rain massage it, craned his neck, and watched the river rise, the current racing. He glared around at all the goblins who were waiting for his next words, his leadership.

"Direfang leaving? Not now, but later?" It was the older goblin again. She'd squeezed her eyes shut against the pounding rain, but she was turning her head this way and that to enjoy the refreshing wetness of it. "After the sickness, Direfang go?"

The hobgoblin scanned the faces of the goblins pressed closest. The rain and the darkness shadowed their expressions and muted their whispered conversations.

"Leaving?" asked the persistent goblin worriedly. "Direfang can't leave."

Direfang made his way through the crowd and toward the black willow. He shivered as he stepped beneath its dead branches, shuffling now and then to avoid bumping into the sick. He couldn't see them well, all but dark lumps against the dark ground. Yet he could hear them: moaning, whimpering, coughing, vomiting. And he could smell them; the stench was a wall he pressed through.

The rain continued to come down hard but not hard enough to squash the stink or drown out the sounds of the ill ones' misery. He found Leftear's corpse and Upana's too. He bent to pick up the two bodies then noticed that several more of the sick goblins near them were dead—not from any of the wizard's spells, but from the illness. He pressed his head against the black willow's trunk and let out a sob. It was a weakness to cry, but in the darkness only the closest sick goblins could see him. And Direfang knew they would die soon, telling no one of his shame.

His shoulders shook in grief over the dead and dying, over the ragtag army that was so difficult to control, and over the whole of his life that had consisted of nothing good—only a dozen free years followed by many more of slavery and brutal beatings, relentless hard work, and finally his horrible situation. He dropped to his knees, scraping his face against the rotting bark. The smell of blood was stronger close to the ground.

A goblin cried out softly, and Direfang reached to his right, feeling the goblin and touching blood and massive boils. He didn't pull his hand away; rather he rubbed the goblin's forehead and reached to touch others that were near.

Let the sickness take me, he thought. Let it end all of this.

***

The early-morning sky shimmered a soft pink, the color of the roses that used to grow in barrels outside the tavern in Steel Town. Mist curled across the top of the river and twined around tree trunks, hinting that the sun would burn the mist off soon and make for a hot day.

Grallik and Horace sat together on a piece of slate on the riverbank, backs to the water and staring at the dead black willow. Bodies were piled like cordwood against its trunk. Kenosh's was among them.

"The last of my talon," Grallik said dully. His face and arms were purple with bruises from the pummeling the goblins had given him the previous night. His leg carried an ugly welt where a goblin kicked him because he'd let the goats run away.

Horace had fared worse. The Ergothian favored his left side and held his chin in his hands. His bruises were conspicuous, even on his dark face, his eyelids were swollen. A gash ran from his right ear to his throat, and it was only just crusting.

"Kenosh was a loyal knight," Horace said finally.

"I will miss him. The best of my talon, he was."

The priest let out a sigh. "Perhaps we will join him soon enough, Gray Robe. The plague spreads, and I can do nothing to even slow it down."

Grallik rubbed at the corner of his lip, where an ugly scab was forming. "It was the dwarf village, wasn't it? That's where the plague came from."

"Aye, the spoils from the Cradle were tainted."

The wizard hung his head. "I . . . I am sorry I brought you into this mess, Horace. I was thinking of myself and—"

"No." Horace cocked his head to study the wizard. "The Sea Mother brought me into this situation, Gray Robe.

And if we survive this predicament, it will be because she wills it."

"Wizard!" Direfang shouted from nearby. "Be fast!"

"The Foreman calls," the wizard said with a deep sigh. "So much for this respite." Grallik carefully stood and tested his legs. "Coming, Foreman!" He called forth a familiar spell as he moved, pointing a slender finger at the black willow and closing his eyes when a gout of flame shot down to catch the top of the tree. "Burning the dead, as you requested, Foreman Direfang."

Before the sun chased the blush from the sky, the tree and all the bodies beneath it had turned to ash.

24

HALF OF THE ARMY

Horace was becoming increasingly familiar with the goblin tongue, though he continued to stumble over some of the words.

"My healing skills are considerable," the priest told the gathering in occasionally halting speech. "But I cannot stop the ravages of this plague. The dwarf village was thick with the disease, and you carried it away with you. You wear it on the clothes you took, the blankets, the shoes, you eat it in the food you stole from the homes. We should have realized something was amiss when the population of the Cradle seemed so small."

He paused. "And now your numbers are dwindling as well."

There were reeds along that stretch of river, dry with the summer, and when the wind gusted, they clattered like finger bones shaken in a pot. Horace listened to the rustling reeds for a moment and dropped his gaze to a patch of ground, black from blood that dying goblins had coughed up.

"I don't know why some of us have been spared," he continued, stepping forward to stand next to Direfang. "We should separate from those already sick. To help stop the spread." For the most part, that had already been done; there was a dividing line, a crack in the ground that ran

195

perpendicular to the river and stretched toward a copse of birch trees. "I will continue to minister to the sick ones, at the very least to ease their passing. And when the plague has run its course, we can move on."

Saro-Saro was not among the sick. He strode up to Direfang, chest thrust out importantly; Pippa followed at his side. He glowered at the priest and tipped his chin up.

"This clan will not stay here and risk the sickness. We will not listen to the skull man." He waved imperiously to indicate all the yellow-skinned goblins behind him. "This clan will not die, nor will the Flamegrass goblins. This clan—all the clans—will leave today."

"Saro-Saro should lead!" Pippa cried. It was the first time any goblin had so openly questioned Direfang's authority. "Direfang must step aside! It is time for Saro-Saro!"

A swell of protest rose from those loyal to Direfang, but chants of "Saro-Saro" rose in volume as well.

"Lead, then!" Direfang spit, jabbing a finger at Saro-Saro and nearly toppling the old goblin over with his vehemence. "Take the damnable task. And take whoever will follow. Die on the march along the river." The hobgoblin's face was slick with anger.

"Not *whoever* will follow," Saro-Saro shot back. "All!"

Horace nervously backed away from the arguing goblins, finding Grallik sitting on the slab of slate on the riverbank. The priest sat next to the wizard, closing his eyes and concentrating on the rustling of the dry reeds, so difficult to hear over the chatter.

"It is good, Gray Robe, that you do not speak their language. The words are ugly and troublesome today," Horace whispered.

Grallik nodded, pricking his ears, trying to pick out the few words he could understand.

Pippa had pushed her way up close to Direfang and stood there, next to Saro-Saro, glaring at the hobgoblin leader.

"It is good that Direfang does not want to lead," Pippa declared smugly. "Good that Direfang is stepping aside without a fight. Direfang lives that way. The weak way. Direfang does not have to die so that strong Saro-Saro can lead."

DEATH MARCH

The hobgoblin's supporters also pressed forward, sticking their angry faces close to members of Saro-Saro's clan and the Flamegrass clan. Direfang felt detached from the argument, wishing that Saro-Saro would just leave and take all the goblins with him. He thought of Mudwort and searched the gathering for the shaman, finally seeing her and Boliver well to the north, hands thrust into the earth and paying no attention to the disturbance.

Pippa had climbed on the shoulders of a Flamegrass goblin and was raising her fist in the air. "Saro-Saro leads!"

"Leads where?" shouted a red-skinned goblin called Skakee. She was young, born in the slave pens, and she'd worked all her shifts under Direfang. "Saro-Saro leads the clans to the Abyss?"

"Leads where?" more goblins shouted; some of them had never liked the insolent Pippa, others were simply curious to know where Saro-Saro was going to take them if he was becoming the leader.

"South!" Saro-Saro proclaimed decisively. The throng quieted down to hear him. Even his opponents stopped to listen. "Away from here and the sickness. Together the clans will build a nation."

"With Saro-Saro as its king!" Pippa cried.

Horace shook his head and whispered to Grallik. "Gray Robe, if they leave now, they will spread this plague to cities to the south. Nor can they march very far with so many of them sick."

The wizard shook his head ruefully. "Look at them. *Really* look at them. I don't have to understand their language to understand what's going on. It's some kind of clan rivalry. The yellow ones seem to prefer that old goblin as their leader."

"He's called Saro-Saro," Horace supplied.

"But there are not so many in the clans that support him. Most of the goblins and hobgoblins stand with the foreman, and I think they will wait for the illness to pass. Some are too tired and sick to go. Most will stay and not spread this damnable disease."

The priest was staring at Pippa. She herself had just started coughing and raised her fist to cover her mouth.

Black spots showed under her arm. The goblin she stood upon coughed also.

"Soon there will be fewer on both sides, Gray Robe," Horace said, agreeing with Grallik. "Another clan of goblins joined this mob this morning. But soon nothing will matter for many of them."

The debate continued to rage, Direfang standing in the midst of the clans, arms crossed indifferently over his chest with his gaze locked most of the time on Mudwort and Boliver. The hobgoblin answered a few questions from time to time. But for the most part, he remained quiet and neutral, just listening to others.

Horace pointed to Direfang, speaking almost admiringly. "The foreman dreams, I think, of being away from all of this."

Grallik studied a tear in the leather along one tip of his boot. "I never envisioned this disaster when we left Steel Town," he said softly. "I, too, had dreams. I thought I would learn goblin magic, and it would benefit us all. Just yesterday I thought I had convinced Foreman Direfang that I knew a faster route to the Qualinesti Forest. I still believed we could escape all these problems."

Horace raised an eyebrow. "Your home, yes, the forest?"

"The home of my youth. By the sea," Grallik admitted. "I was going to find a way to get us all there, safely."

Horace stood. "The sea." He shifted back and forth on the balls of his feet. "Zeboim's element. Yes, I see now. There would be hope and promise in that path. I must talk to the foreman." He pushed his way through the squabbling goblins to reach Direfang.

A fire burned steadily for the next several days as goblin corpses were burned, remains scattered, and ceremonies held to honor the dead. So many had sickened in the meantime that the talk of leaving and of Saro-Saro leading was almost forgotten.

Pippa, Saro-Saro's main cheerleader, was one of those who died fastest.

"Pippa is remembered," Saro-Saro declared at the naming ceremony. "Pippa was loyal and smiled and chattered loudly often. Pippa loved Spikehollow."

"Pippa is remembered," Skakee repeated. "Pippa will be reborn healthy and far from this sad place."

Direfang had seen too many dead bodies burned. He did not directly participate in the ceremony that included Pippa, though even he hovered at the edge of the crowd and listened respectfully.

"Bignose is remembered. An old one, Bignose was born in the Before Time. Good that Bignose died free."

"Zeek is remembered. Zeek bragged and scratched in the dirt. Remember bragging Zeek."

"Urknor feared storms and the volcanoes. Urknor ate worms and grubs and rarely shared. Urknor is remembered."

"Bosti is remembered. Bosti lied often, and Bosti stole. But Bosti fought well and killed two Dark Knights in Steel Town. Bosti the Brave Liar is remembered."

The names of the some of the dead were unknown, particularly those from clans that had recently joined with the goblins from the rebellion, and the dead ones from new clans were honored with speeches about the march through the mountains and about how good it was to die outside of Steel Town and so far from the hated iron mine.

"Kenosh is remembered too." Horace murmured those words aloud, but he stood well away from the goblins, praying to Zeboim at the riverbank. He prayed for Kenosh, but he also prayed for the souls of the dead goblins; mostly he prayed for himself and Grallik, whose fates would be grim if left to the whim of Saro-Saro.

Roughly half of the goblin force had died to the plague in less than a week, and not quite one thousand remained. Some of the survivors had caught the disease and recovered, but Horace took no credit for that. It was a mystery why some few recovered, while most died. Some still carried hints of the disease, in their coughs and black spots, but their symptoms had not worsened.

And so Direfang finally had declared it was time to move on.

"Follow Saro-Saro," he said after that last naming ceremony, raising his voice so all heard him clearly. "Saro-Saro can be the leader now." The hobgoblin then struck off to the south without another word, Mudwort and Boliver loping behind him. After a moment's hesitation, Grallik and Horace headed out too, the latter praying fervently to Zeboim that Saro-Saro's clan members would not claim them and keep them from following Direfang.

To the humans' surprise, nearly all the goblins fell in line behind them, still arguing about who should lead and where they should go. Less than one hundred lagged behind, clustered around Saro-Saro and proclaiming their steadfastness to the yellow-skinned goblin.

Yet as the main force of goblins continued to move farther away, more and more of Saro-Saro's clan peeled off and hurried to join the larger body. In the end even the old goblin and the handful of his most loyal supporters grudgingly joined the mass movement. They wore angry, contemptuous expressions.

"Direfang must die," one of Saro-Saro's clansmen muttered. "That is only solution to Direfang."

"Yes," the old goblin agreed. "Yes, indeed."

Direfang had not expected all the goblins to follow him, but looking over his shoulder, he accepted the inevitable and slowed his pace to accommodate their shorter legs. He thought about his hundreds of dead kinsmen as he walked, the smell of their burned bodies still thick in his nostrils. And he realized that although he had only half of the army that he'd had before, the burden of leadership, the task of bringing all those goblins to a safe homeland, that job, that responsibility was still heavy.

Another dozen died to the illness before they reached the mouth of the river and stood on the shore of the New Sea—where, to their astonishment, another eighteen clans of goblins were waiting for them.

"The call was answered!" called Thya, an overly tall goblin who rushed forward to meet Direfang. "The shaman's call was heard and answered. We've been waiting for you here. Waiting to join the march to a homeland. Together, goblins will be safe and free."

Direfang shuddered to see the many goblins who rushed forward to meet their new comrades. His following was replaced almost as swiftly as it was depleted, it seemed. The sickness would take some, but not all, of them. Many more would join and continue with the goblins following Direfang. The hobgoblin shook his head. So many goblins following him, following him. Following him where?

25

A FEAST OF GEMS

It was early morning; the sun wasn't yet up, and the sky was a pale gray contrast to the dark waters of the inland sea. Many of the goblins busied themselves socializing with the new clans while filling the bottles they'd taken from the glass tree with river water. Others were staring mutely at the sea. No one had ever seen so much water.

"This is a young sea," Horace explained, his face beaded with sweat. He still hadn't recovered his strength; his healing was still in demand. "At least as far as the entire history of the world is concerned, it is young. It was born when the Kingpriest of Istar demanded too many things of the gods. Angered by his insolence, they raised some land masses and sank others. Ansalon's most beautiful plains were among the places the gods drowned with the Sirrion Ocean. The people named the divinely created water the New Sea."

Horace took a deep breath and let the air out slowly. "The dragons have played a part in the formation of this sea too. A section of the eastern part of the New Sea became a swamp, thanks to the great black dragon they called Sable. They say Sable is dead now, and so the swamp slowly is retreating. The New Sea will grow larger again. It is a few thousand feet deep in some places, difficult to navigate in others, particularly where it brushes

202

the great swamp with its tribes of bakali and other lizard-folk."

Horace waded out into the water, Grallik nearby the hobgoblin following both of them closely, listening skeptically.

Direfang scowled. "Keep all those words in the human tongue, skull man. Some clans might not cross this New Sea after learning how deep it is . . . and how dangerous." He looked to the goblins near the shore. "Some will not even come into the shallows to try to lose the plague. And look how many foolish goblins there are now."

"Easily three thousand, I'd wager." The priest's expression grew troubled as he noticed Saro-Saro and a few dozen of his clansmen clustered well back from the shore. But he turned back to stare at the sea. His expression turned serene; he bowed his head and traced a symbol in the air. "I feel the Sea Mother's presence," he said. "Zeboim's breath gently stirs the waves."

Some goblins near them spat at the mention of Zeboim, but Horace and Grallik and Direfang waded farther out, while behind them, a handful of goblins tentatively entered the water.

"May the last vestiges of the plague be washed from all of us. Cleanse us, Sea Mother." Horace traced another symbol in the stirring surf, his fingers playing along the top of the water. Then he closed his eyes and prayed at length. Grallik, too, bowed his head, though he was not given to praying even in the most dire times.

Direfang motioned for other goblins to join the priest in the shallows. Some refused, terrified at the immenseness of the New Sea. They huddled in groups on the shore, watching as, gradually, more and more of their fellows edged out until the waves sloshed around their waists. Some of them playfully slapped at the water.

Grallik's eyes sought out Mudwort. The shaman was one of the hesitant ones, he noted, wrinkling her nose and looking around for Boliver. But he was already out in the water. She raised her lip in a brave snarl and stepped from the shore until the water rose around her ankles, then her knees, and finally her waist. She felt the pouches at her side shift in the current, and she placed her hands on them protectively. A little farther, and the water was up to her chest. She'd go no deeper as she didn't know how to swim.

"Sink," she said with a sneer. "Sink and die and be food for the fishes. Knights would be good food for fishes."

Skakee quickly joined Mudwort, her youthful exuberance apparent; she seemed unafraid. Skakee held her breath and dipped her head in the water, came up and shook herself out, then splashed around and dunked again until Mudwort became annoyed.

Mudwort moved away from the others and peered back at the bank. Saro-Saro and some of his clan members were still huddled there. She couldn't hear their conversation over the lapping water, but she suspected the words were not good. She squinted to study the old goblin, hoping to see him coughing, with black spots on his arms. He'd pose no threat to Direfang if he were dead.

Saro-Saro caught Mudwort staring at him and gave her the evil eye, turning his back so she could not see his face.

Many of the goblins stayed in the water while the priest prayed and continued to trace symbols in the air. Grallik and Direfang waded back to shore and plopped on the ground.

Some risked speaking to Horace, but he ignored their words and dropped to his knees, the water swirling around his chin.

Gulls dipped down, finding small fish along the surface. Their cries were at the same time harsh and musical, and some of the goblins imitated the noise. A bell sounded far off, and Grallik told Direfang it was a ship's bell. Direfang waited to hear more. He knew Grallik knew much about the sea and wanted to talk.

"They say nothing lives below two hundred feet," Grallik said. "It is not that way with all water, but with this body. They say that the depths here are far saltier and colder and hide caverns and all manner of things. But fish are plentiful near the surface."

"You know this how?" asked Direfang.

"I traveled it once, when I was young, and the captain talked a lot. I guess I paid attention." Looking out, he saw that

Horace had finished his praying; he was splashing seawater on his face, coaxing the goblins to do the same. "I disembarked at a Dark Knight outpost to the west. And I haven't seen this sea or any other for nearly forty years."

Direfang grunted. Probably that was interesting talk for humans, but not for him.

"My plan, Foreman," Grallik began hesitantly. "The one I mentioned to you earlier. Perhaps we should speak of it now."

"It is impossible now." Direfang's eyes were dark and sad, and his brow deeply furrowed. "Too many goblins. All of it impossible." The hobgoblin let out a deep breath, a sigh that was almost a moan.

Grallik was taken aback. The hobgoblin suddenly seemed so lost, so uncertain. He opened his mouth to say something, but Direfang waved his words away.

"There is a shorter way to the Qualinesti Forest." Direfang gazed at the water, straining to see an opposite shore. He looked east, where the mountains curved around the New Sea and led to ogre country and the swamp . . . eventually, if his recollection of maps was correct, that path would lead to the Plains of Dust.

"Yes, the shorter way you spoke of before." Grallik gestured west, and the hobgoblin followed his gesture with his eyes, sweeping the shoreline. "It is not impossible, Foreman. Difficult, oh yes, very difficult. But it is not impossible. Not if—"

Just then, at the edge of his vision far down the shoreline, Direfang made out the silhouettes of buildings and ships.

"Mudwort!" the hobgoblin stood and called. "Mudwort, be fast!"

"Yes," Grallik said, noticing Direfang's concern. "You'd best move these goblins back behind the trees. Wouldn't do for a ship to see thousands of goblins so close to that town. Might spook the people and rouse whatever passes for a local militia. You don't need a fight. Oh, you very well could conquer the town with these numbers, but then trouble would come looking for you."

Direfang yelled again for Mudwort. Eventually, she came out of the water and drew near. He pointed to her pouches. The red-skinned goblin bristled; her pouches were none of the hobgoblin's business.

"Give me one," he barked.

"Direfang notices too much," Mudwort hissed. She untied a pouch, the one she guessed had the faceted blue stones in it. She liked the uncut ones better. "Here." She tossed the pouch, which was sodden, to him.

"One more," he said. "Hand it over."

She growled but complied, again giving him one with faceted stones.

"The rest belong to Mudwort, probably," Direfang said.

Her nostrils flared and her eyes narrowed to thin slits, showing her displeasure. They all belonged to Mudwort was the way she looked at it, and Direfang only got what she gave to him.

The wizard watched the exchange with undisguised fascination. Direfang opened one of the sodden pouches and took out one of cut stones. He showed it to the wizard before putting it back in the pouch and addressing Mudwort. "You want to go to the Qualinesti Forest, don't you? Getting there will cost these gems."

Direfang passed the sodden pouches to the wizard. "Men value these. Tell me, then: Is this enough to pay for passage on a ship for everyone? For three thousand?"

"It will take more than one ship." The wizard opened the two pouches and could not hide his astonishment at the number and variety of stones. The wet gems caught the morning light and sparkled. "But yes, these should be enough," he said, knowing full well it was far more than enough. "Enough for passage and supplies. See, Foreman? I told you it was not impossible."

"Supplies." Direfang nodded. "Passage and much food. It will take an awful lot of food." The hobgoblin paused. "And this passage you speak of . . ."

Grallik rubbed at his chin and hefted the pouches filled with stones. "Foreman, I will have to go to the town and make the arrangements; I will have to bring the ships to you. It wouldn't do for three thousand goblins to march into that town and—"

Boliver came up, slogging toward the three of them, eyeing Direfang. He caught on quickly; he knew the human tongue, having learned it by listening in Steel Town, as Direfang had.

"Direfang, the wizard and the skull man cannot be trusted to go into that town." Boliver drew in a deep breath and looked to the shore, where Saro-Saro was still huddled with his clansmen. "The wizard and the skull man will escape from us and—"

Mudwort tapped Boliver on the arm. "The wizard—Grallik—will return, Boliver. I know this. He has his reasons to return." She looked hard at Grallik, who nodded.

"I promise to return," Grallik said.

"The wizard has to come back," Mudwort added softly to Boliver, "because the wizard wants to learn stone magic."

Boliver raised an eyebrow, still looking dubious.

"The skull man will stay here with us," Direfang commanded. "Only the wizard goes. Another reason for him to return, loyalty to his friend." He glanced at Mudwort, seeking some approval of his strategy.

"Already told you, Direfang," she huffed. "The wizard will come back. The wizard will arrange passage and lots of food." She touched her ragged tunic. "And clothes, Grallik. Passage and food and clothes. Make sure that you bring a lot of clothes."

"These blue gems will buy those things." He gently shook the pouches.

"Yes, clothes," Horace agreed. He had silently joined them, the priest's bare chest glistening. The water on his face had dried, leaving behind traces of salty white powder. "I should be the one who goes into the town, you know. I am more familiar with ships and sailors—and with contracts. I am certain—"

"But the wizard is willing to go," Direfang said. "And he has the best reasons to return. Mudwort believes that."

"Indeed," Grallik said. He drew his head back and

watched a *V* of birds flying east toward the mountains. "I will go right away. Perhaps I will be able to return by this evening," Grallik said. "If I have managed to find suitable ships by then."

Direfang growled. "Need those ships right away, wizard."

Grallik shook his head. "I said I would bring the ships to you, but I don't think that's a wise thing to do in daylight. First I'll make the arrangements." His gaze swept over the many goblins who still bobbed in the shallows. "Too many ships on the sea then, too many eyes in that port. You will have to trust my judgment."

Direfang snorted but said nothing.

"Meanwhile," suggested Horace, following Grallik's eyes, "perhaps we should retreat to the cover of trees."

Boliver spoke up harshly. "No. Leave the goblins in the sea while the Gray Robe is gone. Leave them in as long as they can stand it, Foreman Direfang. Until their skin looks withered like prunes and they can't feel their toes. Let us hope the water washes away the plague. But they are happy now. Let them be happy. Leave them in until ships come this way and force them to hide."

"Yes, happy goblins," said Mudwort, who was already tired of their tedious discussion. "That is good."

Direfang nodded, looking over toward Saro-Saro, who still refused to enter the water. He was closer at that time and couldn't help but notice that the goblin had a black spot on the underside of one arm, and a bump was forming on his neck.

26

Grallik's Day in Port

Grallik weathered the hostile stares of Saro-Saro's clan as he headed to the shore and turned west, toward the town in the distance. As he approached, he could see that the town was larger than he first thought, built on a low hill and apparently sectioned into estates. The harbor was extensive, and so many dozens of masts stood out against the sky that Grallik did not try to count all the ships.

He was pleased for the opportunity to leave the smelly, noisy horde of goblins behind for a while. That was his first taste of freedom since joining Direfang's army.

He pulled off his boots and walked barefoot in the sand. His sore feet still ached and were riddled with blisters that he doubted would ever fully heal. After half a mile he threw the well-worn boots into the sea. The uncut gems in the pouches would buy him the best boots in the town—would buy him anything.

He couldn't help but smile.

Another man, even Horace no doubt, would have absconded with the gems and booked passage on a ship, fled the damnable goblins, whose number seemed to multiply at every turn, leaving them all behind, stranded at the mouth of the river. Horace might even believe that Zeboim had gifted him with the gems and freedom. But Mudwort was

209

right. She knew Grallik would return, hoping she would share her magic. And because Direfang trusted Mudwort, the wizard had been given the task and allowed that blissful time alone.

"I really should leave them all," he mused. "Forget the magic the little red goblin casts. Live like a prince." But he knew he would do as he had promised. Magic meant more to him than the gems. And the magic that Mudwort practiced was priceless.

"Where did that goblin get all of these gems?" Reorx's Cradle, of course, he realized, thinking it over. No one in Steel Town possessed such valuables. And she had more. Grallik had seen the two other pouches at her waist. "That little monster has a fortune."

Away from the goblins, the air smelled better; it was salt-tinged from the sea and redolent of fish. The sea air was such a welcome change that Grallik breathed as deeply as he could.

The early sky was empty of clouds and growing bluer as the sun peeked farther over the horizon. The breeze was faint and came from the west, bringing with it a hint of baking bread. The wizard's stomach rumbled.

"New boots," he said. "A warm meal and wine. New clothes and . . . clothes . . ."

He examined his threadbare undertunic, which was stained, ripped, and bloody. His hair was matted and filthy, and the stubble on his face was thick. If, looking like that, he approached any shopkeeper in whatever passed for the town's merchant district, if he sought out any ship's captain, any sane person would think him a beggar. If he presented even a single gem to buy something, they would most certainly declare him a thief, call the watch, and throw him in a dungeon. They would confiscate the fortune he carried.

"A raggedy, raggedy man I am," he said, almost merrily, thinking over the problem. "Whatever to do about it?"

He skirted the waterfront and slipped down an alley between a rickety tavern and a bait shop. He hugged the wall and waited, his mind whirling. He smelled garbage; enough of it was piled outside the tavern's side door. But he also smelled cinnamon, and he scanned the street beyond and spotted a bakery. Again his stomach growled. It hadn't taken him long to walk there, and it was still so early that not many people were walking around. Behind him, toward the dock, sailors and fishermen had begun working on their boats, and smaller ships were putting out to sea. But toward the heart of the city, people were just waking up—or still slept.

Grallik waited.

Minutes later a merchant strolled past the corner where he was crouched, and the wizard was quick to act.

"Good sir!" Grallik remained tucked in the alley but reached out a hand and motioned to the stranger.

The merchant stopped and stared, made a move to keep going, then held his place when he saw Grallik hold up something that caught the light.

"I'll part with this gem for some coins, good sir."

The merchant edged closer, gazing down the street to his right and left, then looking back toward Grallik and peering behind him to make sure no one else hid, waiting in the alley.

"I've need of some coins, good sir." Grallik didn't have to work very hard to get an edge of desperation in his voice. "Help me out. I beg you."

The merchant's eyes gleamed. Greed, Grallik recognized. Finally, the man came close, and Grallik handed him one of the smaller gemstones.

"How did you come by this?" The merchant stared. "A sapphire."

"Yes, it is a sapphire. I've more." Grallik stepped deeper into the alley where the shadows were especially thick.

The merchant hesitated only a moment then followed Grallik. A few minutes later, Grallik was donning the merchant's jacket and trousers and shoving the man's singed body behind the mound of tavern refuse in the alley. Flies, momentarily disturbed, were quick to swarm anew. Grallik put on the merchant's boots, finding them tight and hurtful. He clutched the man's coin pouch and jangled it.

"A fairly wealthy man, were you?" The jacket was of

fine material, yet it was old; the same for the trousers. "You should have spent some of your coin on clothes." Grallik adjusted the shirt and closed the jacket over a burned patch on the chest; Grallik had been forced to aim his fire spell at the man's heart. He looked inside the pouch. "My, my. This will certainly do. You wouldn't spend your coins on clothes, but I will." The merchant had a cap, so Grallik put it on and tucked his filthy hair up and under.

Making sure the man's body was reasonably well concealed, Grallik stepped out on the street and looked around for a clothier's. The outfit wouldn't suit him for very long; someone might recognize it as belonging to the now-deceased merchant. However, it was better to walk around in than his ruined undertunic.

His gait felt stilted because the boots were so tight. He shuffled past a small district of stone and wood buildings, only a few of them two stories tall. Some were residences; most were businesses, marking the place as a thriving port town. The town seemed to offer a little of everything, and Grallik's next stop was a public bath, where he used the first of the merchant's coins. It wouldn't do to bring out any of the precious sapphires there; just one would have paid for a thousand baths.

He slipped into the warm copper tub and washed the salt and dirt and dried sweat off, allowing his mind to drift for several long minutes as a young woman added perfumed oils and began to cut his hair. He'd enjoyed no such bath in years. He'd been afforded few luxuries in Steel Town, nor in his previous post. Though, in his days with the black-robed wizards, he'd enjoyed plenty of costly unnecessary extravagances.

The woman was speaking to him in a low, musical, pleasant voice, but he paid no attention. Instead, he thought about the red-skinned goblin and her promise to teach him her peculiar earth magic. He had no doubt she would live up to her end of the bargain . . . provided he could help lead the goblin horde to the Qualinesti Forest.

"So long I've been from home," he murmured.

"Pardon, sir?"

He stared at her. She was not as young as he first thought, a little plump, and her nose was crooked. Her eyes seemed too small for her face, but it was a sweet, kind face. And her hair was a dull shade of brown that had been cut too short for his liking.

"A shave too."

She was quick to comply, briefly staring at the scars on the left side of his face as she worked, noticing the scars on his left arm and side as well. His beard had grown unevenly because of all of the scars, and he imagined he looked vile to her.

"You're half-elf, sir." She was trying to make polite conversation, though his scars worried her. "Where are you from?"

He wondered if he should answer honestly. "Steel Town," he said after a few moments. "Iverton."

"I've never heard of that place, sir."

"And no one will ever hear of it again," he said softly.

He closed his eyes and felt the razor continue to move slowly across his cheeks. He ought to purchase a shaving kit—two because Horace would also be pleased to be given one. Grallik decided he would not allow himself to look so unkempt ever again.

He refrained from purchasing the woman's company for anything else, though he was sorely tempted. Perhaps, if there was time later, he would return to that soothing bath house. Perhaps there would even be a more comely and younger woman available.

His next stop was at the finest tailor shop in that part of town, one whose windows displayed completed garments. It had been too many years since Grallik had felt soft, new fabric against his fire-scarred skin. With a dozen coins, he purchased a padded linen shirt with brown trim at the elbows and down the front. The shirt fit too loosely, and the tailor offered to take it in. Grallik had spotted nothing in the shop small enough for his gaunt frame.

"I will grow into it," he mused softly, "when I eat properly again." The breeches were green and stopped at mid-calf, inches above the tops of his too-tight boots. The hoodlike hat he purchased helped to conceal his facial scars and matched the breeches. "Can you refer me to a cobbler? The best in town?"

The tailor was quick to give Grallik directions, and the wizard purchased two more outfits before leaving. He burned his purloined clothes in another alley and replaced the stolen boots at the cobbler's. The new ones were soft leather, dyed a brown so dark that they looked nearly black. They laced up to his knees, where he could tuck his breeches in. He bought a pair of comfortable slippers, three pairs of leather gloves, and a backpack to carry his other clothes, the gloves, and the slippers.

The only thing left before finding passage for the goblins was to fill his stomach.

"The finest place to dine in this neighborhood, please," he told the cobbler.

The recommendation was nearby.

Only minutes later, fruit preserves and fresh cheese were sitting in a polished oak bowl in front of him. Grallik had asked for the table farthest from the door so he could watch the rest of the establishment and inspect all the customers as they arrived. The aroma of the place was intoxicating— from the polishing cream used on the walnut furniture, to the scented candles, to the fruit, to the many delights simmering in the kitchen.

Breakfast was being served, but another dozen coins convinced the cook to whip up more substantial fare. His first course was smoked fish on toast rounds. That was followed by roasted turnips, an onion tart, and sautéed cabbage. He had to wait quite some time for the salomene—the rare, twice-cooked fish in a light sauce, complemented by saffron rice and tiny sausages. His feast ended with sugared pears, wafers, and grape juice.

Grallik staggered from the inn, stuffed and sated. His stomach had so shrunken while in the company of the goblins that he was not used to eating so much. On his way to the docks, he stopped in another alley and leaned against a wall and pressed his hands against his stomach. He fought to keep the rich meal down.

"Horace could have shared it with me. He would have enjoyed it." Grallik moaned. "Too bad he couldn't have joined me on this little adventure." Yet the priest might have objected to killing the merchant for his clothes and coins and for putting personal needs—the bath and the meal—ahead of the main job: seeking passage for the goblins. Grallik thought Horace evinced too many scruples for a Dark Knight. But then, thinking it over, again he wondered whether the priest might have gotten it in his head to bolt with the gems, knightly honor notwithstanding.

Grallik chuckled to himself, despite his stomach discomfort. "We're not Dark Knights any longer, though the goblins still think us such. We're hardly men anymore." Grallik and Horace had left the Knighthood when they left Steel Town. They'd left scruples behind.

They'd left everything.

Grallik looked toward the wharf. It was late morning, he guessed, by the length of the shadows. He couldn't spot the sun from his position. But when he looked up and stared around, he spied gulls circling, their cries mingled with the sounds coming from the docks—ships creaking against timbers, sailors shouting, the clomping of boots against the planks and decks.

The odors of fish and shrimp were strong, and while they were not unpleasant, they made his eyes water. That, coupled with his struggling stomach, was too much. Grallik finally stopped resisting and bent over behind a crate of refuse, retching until he felt better. His throat burned and his mouth was filled with a horrid taste, and he was annoyed with himself to have wasted such a fine meal.

"But there will be at least one more fine meal before I leave," he vowed. And it would not be fish; he had a taste for beef, which he hadn't eaten for a long, long time. Yes, he'd return to that inn or, more likely, another on recommendation. He wasn't about to go back to the goblins without having dined well a second time, as he didn't know when he would ever get such an opportunity again.

Grallik swallowed repeatedly in an attempt to get the sour taste out of his mouth. It helped only a little. He brushed at the front of his new shirt and adjusted it at the waist so the folds were more even. Then he headed down toward the wharves.

The gulls were more plentiful as he drew closer, and they acted braver. They dipped down to snatch crumbs from the street that ran parallel to the shore, and they waddled behind passersby, squawking for treats. Pelicans were perched atop timbers and on the roof of one of the bait shops. All over were barrels of fish being off-loaded from boats just arriving. And every place Grallik looked, he saw men working on sails and rigging, painting trim, and hurrying from ships to the shore and back again.

Grallik felt almost dizzy, drinking it all in. He'd been in port towns only a few times, and those were in years long past. He'd not been so interested in the ships then; he'd preferred the inland for his Dark Knight postings. So he'd never really paid attention before to the activities along the docks. It was a blur of sound and color, and he simply stood and gaped for a time.

If the red-skinned goblin were looking in on him—as he well knew she could do with her seeing spells—he hoped she was watching him right then. He had needed a bath and clothes and something to eat. Then she would see him going about the business of transporting Direfang's followers to the Qualinesti Forest.

Grallik had few fond memories of his former home, and he had never expected to return there. But Mudwort sought something in those woods, and whatever interested her interested him. He steepled his fingers and looked from one ship to the next.

Now *there* was an amazing vessel! The largest in port, it bore four masts with blue pennants flying from the top of each one. There were three crow's nests, with men atop each of them, even though it looked as though the ship were not leaving anytime soon. Grallik walked along a plank sidewalk so he could better see the ship. The *Mercy Corvan,* it was called, and along the top at the back were ornate carvings of horses pulling a man riding in a chariot. The carved man was dressed in a flowing robe; his left shoulder and arm were exposed. Birds with human faces were perched on his arm, all expertly rendered and painted garishly. There were windows rather than portholes, and the glass gleamed like diamonds in the bright sun.

Sailors steadily worked on the deck, some painting rails that looked as if they were in no need of painting. Most of the sailors were dark skinned.

"Ergothians," Grallik said to himself. "Horace's people." The wizard was glad then the priest hadn't come along on his errand. Horace had made it clear he wanted to return home, and that vessel would have lured him. Ergothians were noted for their ship building, and the *Corvan* put the others in port to shame. But what was such a fine, fine ship doing in that small town? Grallik wondered about that, briefly, but knew, more important, that a ship of that impressive size could easily accommodate a significant number of goblins and hobgoblins. That was the ship for him.

Grallik hefted one of the pouches filled with sapphires, about to make his move. Then he hesitated. That particular ship was too . . .

"Perfect," he pronounced. "Too fine and fancy." While it would well suit him—and it would delight Horace—it would be too conspicuous for a cargo of goblins, so he moved on, looking.

Grallik knew nothing about ships other than which ones looked bigger, flashier, or cleaner. He couldn't put a name to the type of any of them. He couldn't guess how fast they'd run, how seaworthy they might be. He knew he was not well suited to his task, while the priest would have been the right man. Ergothians were all sea barbarians, at home on the waves. How Horace got stuck in a desolate, dry mining camp in the middle of Neraka was puzzling. Grallik would have to remember to ask him about that later.

Grallik required several big ships, not just one, anyway; they needn't all be as huge as the *Mercy Corvan*. Again he wondered briefly just what a ship that size was doing in the New Sea, particularly at a town so far to the east. But it wasn't his concern, he decided, so he moved along to the farthest dock west.

"That could do."

The ship he was staring at had a similar form to the *Mercy Corvan*, but it was not as long, and it did not seem to sit as heavy in the water. It boasted three masts, though the sails were down on all of them, and only one pennant, which was blue and white striped and fluttering dog-eared from a post at the back.

"*Clare* could be just one of those I'm looking for."

For that was the ship's name, painted in red, flowing script on the bow. Another name had been initially etched beneath that, but the paint had been scraped off so only a trace of a few gray letters could be seen. The *Clare* was not in the same tip-top condition as the *Corvan;* her paint was peeling on the trim, looking like fish scales baking in the sun. The wood appeared more weathered, lines were frayed here and there. Not as seaworthy, Grallik suspected, but seaworthy enough for the New Sea.

Not so many sailors were busy on her decks, and those he could see were in well-worn clothes.

"Perfect indeed." He headed toward the *Clare.*

The crew looked . . . well, they looked hungry, needy. The ship was definitely in need of funds, and his would be a well-paying venture. There wouldn't be many questions asked, Grallik hoped. And perhaps the sailors would point him to other ships that could be just as easily rented.

"Is the captain here?" Grallik cupped his hand over his eyes and peered up the rail.

"Aye. Whatcha want with 'im?" The sailor who answered was a half-ogre with thick stubble on his chin.

"I'll take that matter up with him," Grallik returned brusquely.

"You'll find 'im in the Tattered Sail," the half-ogre shot back. "Ask for Gerrold."

Grallik remained on the dock for a few more minutes, pacing up and down and giving the *Clare* a closer inspection. She could certainly hold a lot of goblins. Across from the *Clare* rested a ship of similar length and draft called *The Elizabeth,* and next to her, an ungainly looking vessel, obviously a merchantman, called *Linda's Grady.* Would the three be enough? Probably not, he mouthed, recalling an image of all the goblins frolicking in the surf. He glanced around at other ships that were near and far.

"Gerrold is his name," the half-ogre called, rousing Grallik from his reverie.

The wizard nodded and went in search of the tavern, found Gerrold, and made a deal that would put Gerrold in charge of the expedition.

Later in the afternoon, he visited several shops and steadily paid out small sapphires to purchase plenty of barrels of water, one hundred crates of dried meat, sacks upon sacks of fruit, bags of flour, hundreds of chickens—all he could find in town—and a few milking goats, and had all delivered to Gerrold at the *Clare*, who had the rest dispersed among *The Elizabeth, Linda's Grady, Star of Lunitari, Wavechaser, Shinare's Prayer,* and *The Balifor Breeze.*

Six ships, he'd settled on. Well more than enough. Grallik had decided to err on the side of excess in the event one or more of the captains backed out when they laid eyes on their passengers.

Back in the heart of the merchant district, he purchased the entire stock of several clothiers', everything the city's dozen cobblers had, and all the blankets three weavers displayed, along with crates of spun yarn in the hopes some of the goblins could learn how to knit. Rumors flew around the port about the wealthy, scarred half-elf who was buying enough to feed and clothe an entire town. An entire army was more like it, Grallik thought, bemused.

The rumblings made the citizens keep their distance and show him respect, so he did nothing to squelch the rumors.

He took care to find garments and boots that would likely fit Horace and the near seven-foot-tall Direfang. He hoped that would put him in better stead with the irascible hobgoblin leader. The special clothes he ordered wrapped in canvas and tied securely with twine to keep them separate from the rest of the goods.

From listening to the men on the dock, he learned he needed rum to mix with the drinking water in order to keep it from becoming fouled during the journey. So he purchased dozens upon dozens of casks, and he added to that a case of the finest wine the port town offered, on which he scrawled his name.

He returned to the tailor's he'd visited early in the morning and had him sew a secret pocket into his shirt. There he hid some of the fortune remaining—a dozen small sapphires—in the event he needed them at some point in the future.

There were a few more stops: a chandler for cases of candles and oil, which might come in handy; bakers for loaves upon loaves of bread, which would have to be eaten relatively quickly while they were fresh; he doubted that would be a problem; and a blacksmith's for an assortment of tools simply because Grallik thought hammers and nails and such might be useful eventually.

He purchased lanterns, goose-down pillows, wheels of cheese, tins of tobacco, three hundred pounds of hard candy—all that the candy maker had on hand—three hundred tanned cow hides from a merchantman who had just come ashore, and two shaving kits and several bars of soap, which he tucked in his backpack for himself and Horace. He also acquired several maps—of the coast around the New Sea, the Kharolis Mountains, the northern section of the Qualinesti Forest (he could find none of the entire territory), and an old map of what the world had looked like before the Chaos War. He expected Direfang to be quite pleased with the maps.

Finally, he purchased several chests of books; he didn't bother to look at the topics or titles. Grallik had lost all of his precious tomes in the earthquakes in Steel Town; many of them were spellbooks, but some were simply interesting treatises on the Dark Knights, Nerakan history, or tales of the gods. He relished reading and knew Horace did too. And he could justify the books, saying that Direfang himself knew how to read; he might even want to use the books to teach some of the goblins to read also.

One last stop: a cook shop recommended by Captain Gerrold. Exhausted from his extensive shopping expedition, he settled at a table far from the door, a habit he'd picked up in Steel Town's only tavern. His timing was excellent; after the serving girl brought out a plate of bread, soft cheese, and quince marmalade, people started arriving in droves for the evening meal.

Grallik was careful not to eat too much, limiting himself to the venison custard. There were bits of bacon in it, and bacon was something he hadn't enjoyed since his posting to Steel Town. There was also wine, cinnamon, ginger, saffron, dates, and prunes; he savored all the ingredients. He finished his meal with a torte made of ground cherries, cheese, sugar, and rose petals.

"Aye, it will be a long while before I have such divine fare," he told the serving girl. "A glass of wine, and I'll be on my way."

The sun was just setting as he made his way back to the *Clare*. He strode up the plank and greeted Gerrold, giving him the signal to motion for the crew to make ready to leave the port. The other five ships he'd made arrangements with were waiting in the harbor; they would follow the *Clare*. The wind was strong, and the sails snapped and billowed as they were raised.

"Everything's loaded in the holds." That came from the half-ogre Grallik had met earlier. His name, he had learned, was K'lars, and he served as the bosun's mate. "A lot of food, you've bought. All manner of things. Quite a lot of ships you've acquired too."

Grallik stood at the rail, wrapped his long fingers around the wood, and looked up to see the sky full of gulls and blackbirds.

"We're picking up many passengers," Grallik said when he heard K'lars step closer. "Captain Gerrold is well aware of the arrangements."

"And these passengers . . ."

"Just set your course for the mouth of the river to the east. I don't know the name of the river." Grallik hadn't even bothered to ask the name of the town. He knew he could find the town later, though, if he wanted. It would be on one of the maps he had bought.

"All these passengers are waiting there, at the river?"

"Yes," Grallik answered tersely.

"Didn't want to come to town to get on these ships? What's the matter with 'em?"

Grallik had already begun to dislike the half-ogre who was too curious for his own good. He turned and glared at him. "You're being paid to crew this ship," he answered. "Paid better than you ever were paid before. But I'm not paying you to ask questions."

"It's your ship," K'lars admitted, bowing slightly. He walked away, barking orders to the men in the rigging. "These are all your ships."

"Only until we reach the mouth of the river is this my ship," Grallik muttered under his breath. "Then Foreman Direfang will reclaim the leadership of this ship and all the others, for certain."

But K'lars was right. Grallik hadn't simply purchased passage for the goblins. He'd purchased the ships outright.

27

THE BEAR

It was a fat bird with short wings, all of it the color of the earth. An ugly bird, Saarh thought, but it might be tasty, and there looked to be a good amount of flesh on it. She crawled toward the fat bird through ferns damp from the previous night's rain. She took in the smells as she went, appreciating the flowers the best. All along that part of the forest floor were ground-hugging, three-leafed plants with tiny white and red blooms. They were beautiful flowers, though they had settled sourly in her mouth when she tasted them. She was quickly learning what was edible and what was not.

The fat bird was the size of her head, and it was poking at something at its feet. Bugs, probably, she thought. Saarh didn't much care for bugs, but some beetles were all right; the big green and black ones were all right if she was hungry enough.

The bird fluffed its tail, startling her. But Saarh held her position, peering through the fronds and discovering that it wasn't so ugly after all. Its tail was not like that of other forest birds. It was fan shaped, showing black and white stripes. The bird ruffled the feathers around its neck, those the color of mud and looking soft and contrasting sharply with an orange line she hadn't noticed before around its eyes. No doubt the bird was alerted to her presence, because

223

it pawed at the ground nervously, yet it hadn't been spooked so much to make it fly away.

Perhaps what it was nibbling at was too tasty to give up easily, Saarh thought. Or maybe the bird was too fat to spring away and fly. She held her breath and continued to watch the fat bird, marveling at the play of dark colors across its body when a stream of sunlight came through the branches and splashed across it.

A beautiful bird, really, Saarh decided. Pity she was going to have to kill it. The goblin shaman was hungry, but she waited, studying the bird a while longer. It ate a little more of whatever was on the ground in front of it before waddling into a thicket. The light was dim there, the branches directly overhead were tightly woven.

Saarh crawled closer, careful not to make a sound. She held her breath when she caught sight of the bird again. It had settled itself on a patch of tiny twigs and dead leaves, fluffing its feathers and craning its neck around to preen itself. The shaman's keen eyes noticed thick bands of dark yellow on its breast.

It was a beautiful, beautiful bird, which had conveniently made its nest on the ground.

When she was near enough that she could smell it—a musky scent that pleasantly filled her nostrils—Saarh stuck her thumb in the ground and made a clacking sound. The bird spooked that time, jumping off its nest, wings flapping and head bobbing up and down and beak opening. The bird appeared more comical than menacing, and Saarh even giggled a little as she cast a spell.

The bird skittered back and forth in front of its nest, still flapping but not flying away, being protective, and also being totally unaware that the ground was turning to mud around its feet. A moment more and the mud oozed up over its talons then instantly hardened, trapping it.

Saarh stood and brushed the dirt from her hands and stomach, walking toward the terrified, angry, squawking bird and playing with the beads of one of her necklaces as she went. She stopped directly over the bird, admiring its feathers, then grabbed and wrung its neck, tugging the bird free and starting to pluck its feathers.

She set aside the prettiest feathers as she worked, thinking she might make them into another necklace or give them to Brab as a gift. Brab was the crooked-faced goblin who kept closest company with her. He was among the throng of goblins tearing up small trees to fashion them into tools and torches and firewood. He was occupying the entire clan so she could have that precious time alone.

The bird would taste good after being cooked over some of that firewood, but then she would have to share the food. So Saarh ate it raw, careful to pick out its organs, which she thought tasted too salty. When she'd consumed most of the sweet flesh, she set a few strips aside for Brab, wrapping them in maple leaves and tying the small bundle with long strands of grass. The feathers she stuffed into a pouch that dangled from her newest necklace.

Finished with those tasks, she crept toward the nest. She'd not heard any cheeping sounds, so she knew there were no baby birds. She grinned wide when she saw the eggs—eight of them, each about the size of her thumb—a special treat. She sat with her legs protectively wrapped around the nest, one by one picking up the eggs, registering their warmth, then digging a claw into each one so she could break it and suck out the liquid.

Thoroughly sated, she rose and stretched, declaring it a very good morning indeed. She wasn't ready to return to the goblins, though she was curious about their progress. She was more curious about the power she'd sensed in the forest, which was the ultimate reason she'd brought them all there.

She walked west. The air was moist, a carryover from the previous day's deluge. The ground was damp but not muddy. Saarh discovered it was coolest up against the trunk, where the leaves held the summer sun at bay. Between knobby roots, the ground cover was thick with low-growing plants that boasted tiny, teardrop-shaped leaves. They looked so delicate, Saarh hesitated to walk on them.

There were few truly large trees, so Saarh knew the forest was young. But she also knew it could grow into

JEAN RABE

something magnificent; her magic had revealed that to her. She wanted her tribe to grow with the forest. A few trees ahead tilted precariously, nearly blown over in the previous day's storm. She continued walking, seeing one recently felled, the leaves still vibrant, the broken roots sticking out in all directions. Farther along she spotted a tree growing through a wide crack in a big rock. Curious, she touched its bark, feeling bumps and ridges and finding a sap that smelled rich. A tree nearby had stringy pieces of bark that she could pull off in thin strips.

Saarh intended to bring Brab that way later and show him the amazing plants. She stopped when something chattered at her. An unfamiliar sound, she tipped her head back and searched through the branches.

The creature making the noise was small and looked vaguely ratlike. She'd seen plenty of rats before, but this one was light brown, its tail incredibly bushy. Its small ears were pressed forward against the sides of its head, and it held a nut in its front paws.

Saarh watched it while it chattered loudly and scampered back and forth, putting the nut in its mouth so that one side of its face bulged.

"Scolding." She realized the creature was angry that she had intruded into its territory. "Maybe tasty." Saarh enjoyed cooked rats. But she patted her full stomach and moved along.

She came to another fallen tree large enough to sit on. Black bugs the size of her little finger scampered across the rotting wood, and she noted the small footprints of animals that likely lived beneath the log. A small tree had sprouted from the dead one, and Saarh thought that odd; all the other trees she'd seen grew from the earth. She shook her head. No, not all the trees, there had been that tree growing through the rock.

"Trees are amazing," she said. "Better than the stone of the caves."

There were thorny plants in that section of the woods and ones with supple stems and white, fist-sized flowers. More flowers, purple ones with yellow centers, grew on vines that hung from high branches. Tall grasses grew everywhere, and Saarh spotted a clump that had been chewed on by some creature. When she returned to the tribe, she intended to tell Brab to gather a party and explore, collecting plants and determining which were edible. And they'd catch insects, too, and learn which were the most tasty.

"A good home," she pronounced, pleased that she had brought the goblins out of the caverns and to a place so abundant with space and food and good smells. "And a safe one."

She'd seen no sign of dwarves or umber hulks—both races she was familiar with and hated. In significant numbers, they could threaten her tribe. During previous trips she'd not spotted anything in the woods that might pose a problem. It was a place where apparently even young-lings could wander freely.

"A powerful place." She'd been walking west because the arcane pulse that drew her out of the caverns still emanated from that direction. She hoped to find the source of that pulse that day. If it was too far away, she'd have to return to the tribe and move them in that direction. But she hoped that would not be necessary.

Saarh hadn't traveled more than another mile before something else drew her attention. She'd never heard such a noise before, a "maaawww" that reverberated throughout the clearing she had entered. It sounded powerful, maybe fierce, but it wasn't associated with the arcane thing she was seeking.

"What is it? What, what, what?" She headed toward the *maaawww*ing sound, veering a little to the south. She cursed herself for always being so curious, but she knew she would not be able to go on without finding the source of the sound.

A dozen steps later, and through a gap in some small flowering bushes, Saarh saw the *maaawww*ing beast.

"A bear."

She'd seen a few in her younger years in the high caves in the mountain. She figured they were creatures of the range, and she'd not thought to find them in the woods.

It was not terribly large, no more than the weight of four grown goblins, so she thought it might be a youngling. It had caught a small deer and had its snout stuck in its belly, feasting.

Saarh thought the young bear was a magnificent creature, with thick fur the color of mud, but silvery on the ends around its neck and hindquarters. It raised its head, blood dripping from its jaws, and made the *maaawww*ing sound again. It had a short, stubby tail, like the cave bears she'd seen, and a muscular hump on its shoulders. Its legs rippled as it tore into the deer more fiercely.

She'd seen enough, and she'd tell Brab about the sighting. But it was back to business; she promised herself no more distractions. She had started to withdraw when a throaty growl sounded, so loud that she felt the ripples of it against the bottoms of her feet. It was accompanied by a crashing sound and the appearance of a second bear, easily five times the size of the first.

Saarh stood rooted in awe. Terror seized her when she realized the great bear was charging straight at her. The shaman acted instinctively. She raised her right arm toward the clouds while dropping to a crouch and thrusting her fingers into the earth. The sky crackled with energy, and lightning flickered down, a thin bolt striking the large bear and another striking the top of a spindly oak. The ground surged around her fingers and churned outward in a growing ripple that turned to a mound right in front of the bear.

The creature reared in pain from the lightning. Saarh could feel its heart, hammering so wildly, she thought it would burst. She called down another bolt, which whipped its neck. The bear was knocked aside. The stench of burned flesh and fur filled the air, along with the smell of something acrid that the lightning had left behind.

Its claws were nearly as long as Saarh's forearm, and she knew if the bear took a swipe at her, it would slay her instantly. Its head was round and large, its mouth filled with wicked, white teeth that flashed and sparkled because of the lightning. The creature's growl had turned into a whimper of pain, however, as it slumped forward on the mound of earth Saarh had summoned.

Behind it, the smaller bear made a mewling sound, looking to its dead parent, then staring at the goblin. It raised its bloodstained lips and thundered forward. Saarh sent out another ripple of earth, that one uprooting a small tree and sending it into the small bear's path. It only slowed the creature, but that was enough time for her to call down a final bolt of lightning to slay it.

Above, the sky darkened and lightning flickered in the thick clouds. Saarh's magic had touched off another storm. As the wet drops started to fall, she shook out her hands, stood, and turned east.

Finding the source of the arcane pulse would have to wait. She needed to return to her tribe and direct them there. No use letting the bear carcasses go to waste; they would feed plenty of her people.

Mudwort sat in the sand, the waves surging in to cover her legs, then the water retreating and taking some of the beach with it. Her hands were thrust down at her sides, fingers buried and senses far from the shore of the New Sea, observing Saarh.

She was upset that Saarh had not found the arcane something that was drawing her westward. But at the same time, she was captivated by the shaman's ability to pull lightning out of the clouds. Had the shaman not tarried and found the bears, Mudwort might not have learned about such wonderful magic.

Mudwort released the image and tugged her hands free of the sand. The seeing was no longer interesting. She had no inclination to watch Saarh retrieve the goblin tribe and watch them all devour the bears. But she would look in on the shaman later.

Mudwort looked up at the sky. There were thick white clouds up there, just as there had been over the Qualinesti Forest in her vision. Some had gray bellies full of water. She concentrated, her brow wrinkling in a painful-looking expression. She could send her senses so easily into the earth and across time. Could she, she wondered for the first time, also send her senses skyward?

Mudwort had never been taught magic, as she knew the Dark Knight wizard had. She accidentally learned of her arcane ability years earlier, shortly after being captured by the ogres and sold to work in Steel Town. During long hours in the mines, she started imagining that the stone was talking to her. At first she thought she was going mad. The goblins around her thought so too, telling everyone she had a sour mind. But eventually Mudwort discovered that the stone really was speaking, not exactly in the way one goblin talks to another, but conveying emotions and impressions.

She steadily and secretly honed her skills, learning to sense where the richest veins of ore were, discovering places where the stone was either weak or especially strong, and finally discovering how to send her senses through the stone to scry on other places and creatures. Mingling her magic with others, such as Boliver, came later, as did moving the earth to dig holes.

Could she work with the sky the way she worked with the earth?

Finally she felt the cloud swirl around her, though she still sat firmly on the sand. Her head throbbed from the effort; it felt like needles were stabbing at her eyes. New magic always affected her that way. However, there was always pain before the reward. Her spine tightened and her arms locked, and for an instant she couldn't breathe. But in the same instant, she felt an odd energy, and she wrapped her thoughts around that energy and tugged.

The cloud directly overhead flickered with silvery threads of light.

She tugged harder, grinding her teeth together and straining as if she were chained and trying to break free. She tugged again and again and watched the silvery threads thicken and flash.

Mudwort couldn't say how long her mind played with the energy in the cloud—hours maybe, as the clouds shifted to the east and she grew increasingly fatigued and achy. Goblins milled around her, curious about she was doing. Some asked her questions, but she couldn't take time to answer them and risk losing her hold on the new magic. They eventually ambled away, muttering to themselves, some returning later only to leave again.

One of the bolts flashed strongly as it arced down and stopped just short of the water. A boom of thunder followed, and Mudwort fell back, her energy sapped and breath returning. An acridness assailed her nostrils, the same scent she'd registered in her seeing spell after Saarh pulled down a bolt.

It was the scent that had hung in the air in Steel Town when the clouds overhead danced with lightning but failed to follow with rain.

The surf swirled over Mudwort's legs and chest and retreated. She listened to the surf shushing, the splashing noises of younglings playing in the water, goblin conversations both in the sea and up on the bank, and human words that she couldn't wholly understand. The latter were being uttered by the priest, who was praying to his insipid god again.

Mudwort pushed herself back into a sitting position just as the surf rushed in again. Her shoulders and upper arms itched, and she saw a white powder on her dry skin and on the little of her tunic that was dry—salt from the sea. Maybe, indeed, the sea was chasing away the last bit of the deathly sickness.

Mudwort stood and waded out to her waist, bracing herself when a small wave came in and tried to knock her over. She was tired of being wet and suspected all the goblins still in the sea were tired of it, save the younglings. But more than her dislike of the sea, she didn't want to catch the plague. She had too many other things to do, such as learning better how to pull the lightning from the clouds.

It was midafternoon, and there had been no sign of the wizard since he left. She remembered him saying he hoped to be back in the evening, after arranging a way to sail them across the New Sea. She knew Direfang was a little skeptical the wizard would return. But she knew he craved her magic too desperately, so he would come back. He was taking a long time.

She sloshed her way farther out, spotting Direfang standing alone, the water up to his chest. She wouldn't go out that far, but she'd get closer to him and attract his attention. She'd show him that she could tug lightning from the clouds. She would practice her new spell until either the wizard returned or she became too exhausted.

Then she would learn how to use the wizard's fire.

Earth magic first. Sky magic soon. Next, fire magic. Her eyes glimmered darkly with the promise of gaining more magic.

No, she decided at the last moment, turning back toward shore; she wouldn't show Direfang her new magic. That would be her secret and her surprise. Perhaps she would show him later.

28

Grallik's Armada

Twilight had claimed the sky by the time the *Clare* and the other five ships neared the mouth of the river. They didn't sail too close to the shore as, even with high tide, the captains were uncertain of the depths.

"Lower the longboats," Gerrold ordered.

There were four on the *Clare,* and Grallik guessed each would hold twenty or so goblins, which meant several trips would be necessary for that ship alone. *Linda's Grady* was the largest of the ships, with a full dozen longboats going over the sides.

Grallik had waited until the last possible moment before informing the Captain Gerrold about the true nature of the passengers he was about to pick up, giving the man a sapphire and promising him another when all the goblins were on board.

"I didn't sign on for goblins," Gerrold said irritably, rubbing his chin. "But I knew this would not be a normal run. Not with us coming here at night, and not after being paid so well. I suspect Captain Ghanger knew something odd was happening too." He referred to the captain of the big merchantman, a sea elf who spent as much time over the side as on the deck. "And I know damn well R'chet had to be suspicious—not that he'd object, given what you're paying."

233

"I paid well," Grallik echoed. "I bought these ships."

Gerrold wasn't the owner of the *Clare,* but earlier in the day he'd pointed Grallik to a wealthy merchant who owned her and three of the other ships he had engaged. The merchant was willing to part with the *Clare* for seven of the stones—a price Grallik considered outrageous, but in the end he handed them over. The rest of the ships commanded similar prices. Owning the ships would guarantee the sailors would have no choice but to accept the "cargo." The *Clare* and the others could be sold later, though no doubt at a loss, at some port town near the forest where they were headed, though Grallik hoped Direfang might see the wisdom in keeping at least one.

The wizard kept the existing crews after changing fifteen more sapphires for steel pieces and distributing them evenly among the veteran seafarers. The pay was many times over what the sailors would have earned otherwise for a voyage to the Qualinesti Forest—or to anywhere else in the world for that matter. He hoped that steel would buy their loyalty, although he expected plenty of grumbling and complaints when the goblins materialized.

"Lower all of them," Gerrold barked his commands. "Our . . . *passengers* . . . gentlemen, are goblins. No questions. No arguments."

But there were arguments, of course, fast and heated ones, and the captain let them run their course for several minutes before silencing the sailors with a violent gesture. Grallik decided to accompany the longboats and climbed in the first one over the side.

"We've been compensated well to take the goblins on. The owner of our fair *Clare,*" he nodded toward Grallik, "has been more than generous. We certainly can stomach the foul beasties for a few weeks. No worse than hauling cattle, gentlemen. And he's promised they'll not be too much trouble."

Oh, they'll be some trouble, I suspect, Grallik thought as his longboat touched the water.

Bosun's mate K'lars commanded that longboat. The half-ogre shielded his thick brow with his hand and peered toward the river's mouth. The clouds were high and thin, so the moonlight revealed the army of goblins gathered on the shore. K'lars growled softly deep in his throat.

"Goblins," he muttered. "Rats what walk on two legs, they are."

"Why are we hauling 'em to the Qualinesti Forest?" one of the oarsmen asked. "What's wrong with the woods over there?" He gestured to the trees west of the river.

"What's wrong with the mountains?" asked another. "Or the Abyss, for that matter? And why'd you need so many ships for 'em?"

Grallik didn't reply.

"By the gods!" K'lars shouted when he got closer and saw the spreading mass of goblins. "There must be thousands."

"Yes," Grallik said dryly. His shoulders sagged when he realized there were more goblins on the shore than when he'd left them in the morning. Somehow hundreds more had heard the "call" that Mudwort was sending out.

"Four thousand, I'd guess," K'lars said. He shuddered and spit. "Four thousand, five maybe. Rats, all of them."

Minutes later, the first wave of goblins climbed into the longboats, chattering and hissing, unnerving the sailors, and crowding in the center of the boats to keep away from the water. Not one had been *on* the water before, and several of them retched from seasickness before they even made it to the ships.

Staring around at the sailors and other goblins almost contemptuously, Mudwort was among those who climbed into the first boat, settling herself almost regally amid the others.

Yet there were screams and shouts when the first longboat reached the *Wavechaser*, captained by a minotaur named R'chet. It took an overly tall goblin called Thya to calm the panicked goblins down.

Horace remained on the shore with Direfang, who was trying to convince some of the goblins most reluctant to accept the strategy of the sea crossing, when the longboats returned for a second trip.

"Rather walk some more," Skakee argued. "Walking is better. Can't swim, Direfang. Walk to the Qualinesti Forest. Walk, walk, walk."

"Can't swim," voice after voice echoed.

"You don't have to swim," Horace said, stepping close to Direfang and lending his support to the hobgoblin leader. The priest spoke slowly and clearly in the goblin tongue. "The ship does it for you." He cupped his hands together, imitating the vessel, raising his voice so many could hear. "It will carry you across the water and—"

"What if it sinks?" Skakee asked. She shivered at the notion. "If it sinks, all the goblins will drown."

Direfang spoke in Horace's ear, and the priest began a spell. Horace had relied on variations of the spell whenever the goblins became unruly in Steel Town. There had been three other priests in the mining camp, and all of them used similar enchantments on the goblins and hobgoblins from time to time. The divine coercion had been particularly useful after the earthquakes struck, keeping some of the goblins from escaping; it worked best on those with simple minds, the priest told Direfang.

"No fear," Horace intoned. "Have no fear of the longboats and the great ship. Have no fear of the water on which we will sail." The words were repeated, the sound was rich and melodic, almost like a song, and the goblins nearest to the priest were listening intently. "The sea belongs to Zeboim, and she will keep us safe."

Even Direfang found himself caught up in the priest's incantation.

"Safe," Skakee said. "Have no fear of the water. Zeboim."

"Have no fear of the great ship," Two-chins said. He swayed back and forth in time with the bobbing of the long-boats. "Safe, safe, safe."

Direfang shivered. The hobgoblin was thankful for the priest's incantation in that instance. But it worried him that Horace retained the power to sway the simple minds of the goblins.

"Into the boats," Direfang ordered.

"Safe in the boats," Skakee echoed. She was quick to climb into the closest boat, settling herself next to a sailor who was clearly repulsed by her presence. Regardless, she plucked at his shirtsleeve and oohed over the colorful stripes in the material.

Death March

"Skull man, watch the sailors," Direfang cautioned.

"Aye, Foreman. My spell can soothe the men too."

Despite Horace's enchantment, eighteen goblins refused to budge from the sand. They saw what was happening to the others; they refused to look the priest in the eye, and they plugged their ears with their fingers, managing to resist his persuasive words.

"Stay, then," Direfang pronounced.

Most of the stubborn goblins were from the Fishgatherer clan, but a few were Flamegrass clansmen. One was a tall, sturdy young goblin whom Direfang hated to leave behind.

"Stay and hide," Direfang warned them. "Stay and be hale," he said finally, his anger softening.

He and the priest were the last to step into one of the crowded longboats.

"They will not fare well on their own," Horace warned. He watched the eighteen back away until they disappeared into the shadows. "If they are not careful, ogres will catch them and sell them again."

"But not to the Dark Knights in Steel Town."

"No," Horace admitted. "Iverton is shattered and buried in ash."

Direfang looked to the *Clare,* then to the five other ships beyond it, eyes lingering on the *Wavechaser* with its largely minotaur crew. For all his bravado and despite the priest's spell, which had bolstered his own confidence, the hobgoblin felt anxious and uncertain. It no longer seemed like such a good idea. "Walk, walk, walk," Skakee's words echoed in his mind. The longboat carrying Direfang and Horace and the last of the goblins veered over to the *Clare.*

Ahead, against the hull of the *Clare,* goblins were clambering out of another longboat and up a boarding net. The sailors yelled at them to wait, that the entire boat would be pulled up. But the goblins could not understand the men and tried to climb over each other in their haste and fear.

"No!" Direfang stood in his longboat, setting it to rocking as he pointed toward the boarding net. "Take care!" He shouted in the goblin tongue. "Slow and easy. Do not—"

Three goblins tumbled from the net, one falling back into the longboat and caught by her kinsmen. The other two were not so lucky and plopped into the sea. Spindly limbs flailed for purchase, touching the net and the side of the boat, before going under.

The sailors in Direfang's boat rowed faster, shouting to the deck of the *Clare* that some of their passengers had fallen into the sea. Two more goblins tumbled over the sides of the longboat in their clumsy attempts to help their drowning fellows. The sailors shouted and pointed but made only feeble rescue efforts.

"Four lost all together," Direfang pronounced minutes later when they had all assembled on the deck of the *Clare*. "Drowned and gone. Perhaps more were lost getting on the other ships. So dark, I cannot see, and so far, one ship from the other, I cannot hear."

"They use mirrors and lanterns to signal each other, Foreman." Horace pointed to a signal light on the *Clare* and to a responding signal from *Linda's Grady*. "I can read some of it, most of it. Your ships are on course. All . . . at the moment . . . is well."

"Some foolish goblins will drown," Grallik said, standing behind Horace and Grallik. "You or I cannot be on each ship to keep all of them safe. We have done the best we can."

"Dark Knights such as you," glowered Direfang, "cannot begin to understand the profound sadness of the loss of goblins to the sea."

Horace shook his head. "I understand your beliefs, Foreman. I know that goblins believe that after death their spirits return to their bodies as long as those bodies remain whole. It's why you burn the dead and spread the ashes, so the spirits have nothing to come back to and must move on. I respect that belief."

If Direfang was surprised that the human understood goblin custom, or paid respect to it, his stern face did not show it.

"You think the spirits will return to those bodies that have plunged to the bottom of the New Sea and will be trapped forever, don't you?" The priest shook his head as he joined Direfang at the rail, staring out at the rising and falling waves. "The bodies will not remain intact, Foreman. Zeboim will take care of that."

"Yes, the fish will eat the dead and scatter the bones," Direfang said. But will they do it soon enough? he wondered to himself. Before the spirits return? And what does a damn Dark Knight know anyway? He pushed away from the rail, heading toward the capstan.

"As I said," Horace repeated in a whisper as Grallik came up to stand beside him. "Zeboim will take care of everything."

Hours later, Horace was still at the port rail. He had not been so happy in years. His elbows were propped at the rail, his eyes were closed, and there was a sublime expression on his face. His mouth moved, some prayer of thanks to Zeboim, Grallik guessed.

"The goblins are below now, all of them," Grallik reported. "I understand they are happy to be out of sight of the water, but they are not happy to be in a 'wooden cave,' as some of them are calling the ship. I do not know how the goblins are faring on the other ships, but Captain Gerrold has told me that R'chet speaks the goblin tongue, as does the first mate on *The Elizabeth*. That will be some help, I would hope, in calming the creatures."

The priest gave no indication he had even heard him.

"Save for Foreman Direfang, Horace. He is not below. He hovers behind the captain at the wheel. The foreman is nervous," Grallik said. "I've never seen him like this. He fears the water as much as the goblins and hates being on this ship."

"And does that make you nervous too?" Horace asked without opening his eyes.

Grallik shrugged. "He leads the goblins. The ship makes him vulnerable. And, yes, I guess that does make me nervous."

Horace leaned out farther and sucked in a deep breath. He

held it as long as possible then released it, whistling through his teeth. "How was your day in port, Gray Robe?"

"Glorious." Grallik remembered the clothes and boots he'd purchased for the priest. The captain was keeping that private bundle in his cabin, out of sight of curious goblins. He was surprised Horace had not asked him about his own fine clothing—his bulging new backpack and boots and top-quality attire. "I hadn't realized how badly I'd missed . . . civilization, Horace. I ate two cooked meals, spiced perfectly. You would have enjoyed them. And there were people . . . colorful, talkative people. A welcome change from the bickering and chattering of goblins."

"I hadn't realized how badly I'd missed the sea." The priest finally opened his eyes and angled his face to look at Grallik. Then he fumbled with a small pouch at his waist and pulled out a pipe, tamping some tobacco into the bowl. Grallik stared at the priest. "A gift from Mudwort," Horace explained. "I don't want to know where the little goblin got it."

"Mudwort." Grallik's thoughts never strayed far from the shaman. He had seen her come aboard the *Clare,* the lead ship, but had lost track of her during all the hubbub of boarding. He was meeting her price—helping to take the goblins to the Qualinesti Forest. He would look for her in the morning and seek her part of the bargain.

"I'll not be joining you in the Qualinesti Forest, Gray Robe. I'll not let you or the foreman persuade me." Horace held the pipe out for Grallik to light.

With raised eyebrows the wizard touched his finger to the bowl, and the tobacco glowed.

"I've other plans," the priest explained, contentedly puffing on the pipe and watching the wisp of smoke spiral up.

Grallik opened his mouth to ask about those plans but thought better of it. It was not the time to argue with Horace, or to remind the priest that he was a slave to the goblins and might have no real say in his ultimate destiny.

"I'm staying here," Horace continued, unprompted. "On the water, where I belong. On this very ship perhaps. It is a fine ship, though a little overburdened at the moment." He took a long puff. "It's the sail configuration, I think, that makes it drag."

The wizard turned and walked toward the stern, as the priest blathered on to himself about attach points for the top mast.

"I doubt you'll be leaving our company, 'skull man,' " Grallik muttered when Horace was out of earshot. "I've no intention of leaving Mudwort, and I don't think it wise to be the only human among these goblins. So you will not be going anywhere, my friend."

The *Clare* had two levels of cargo holds, and the goblins occupied the largest at the bottom. A share of the goods Grallik had purchased was on the higher level, and Direfang had appointed two hobgoblins to guard those goods from both the goblins and sailors.

Seven hundred fifty two goblins were packed into that hold, and there were even more packed into holds on some of the other ships, especially the big minotaur-manned vessel. Direfang had counted the number there a little while earlier when the oil lamps hanging from the ceiling were turned bright. At the moment only one lamp burned, that from the top of the stairs. The hobgoblin had logged the number of goblins in the book the dwarf had drawn her maps in.

"Seven hundred and fifty two," Direfang mused. Where had all the many, many goblins come from? The mountains, east to the sea, from the far north; he'd vaguely listened to the clans talk about their former homes and the call that had summoned them. "So many. Too many."

He listened to the wooden bones of the ship softly groan, thinking the sound vaguely comforting. His keen hearing picked up the sound of his hobgoblin guards striding overhead. He suspected they were poking through some of Grallik's myriad purchases. They were loyal, though, and he knew they would not eat much.

He couldn't see Mudwort, though he'd spotted her down there earlier, whispering to Graytoes. He'd wanted to put

Mudwort in charge of the goblins on *The Elizabeth* or *Linda's Grady,* but she'd preferred to stay close to Direfang. And Direfang did not trust Saro-Saro, Grallik, or Horace enough to have them on a ship other than his. So they were all there, friends and enemies, and some friends who might very well become enemies.

"Mudwort?" She would be sleeping where the shadows were the thickest or where she might find some nook that afforded her a little privacy. He'd look for her later, maybe wait until morning.

His ruminations were interrupted by Two-chins. The goblin suddenly stood, swayed unsteadily on his feet, held his stomach, then bent over and vomited, the bile splashing over the goblin and spattering his kinsmen nearby. After a bit of arguing and shuffling to find a clean place of floor, the hold grew quiet again.

Was this a mistake? Direfang wondered.

He was not wondering about leaving Steel Town; they were right to abandon that hellish life. So many, many dead—more than a thousand lost to the earthquakes, more lost in the mountains to the volcanoes. Some left with Hurbear; Direfang hoped they were safe somewhere. Dozens were dead to the tylor—his fault for ordering the charge. Hundreds fell to the malady the skull man called a plague.

Had it been a mistake to take them into the mountains?

Would things have turned out better if he'd led them north? There were volcanoes there too. But perhaps they did not all erupt as violently. The mountains didn't stretch as far to the north; he remembered that from the Dark Knight maps. He knew men were more numerous there. But he hadn't anticipated the tylor and the plague. If he'd taken them north, would more of them be alive?

"A mistake," he whispered in the human tongue. "Too, too many dead."

Direfang sat on a step that led down to the lower cargo hold, his feet touching the floor. He stared into the shadows where the goblins were huddled in clusters corresponding to their clans, most of them trying to sleep. He rubbed his thumbs over the pouch that Grallik had returned to him; the wizard had spent all but five gems. Direfang was pleased the wizard had done his job well, managing to purchase ships. It felt good to own something.

Graytoes sat near Direfang, cradling the dwarf baby and making cooing sounds to it.

"Goats above," she said, beaming. "Saw the goats. Goat milk for this baby. For Umay. And for other younglings."

Direfang nodded.

"Umay," Graytoes repeated. She made a clicking noise with her teeth, and the baby gurgled happily.

"It is a good name," Direfang said.

"For a very good baby." Graytoes rocked the child and started singing an old goblin tune about war and death. She did not know any lullabies.

"A horrible mistake," Direfang whispered.

Graytoes looked up in surprise, interrupting her singing. She didn't understand many human words, but she knew *mistake*.

"What is a mistake?" she asked, pushing out her bottom lip. "Not Umay!"

"No, that was not a mistake." Direfang gave her a rare smile. She'd not whimpered about Moon-eye since taking the baby from Reorx's Cradle. At least that was one good thing that had happened on the journey. "Shh. Time to rest, Graytoes."

She settled herself against a snoring hobgoblin, reclining against his stomach and holding the baby close. It cooed pleasantly.

Direfang's head bobbed forward until his chin touched his chest. He had stayed up on the deck for a few hours, until his legs got sore from standing so long and he feared he would get sick in front of the sailors. He worried about the goblins on the other ships and was frustrated that he had no way to communicate with them. He didn't want to show his frustration or his fears to the sailors on the *Clare,* so he had eventually gone down to the hold, wanting to check on his kinsmen. His stomach still roiled, and he was thankful he'd not eaten much that day. He could smell the vomit everywhere from goblins who'd gotten sick from the rocking of the ship.

He also smelled their familiar musky scent in the close air. They did not stink as much, most of them wading in the sea for hours at the priest's direction in an effort to rid themselves of the plague germs. But he smelled the salt and the wood of the ship.

Their clothes were stiff from the saltwater, as was his ragged tunic. He pawed at his arms, brushing more salt away. His feet still ached, though he liked the feel of the smooth oak against his soles.

Coming that way, to the south, probably a mistake, he thought. The tylor, Reorx's Cradle—the monster and the village that spread the plague. Those deaths were on his hands.

But the ship . . . that might not be a mistake, he reflected, trying to rally his spirits. It would be a chance to rest, to give his feet time to mend, an opportunity for the goblins to eat and not complain about walking on a mountain.

A shout from above roused him.

"Foreman! Trouble's coming!" It was the priest, Horace, calling to Direfang from the top of the stairs. "You'd best hurry."

29

Rough Waters

Direfang hadn't meant to, but he had fallen asleep in the hold. The sky was lightening as he climbed up on deck. Above him the sails snapped, startling him, and the ship rose on a wave. He couldn't keep his balance and dropped to his knees; a pair of sailors working the lines nearby laughed at his clumsiness.

"The beastie has no sea legs," a gangly human chortled. "They're all puking below. I heard a lot of them giving up their dinner last night."

"Two weeks and we'll be clear o' them," his companion said. "Then we'll scrub the hold three or four times to make sure we get all the fleas. Bet *The Balifor Breeze* is faring worse. They got most of the hobs."

Direfang stood, bracing himself when the ship rode up on another wave. He sneered at the two men, who were oblivious to the fact that he understood their tongue. They continued to deride the goblin passengers as Horace hurried back from the wheel and took Direfang's arm.

"Foreman, you need to see the captain." Horace tugged him toward the wheel. "There's trouble, I say!"

The ship rose again, the bow coming down just as a wave washed over it, the spray washing over Direfang and Horace and making the deck slippery. The hobgoblin tugged his arm free and lengthened his stride, coming up to Captain

245

Gerrold just as a sailor in the crow's nest barked down "Still following us, she is! Following all o' us!"

The captain turned at Direfang's approach. His eyes were hard, and the lines on his tanned face reminded the hobgoblin of tree bark.

"What trouble?" Direfang steadied himself as the bow rose again.

The captain raised an eyebrow and twisted the wheel to port. "You speak Common?"

"If that's what you call your language, yes."

"The storm is one trouble," the captain replied. "It's coming up quick. A sharp freshening, feel it? The wind shifted on us, and we're tacking through it, but it's going to be rough sailing for a while. You'll need to explain that to your . . . fellows. I pray my counterparts will be able to handle the others."

Direfang looked up through gaps in the sails, spying a thick bank of clouds and smelling a sweetness in the air that hinted at heavy rain. He saw the sails of the other five ships, spread out and drawing close to the *Clare*. In fact, it appeared that the five were gaining and were going to overtake the lead ship.

"The storms here . . . on this inland sea . . . they ain't so bad as what you'll come into on open water." Captain Gerrold forced the wheel to starboard and closed his eyes as another wave washed across the bow. "This is nothing for the *Clare* . . ."

"Foreman Direfang," Horace supplied. "His name is Direfang."

The captain made a humming sound, as if to say that was an interesting name. "What concerns me is that ship that is following us . . . Foreman Direfang. That's why I'm slowing, letting the others catch up and get ahead. We've got a wizard with us, I know, and so we'll need to organize a defense if such is needed."

Direfang turned, but he couldn't see anything beyond the masts and lines, and the men moving around on the other ships. The water looked as gray as the sky, broken by only chunks of white foam.

"Oh, she's back there, Direfang." The captain paused. "How is it you know Common, may I ask? I'd not think your kind—"

"This ship that follows us," Direfang said, ignoring the question. "Why is it of concern? Aren't there many ships that sail this route?"

The captain wrapped the fingers of his right hand around the king spoke. "She's a sloop with one mast, not close to *Clare*'s size, not as big as any in your armada. But her bowsprit's as long as her hull, and I'd wager she could make double our speed in fair weather. She's built for the shallows, her draft but a whisper. If the wind weren't against her, she'd easily overtake all of us. But she's been catching up, and with the freshening, she will."

"And that is what she intends to do?" That came from Horace. He squinted into the grayness of the sea and sky. "What makes you think that?"

Captain Gerrold gave a clipped laugh. "Her name's the *Blithe Dagger*. I saw her in port yesterday. She pulled in for supplies, left a few hours ahead of us. Thought she was gone from these waters, but she must have been waiting for us. Must have caught word that Grallik N'sera bought the *Clare*, bought five other ships and lots of things with the gemstones he was spending around the docks. Drew quite the interest, all those sparkling blue stones." Gerrold paused and looked up at a flight of gulls struggling against the wind. "The *Blithe Dagger*'s full of your kind, Horace, if you don't mind my saying. Sea barbarians from Ergoth." He let the silence settle a moment. "Pirates, Direfang. The *Blithe Dagger* will pose a far greater threat than the storm. Even though we're five ships, she can come in and pick us off, one at a time."

Horace's eyes grew wide.

"They know they'll get a good haul from us, worth the risks," Captain Gerrold continued. "Whatever gemstones Grallik has left, the hold full of supplies, goblins that can be sold as slaves."

"You sound already defeated." Horace's face showed a mix of anger and disbelief.

"Oh, I'll not give up without a fight," the captain averred. "I've ordered all my men armed. But we're a merchantman, all of these ships Grallik bought are merchantmen, not men-o-war, and the *Blithe Dagger*'s captain . . . well, she's an old Black Robe. Her spells alone could well sink us—that is, if they wanted to sink us."

"A Black Robe." The words hissed out between Direfang's teeth. He spun, nearly losing his footing on the slippery deck. "Skull man, where is the wizard?"

"In the captain's cabin," Horace answered quickly. "Sleeping."

"Well, it's time to wake him up," said the hobgoblin as he turned and headed toward the second level, struggling to keep his footing.

The ship pitched with a high wave. Lightning flickered overhead, looking like thin, gold threads against the gray sky. Direfang could barely hear the thunder over the flapping sails, and he worried about the other ships. "Walk, walk, walk," he remembered Skakee saying. "Indeed," he said, looking around gloomily. "This army should have walked."

He approached an ornate door on the second level at the end of a narrow corridor faintly lit by a lantern that constantly wobbled and clanked. Direfang's shoulders rubbed against the walls, and he turned sideways to avoid knocking the lantern down. He stopped midway as the half-ogre K'lars exited a nearby bunk room and tried to squeeze by. In the end, K'lars stepped back, letting Direfang pass.

"Wizard!" The knob was polished brass and in the shape of a ship, too small for Direfang's big hand. He fumbled with it then shoved the door open just as the ship's bow rose so high, it pitched him off his feet. He tumbled forward, into a table that had been bolted to the floor. "Wizard!"

Direfang pulled himself up and leaned against the table. He could barely stand upright in the room, less than an inch separating the top of his head from the ceiling. Everything was polished mahogany, smelling and looking rich—the table, desk, the large bed from which the wizard was rising. At the back of the room, windows looked out onto the sea; the roiling waves setting the hobgoblin's stomach to spinning.

He stumbled around the table and went to the windows, shouting for Grallik to hurry and get up.

"Foreman, I've packages in here for you . . . and maps. I mentioned them to you last night and—"

Direfang snarled.

"I realized I should have asked permission to sleep here rather than in the hold. I just thought—"

"Wizard, see that ship?" Direfang stabbed a finger at a window pane. The sloop was hard to make out, everything so gray and the *Clare* pitching and rolling. And the hobgoblin talked so fast, about a pirate wizard and the swift, single-masted ship and Ergothians. He occasionally slipped into the goblin tongue.

But Grallik caught the gist of it and immediately stood and dressed. He followed the hobgoblin back through the narrow hallway. At the stairs, goblins were streaming up, complaining of the rocking ship and cursing Direfang for leading them onto stormy seas.

"Down!" he ordered. "Safer below in the hold. It's a storm coming. Better to stay below than fall off the ship."

That last scared them, and those who hadn't yet climbed up to the top hastily beat a retreat.

"Except Mudwort!" Direfang shouted down the stairs. "Get Mudwort. Be fast!" He repeated the order before shoving Grallik up the stairs. Then he followed, holding onto the top rung as the ship climbed a wave and crashed down. His feet lost their purchase, and his legs banged hard into the stairs. But his fingers gripped the rung tighter and he slowly pulled himself up.

Chaos ruled on the *Clare*'s deck, and Direfang blinked furiously in an effort to see all that was going on. In the short time he'd been belowdecks, the rain had started to pour. The rain came down hard at an angle, looking like a wall of water and splashing back up from the deck. At the same time, waves were washing over the port rail. Lines were whipping around, and sailors worked to secure them. Sails were being lowered; one of the larger ones had a rent in it. Everywhere men were moving, slipping, sliding, but the grizzled sailors knew their jobs, and none of them fell or were knocked over.

Direfang could vaguely make out his other ships, *The Elizabeth* and *Shinare's Prayer* just passing the *Clare*. No goblins were on those decks, he noted with a mix of fear and relief. Then he saw those ships lower their sails, and his heart thudded in terror.

Direfang lumbered forward, intending to order the captain to relay the message to raise those sails and fast. How could any of his ships hope to outdistance the *Blithe Dagger* dead in the water? But then he knew they were guarding against ripped or torn sails; the ships risked being shredded by the strong storm. He swung around, looking for the wizard, and saw him stumble past the center mast on his way to the stern. Direfang followed, grabbing onto lines and sailors and coils of rope to keep from falling.

The several goblins that had made it up on deck were huddled together near the capstan. They hissed and gestured wildly to Direfang, but the hobgoblin went past them. "Go below!" he shouted, not certain they could hear him over all the ruckus. He lost sight of the wizard for a moment when another wave crashed over.

He thought he heard someone shout that a man had gone overboard.

"Don't let it be the wizard," he muttered.

Then he heard goblins scream as the ship rolled to starboard, the wind keening and the rain coming even harder. He leaped to grab the port rail, wrapping his arms around it and feeling his feet fly free. It felt as if his stomach were rising into his throat. He closed his eyes as a wave pummeled him. His eyes burned from the salty water, and when he opened them, all he saw was a wall of gray. A moment more, and the ship righted itself. Dizzy, he stood, still holding the rail, gripping it tighter still when another wave came.

A mistake, he thought, choking on swallowed water. This ship was a horrid mistake.

"Foreman!" the wizard called to him.

Direfang squinted, seeing shapes in the rain but not

able to differentiate one from another. He tasted blood and realized he'd bitten his tongue. The saltwater worsened the pain. Spitting, he shuffled toward the stern, ducking once to avoid a flailing line, digging his claws into the rail so tightly that he felt the wood splinter against his palm.

Finally he saw the wizard, holding on to a post on the spar deck. The *Clare* rose and fell, threatening to pitch Direfang over the side, but he fought his way to the center, grabbing tightly to the aft mast and yelling for Grallik. Direfang could barely hear his own voice and succeeded only in growing hoarse and swallowing rain and seawater. He held his chin tight to his chest and took several deep breaths, then pushed off of the mast and staggered toward the short flight of stairs that would take him up to the spar deck.

Grallik stood there with two sailors, who were steadying the wizard as he worked his fingers as though weaving a web. He mouthed the words to a spell and squinted through the rain to spy the prow of the pirate vessel steadily approaching through the heavy storm. Direfang lunged for the stern rail, holding tight to it just as the *Clare* climbed another wave and crashed down.

The *Blithe Dagger* was under full sail. Its main canvas held steady, as though unaffected by the storm. Its pennant flapped only slightly.

"Magic," one of the sailors cursed. "The ship that dogs us is enchanted."

"Can't be, not an entire ship," the other replied as he grabbed Grallik's belt to help steady the wizard. "But her captain . . . it's said the captain is a sorceress and can keep the ship dry and steady in any gale. Might as well strike the colors and surrender. She'll take all six of these ships in time."

"Aye, surrender and pray to Zeboim the pirates let us live," said the first.

Direfang gaped when he finally caught a good look at the *Blithe Dagger*. It was as the one sailor said. The ship appeared dry. The rain seemed to be held at bay by some force; he could see it veer off just shy of the ship. The enemy vessel wasn't nearly as large as the *Clare,* with only one mast and a square topsail. He saw men and women crowded at the bow, grappling hooks and lines ready. The ship closed fast.

"Wizard, bring down some fire!" Direfang howled.

Grallik was busy doing just that. Just then a column of flame shot down, aimed at the bow of the *Blithe Dagger,* where all the sailors stood. Steam hissed around the column, clouds roiling away from the flames, the crackling of which could be heard through the storm.

"More!" Direfang encouraged. The sailors holding Grallik up added their encouragement. "Bring down . . ." But the words died in the hobgoblin's throat.

The column of flame clearly had struck its mark, but it caused the ship and its crew no apparent harm.

"Their sorceress," Grallik gasped. "she's protected them from flames too . . . fire and the storm. She bends the elements, Foreman." Still, he tried to send more fire strikes at the *Blithe Dagger,* concentrating on the sails, with the same result.

"Hold him," one of the sailors said to Direfang. He tromped away from the wizard. "I've got to report to Captain Gerrold, tell him we're all but done." He disappeared down the steps toward the main deck.

"I'll not give up," Grallik said to the hobgoblin leader. His face was drawn together as he pointed at the enemy ship, which loomed frighteningly close. Fire shot from his fingers, striking the bowsprit and sending steam hissing in all directions.

Direfang grabbed Grallik's tunic with one hand and with the other squeezed the stern rail as hard as he could.

Once more the wizard drew his best fire down on the ship.

"Nothing!" the hobgoblin spit. "Your pathetic fire magic does nothing."

The sounds grew louder—the thrumming of the thunder and the groans of the wood, a snap, followed by sailors yelling that a mast had broken. There was a crash, and Direfang knew it was the mast falling; he didn't have to look to confirm it. There were shouts from the *Clare*'s crew, feet pounding over the deck; the wind howled amid the constant rain and roaring of the waves. The sailor helping to hold Grallik began praying aloud to Zeboim, nearly shouting the words.

"Your god won't listen," Direfang muttered. "The gods never listen. Worthless and empty, the gods."

He heard shouts coming from the deck of the *Blithe Dagger* and saw a tall Ergothian dressed in red swing the grapple above his head. The man meant to catch the stern rail of the *Clare*.

"They're getting ready to board us," Grallik said, abandoning the fire spell he'd started. "The sorceress . . . do you see her?" He gestured with his head.

Direfang saw a woman dressed in a black robe, blood-red cloak gently billowing around her. She was the only one who didn't have a weapon strapped to her waist or in her hand. Her head was shaved, a gold circlet sitting on it like a crown. Her eyes caught his; he saw her smile, and a shiver raced down his spine.

"She'll kill us," Grallik continued. "Her ship's not big enough to haul your goblins. She'll kill you and strip everything valuable. She's not a slaver."

"Aye," the sailor who had been praying to Zeboim agreed. "And then she'll sink the fair *Clare*."

A mistake, Direfang thought, swallowing hard. He'd doomed all of them by agreeing to the shortcut to the Qualinesti Forest. His entire life was a mistake, he thought. Thousands of goblins would perish because of him.

The grapple hook sailed out, narrowly missing the *Clare*.

"Closer!" the enemy sailor bellowed. He tugged the hook back and sent it circling his head again.

Whooping erupted from the *Blithe Dagger*'s deck as the hook sailed out again, that time catching hold somewhere below the rail, where Direfang and Grallik could not see it. Cheers followed, and the hobgoblin watched the sorceress disappear in the crowd.

Then the cheers turned to yelps of surprise as a glittering fork of lightning struck their lone mast. It was followed by a second bolt, that one splitting the mast in two. A third struck the port side above the waterline. The sails flapped like sheets hung out on a clothesline, one tugging free and floating into the storm, the other coming down with part of the mast, covering some of the crew.

Hands reached up to clutch Direfang's ragged tunic, and he looked down to see Mudwort's face twisted into an ugly expression, as if she'd eaten something terribly bitter. She sucked her lower lip into her mouth just as another bolt arced down, that time lancing off the bowsprit. The *Blithe Dagger* rocked to its port side, spilling some of the enemy sailors, who were instantly lost in the churning water.

Mudwort murmured something, but Direfang couldn't hear. He shrugged and cocked his head.

She raised her voice. "Can't find Boliver! Need Boliver to help with this magic!"

The wizard was staring at her in surprise. So did Direfang. "The lightning? Mudwort made the lightning?" Disbelief was heavy in his voice.

Mudwort grinned wide. "Not all of it! Just what touches that ship. Just some of the lightning. A little is maybe enough." She closed her eyes, and her face took on an even more pained countenance. A heartbeat later, thin threads of lightning flickered overhead and raced down to again strike the *Blithe Dagger*'s port side. The ship listed farther and more sailors tumbled into the sea, but some lucky ones managed to grab on to sail to keep from going over the side.

Lightning continued to flash overhead, but it stayed high. The thunder that followed shook the deck under Direfang's feet. There were more whoops and cheers, but that time they came from the sailors on the *Clare* and the nearby *Shinare's Prayer*.

"She's sinking! The damn pirate's going under!" someone behind Direfang yelled. It was K'lars, the half-ogre bosun's mate. He clomped to the rail, shifting his balance as the deck pitched. He slapped Grallik on the back. "Wizard, you did it! You bested the *Dagger!*"

Grallik shook his head and opened his mouth to reject

the praise, but Mudwort squeezed between the wizard and Direfang and tugged on the wizard's trousers. She shook her head and narrowed her eyes, drew a finger to her lip, then looked back out to the *Blithe Dagger*.

K'lars slapped Grallik on the back again. "Captain Gerrold said it was your magic, said if anyone could save us from the *Dagger*'s sorceress, it would be one of her own kind."

The wizard stared helplessly at Mudwort, who shook her head and made a shushing sound. "Tired," she said. "Done with the magic for a time." She sagged against Grallik's leg.

The *Clare* continued to rise and fall with the waves, and despite the storm, sailors scurried from one end of the ship to the other, still working with errant lines, lashing the sails tighter, throwing extra lines around the water barrels. Orders were screamed by sailors Direfang couldn't see. More orders were shouted on *Shinare's Prayer* and *The Elizabeth*, the voices carrying over the waves.

Direfang turned, his back to the stern rail, fingers still holding tight. He could make no sense of all the activity, and he was still trying to comprehend what Mudwort had managed to do with her magic lightning. He would ask her about that later.

It was time to get to a safer spot. He waited until the ship rose with another high wave and braced himself. Then he pushed off the rail and wobbled toward the stairs, locking his hands to the railing as he slowly climbed down to the main deck. Setting his sights on the aft mast, he bolted for it, grabbing the lines that wrapped around it and looking for the priest or the captain.

The captain spotted him and came over, leaning down and speaking in hushed tones to the hobgoblin leader, whose face twisted. He stared out at the seas, beyond the *Blithe Dagger*, suddenly looking anguished, defeated. The captain whirled away to see to business.

Direfang stayed there for long minutes, feeling sicker than he'd thought possible and wanting desperately to feel ground beneath his feet. "Walk, walk, walk," that's what Skakee had told him the day before on the shore. How he wished he would have listened to her. The threat from the

Blithe Dagger might be past, but the storm still raged, and the hobgoblin believed it was strong enough to tear the *Clare* apart.

K'lars stomped past him, gesturing and hollering, and Direfang had to concentrate to hear the orders. His eyes popped wide when he realized the half-ogre was telling sailors to launch the longboats.

"You can't mean to rescue those men!" Grallik complained. The wizard had followed the half-ogre. "They're pirates! Let them drown."

The half-ogre grabbed the side of one of the longboats, holding it steady as several sailors waited to climb in.

"I've no intention of saving them," K'lars snapped. "In fact, we'll finish off any who're still breathing. But the *Blithe Dagger*'s certain to have treasure aboard her, and that I aim to rescue before she goes under!"

Grallik persisted, tugging at the half-ogre's sleeve. "This is madness. Remember, this is my ship! I'm paying you, and—"

K'lars looked to Direfang, who still clutched the lines. "I heard you tell Captain Gerrold the ship belonged to the hobgoblin there. And he ain't told us to stay put. Besides, that last bit of the storm you called down on their ship blasted a wide hole. We've got to hurry." The half-ogre climbed in and winched the longboat down. A second boat was lowered moments behind. Two more boats were lowered from *The Elizabeth,* with that ship's sailors intent on the same goal.

Grallik staggered toward Direfang, finding a lashed water barrel to hold on to. "You should've ordered him to stop . . . told the captain to keep them all here. This storm is bad enough."

Direfang closed his eyes and fought to stay conscious. The tumultuously rocking deck was sapping his strength and making him dizzier by the minute. The wizard continued to shout at him, but the hobgoblin shut out the words, listening instead to his own pounding heart.

"A horrible mistake," Direfang muttered.

"What's a mistake?" Grallik shouted.

DEATH MARCH

"This. All of this. Captain Gerrold just told me that *Shinare's Prayer* went down in the storm. Well more than five hundred goblins lost, wizard. Well more than that."

30

DIVIDING THE SPOILS

Three survivors from the *Shinare's Prayer*. All goblins. They're below." K'lars paced in the captain's cabin. "It wasn't just the storm that got them. One of the mates on *The Elizabeth* said the sorceress from the *Dagger* had done something to twist the wood of their hull, split it wide. Sorceress would've looted the ship, no doubt, but the storm helped it under too quick. The *Dagger* followed, praise Zeboim."

"And the sorceress?" Captain Gerrold regarded K'lars.

"Nowhere to be seen. Didn't see her in the water. Nothing."

Gerrold sat at his table, an array of jewelry spread in front of him, all glittering in the light of a lantern that hung from the ceiling and swung with the movement of the ship. They were past the storm, but the sea was still choppy in the strong wind. Everything outside the windows still looked gray.

"She used her magic to get free, I'll wager," the half-ogre continued. "Maybe got some of her men free with her. Couldn't tell if any longboats had been launched. Don't know how many the *Dagger* had. We found only a few survivors, but they didn't survive long."

Direfang sat opposite the captain, staring at the jewelry not because he was interested in such gewgaws, but because it was something to fixate on that didn't move. Grallik had

258

hovered behind him for a time, but the hobgoblin had dismissed him, telling the wizard to go help Horace tend to any goblins and sailors who'd been injured by being tossed around in the storm.

K'lars's pacing was rhythmic and seemed to echo the sweep of the lantern. His course took him around the table, to the bay of windows, and back. "Don't like the notion that the sorceress is still out there, somewhere, mad now. Could come for us, you know, Captain. Such as she would look for some measure of vengeance."

"She'd have to get herself another ship for that, wouldn't she?" Captain Gerrold steepled his fingers under his chin and stretched his legs out under the table. He brushed his feet against Direfang's and shifted to give the still-silent hobgoblin more room. "And if Grallik N'sera was able to sink her ship once by bringing down the storm and sheering the mast and poking a hole in the side, I think she'd avoid the *Clare* for all the rest of her days."

K'lars stopped pacing and stood against a side of the table. His gaze shifted from Direfang to Gerrold. He tapped a thick finger at the edge, a gesture also in time with the swaying of the lantern.

"I've got Leath in charge of repairing our mast," K'lars said. "Lost one of the longboats. Lost two men before that. A couple of them goblins went flying over the port rail. Don't know who or how many exactly." He looked at Direfang when he said that.

The hobgoblin continued to stare at the jewelry, though he winced at the report.

"Some losses on *Linda's Grady;* bosun's mate on *The Elizabeth* went over. We're sailing with two masts at the moment. Slower going, but at least we're going. The other ships are ahead of us, but we're keeping them in sight." K'lars tapped two fingers and sucked in a breath. "That priest . . ."

"The Ergothian's name is Horace," Gerrold supplied.

"Yes, Horace. Fine. He's seeing to Dargweller and Nate. They got hit by a spar when the mast broke. Nate's got a bad gash. I figure it was the sorceress what did it. Mast was shorn clean, like someone'd taken a big saw to it. Not a break caused by the wind, that's for certain." K'lars cleared his throat. "So this booty . . ." He nodded toward the jewelry then cocked his head backward to indicate the other seven chests stacked near the captain's bunk. "Who's it belong to . . . us . . . or him?" He nodded to Direfang.

Captain Gerrold placed his hands on the table, cupping the edge. He waited until Direfang looked up.

"What's customary?" the hobgoblin asked.

Gerrold's smile reached his eyes. "Not that we're pirates ourselves, mind you. The *Clare*'s a respectable ship, a merchantman. But typically such booty is divided among the crew. Three shares to the captain, four to the owner, a share and a half to the first mate and the healer, that would be the priest in this case . . . that's customary." He leaned close. "But you haven't told me," he added confidentially. "How did you learn to speak Common? You speak it as well as any of my men. As well as any man I know, for that matter."

The captain had asked the question after the goblins boarded yesterday, but Direfang had ignored it then.

"The priest doesn't get a share." The hobgoblin dropped his gaze to the jewelry and told Gerrold and K'lars a little about his capture by the ogres, his life as a slave in Steel Town, and their escape. He made it clear that the priest and wizard were beholden to him and wouldn't get special treatment. He did not mention how many goblins had died along the way to reach the shore of the New Sea.

"So you learned Common by listening to the Dark Knights?" Gerrold seemed genuinely impressed. "Do you read too?"

Direfang gave him a nod.

"Remarkable. I have to admit . . . Direfang . . . that until I'd met you, I'd considered goblins foul little creatures. Hobgoblins too . . . though not so little."

"Rats what walk on two legs," K'lars interjected.

Direfang's lips curled imperceptibly.

Gerrold cut the half-ogre a cross look. "But you're civilized. Not what I expected. So I was wrong about hobgoblins, I admit that. And Grallik N'sera and the priest answer to you?"

"My slaves now," Direfang said.

"A fair turnabout," Gerrold replied evenly. "More than fair."

Silence settled among the three for a while. The ship groaned softly as it continued to rise and fall with the swells; the handle that held the lantern creaked in time with it. From above came the sounds of men walking across the deck and working on the mast, the snap of the sails, and the occasional shouted order.

Fainter, from below, came goblin conversations; only Direfang could understand the jumble of words, and he pushed the chatter aside. Beyond the door to the captain's cabin, footsteps sounded in the hallway and the clank of pots was heard. The faint smell of meat and potatoes cooking tickled the hobgoblin's nose.

Finally, Gerrold spoke again. "I lost my first mate a few months back. Never replaced him. K'lars has been filling the role as needed and occupies that cabin. He merits his share and a half. I've moved a few sailors into the bosun's quarters, but I'll order them out. Give you the room. Not as nice as this, but it's . . . customary . . . for the captain to have the best accommodations."

Direfang shook his head.

"He'd rather stay with the rest of them," K'lars growled.

"It's better that way," Direfang admitted. "The clans are not taking this voyage well. No way to know how the clans on the ships are faring."

"Yes, the voyage to the Qualinesti Forest." Gerrold rose, still keeping his hands on the table. "Why there, if I may ask? And—"

"And why this ship?" Direfang finished for him.

Gerrold shook his head. "No, I've figured that much out. Taking the *Clare* and these others is far faster than walking. And the *Clare, The Elizabeth* . . . they were all that could be bought."

Direfang laughed bitterly.

"Two weeks, and we'll have you on the forest shore,

luck willing. Maybe less than that, but this storm has set us back." Gerrold stepped away from the table and walked to a cabinet. It was latched to keep the doors from banging open on rough waters. Everything in the cabin seemed latched or nailed down. "Would have taken you two months, maybe a little more, if you'd try to walk there."

"Months?" The word came out as a croak. Direfang's throat went instantly dry. "Only two months?" The hobgoblin had thought the world so vast on the Dark Knight maps that it could take two years at best. With a stony look, he said no more—one more mistake he'd made.

Gerrold returned with a map, unrolling it and spreading it on top of the jewelry. He fished underneath it, coming up with four heavy bracelets to set on the corners.

It was like one of the maps Direfang had remembered from the hours he spent hovering around the Dark Knights in Steel Town. But there was more detail to Gerrold's, and the light was better so he could read the names of towns and rivers and other landscape features.

Direfang bent over to peer at the map. "Is this one of the maps the wizard bought?" the hobgoblin leader asked.

"No, those are over there. With several packages he said were for you and the priest. I would like to take a look at those maps too . . . with your permission." He gestured to the corner where a jumble of scroll tubes, satchels, and bundles nested.

Direfang did not even look where Gerrold pointed; his gaze remained fixed on the map.

"We're here." Gerrold stabbed his finger at a spot close to the northern shore. "The wind blew us here, and so we're following the coast. It's deep all along this part, so we ought to be fine. We'll cut toward the center as we near this island, Schallsea. I've signaled to the other ships also to head for Schallsea."

Direfang spotted a scale, something he'd not been close enough to see on the Dark Knight maps. It made the world smaller than he thought. "Two months." He laughed aloud at his own stupidity. "Walk, walk, walk. Should have walked."

DEATH MARCH

"Certainly you would have avoided seasickness," Gerrold averred. "Saved you quite a few of those sapphires too." He turned his head and listened to something overhead. "Sound's like it's up."

"Aye," K'lars said. "I'll take a look." He left, closing the door behind himself, his footfalls receding.

The captain removed the bracelets and rolled up his map, replacing it then walking over to another cabinet. He retrieved a fluted red bottle and two thick glasses, brought them back to the table, and sat heavily.

"Sweet cherry wine," he said, pouring Direfang a glass first, then one for himself. "With a little extra: rosemary, fennel seeds, sage, lemon peels—distilled and aged to perfection." He took a sip and closed his eyes appreciatively. "I've some stout and pine drink too. But they pale to this."

Direfang copied him, finding the liquid heady and like warm syrup on his tongue. It would be easy to down it in one gulp; he'd never tasted anything so sweet. But he'd seen men in Steel Town after too much drink, and he didn't want to dull his senses or show any weakness to the captain.

"It is good indeed," Direfang pronounced, thinking he should say something about the drink.

"Aye, it is that." Gerrold held his finger against his lips. "Shh. I don't share it often. Not even K'lars knows I have this." He took another sip and held it in his mouth, savoring it before finally swallowing. "So tell me, Direfang, why all the secrecy? Why the Qualinesti Forest?"

The captain was not one to let a question go unanswered, the hobgoblin decided. He took another careful swallow and set the glass down on the table between two gold necklaces. "The place is supposedly empty of elves," he began. "A place free of ogres too. A place to be free. Mudwort says we should go there, says it is the best place. And Mudwort is to be trusted." He held onto the base of the glass, his thumbs slowly circling against the smooth crystal. "It is a place to build a nation, and a place to be left alone."

Direfang surprised himself, confiding in a human. It couldn't be the drink; he'd not yet had enough to muddle his senses. But the captain had a genial, easy nature . . . when away from the ship's wheel. And he spoke to Direfang as an equal, in a manner that not even the Dark Knight priest and wizard exhibited. Perhaps it was that easygoing manner that coaxed so many words out of the hobgoblin.

He told Gerrold tales about the difficult work in the mines, and after he finished his first glass and they'd both started on their second, he revealed some of the atrocities he'd witnessed, including a Dark Knight priest magically slaying Graytoes' unborn baby.

"Not all men are so ugly," Gerrold remarked. He ran his finger around the lip of the glass, producing a faint humming sound. "Though I trust that you're making a good move, heading to the forest. Big enough to lose yourself in, despite the thousands of goblins you've with you. And the elves abandoned the forest, most of them anyway. Not all men are ugly, you should know. But most of them are thick with prejudice and won't accept you and your kin. Keep on hunting you and enslaving you. Best that you do as you prefer, go to Qualinesti, build a nation and hide away there."

"Why so sympathetic?" Direfang hadn't meant to ask the question aloud. He thought it bordered on being rude, yet he blurted it out.

Gerrold shrugged then tipped his glass up and drained it. "My father served on a ship, not quite so fine as this one. He was pressed into the work, never to see me or my mother again. I don't know if he's still alive. So I understand slavery. And I understand men. The body is a shell that conceals the inside, Direfang. Mine, yours, K'lars's. See, K'lars doesn't get on well in most places. People don't like the looks of him. The minotaurs on the *Wavechaser,* they have it worse in spots. I've other mates of mixed . . . parentage. It's what's inside the shell that counts, I've learned." He poured the rest of the wine, dividing it between his and the hobgoblin's glasses. "Was it this priest who killed the baby?"

Direfang shook his head and glanced down, seeing his reflection on the surface of the wine. "This priest was the least of Steel Town's evils."

Gerrold worked a kink out of his neck and wrapped his

right hand around his glass. The fingers of his left hand played slowly over the links of a thick necklace. "The priest . . . Horace . . . I don't think he wants to be a slave anymore. He wants to join my crew."

The hobgoblin looked surprised, turning the glass, his reflection distorted by the ripples in the wine. "Fine. But only after the *Clare* reaches the Qualinesti Forest. A slave until then."

"And the wizard . . . Grallik N'sera?"

Direfang took a long pull on the wine, letting it ease down his throat. He felt warm, and his tongue felt thick. He'd not planned to drink so much that his senses whirled.

"The wizard bought this ship," the hobgoblin said. His words sounded thick too.

"Bought it for you, Direfang, I understand. With gems worth more than our take from the *Blithe Dagger*."

"Won't need the ship beyond the Qualinesti Forest."

"Then I could buy it back from you," Gerrold suggested. "Everything I have here for the *Clare*. Though that would be a bargain for me and a bit of a loss for you, given what you paid the original owner."

"So be it. Fine." Direfang took another pull. The wine had relaxed him. He didn't mind quite so much the rocking of the *Clare* anymore.

"And I ask again, the wizard? Grallik N'sera?"

Direfang raised an eyebrow. The captain was a persistent devil.

"What about the wizard? Why does he interest you so much?" the hobgoblin asked.

"Will he remain your slave after we reach the Qualinesti Forest?"

Direfang finished the wine and rose from his chair, careful to hold on to the table to steady himself. He'd not had anything so strong since . . . well, probably never, he realized. He grunted at the captain. Some questions he still wouldn't answer. The hobgoblin leader shuffled over to the corner where the packs and scroll tubes were piled up, and began to riffle through his treasures.

31

THE WOODEN RELIC

Mudwort's stomach clenched. She sat in the hold on a tall crate at the prow, as alone as possible in the crowded wooden cave. The motion was worse there with the ship rising and falling. It was not so pronounced at the opposite end, where most of the goblins huddled, including Saro-Saro, who was wrapped in his green blanket, his head on a pillow he found somewhere, trying to sleep.

She didn't like the close air and longed terribly for a fresh breeze that would carry away some of the mustiness of her kinsmen. The smell from all the bodies crammed together was strong and clung bitterly to her tongue. No amount of spitting would get rid of it. She breathed shallowly and cupped her hands over her mouth to keep out the foulest of the aroma. Added to everything was the smell of waste and vomit, which hung heavy in the room as some of the goblins were perpetually sick from the motion of the ship. And a dozen seemed to be still sick from the illness that had taken so many by the river.

"S'dards, not to have washed with the skull man in the sea," she muttered. "S'dard Direfang, not to wash the sick ones over the side now." The hobgoblin had to know that some of Saro-Saro's and Cattail's clans were ill with spots, she thought. Though she hadn't seen the hobgoblin down in the hold since the beginning of the trip. Maybe he was

266

oblivious that the illness lingered. *"S'dard* Direfang."

How could her fellow goblins not be bothered by the nasty smells in the stale, close air? They seemed more worried about the sea. Perhaps it was because their senses of smell were not as keen as hers. Perhaps it was because so many of them slept and were oblivious.

Not all of the goblins were down in the hold breathing all of that fetid atmosphere. Some were in the galley; the cook had demanded they eat in shifts. The goblins did not argue about which clan should go first; they were subdued from the storm and the loss of their kinsmen to the storm. And they were grateful for something cooked that was certain to be tasty.

Seven members of the Rockbridge clan—the only members of that clan to survive the earthquakes—were on the level above, inventorying the food and goods at Direfang's request. It was a useless task, as there was no way to alter what had been purchased, and it was likely the clansmen would forget the numbers of the various whatnots they counted, thought Mudwort. Perhaps the exercise was merely intended to give those goblins something to do.

Despite goblins being washed over the rail, more continued to venture up on deck, too curious for their own good, Mudwort thought. A big wave would take care of the too-curious ones; she wished again it would take care of the dozen or so who were sick with spots.

She had not enjoyed her brief foray on the deck, which was why she preferred to wallow in the conditions down there. However, she had found some pleasure in calling down the lightning and ruining the pursuing pirate ship. She was angry at herself for letting the wizard take all the credit for her ingenious, destructive magic. At the time she'd not wanted anyone to know she'd discovered such a powerful, new enchantment. She liked to keep secrets. But then she thought she might have gained some more respect because of her heroism and perhaps a spot in a cabin above where conditions had to be better.

Boliver had been elusive; she'd inquired about him among the others several times in the past few hours.

He wasn't a member of the Rockbridge clan, so he was not conducting the useless inventory directly overhead. Neither was he down there. She hoped he hadn't perished in the storm.

She hadn't remembered seeing him get into one of the longboats at the mouth of the river, so he might have been one of the stubborn eighteen who remained on the shore. Boliver was stubborn; that was possible. Or he might have been tossed over the side during the storm. Her magical scrying told her he was not on one of the other ships either. A mystery—the disappearance of Boliver.

Mudwort's stomach clenched tighter because she missed her friend. Boliver and Moon-eye had been the only goblins she really talked to. She'd spent quite a bit of time with Boliver since leaving Steel Town, mingling magic and learning more than a little from him. She enjoyed his company because he was a smart goblin and because joining their spells had been so effortless. He'd been a shaman for his clan in the Before Time, and she suspected he was more powerful than she.

She thought he'd been left behind on the shore, too frightened of the sea to get in a longboat. She could use her seeing spell to look for him in the pine woods to be certain. But she was weary right then, drained of some power. The attack on the pirate ship had left her in need of rest. And if Boliver was dead or gone, then she would find out soon enough.

She tried to relax rather than concentrate on her assorted complaints and the mystery of her absent friend. The wood of the crate felt good against the backs of her legs, the wood of the prow against her neck and shoulders. The ship rocked ceaselessly and creaked constantly, however, an unpleasant, worrisome sound. Yet the noise was enough to keep some of the snores and chittering of the goblins at bay.

She closed her eyes and tried to sleep.

Saarh was with Brab, the crooked-faced goblin, in the heart of the young forest. The clan was nearby, digging bowl-shaped depressions in the earth between clumps of willowy birch and ash trees. It had rained earlier, shortly after dawn, but it was not a long or intense storm.

The rain made all the greens and browns brighter, fed the ever-thirsty trilliums so close to the ground, brought out rich and wonderful scents, and, above all, made the earth soft for digging. Saarh's goblins were making homes; they would circle their depressions with stones and small logs, and later weave branches to cover them to keep out the worst of future rains. Saarh's goblins had never constructed such dwellings before, but she'd seen things like that in her seeing spells, and she decided the clansmen would feel safer sleeping in the earth pockets.

Busy, the goblins did not need her for a while, so Saarh and her consort wandered west.

"Ril bore a youngling last night," the crooked-faced goblin told her.

Saarh nodded, though she had been unaware of the news. "Yes, Brab, a fine youngling that will grow strong in these woods." She'd been using her magic to search through the earth, trying to pinpoint the power she searched for. It lay in that direction; she felt the pull.

"Others will bear younglings in the next few months," he continued. "The food is plentiful here, so no more younglings should die from shrunken bellies."

"No, never again, that is to be hoped." The clan had lost a few babies recently, when the food in the caves became scarce. Saarh could have led them to other chambers, where the great urkhan worms laired. Even a young worm would have fed the clan for days and days.

But there was no lure of power in the chambers.

When Saarh picked up her pace, the crooked-faced goblin struggled to keep up. Brab dragged his right leg; the foot of his right leg was turned outward and gave him an odd, halting gait. He fell behind after a while, and she did not slow to accommodate him, as she always had before in the caves. Still, he did not quit following her. He looked to the ground to find her footprints. Looking slowed him even further.

She stopped in the late afternoon, when her legs tired and her stomach growled in protest. Saarh thought about the clan she'd brought with her and wondered how their digging project was progressing. She'd been walking for a few hours, and she hoped they had not grown bored with the task. They always needed prodding and encouragement, she thought with a sigh. Leadership—that was what they needed. She sat on a large, flat rock and rubbed her thighs, turning her head this way and that and rolling her shoulders.

She heard a peculiar noise and sat still. She had nothing in her memory to compare it to—a good-sounding noise. It was accompanied by a soft splashing that meant water running nearby. Thirsty and ever-curious, Saarh slid off the rock and crept to the north. She was careful and stayed low, not wanting to find something as large as more bears on that trip. She didn't fear bears and enjoyed their meat, but she did not want to waste time slaying more of them, even though she was hungry.

As it was, Saarh cursed herself for indulging in an investigation that had gone on too long and far. But the noise was very near, and she reminded herself that she was thirsty. Almost immediately she saw the stream and the thing in it making the noise. It looked like no bird she'd seen before, and its nasal squawking and clacking was not like typical birdsong. Its feathers were black under its chin and on its back. Its cheeks and back were a chestnut brown, mottled with tiny white feathers in places, particularly on its breast. The creature's beak was flat and rounded and long, a yellowish shade, and its legs ended in feet that were scalloped like a bat's wings. The creature was eating tadpoles and water insects and was happily unaware of the watching goblin.

"Weet," she whispered, mimicking the sound it made. She smiled as it splashed in the water, throwing droplets up over its back and seeing them bead up all over. Fumbling on the ground at her feet, she picked up a rock. Raising it and taking careful aim, she threw the rock with as much strength as she could summon, striking the strange-looking bird on the side of its head and dropping it.

She scurried forward, sat in the stream, grabbed the dead creature up, and started plucking its feathers. Then she bit into its belly. The bird-creature tasted much better than bear, and she was certain it would be even better cooked. Selecting some of the better feathers, she put them in her pouch and pictured the thing when it had splashed in the water. She would describe it to the clan later, so they could add it to the list of creatures they desired to hunt.

There might be a nest nearby filled with sweet eggs. But she'd already spent too much time away from her quest and would not look. Saarh left the half-eaten carcass and hurried farther west, always following the intermittent pulse of the interesting thing.

After another few hours, she realized she had strayed too far and that she would not make it back to her clan by evening. It was nearing sunset, and she had let herself be tugged for miles. Hungry again, she wished she would have brought the rest of the bird-creature with her. Too, she regretted not taking more of the feathers.

What if she didn't reach the *something* that day? Or the next? She couldn't keep returning to the clan and retracing her steps west if it was so far away. No, she shook her head. She would not return to the clan until she found the *something*. The pull on her had become too strong.

Saarh slept little that night, by a bush with bright purple berries that tasted delicious. If she came back that way, she would take some of the berries and leaves with her to show the clan so they could look for similar bushes. There were owls in the trees above her, and they had hooted loudly and often, waking her several times. Deer had passed nearby, nibbling on leaves and rustling ferns. She knew that deer were good-tasting too, and easier to kill than bears, but the berries were enough for the moment.

It was midmorning when she stopped again for a brief rest and to eat different berries that she'd found growing beneath a young willow. They were clusters of tiny red globes that tasted very sweet. She ate too many of them, cleaning almost all of them off the bush, and paid for it with a sour stomach that forced her to curl into a ball and moan for a while. If it hadn't been for her sickening, the crooked-faced goblin would not have caught up.

Brab was tired, having walked relentlessly through the night, and just as hungry because he'd not stopped to eat. He slumped beside her and ran his fingers along her side, offering comfort for her ailing stomach. While she slept briefly, he finished the berries on the bush and nestled himself next to her, draping an arm across her side so she would wake him if she moved.

By sunset that day, Saarh found the source of the arcane power. She'd walked slower that time, grateful for Brab's company and the opportunity to tell someone about the tasty bird-creature with the odd beak. She showed him the feathers as they neared the clearing; then when they fluttered from her fingers, she gasped and dropped to her knees and closed her eyes, stretching out her hands toward an old oak—the largest tree she'd come across in that young forest. The tree was older than anything that surrounded it, older than Saarh, perhaps as old as the damp ground beneath her knees.

"This is it? The tree?" The crooked-faced goblin stared at the oak with a mix of wonder and disgust. It was the ugliest tree he'd seen in the woods. The trunk was not straight, it leaned to the north, and its lowest branches were dead. The bark was thick and corky, and its leaves were oval shaped with bristly edges. The acorns were big, and the cups that held them looked spiky and itchy.

"All this walking and walking and not eating enough was to find this ugly tree?" Brab sat next to her, cross-legged and holding his chin in his palms. Disappointment was writ plain on his crooked face. "Too much walking for such a big, ugly tree, if you ask me. The clan will not come here, not after digging so many burrows and establishing a home in the clearing back there. The clan would find this an ugly, dying thing too. The clan would be angry."

He didn't say anything for a time and rested his legs and feet while she remained kneeling and facing the tree. Finally she raised her hands toward the tree, and after she held that pose for several minutes, she made a slashing gesture with her fingers.

The crooked-faced goblin realized Saarh had been casting a spell.

Her magical gesture split the oak's trunk as easily as a sharp knife could split the belly of a piglet. The cracking sound startled both of them. But the greater surprise came when the tree shriveled to a woody pulp, the leaves vanished, and standing there where the trunk had been just a moment before, was a spear.

"Someone hid this," Saarh said. "Made the tree grow around it. But it was not so well hidden that it could not be found."

The crooked-faced goblin said nothing, his throat tight and dry.

Saarh stood and slowly approached the spear, a reverence in her bearing. She bowed to the spear then stretched a hand out, fingers tingling from the energy the thing exuded.

The wooden spear hovered a hand-breadth above the ground. It was green, as if it had been fashioned from a too-young tree whose bark had been stripped. Slivers of gold, silver, and platinum were inlaid along the shaft, forming designs that matched some of those the goblins had carved in the dome ceiling under the mountain. Tiny gems that sparkled in the last rays of the sun were sprinkled among the precious metal runes. They were diamonds mostly; Saarh was familiar with those gemstones that could be found in the warrens in the Kharolis. But there were also emeralds as bright and dark green as sugar maple leaves coated by rainwater. And there were a few yellow-hued stones that looked like shards of sunlight caught on the surface of a stream.

The tip was metal, not one of the precious kinds that formed the runes on the shaft, but something stronger and sharper than anything Saarh had ever known. It gleamed dully, and when she bent close to the ground to look at the tip, she observed her own reflection. Above the spear tip was a silver band that held small rings. Feathers dangled from the rings, dark yellow ones shot through with rich browns and vibrant greens.

"Chislev's symbol, these feathers," Saarh said in awe. "Chislev's spear, this."

Behind her, the crooked-faced goblin gasped. "The weapon of a god?"

"The only weapon this god wielded," she softly returned. She stood upright again and pushed her hand forward, through an unseen force that held the spear poised above the earth. The shaman slowly wrapped the fingers of her right hand around the shaft. The power in the weapon flowed into her.

Mudwort had not been able to sleep, so she'd looked in on the shaman of long-ago. She'd used one of the uncut blue stones to help in the seeing spell as there were no rocks or earth beneath her to channel the magic through. Mudwort needed to send her magic through stone if she wanted to sustain a spell for more than a few minutes.

So that journey into the past had taken more than a few minutes. Indeed, Mudwort had been caught up in the enchantment for the better part of two days. Her throat and mouth were dry from lack of water, and her stomach ached because she had not eaten in a while. That no one had disturbed her during those two days surprised her. But then, she'd been sprawled against the crate, where the rocking sea was felt stronger than elsewhere. And she was still a loner and a member of none of the other clans.

She needed food, so she slipped off the crate, standing still for a few moments as her legs protested moving after being locked for so many hours in a rigid position. She nearly toppled into another crate, as she was dizzy from the ship and her hunger, and the stink in the air was palpable. Disgusting.

She climbed the stairs and headed to the galley. Something was cooking, meat and vegetables; the smell of potatoes set her mouth to watering. She didn't care what the cook had thrown in the pot—she would eat her fill, and she would sleep and dream about Chislev's spear.

What had once tugged the goblin who lived in the long-ago time tugged Mudwort.

32

POLITICAL ILLS

Direfang must come now. Be fast." Thus spoke a yellow-skinned goblin from Saro-Saro's clan. Direfang could not recall her name, but he'd seen her hovering around the old goblin often enough.

The hobgoblin was standing on the deck of the *Clare*, leaning against the stern railing and watching the waves. It was somehow more relaxing, less unsettling to his stomach, than standing at the bow of the ship, and fewer sailors bothered him.

Direfang shook his head. Nearby was a signaler who'd been sending a message to *Linda's Grady* at the hobgoblin's request. *Linda's Grady* trailed the *Clare* at the moment, and through the signaler, Direfang had learned that things were reasonably calm and secure aboard the other ship.

"Direfang must come now. Be fast."

The hobgoblin let out a deep sigh, digging his nails into the railing. He could feel the gouges where he'd already marred the wood.

"How necessary is this thing that needs attention?" Direfang wanted to address the goblin by name, but try as he may, he couldn't remember it. "Is something wrong?"

He did not even glance at her as he spoke, keeping his eyes on the water and on *Linda's Grady*. The air was fresh and brisk there. And in the few days since they'd

275

left the mouth of the river, he'd learned to enjoy listening to the sounds of the sails moving in the wind punctuated by the cries of seagulls.

"Necessary, Direfang. Be fast." She prodded him in the leg so he would look at her, gave him a serious stare, then spun about on shoes she'd appropriated from the dwarf village. As other goblins had, she'd tied them on with twine so they would not fall off. But they noisily slapped as she walked away. "Be fast now, Direfang. Very fast." She looked over her shoulder to make sure he followed.

On the level below deck he paused outside the galley. Mudwort was eating there, alone at a table. The priest and wizard were at another table, their plates empty but smeared with some sort of gravy. Grallik was sipping a mug of something. Horace's head was bowed in prayer. Sailors toiled around them, cleaning up platters from an earlier shift, taking the dishes to a table and heaping on more food for the second wave of hungry goblins. The hobgoblin knew the cook and the sailors were not pleased at feeding so many mouths. But Grallik had bought enough food, and enough steel pieces had been spread around to keep the complaints muted and limited. Direfang wondered if the other ships also had enough food.

"No time for food, Direfang. Be fast." Saro-Saro's messenger shook a finger at him and started down the flight of stairs that led to the lower hold.

Direfang had not spoken to Mudwort since she had brought the lightning down on the *Blithe Dagger* and given the wizard credit for that magic. He wanted to sit with her, eat, and discuss the Qualinesti Forest—telling her it was much closer than he had imagined. He was looking forward to reaching land, but he had an important task he wanted her to attend to well before the ship stopped. He needed her to use her seeing spell again.

"Later," he muttered aloud, meaning, later he would catch up with Mudwort.

"No, now," the yellow-skinned goblin insisted, overhearing him as she stopped and turned halfway down on the steps. "Be fast."

DEATH MARCH

Direfang was quick to follow her; if truth be told, he was genuinely curious what was happening that was so urgent in the hold. He took a deep breath before going down, knowing well the air would be thick and foul, and closing his eyes so when he reached the bottom he could open them and more easily adjust to the darkness.

Only a few lanterns were lit at midpoint in the hold. No goblins clustered directly under them, as they seemed to prefer the darkness in the recesses of the wooden cave. The air was worse than the hobgoblin had expected, far, far worse than on his previous visit there. Not even the slave pens in Steel Town had reeked so badly, but then there was always air stirring around the pens in the mining camp.

He coughed to clear his throat and followed the beckoning goblin. Direfang nodded to Two-chins and Rustymane and grunted a hello to Cattail, who'd been discussing the upcoming meal with some of her Flamegrass clan members. The discussion stopped and they started whispering as he passed by. Goblins always had secrets, he mused.

The air grew worse the farther he went toward the rear of the hold, stepping between goblins and hobgoblins and seeing Saro-Saro surrounded by his clan at the very back of the packed group. The old goblin was stretched out, his green cloak covering him like a blanket. The goblin who'd led Direfang down there went over to Saro-Saro and dabbed his forehead with the hem of her dress.

Saro-Saro turned his head and caught Direfang's shocked expression. The old clan leader was clearly dying.

The skin of his face was sunken to such a degree that he looked skeletal, and even though little light reached back there, Direfang could see the telltale black splotches. There were large black knobs on Saro-Saro's neck, of the sort that had decorated the limbs and necks of many of the goblins who'd died from the plague.

"Should have went into the sea with the priest," Direfang said reproachfully as he neared, standing over Saro-Saro, but not too close. He shook his head at the clan members who still hovered close by; they risked getting the sickness by touching the old goblin.

Some of them had already caught it. Direfang heard coughs muffled by cupped hands; several goblins were sweating profusely. It was overly warm in the hold with the press of bodies, but the ones who sweated there were wrapped in cloaks and blankets, shivering.

"Leave," Saro-Saro gestured forcefully to the clansmen nearest him. "It is time to speak to Direfang alone."

"No." Direfang held his hands out to his sides to block some of them from leaving. "The sick should stay here, away from the others. This one and this one stay. This one too." He pointed to seven or eight more, making it about a dozen, with Saro-Saro, who were visibly afflicted. "The rest of you, go up on the top deck. The air is good there. Cause no trouble with the sailors, and be fast."

The healthy ones protested at being sent to the top deck of the ship, where they feared the waves and water, but Direfang insisted.

The hobgoblin leader waited until the healthy clan members shuffled past; then he sat, keeping an arm's length from Saro-Saro. The clan leader turned his head so he could better see the hobgoblin.

"Dying," Saro-Saro said. "I am."

"Yes."

"The skull man said he could not help. The skull man's magic is weak and used up."

"Perhaps the skull man used too much of his precious magic healing goblins by the river days past." Direfang heard goblins shifting around behind him, turned his head, and caught several edging close, trying to eavesdrop. He glared at them, and they backed away a little, but the hold was crowded and they could not go far.

"The skull man said four days, maybe five."

"Before this ship reaches the forest."

Saro-Saro nodded. "Will never see the forest because the skull man's magic is weak. Will never see anything beyond this wooden cave, this hole made by sailing men." He spoke softer, and the hobgoblin leaned closer out of respect for the old clan leader. "Slave for too long, Direfang. Too many years toiling for the hated Dark Knights. Should have had a better life. Deserved one, didn't I? We?"

The hobgoblin had only a choked reply. He nearly reached out to touch Saro-Saro in sympathy but stopped himself and set his hands instead on his knees.

"Should have died, maybe, to the earthquakes. Would have been faster death and would not have hurt so much." Saro-Saro's voice dropped even lower, and Direfang crept forward just a little and saw that the pillow Saro-Saro's head was on was crusted with blood and vomit. "This sickness, Direfang, it ruined all the plans. My plans."

What foolish plans? Direfang wondered to himself, but he thought he would humor the dying goblin by nodding agreement. "Perhaps after this ship reaches the forest, the clan can still—"

Saro-Saro shook his head. He coughed once and made a gasping, raspy sound that caused some of his ill clansmen to shrink back against the hull. "No, Direfang." The goblin coughed again, deeper and racking, his body writhing from the spasm.

Direfang held his breath and looked at the once-proud clan leader. He heard whispers behind him; two Woodcutter clan members were speculating that Saro-Saro likely would not live out the day. The hobgoblin cut a cross look over his shoulder, silencing the two.

The coughing subsided and Saro-Saro tried to speak again. His voice cracked, and the words sounded like leaves blowing across a dry riverbed.

Direfang saw that one of the black knobs on the old goblin's neck had ruptured and was oozing an ugly green pus. He breathed only slightly, not wanting to inhale any of the sickness. The stench was so awful that he clenched his teeth and fought to keep from retching.

A goblin named Uren knelt at Saro-Saro's shoulder. Uren had often worked under Direfang at the Dark Knight mine and had distinguished himself by rarely complaining and sometimes helping older goblins heft their ore sacks. Uren did not yet have knobs on his neck, but he sweated heavily, and he shivered so hard, his teeth chattered. There were a few black spots on his cheek.

The old goblin broke into another coughing spasm, and Direfang closed his eyes at the terrible sight. He heard other goblins coughing, though not as loud or hurtful sounding, heard a baby cry—the sound so rare down there that he knew it must be Graytoes' Umay. He heard shuffling near him, felt something brush up against his back, and as he turned, he felt fingers dig into his legs.

Direfang's eyes flew open, and he tried to scoot back as two goblins behind him, their clawed hands on his shoulders, forced him to his knees. Somehow Saro-Saro had managed to rally and was struggling to sit up with the help of Uren. The old goblin was the one who had dug his claws into Direfang's legs, poking through the thin material of his leggings and finding flesh beneath. Saro-Saro pulled himself close the hobgoblin even as Direfang tried to shove away.

Saro-Saro scratched Direfang's chest and spit in his face. At last Direfang threw off the goblins behind him and lurched to his feet then fell forward when the ship tossed. Saro-Saro continued to claw and spit at Direfang, reaching for him futilely. Uren and two other ill members of Saro-Saro's clan piled on top of the hobgoblin.

"Die too, Direfang," Saro-Saro rasped. "Join me in death." A thick line of blood dripped over his lip. "Should have died on the mountain, you. Were supposed to die there."

"Should have died, Direfang, so Saro-Saro could lead this army," Uren hissed. "If Saro-Saro cannot lead, Direfang will not either!"

Direfang kicked out, knocking Saro-Saro away. The clan leader landed heavily on his back and started coughing wildly again, with the sick ones around him forgetting Direfang and huddling close to Saro-Saro. But the goblins behind the hobgoblin leader surged forward. Direfang spun to face them before realizing they were coming to his aid, indeed were going to brave the sickness to help him.

"Stay back!" He shouted at them all, glaring. "Farther back!" He waved a fist at the goblins, who backed away slowly and pressed together toward the center of the hold. "It is not safe here."

Saro-Saro continued to cough frantically behind him, Uren joining in.

Two-chins was farther back in the hold, and he climbed on the shoulders of another goblin so he could better see what was going on.

"Get the skull man," Direfang called, spotting Two-chins. "Be fast." Once more the goblins tried to edge closer, partly out of curiosity and partly because some of them wished to help. "Stay back." Softer, he said, "Stay away from the sickness and stay well."

"Stay well, stay well." The advice was passed back through the throng.

"Will Direfang die too?" Rustymane, a hobgoblin who also had worked as a foreman in the mine, spoke for the others, fearfully.

"Everything dies," another hobgoblin answered stoically.

"But will Direfang die of the sickness?" Rustymane persisted.

"Maybe," Direfang growled. "Maybe me, you, all of us."

"Saro-Saro must account for this!" Rustymane insisted.

"Saro-Saro is dying," Skakee chimed in. "Like Direfang will die now, I think. Saro-Saro's blood and sickness is mixed in Direfang's wounds. It will be an empty, sad forest without Direfang."

The goblins quieted. Some of them stared in disbelief that Saro-Saro would do such a thing to Direfang, purposely spreading the foul illness. Others looked grief-stricken and angry. A few trembled in fear and tried to squeeze their way to the front of the hold, wanting to get as far away from the sick and dying ones as possible.

"Please, Two-chins," Direfang pleaded. "Get the skull man. Be fast."

Two-chins climbed off his kinsman's shoulders, eyes on Direfang as he backed toward the stairs.

"Be fast!" echoed Graytoes. "Be very fast!"

33

DEATH ON THE NEW SEA

Direfang's growls kept the dozen ill clansmen an arm's distance away. He could barely stand upright in that section of the hold; the top of his head brushed the low ceiling. The ropy muscles in his arms bunched, and he clenched and unclenched his hands in a silent fury that raised his temperature and quickened his heart.

He wanted to shout oaths at Saro-Saro and his foul clansmen, telling them they were all fools. He'd led them from Steel Town and into the mountains, at one point giving everyone the option of going their own way, perhaps in clans, perhaps scattering. He practically begged them to leave him alone; that was his deepest desire. Some goblins did leave then, Hurbear's clan. Direfang wished he would have followed Hurbear.

Direfang wasn't sure how that had all happened. Whose idea was it that he should lead the goblins to a new home-land? A foreman in the Dark Knight mines, they'd been following his orders for a few years, yes. But there had been other sturdy foremen, such as Rustymane, who stared at him at that moment with a vacant expression.

Was it because it was he who had urged them to rebel and flee the mining camp? They'd followed him then, so they kept on following. Then more and more and more kept arriving, thousands. That was Mudwort's doing. He trusted

282

Mudwort, but she shouldn't have told so many others to come and follow him.

Mudwort said the goblins felt they owed their lives to him.

So he felt responsible, even for Saro-Saro and his vile bunch.

Direfang's legs stung where the old goblin's claws had ripped the flesh. His shoulders ached where Uren and a few others had bitten and scratched him. He felt Saro-Saro's bloody spittle drying on his face and wondered if the illness that was claiming the old goblin was even then wending its way into his body. Half of the offending goblins had knives they'd taken from Steel Town or the ogre village they'd raided; why hadn't they just killed him swiftly with their knives?

Because Saro-Saro didn't want Direfang to die fast, the hobgoblin knew. The clan leader wanted Direfang to catch the illness and suffer as he was suffering. Well, suffering was nothing new to Direfang, he thought bitterly. His life had been nothing but suffering, the thick scars and his mangled ear a testament to that.

The main reason for the ignominious attack was because Saro-Saro had wanted to be the leader. His illness would prevent that.

Direfang gave a low moan, startling the others who were closest by, sending them back a few steps. If Saro-Saro had expressed such a desire when they'd first left Steel Town, the hobgoblin leader reflected ruefully, Direfang would have eagerly relented.

"Who will lead now, Saro-Saro? If not you or me?" Direfang's words were plaintive and couldn't be heard by many goblins in the hold.

"It doesn't matter," the dying, old goblin hissed. "Does not matter," Saro-Saro repeated. "Just that it will not be Direfang."

The hobgoblin leader suddenly felt a weakness in his legs. Did the illness strike that quickly? Or was the ship making him dizzy again? He felt as if he were floating, lifted by his pounding heart and the swells the *Clare* climbed. A few hundred goblins watched him, not a one speaking, all of them staring at him and Saro-Saro.

Rustymane edged closer. Rustymane could lead, Direfang thought, staring at his old friend. He'd been a good foreman, though not for more than a handful of months before the earthquakes struck. Rustymane had reddish, wiry hair and only a few scars on his face and arms. His hands were large, the fingers stubby. His wide eyes held a hint of kindness, tears now threatening at the edges.

Direfang turned his head to stare angrily at Saro-Saro. The old goblin was propped up on his pillow, Uren at his shoulder, both of them coughing and sweating and shivering in the meager light that reached that far end of the ship. The others in bad condition surrounding them also shivered, the closest ones glaring at Direfang. He continued to clench and unclench his fists, wanting to lash out at the clansmen and hurt them as they had hurt and betrayed him. But he could do nothing worse to them that what they already suffered.

"The knives. Set the knives down." Direfang spoke fiercely, snarling for emphasis. "The knives. Be fast."

They did lay down their knives, to the hobgoblin's surprise. He stalked forward, using his feet to kick the knives behind him and well away from Saro-Saro's band of diseased loyalists. He heard scrabbling and knew other goblins were snatching up the weapons behind him.

No one spoke for long minutes then, though he could hear his own breathing, fast in his anger and exertion, and he could hear the forced breathing of Saro-Saro and Uren also. He heard the groaning of the wooden ship and hurried footsteps from overhead. Someone heavy was coming down the steps.

"Skull man, take care," Direfang cautioned.

None of the goblins spoke as Horace threaded his way through them.

"Foreman Direfang . . ."

Rustymane had moved up alongside the priest and was relating the tale of Saro-Saro's attack.

Horace looked different that day. He was dressed in a pale green tunic that draped to mid-thigh, with dark blue leggings that were tucked in the tops of a pair of shiny, brown boots. A black vest with faint green and blue embroidered leaves at the shoulders fit a little too tightly. The clothes had been purchased by Grallik, the hobgoblin knew. Direfang thought it fortunate that he'd not yet changed into the clothes Grallik said had been purchased for him. The clothes would be contaminated if he had the sickness.

The priest looked as though he'd swallowed something bitter after listening to Rustymane. He squinted, not seeing as well as the goblins could in the relative darkness of the hold.

"I'd thought the sickness past," he said with genuine regret. "I thought we'd left it on the shore of the New Sea. The salt cleansing the last trace. With Zeboim's blessings . . ."

"The sea. Zeboim. Did nothing for Saro-Saro," Direfang finished.

Horace changed his expression, trying to look optimistic. "Foreman, you've weathered being near the ill before, under the black willow along the river where so many goblins died. You will weather this. You are healthy and you have willpower and—"

Direfang gestured toward Saro-Saro and Uren and their followers. "What of these goblins? Can Saro-Saro's clansmen be healed?"

"I thought . . ." Horace shifted so he could better see around Direfang. "I thought I should start by helping you."

Direfang shook his head, beckoning Horace forward. He ordered the healthy goblins back, sending some up to the galley and more of the stout-hearted up on deck. "Do not get in the sailors' way," he cautioned. When the shuffling was finished, about three hundred and fifty remained below, and they kept as much distance as possible from Direfang and Horace and the coughing, spasming ill. Yet because there was more room in the hold, the air was not so thick anymore.

"Help those first," Direfang told the priest. "But only if there is a chance the clansmen can be healed. Only *if*, skull man."

Horace, nodding grimly, tended to Uren first. Saro-Saro lay quietly, shivering, staring hatefully at Direfang. "You should have called for me earlier," the priest said to those in Saro-Saro's clan who were afflicted. He spoke bluntly, irritably, in the goblin tongue. "This has progressed beyond the power of my magic. I do not think I can do anything for you. Why, in the name of all the Sea Mother counts holy, did you not call for me before now?"

Uren coughed into his hands, blood dripping onto his fingers. He wiped the blood on his shirt, which was already smeared with blood and vomit. "Thought this maybe was sickness from the water, skull man. The up and down, side to side. The wind and whoosh and—"

"No, not seasickness. Clearly," Horace answered. He coughed too but not from the plague. The stench from the waste and the disease made simple breathing difficult for the priest.

"Some got well before," Uren said hopefully. "Back by the river. Some got sick, then got well. Some of those are down here." He gestured with a bloody hand toward a group of Saro-Saro's clansmen who stood well back from the sick. "Watched them get well."

"A few," Horace admitted. "But not many. Don't know why. The plague killed nearly everyone else it touched." The priest seemed weary and defeated. "I will try to ease some of your suffering." He looked solemnly at Saro-Saro, and the old goblin nodded in understanding. "But I cannot heal you. The illness has taken too firm a hold. I can bless you, pray to Zeboim that your spirits—"

"Stop!" Direfang barked when he heard Horace's words. "Your healing will not help Saro-Saro and those others?"

Horace shook his head. "Sorry. No. More skilled healers than I could perhaps do something. But I will try to take away some of the pain and—"

"Will the illness spread? To the ones who are healthy?"

Horace shrugged, but his glum look told Direfang that it was likely.

"Perhaps this hold can be cleansed. To help?"

"Well, yes, I've spells that can—"

"Then forget the healing. Do this cleansing. Worry about the healthy, forget the dying."

DEATH MARCH

Direfang clomped past the priest and grabbed up Uren and another goblin who was close to him. Tucking the two under one arm, he grabbed two more with the other. They squirmed against him, kicking and biting and drawing more blood. But the illness had taken some of their strength. Direfang headed toward the stairs.

"Stay away. Stay back from the sick," Direfang called over his shoulder to the healthy ones. "Use your knives to keep the sick back there. Understand?" He didn't wait to hear the replies.

Two-chins had been hovering on the stairs, trying to take everything in. He followed Direfang up the stairs, trailed by Two-chins' mate. More goblins started up, but Rustymane cried out.

"Wait!" he shouted, stomping to the stairs and pushing goblins away. "Wait until Direfang comes back. Wait and keep the sick from leaving. Direfang means to protect all of the clans. Direfang will—"

"What will Direfang do with Uren and . . . ?" Graytoes had squeezed between two hobgoblins. She looked up at Rustymane, holding Umay close, the baby sleeping despite the ruckus. "What will Direfang do?"

Rustymane growled softly, silencing her and the other restless goblins.

Meanwhile Direfang had wrestled the four plague-ridden goblins up to the deck. He gulped in the fresh, salt-tinged air, gathering his strength. He ignored the shouts of the goblins gathered around the main mast. K'lars was at the capstan, huddled over some device. The half-ogre stopped what he was doing and headed over to Direfang.

"What are you doing?" K'lars nearly had caught up before Direfang spun around to confront him.

"Stay back. See the sickness?" Direfang gestured with his head to Uren, held tight though squirming under his armpit. "Stay back and stay well." Then Direfang reached the port rail and one by one hurled the goblins over the side. "The sickness ends here."

The hobgoblin returned belowdecks, making two more trips, Horace following him on the last one, his wide

287

eyes disbelieving. The goblins protested and screamed as Direfang pitched them over the rail, all save the last—Saro-Saro, who had grown too weak to resist or say anything. Direfang held the old clan leader like Graytoes cradled Umay. He took no pleasure in what he had to do.

"Die free, Saro-Saro," Direfang said bitterly. He coughed, and he saw Saro-Saro's eyes sparkle with the hope that the illness had quickly taken hold of the hobgoblin. "Die fast, old one." Then he dropped Saro-Saro over the rail, the goblin striking the side of the ship before hitting the water and immediately going under the swirling waves. None of the goblins had known how to swim, so the strongest of them bobbed only once or twice before drowning quickly.

Horace gripped the rail and stared at the spot where Saro-Saro had been. "I-I-I don't understand, Foreman Direfang. To kill them like this . . ."

"The illness, this plague, had already killed those goblins and enough others," Direfang said vehemently. He motioned to the goblins edging away from the mast. "Stay back and stay well."

Two-chins' mate spoke a little of the human tongue, and she tried to explain to K'lars about the plague and the goblins who were sick in the hold and who were now lying at the bottom of the New Sea, she hoped being devoured by the fishes.

The half-ogre's eyes widened. He stared angrily at Direfang and took a step toward the hobgoblin leader. "No one told me or Captain Gerrold about any plague. No amount of coin would have gotten you this ship or the other ships, I'm certain, if we had known—"

Horace cut him off, interposing himself between the half-ogre and Direfang. The half-ogre thrust a hand against the priest's shoulder, but Horace stood firm and spoke forcefully.

"We thought the plague had passed, I promise you," Horace said. "We'd not have come on this ship if we thought there was a threat to you. Zeboim is your goddess; you follow her, same as I do. I swear on the silvery hair of the Sea Mother that no harm was meant and that my best efforts will go toward ensuring that no harm shall result to you—"

"*No!*" Two-chins flailed his arms in the air then pointed to the rail.

Direfang was climbing over.

"Rustymane," Direfang rasped. "Rustymane can lead now. The skull man can cleanse the hold." The hobgoblin coughed and wiped at the line of bloody drool spilling over his bottom lip. "The mistakes end here. My responsibility ends. The illness ends here."

He dropped over the rail.

34

THE SPEAR OF CHISLEV

Mudwort was oblivious to the commotion on deck. She'd heard goblins tromping past the galley door and caught a glimpse of Direfang. She'd noted the surge of goblins piling into the galley and crowding on the benches, waiting for food.

The wizard sat across from her; he'd moved from his table to hers when Two-chins came in to get the priest.

"More room!" Mudwort told a goblin who tried to sit next to her. She stretched and reached out her arm, indicating the goblin should give her that much extra space. "Farther away," she repeated to the hobgoblin who started to settle in next to Grallik. She added a withering glance and thrummed her fingers against the table. The goblin and hobgoblin complied.

The plate in front of her had been licked clean. For nearly two days, she'd been caught up in her latest seeing spell, and it had left her famished and tired. Sated, her eyelids drooped and she yawned.

"Talk about Chislev," she said to Grallik, her head bobbing forward. She forced herself to stay awake. "Talk clear, wizard, and talk slow." Mudwort's command of the human's language was limited.

"You should be talking to Horace," the wizard said. "Horace is a follower of Zeboim, but there's a part of him that respects all the gods. He's a scholar of the divine, Mudwort, and he—"

She stuffed her fist in her mouth as she yawned again, shook her head vehemently, and fixed him with a narrowed gaze. "Did not ask the skull man. Will not ask the skull man." She slammed her fist against the table, making her empty plate jump. The others around them edged away. "Tell me about Chislev. It is important."

Grallik's eyes widened. He'd been watching her, and he'd heard her repeat "Chislev" once during one of her far-seeing enchantments.

"She—"

"Chislev is female?"

Grallik nodded.

"There is power in females," Mudwort said. "But not in gods. Goblins do not—"

"Believe in them, I know." Grallik rubbed at a smudge on the table and looked up as a sailor came around with a kettle, ladling out more helpings of a meat and potato stew onto plates. The air filled with slurping and belching sounds, appreciative chatter, and plates clanking against the table to hurry the sailor.

"Chislev. Talk some more, wizard." Mudwort yawned wide. "More about this female god."

"She is called the Beast and also Kisla, the Mother of Sea Creatures, which is why you should ask Horace about her. Some call her the Wild One as she represents nature."

"And power?"

"Aye, the wild goddess represents that too."

Mudwort nodded, beginning to understand Saarh's interest in Chislev's spear. Saarh seemed very in touch with nature and eager to accumulate arcane power.

Grallik pursed his lips, searching his memory for what he had heard about Chislev. "Worshipers associate colors with her—"

"Yellow," Mudwort supplied, remembering the colors on the spear in her vision of Saarh. "Brown too. Mostly green."

"You know much," Grallik said, "for one who does not believe in Chislev."

Mudwort glared at him. "More, wizard."

Grallik nodded to the sailor, who ladled more of the stew on his plate. "Another helping, yes, a small one." The wizard stirred a spoon in the stew and noticed that not a single goblin had asked for or been given a spoon. He smiled about that.

"Chislev's symbol is a feather, of her colors. Her weapon, the short spear." He didn't notice Mudwort's eyes widen, or see her mouth, "My spear."

He ate a spoonful of the stew. "Most of her worshipers are farmers and hunters, druids too, some bands of elves, and I believe the centaurs of the plains. It is said that the seasons march on her whim, that summer comes when she is passionate, winter when she wraps herself in melancholy. When she is angry, she shows it in violent storms."

One of the sailors carrying the stew pots stopped at Grallik's shoulder. "You speak of Chislev," he said, frowning. "I favor Zeboim, who despises the Mother of Sea Creatures. It was Zeboim's will that we got through that last blow with nary a problem." He moved on.

Grallik took a few more spoonfuls of the stew and continued his explanation. "Chislev doesn't have priests in the same sense as Krynn's other gods. Hers are the druids, and they protect the forests. As that sailor said, she is known to dislike Zeboim. Their ill will was fostered in the All-Saint's War when Zeboim defeated her. I know little else, Mudwort. As I told you, Horace could—"

Mudwort had been fighting off sleep for too long. Her head plopped onto her empty plate, and she started to snore.

Grallik shrugged and kept eating.

"Rude things, ain't they?" said another sailor passing by with slices of bread. "K'lars calls them rats what walk on two legs."

"Be careful," Grallik hissed. "A few of those *rats* can understand every word you say." He fell to finishing his plate of stew, the clatter of plates and pitchers and the goblin chatter rising all around him.

DEATH MARCH

Direfang struck the cold sea and dropped like a heavy stone. After a moment, however, the water buoyed him up again, just as he'd seen happen with the goblins he'd thrown over. His reflexes caused him to gasp and gulp in the sweet air—his last breaths, probably.

In truth, he didn't want to die. But more than that, he didn't want to suffer the way Saro-Saro and the other stricken goblins had languished, didn't want his already-ugly body to become covered with the large, black, oozing knobs. He didn't want to cough up great gobs of blood. A quick death was better. And it was better that the plague end with him than spread to his comrades.

The saltwater stung the slashes on his arms and legs, and it made his tattered clothes heavy and worked to pull him down again. Direfang was at the same time terrified of dying and furious at Saro-Saro for bringing about such a sorry end to his miserable life. He raged at the circumstances that had caused all of it, yet it had been his decision to swarm into Reorx's Cradle and take away the foul sickness. He'd survived so much—the years of tortuous labor at the mining camp, the beatings, the night they poured salt in his wounds and cut off his left ear, the earthquakes, the lava, the fight with the tylor—all to be murdered by some foul disease.

He slipped under gradually. He felt a buzzing in his ears, then a quick thrumming, which he guessed was his heart beating. He briefly kicked with his legs, feeling himself rise again then drew his legs together, deciding to resist the instinct to survive.

The plague ends here, he thought.

Direfang opened his eyes, astonished that he could see under water. The world down there was a green-gray with a few slender, shadowy shapes passing through it: fish. It was colder than he had expected, but he welcomed that—the air in the ship's hold had been cloying and hot. He swallowed the water, thinking it really had no taste to it. He felt heavy, full of water, and very cold.

Then the world turned black just as he felt himself pulled upward again.

"Got him!" K'lars shouted, his booming voice carrying

across the chop. "Heavy, this big rat is!" The half-ogre treaded water several dozen feet behind the *Clare*.

A longboat was being lowered with four sailors in it. The *Clare* had dropped its sails when Direfang started heaving sick goblins overboard. K'lars had followed Direfang into the sea a heartbeat after the hobgoblin leader had jumped to what he believed was a certain death. But the ship did not stop immediately and was drifting ahead, so the longboat was needed to go back and retrieve the pair.

"Hurry it, will you?" K'lars called. "I said he's heavy!" The sailor had grabbed Direfang under one armpit and was lifting his head above the water as best he could. The two were of similar build and size, both nearly seven feet tall. But the hobgoblin was dead weight, and twice the half-ogre lost his grip and fumbled with his burden, briefly sinking, before the longboat arrived.

"You pull 'im up. He's an anchor, that's for sure." K'lars waited until they had Direfang in the center of the boat; then he dragged himself in. The hobgoblin leader's eyes were shut, and he lay still as stone. "The cook better make something special for me for dinner after I risked my own sorry hide to save this big rat."

Once on the ship, they turned Direfang on his side, and K'lars struck him in the center of his back. The hobgoblin coughed once, his eyes opening, the water rushing out of his mouth. He coughed again, blinked, and struggled to rise. K'lars helped him up.

"Raise the sails!" Captain Gerrold set his fists against his hips and watched as Horace inspected the wet, dazed hobgoblin. "Get back you, all of you."

But the goblins who'd been gathered amidships didn't understand the commands in Common and clustered around Direfang.

"Get them below," Gerrold said, looking daggers at Direfang. "All of them. I don't want a single one getting tangled in my lines or tripping my sailors. Don't want another one jumping over the side either . . . or being tossed over like garbage."

Direfang looked around slowly, still half in a daze. The

eyes of the goblins shifted away as most of them drifted off, following the captain's orders. The hobgoblin leader met the angry stare of Gerrold.

"The illness is in here." He stabbed his thumb at his chest. "And it spreads like a fire over a mound of dead. The illness will move to here and here and here"—he pointed to the men who were wet and apparently had helped him into the longboat—"and there; sooner or later the illness will spread to them." He gestured to K'lars, giving him a nod. "Don't doom this ship. And look to the other ships. If there is more plague with the goblins—"

Gerrold stormed forward and grabbed Direfang's tunic at the breastbone. "Doom? The plague was brought on the *Clare,* and you throwing yourself overboard won't get rid of it. The damnable thing is in deep in the hold and probably seeping into the very wood of the ship." Spittle flew from the captain's lips, his face twisting with anger. "I didn't order your rescue for any noble reason, hob. I need you to control these goblins. They seem to follow you. We'll be arriving at your damnable forest soon enough. But first we're going to the lady's island, Schallsea Island, like I'd planned. Not just for new line and sails now. I mean to rid *my* ship and *my* men of this insidious disease. Everything and everyone must be made whole or die."

He released his grip on the hobgoblin, pivoted on his leather heels, and returned to the wheel.

"Takes something to get the captain mad," K'lars said in a low voice. "Did you hear him call the *Clare* his ship? I think he just bought it from you, Direfang. Paid you in full when he had us haul your sorry hide out of the sea and changed his course for the lady's island. Bought it with the lady's healing hands, the captain did."

Direfang gaped dully at the sailor, shivering, whether from the illness or his ordeal, he couldn't say.

K'lars beckoned to Horace. "I think maybe you better get this big rat into the hold with all of the other rats, eh? Best right now if the captain doesn't see much of them. Captain Gerrold's got a mad streak on that'll take this ship to the Blood Sea and back."

Horace gestured to Direfang, and the hobgoblin slowly followed him toward the stairs.

"Schallsea Island?" Horace asked.

"Aye, the lady's place," K'lars returned.

Direfang followed Horace below.

"Predominantly human," Horace was explaining to Direfang, some minutes later. The hobgoblin sat on the stairs that led into the lower bay. Horace stood facing him. "Schallsea Island is near Abanasinia, separated by the straits. A big island, two hundred or more miles long, but less than half that at its widest point."

The hobgoblin coughed and shivered. He and Horace were as alone as possible, even the most curious of the goblins not wanting to get too close to him—maybe because they were afraid they might catch the illness, maybe because he had disgraced them with his behavior. Word had already spread that Direfang had tossed Saro-Saro and some of his clansmen over the side to their deaths.

Horace's eyes misted. "I visited there in my youth, Schallsea, with my uncle and my oldest brother. A beautiful place with many streams that sparkle like diamonds in the warmest months. Most of the island is inaccessible because of its dangerous cliffs. But there are a handful of harbors, and I'm certain he's taking this ship to the largest. That would be the Port of Schallsea, where my uncle once took his ship. A good thing it's summertime, Foreman. In winter the harbors have been known to freeze solid."

Horace seemed lost in the memory, and his head bobbed in time with the gentle rising and falling of the *Clare*.

"The lady's island, K'lars called it." Direfang coughed again and cursed to feel blood welling at the edge of his lip.

"Aye, the island is said to have been born during the Cataclysm. When the New Sea rose and lands all around this part of the world dropped, one stretch didn't, and they called it Schallsea. After the Chaos War, a famous Hero of the Lance came to it: Goldmoon."

Direfang nodded. He was familiar with some of the old tales.

"That's why these sailors call it the lady's island, Foreman. This lady, Goldmoon, established the Citadel of Light, which was destroyed not too many years ago. Last I heard, it was being rebuilt, though."

"Why take this ship there?" Direfang's shoulders were slumped, and he wrapped his arms around his chest, trying futilely to warm himself.

"Because Goldmoon attracted many healers to her citadel. There are people there far more skilled in the divine arts than I. If anyone can cure this plague, it would be the priests on that island. Captain Gerrold is smart to head there. I must go and tell Grallik."

"Fine," Direfang muttered. He groaned softly, his chin dropping, and slid forward, his chin striking the floor.

35

THE CITADEL OF LIGHT

There were flowers somewhere; Direfang could smell them. He couldn't see them—something sodden and soft was draped across his eyes. But the flowers smelled sweet, and he knew they must be close by. They mixed pleasantly with the musky scent of himself and with that of grass that had been rained on recently.

Gone were all the abysmal smells that had filled the cramped hold of the ship.

He felt warm but not too warm. His fever had broken, and he could breathe without coughing. His jaw ached, though, and when he ran his tongue around in his mouth, he felt broken teeth and spots of dried blood.

"You hit your head when you fell." It was Horace's voice. "Broke your jaw, which I was able to mend. The mystics here took care of the rest."

Direfang tried to get up, but a few pairs of strong hands pushed him back down.

"Rest." The voice was female and human, to his surprise. "I understand that you can speak Common."

Direfang tried to answer, but his throat was dry. He nodded, dislodging the wet cloth that had been covering his eyes. He blinked then closed his eyes again. The sun was high and bright and hurtful. He struggled to stay awake, but in the end gave in to the smell of the flowers and the feel of the soft breeze that played over his clean, bare skin. He'd registered that his ragged clothes had been removed and that the gouges on his arms and legs had been bandaged.

"Sleep," the woman insisted.

He let himself do just that.

The same woman spoke to him when he awoke again. "You are on Schallsea Island, Direfang, near the Citadel of Light. Horace thought it best to keep you and your brothers outside the citadel and the city." She paused before continuing. "I am Aerlane, once of Solace. And I welcome you to our island."

"Schallsea Island," Horace's voice echoed. The priest must have been nearby as well. "Remember? The captain said he was taking us there. To the citadel."

"Citadel?" The word came out of Direfang's mouth more as a croak. Again the light seemed bright, though not so strong anymore. Still, he closed his eyes. His ears would serve him well enough.

"The citadel is as much a piece of our hearts as it is a construction. It is more spiritual than physical. Most of us worship Mishakal here."

That was a god Direfang had not heard mentioned before.

"How did—?" Again Direfang's voice cracked. Someone dripped water into his mouth, and he greedily swallowed the liquid.

"The sailors brought you and the others here," the woman continued. "Cassandra and Jemtal sent us to tend you. Jemtal was once the same as Horace; he was a former Skull Knight. My sisters and brothers here are all from the Healing Lyceum. More of us are on your ship now."

"Clearing it of the foul plague you brought aboard."

Direfang opened his eyes finally and saw Captain Gerrold standing above him, next to Horace. The hobgoblin sat up, a little wobbly. He found he was in a meadow, the grass tall and mixed with purple and yellow wildflowers. Five women and two men in flowing blue and white robes trimmed in silver stood behind Gerrold. The tallest and oldest, a painfully-thin woman with short, gray hair, had been the main speaker.

Farther back stood four men in chain armor that glimmered under the late-afternoon sun. Had he slept most of the day away? Or how many days?

Spear in one hand, shield in the other, the quartet stood at attention and immediately reminded the hobgoblin of the Dark Knights in Steel Town.

"The Citadel Guardians," the woman explained, following Direfang's gaze. "They are a precaution only. Horace vouches for you."

There were other goblins in the meadow, but they were some distance away, and there were more blue and white–robed men and women in their midst, as well as more of the armed and armored Citadel Guardians.

"Direfang, those goblins over there were found to have traces of the illness, and so the mystics are trying to heal them. They are far more proficient in healing than I," Horace admitted. "Indeed, I envy their divine abilities."

Direfang saw the oddest figure standing near the goblin gathering. It looked like a beast but walked on two legs. Appearing a little taller than Direfang, the figure had gray-green skin covered with thin fur and a head that resembled a hyena's. A red-gray mane sprouted from the top of its head and ran down its neck. It was dressed in a leather jerkin and loose-fitting trousers. If it wore shoes, Direfang couldn't see them for the tall grass.

"Orvago," Aerlane named him, pointing toward the creature. "He is a gnoll, and one of Scanion's druids from the Animism Lyceum."

"A gnoll?" Direfang's eyes widened. Horace nodded to him reassuringly.

"We do not judge here based on one's race," Aerlane said. "It is the heart that matters. Orvago is here because he is curious and because he has embraced nature's arts."

"He is always curious," one of the robed men said.

Captain Gerrold stepped close and locked eyes with the hobgoblin, blocking his view of the gnoll.

Direfang noticed that the captain had changed into a fine shirt and trousers and that his hair was combed and tied tight at the back of his neck.

DEATH MARCH

"That's why I brought them all here, good lady. This one in particular. Good that you do not judge based on a man's shell. And so you saved him, perhaps saved all of us."

"Barely in time for him," she answered.

"I'd not thought Direfang would make it the two days it took us to reach Pelican Cove. The island's reputation spreads far across the waters, and I knew this was the only recourse, despite the distance. I thank you for allowing all of the goblins ashore, trusting woman. There are thousands, I know." He broke eye contact with Direfang, turned, and took her arm, leading her away. "Now, tell me Aerlane, how does construction go on rebuilding the citadel? And can my men lend some of their muscle through the night? Carrying, cleaning, whatever we can do in Mishakal's name. Take advantage of their gratitude now, and of all these goblins. The goblins are little, but they're strong, and there are an awful lot of them."

One of the robed women, who looked little older than a child, knelt next to Direfang. "It was an old, old plague that held you in its grip, one that the healers and mystics here had thought gone from this world. It is good that Gerrold brought you. And good that we can work to rid all of your ships of the last vestiges of this disease. The illness will not pain you and your brothers ever again."

"What is this place?"

The girl passed him a crystal decanter of water and motioned that he should drink.

The water was cool, and he held it in his mouth before swallowing.

"This place? This island? This—"

She cocked her head. "I thought Aerlane explained that. You are on Schallsea Island near the Citadel of Light. What more do you need to know? Everyone has heard of this place, and—"

Horace cleared his throat. "Foreman Direfang has seen little of the world, Qel. He was . . ." The priest hesitated and let a breath whistle out between his teeth. "Until recently he and his kinsmen were slaves."

She frowned first, then suddenly beamed. "Freed slaves?

301

Good. All of the gods' creatures should be free." She helped Direfang stand. The hobgoblin found her surprisingly strong for her size. "The citadel was founded long years ago as a place to develop mystic talents. Now it is a place of learning and healing. But more than priests and druids and scholars call this home. Heartspring is near here, and Captain Gerrold has sent some of his sailors there to take on grain and vegetables. Heartspring is a farming village. Some of your kind are scattered on this island too, and—"

"Goblins? Or hobgoblins?" Direfang found that his full voice was returning. The cool water had soothed his throat and restored his energy. He wondered if there was something enchanted about the water.

"In the wilds are many races, Direfang. A forest surrounds much of the island. Some goblins live here. Captain R'chet has offered to take more goblins on his ship, provided that they can be gathered and that they will not fear the presence of his minotaur crew. The captains tell me they are taking all of you to the Qualinesti Forest, where you will build a nation for your kind."

"Captain Gerrold and the minotaur R'chet speak too much," Direfang growled.

"There must be a hundred or more goblins on this island. To be truthful, they vex the farmers, raiding the fields and taking sheep. No one knows how they got here, but Captain R'chet wonders if a slave ship wrecked on the coast and these goblins are the survivors."

As they walked toward the host of sick goblins, Qel related some of the long history of the citadel to Direfang. "Goldmoon—"

"A Hero of the Lance," Direfang supplied.

"Yes. Goldmoon was looking for a home for her mystics and settled on this island after climbing the Silver Stair. I will tell you about all that later. The dwarves of Hillhome built the initial citadel with its crystal domes. Knights of the Sword helped." She paused. "Very many people helped. But a huge green dragon attacked the citadel during the War of Souls. It was looking for a great magical treasure. Some of the domes collapsed, and others were heavily damaged. But the mystics' spirits were not harmed, and reconstruction is well under way. Some say the citadel will be more beautiful than ever when it is again finished."

The hobgoblin let the rest of her words fade, instead concentrating on the chatter of his kinsmen. He'd found her story interesting but unimportant, and he doubted he would remember it long after that day. He looked around for familiar faces and realized that many of the goblins were pleased and excited to see him.

Two-chins rushed to him first, grabbing at his leg. "Clothes. Direfang needs clothes. Burned the old clothes, the people did."

"Clothes later," Direfang returned. "Back on the ship." He remembered he had that new package of clothes waiting for him in the captain's cabin.

"Could make a goblin home here," Two-chins suggested. "Lots of trees, farms to raid, sheep and goats to—"

"Goats!" That was blurted by Truak. The big hobgoblin stood and smacked his lips. "Like goats a lot, me do."

"Back on the ship," Direfang said. "That is our home for now."

He spoke loudly, making it a command for the others to hear. "The forest that once belonged to the elves is not far now." At least he hoped it wasn't. He tried to picture the map Gerrold had showed him days past. He recalled seeing the island, but he couldn't remember how much sea stretched between the island and the Qualinesti Forest. "Be fast," he added. "Get back on the ship." A part of him worried that Captain Gerrold might sail on without the goblins. He vividly recalled the anger in the man's voice and the fire in his eyes when he accused Direfang of bringing the plague on board his ship.

Looking around, he finally caught sight of Mudwort, who was well east of the assembly. She sat with the wizard; Grallik was hunched over so far that his forehead appeared to be touching hers. A snarl caught in Direfang's throat; he disapproved of Mudwort aligning her magic with that man's.

"Back to the ship, now. Now!" The goblins around

Direfang grumbled only a little, they were so pleased to be healed and happy to have the hobgoblin leader back among them. Two-chins picked a handful of the yellow flowers as he turned to head toward the sea. For his mate, he told Direfang, and he hurried to be one of the first back. The robed men and women slowly followed the goblins down a winding dirt path that stretched toward the sea. The guardians remained, eyes on Direfang and hands clenched tightly on the spears.

Direfang approached Mudwort and sat near her and the wizard. His fingers were twined in the grass, like hers, and after a few minutes, he pulled up a long blade and slid it between two teeth.

"Do what?" Direfang finally asked.

"Looking for goblins." Mudwort answered him in goblinspeak, which kept their words private from the wizard. "Calling the ones hidden on this island. The old, skinny woman asked for this. Wants the goblins away. Says it will be better for the goblins. Says there is no prejudice here. But those last words sound hollow."

Direfang nodded.

"Still," Mudwort continued, "calling the goblins on this island is good. Calling goblins from other places is good too."

Direfang frowned.

"Still summoning them, Mudwort? We don't have enough already?"

She smiled. "Talking through the stone, Direfang. Calling goblins and hobgoblins through the earth. Many more goblins everywhere. Many listening too, and some talk back."

He noticed that her and Grallik's hands were buried in the ground and that the grass had twisted around their wrists. He watched them for quite some time, aware of the guardians still standing rigidly but more aware of the meadow. He'd never felt so at peace before, and he allowed himself time to savor the moment.

Twilight had claimed the sky by the time Direfang heard Grallik and Mudwort stir away from their magic. He'd sat there for hours! His legs were a little stiff, but he shook off the feeling as he stood.

"Past time to return to the ship," he declared brusquely in Common so the wizard would understand. Direfang suddenly wanted to don his new clothes. He felt fully healed, alive again. "Be fast."

Grallik likewise was stiff, picking up first one leg then the other and rubbing them to get the feeling back. "Aye, Foreman." The wizard's eyes glistened like polished black buttons. "Past time it is. And soon enough we'll be in the Qualinesti Forest."

"The Goblin Forest," Mudwort corrected him. She hadn't stood, and her hands remained in the earth. "Go," she told them. "Won't be long now. Just a little bit more."

Direfang started to argue, but the wizard brushed past him, taking the same dirt path. The hobgoblin decided to follow as Mudwort wouldn't listen to him anyway. Stubborn goblin, she was.

"Just a little longer," Mudwort said.

The guardians remained, watching her.

The forest she envisioned had more trees, though they were still all relatively young—hundreds and hundreds of saplings. Mudwort knew Saarh had done something to increase the number of the trees. Everything was more lush and greener, and there were more goblins too, plenty of younglings hanging on their mothers.

They'd built a village, which consisted of dozens of rock and wood-domed homes atop hollowed-out earthen nests.

"How long ago was this?" Mudwort mused, concentrating. "Long time ago to be certain. A long, long time." When her mind had touched the forest as it existed in her time, during the seeing spell she'd just conjured with Grallik, there'd been no trace of the village. So Saarh and her followers had had enough time to build homes.

She'd been careful not to search for the spear, buried somewhere in the ancient woods, wrapped in the once-beautiful piece of cloth. She didn't want Grallik to know about the unusual spear, once wielded by Saarh. She could search for the spear because she was alone, but it was getting late, and she'd better be careful; she might miss the ship. She would find an opportunity to look later.

"The spear of Chislev," Mudwort murmured to herself. "Soon to be Mudwort's."

She took a last magical glance at Saarh, who stood apart from her village, looking up at the twilight sky. Yes, there it was! Chislev's spear was in Saarh's hand, and her consort was at her shoulder. He no longer had the crooked face, and his leg and foot were not twisted. But Mudwort knew it was the same goblin.

"The spear and the power will be Mudwort's very soon."

* * *

A few days later, nearly five thousand goblins stood on the shore of the Qualinesti Forest, watching the longboats row back to the five ships that had brought them to land. More than one hundred fifty goblins had streamed from the woods to join Direfang's ever-growing goblin nation on the journey from Schallsea Island.

Grallik stood closest to the water, hand shielding his eyes as he looked toward the ship and the setting sun. Mudwort stood near the wizard, her back to the sea, peering inland, already wandering off on her own path.

Direfang guessed that the wizard was trying to catch one last sight of Horace on the *Clare*'s deck. He'd heard the wizard arguing hotly with the priest, demanding that he come to the forest with him and Mudwort and Direfang and all the other goblins. The hobgoblin leader had interceded and decreed the priest could go where he wished, that Horace was free.

There were two healers to replace Horace; Direfang was thankful for that. One was the gnoll Orvago, a creature the hobgoblin considered even uglier than his scarred self. The gnoll said he had wanted to come along for the adventure and to make sure the goblins did not damage the "precious woods." Direfang did not object to the creature's presence because if an illness such as the plague came again, he wanted all the help he could get in dealing with it.

The other was the young woman named Qel.

"I was born on Schallsea Island," she had told Direfang as she boarded the *Clare*. "And I need to see something else of the world. Why not start with the ancient woods and the birth of a new nation?"

Direfang suspected her motives were not so innocent and that the mystics at the Citadel wanted her to be their eyes.

"Let the priests watch," he muttered, drawing the curious stare of Graytoes.

Graytoes wiggled her feet in the sand, scampering back when a wave came in and careful not to drop Umay. The baby cooed happily, and Graytoes answered it with meaningless sounds.

"Let the priests watch this nation grow, grow in spite of everything."

The hobgoblin turned away from the sea and led the goblins inland.

36

BERA'S QUEST

The largest ship in port, the *Mercy Corvan* had four masts and blue pennants flying from the top of each one. There were three crow's nests and men in each of them. One was a Dark Knight scout who had scant sailing experience, but he had keen vision.

Bera paced along a plank sidewalk so she could better watch the ship being loaded. The crates and barrels were meager, given the number of knights they would have to feed. No matter how much she berated the local merchants, she knew she could extract little else from them. They told her that a well-dressed half-elf with a heavily scarred face had been through the town seven days past and had purchased practically all goods and supplies. The merchants tried to soothe her ire by suggesting she stop in one of the ports to the west and replenish along the way. But she had already tarried there too long and was anxious for the chase.

Bera stared at the ship. Along the top at the rear were ornate carvings of horses pulling a man in a chariot. The chariot man was dressed in a flowing robe, and his left shoulder and arm were exposed, an ancient style of dress she thought had been favored by the Irda. Birds with human faces were perched on the exposed flesh, all expertly rendered and painted garishly. Only one of those faces looked feminine. There were windows rather than portholes in the ship, the glass gleaming in the bright afternoon sun.

She shuddered, still furious the goblins had eluded her. She'd heard from a few sailors that a half dozen ships had been bought by the fine-dressed half-elf; there were rumors they had picked up passengers along the coast—not humans. Honor, and her orders, demanded that she find the ships, the wizard, the priest, and the fugitive goblins and deliver Dark Knight justice.

Isaam was standing at the railing, supervising the loading of knights and supplies. The wizard's magic had not led Bera there, however; it was the handful of goblins they'd caught along the river to the east. The goblins had crumpled under torture, revealing they'd been part of a much, much larger force, one led by a grizzled hobgoblin who was aided by a former Dark Knight wizard. The goblins had left the larger army because they were afraid of traveling on ships across the New Sea. She'd spared two of the goblins, and they were in *Mercy Corvan*'s hold. After they recovered from their injuries, they might be able to provide additional useful information. If not, she'd see if they could swim.

"The captain wants to leave at high tide."

The words startled Bera, and she turned to see Zoccinder, who had materialized behind her. "I'm well aware," she replied tersely.

"More knights have just arrived at an outpost on the edge of this city," he continued. "Come from the north, they're tired from the forced march. Their commander has turned them over to you, as he's returning to his post. The knights will be at the docks shortly."

"That makes nearly five hundred of us, then." Bera had picked up additional knights along the river. The mission was of the utmost importance. Among other things, her own future depended on its success. "And I've received notice that two ships are sailing from the north."

"An adequate force," Zoccinder pronounced.

"More than adequate to deal with those rats." Bera paused and watched an ungainly penguin waddle down the pier and launch itself into the water. "I'm impatient, Zocci. Let's get moving."

She strode to the gangplank, Zoccinder following, their boot heels clacking in time across the weathered wood.

"We will crush the rats and send a powerful message across the face of Krynn," she whispered. "And we will send the souls of our traitorous brothers to the deepest corner of the Abyss."

TRACY HICKMAN

PRESENTS
THE ANVIL OF TIME

With the power of the Anvil of Time, the Journeyman can travel
the river of time as simply as walking upstream, visiting the
ancient past of Krynn with ease.

VOLUME ONE
THE SELLSWORD
Cam Banks

Vanderjack, a mercenary with a price on his head, agrees out of
desperation to retrieve a priceless treasure for a displaced noble. The
treasure is deep within enemy territory, and he must survive an army of
old foes, a chorus of unhappy ghosts, and the questionable assistance of
a mad gnome to find it.

April 2008

VOLUME TWO
THE SURVIVORS
Dan Willis

A goodhearted dwarf is warned of an apocalyptic flood by the god
Reorx, and he and his motley followers must decide whether the
warning is real—and then survive the disaster that sweeps
through their part of Krynn.

November 2008

RICHARD A. KNAAK

THE OGRE TITANS

The Grand Lord Golgren has been savagely crushing
all opposition to his control of the harsh ogre lands of
Kern and Blöde, first sweeping away rival chieftains, then
rebuilding the capital in his image. For this he has had to
deal with the ogre titans, dark, sorcerous giants who have
contempt for his leadership.

VOLUME ONE
THE BLACK TALON

Among the ogres, where every ritual demands blood and every ally can
become a deadly foe, Golgren seeks whatever advantage he can obtain,
even if it means a possible alliance with the Knights of Solamnia, a
questionable pact with a mysterious wizard, and trusting an elven slave
who might wish him dead.

VOLUME TWO
THE FIRE ROSE

Attacked by enemies on all sides, Golgren must abandon his throne
to undertake the quest for the Fire Rose before Safrag, master
of the Ogre Titans can locate it and claim supremacy
over all ogres—and perhaps all of Krynn.

December 2008

VOLUME THREE
THE GARGOYLE KING

Forced from the throne he has so long coveted, Golgren makes a final
stand for control of the ogre lands against the Titans . . . against an
enemy as ancient and powerful as a god.

December 2009

An action-packed tale of adventure and intrigue from one of the EBERRON® line's finest authors.

DON BASSINGTHWAITE

Legacy of Dhakaan

From the ashes of the long-collapsed Dhakaani Empire, a new king of the goblins will do whatever he can to see the kingdom of Darguun recognized. The Five Nations may not have much love for the descendents of Dhakaan, but they must respect the bloodthirsty warriors.

Book 1
The Doom of Kings
August 2008

The Dragon Below

In the dark places of the wild, there are terrors older than the nations of men. When a chance rescue brings bitter rivals together, two warriors team up on a mission of vengeance. But the enemy waiting for them in the depths of the Shadow Marches is far more sinister than any they've faced before.

Book 1
The Binding Stone

Book 2
The Grieving Tree

Book 3
The Killing Song

FORGOTTEN REALMS®

never been to the
forgotten realms® world ?

SEMBIA:
GATEWAY TO THE REALMS

Opens the door to our most popular world with stories full of
intrigue, adventure, and fascinating characters. Sembia is a land
of wealth and power, where rival families buy and sell everything
imaginable—even life itself. In that unforgiving realm, the
Uskevren family may hold the rarest commodity of all: honor.

BOOK I
The Halls of Stormweather
Edited by Philip Athans

BOOK II
Shadow's Witness
Paul S. Kemp

BOOK III
The Shattered Mask
Richard Lee Byers

BOOK IV
Black Wolf
Dave Gross

BOOK V
Heirs of Prophecy
Lisa Smedman

BOOK VI
Sands of the Soul
Voronica Whitney-Robinson

BOOK VII
Lord of Stormweather
Dave Gross

But even the most honorable family is not without its secrets, and
everyone from the maid to the matriarch has something to hide.